Dear Mouse Friends,
Welcome to the world of

Geronimo Stilton

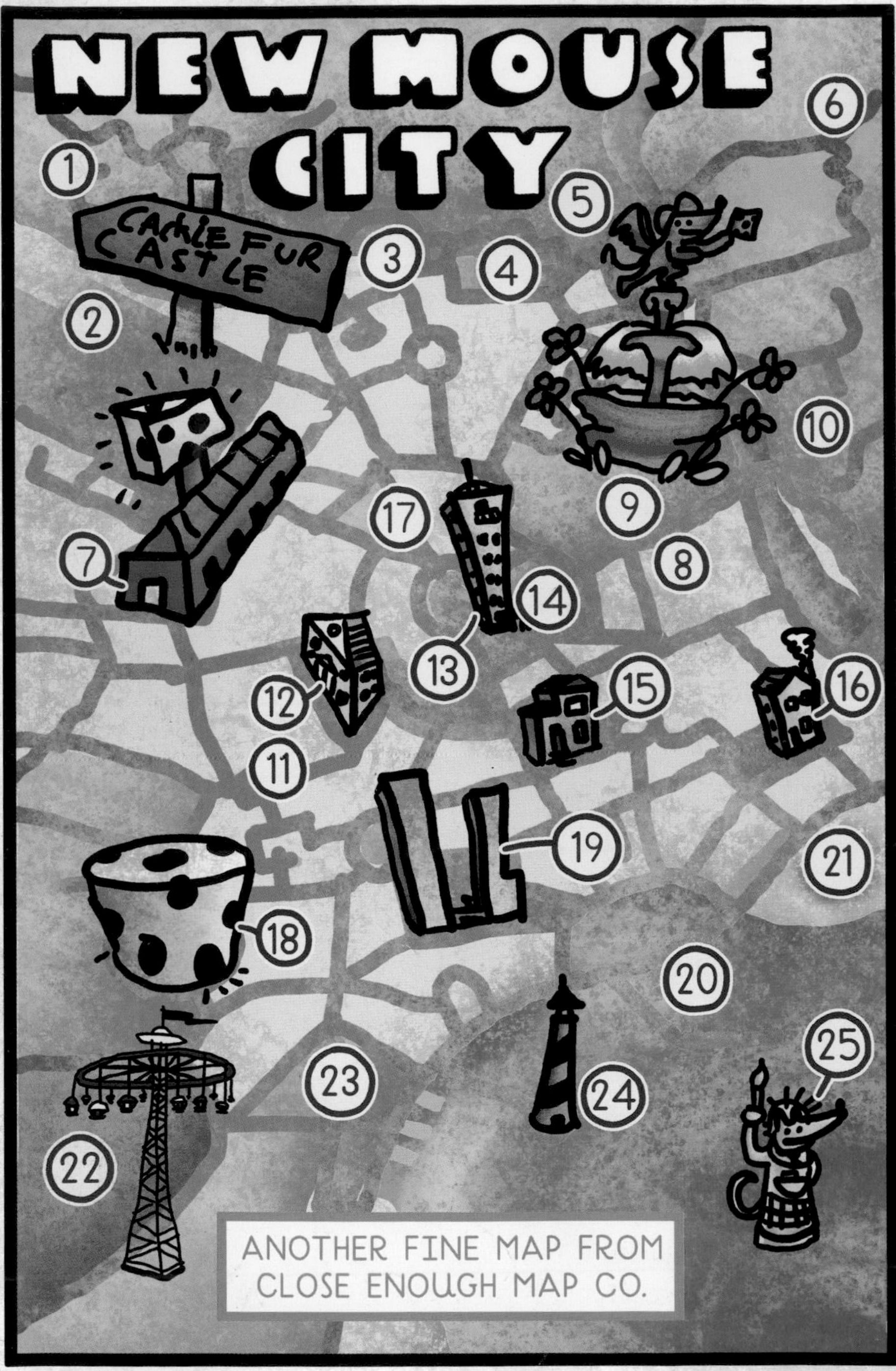
NEW MOUSE CITY
CATTLEFUR CASTLE
1
2
3
4
5
6
7
8
9
10
11
12
13
14
15
16
17
18
19
20
21
22
23
24
25
ANOTHER FINE MAP FROM CLOSE ENOUGH MAP CO.

TABLE OF

Published by Scholastic Inc., *Publishers since 1920*, 557 Broadway, New York, NY 10012. SCHOLASTIC and associated logos are trademarks and/or registered trademarks of Scholastic Inc.

"National Anthem of the Sewers" adapted and composed by Oscar Angleberger

ISBN 978-1-338-72939-9

Text by Geronimo Stilton
Story by Elisabetta Dami
Original title *Brividi felini al luna park*
Cover and Illustrations by Tom Angleberger
Edited by Abigail McAden and Tiffany Colón
Translated by Emily Clement
Color by Corey Barba
Lettering by Kristin Kemper
Book design by Phil Falco and Shivana Sookdeo
Creative Director: Phil Falco
Publisher: David Saylor

10 9 8 7 6 5 4 3 2 1   22 23 24 25 26

Printed in China 127
First edition, May 2022

Geronimo Stilton

THE GRAPHIC NOVEL

LAST RIDE AT LUNA PARK

with **Tom Angleberger**   story by **Elisabetta Dami**

color by **Corey Barba**

graphix

An Imprint of

■Scholastic

1. Cheese Factories
2. Angorat International Airport
3. Comic Book Store
4. Mouse General Hospital
5. WRAT Radio & Television Station
6. Snotnose Castle
7. Cheese Market
8. Grand Hotel
9. Botanical Gardens
10. Petunia Pretty Paws's House
11. *The Daily Rat*
12. *The Rodent's Gazette*
13. Thea's House
14. Cheap Junk for Less
15. Geronimo's House
16. Benjamin's House
17. Public Library
18. Mousidon Square Garden
19. Hercule Poirat's Office
20. New Mouse Harbor
21. Beach
22. Luna Park
23. Shipyard
24. Luna Light House
25. The Statue of Liberty

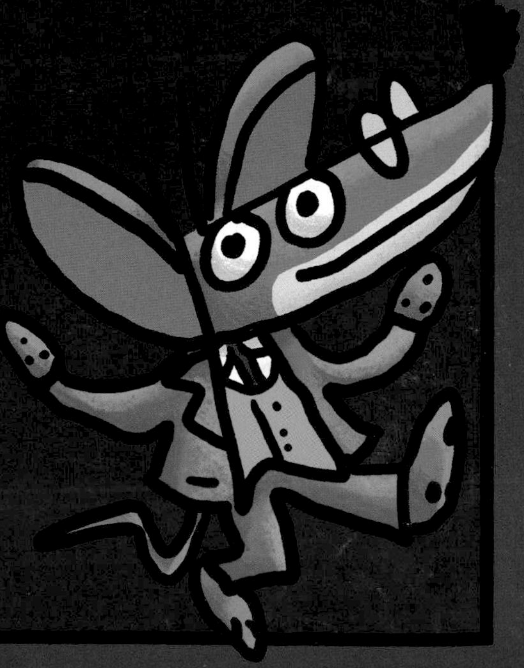

CONTENTS

CHAPTER ONE
EEK!!
A GHOST MOUSE!

Ah, what a **BEAUTIFUL** night for a **MOONLIGHT** stroll...

Oh! I forgot to introduce myself! My name is **Stilton**...

Geronimo Stilton!

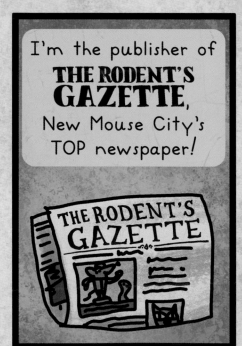

I'm the publisher of **THE RODENT'S GAZETTE**, New Mouse City's TOP newspaper!

THE RODENT'S GAZETTE

And tonight, I stayed up late to work on my novel...

The mouse in the big hat looked up.

"No," he cried. "Not you!!"

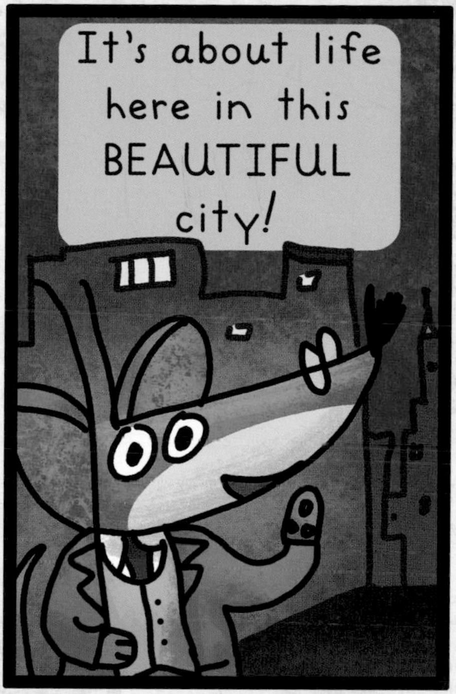
It's about life here in this BEAUTIFUL city!

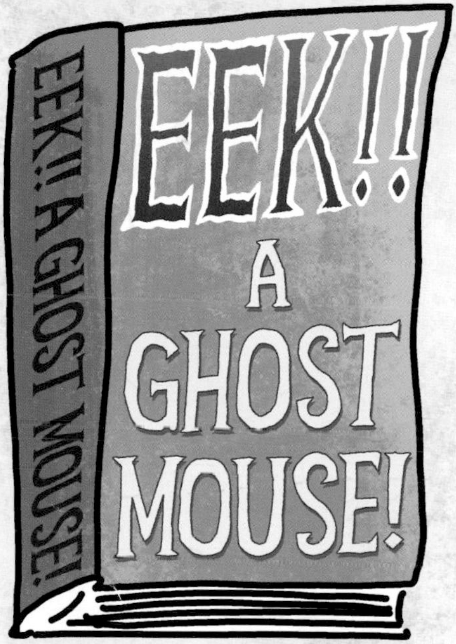
EEK!! A GHOST MOUSE!
EEK!! A GHOST MOUSE!

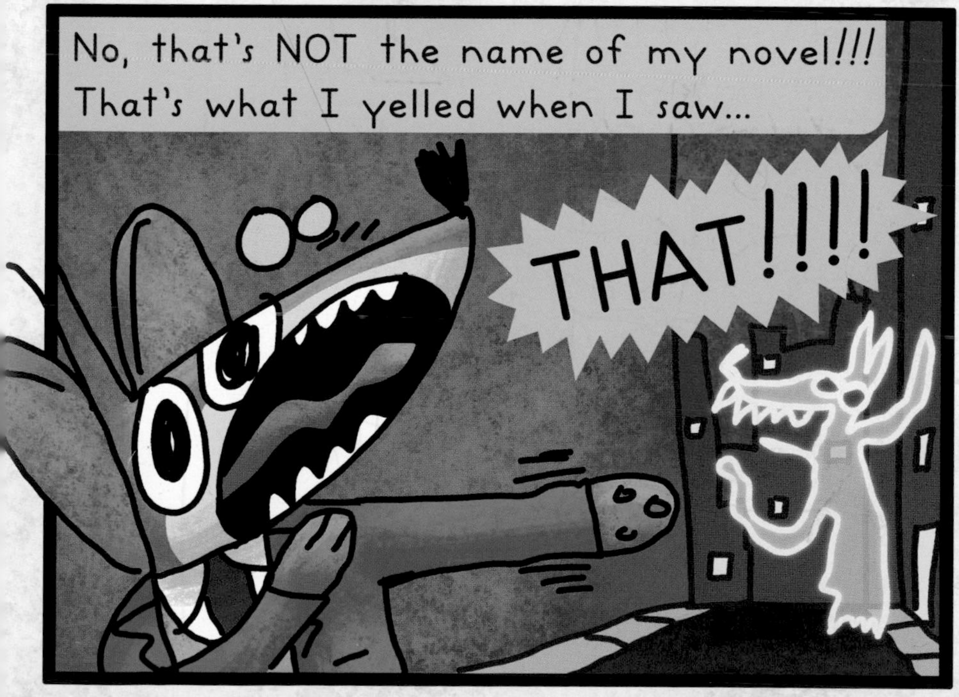
No, that's NOT the name of my novel!!!
That's what I yelled when I saw...
THAT!!!!

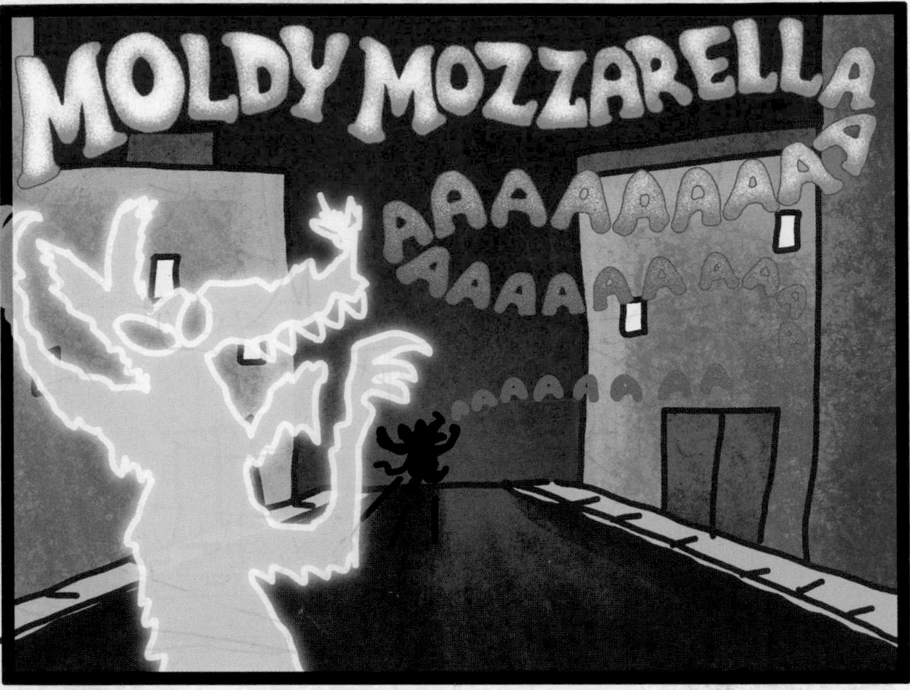
MOLDY MOZZARELLAAAAAAAAAAAAAAAAAAAAAAAAAAAAA

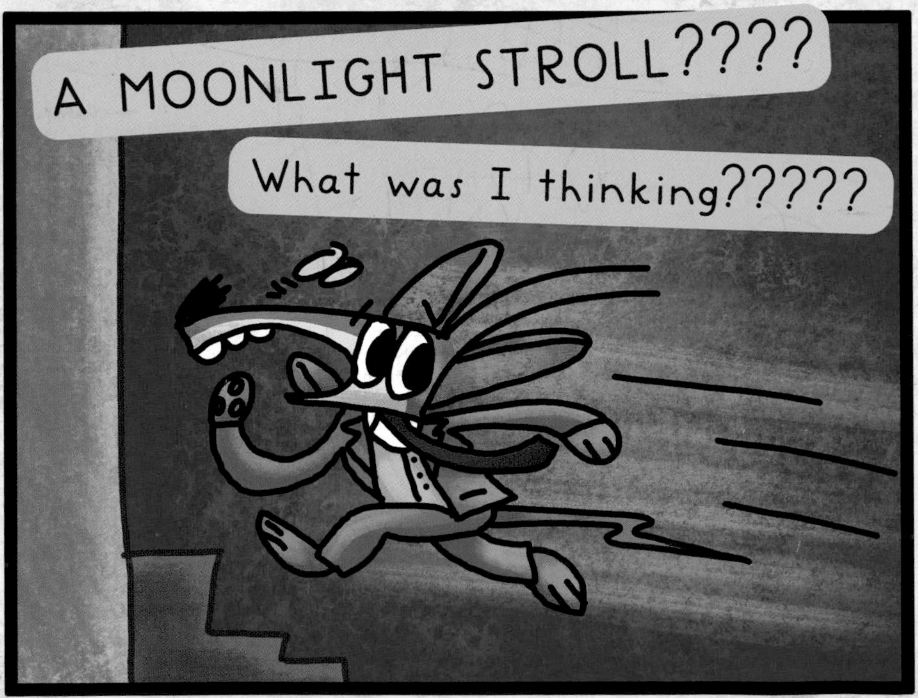
A MOONLIGHT STROLL????
What was I thinking?????

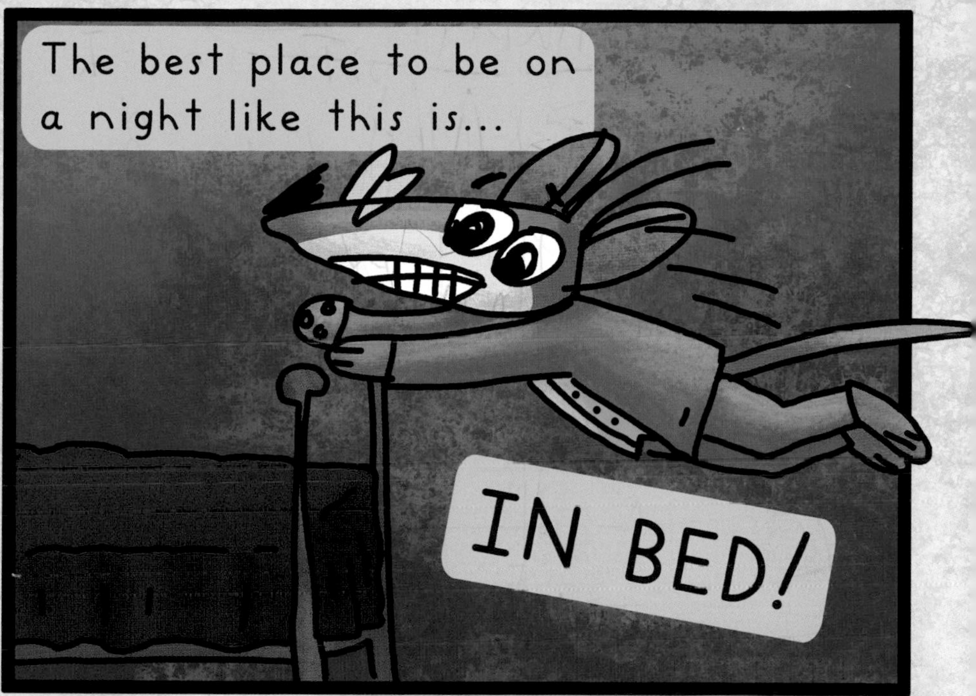
The best place to be on a night like this is...
IN BED!

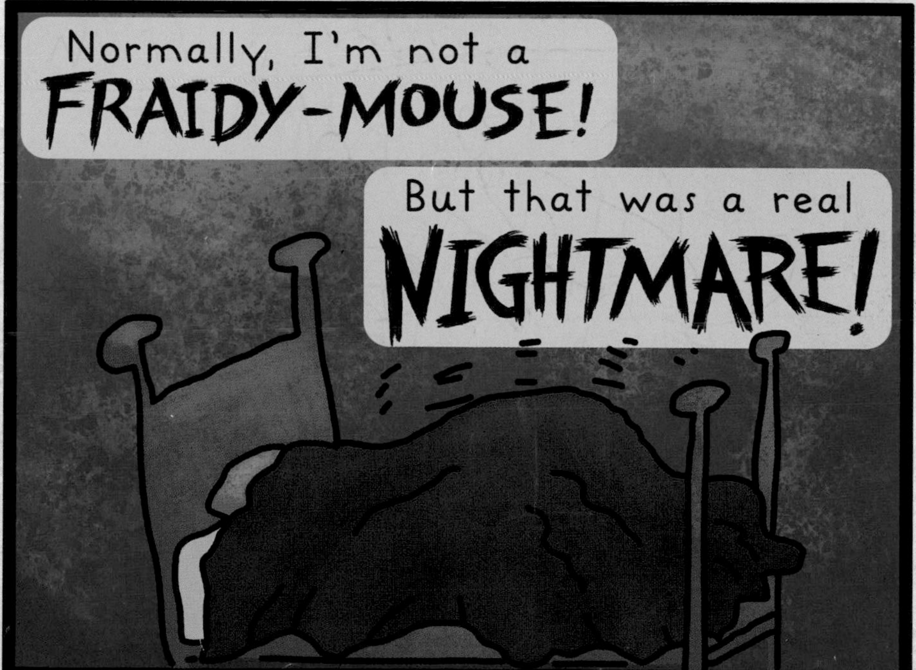
Normally, I'm not a FRAIDY-MOUSE!
But that was a real NIGHTMARE!

CHAPTER TWO

The Next Morning...

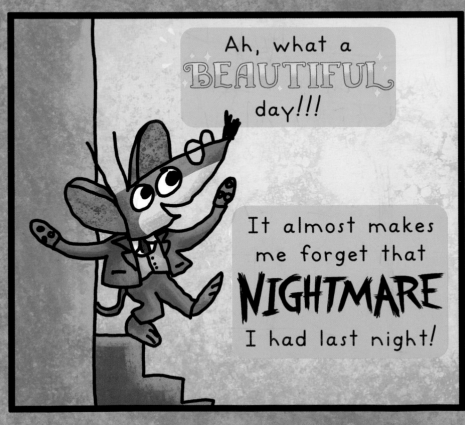

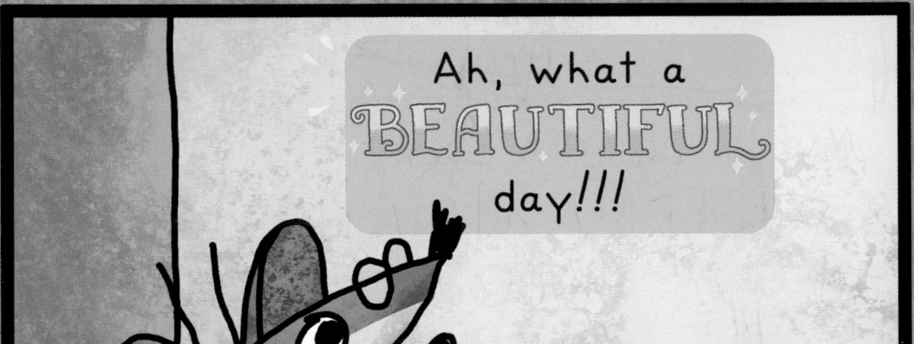
Ah, what a BEAUTIFUL day!!!
It almost makes me forget that NIGHTMARE I had last night!

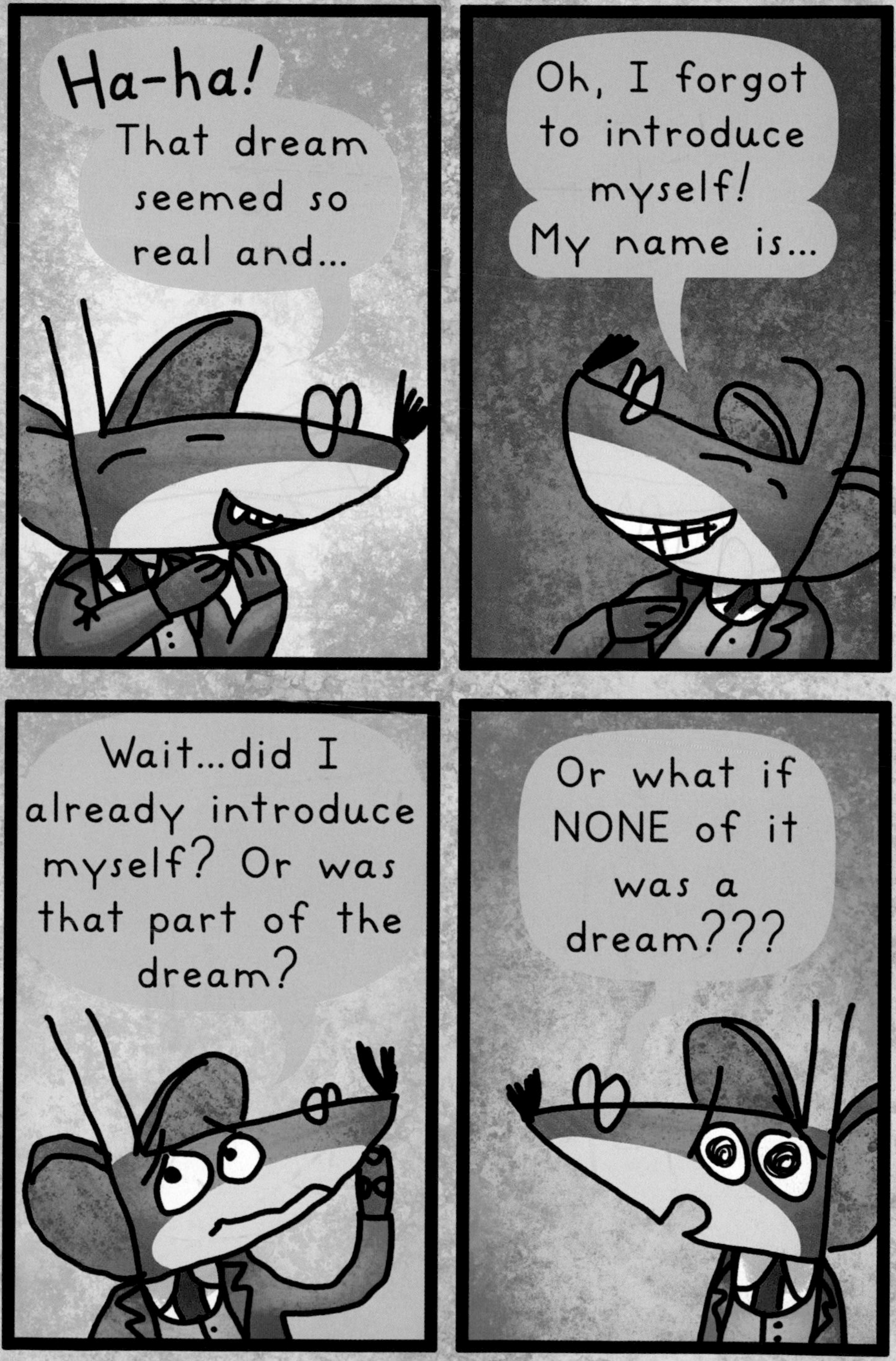
Ha-ha! That dream seemed so real and...
Oh, I forgot to introduce myself! My name is...
Wait...did I already introduce myself? Or was that part of the dream?
Or what if NONE of it was a dream???

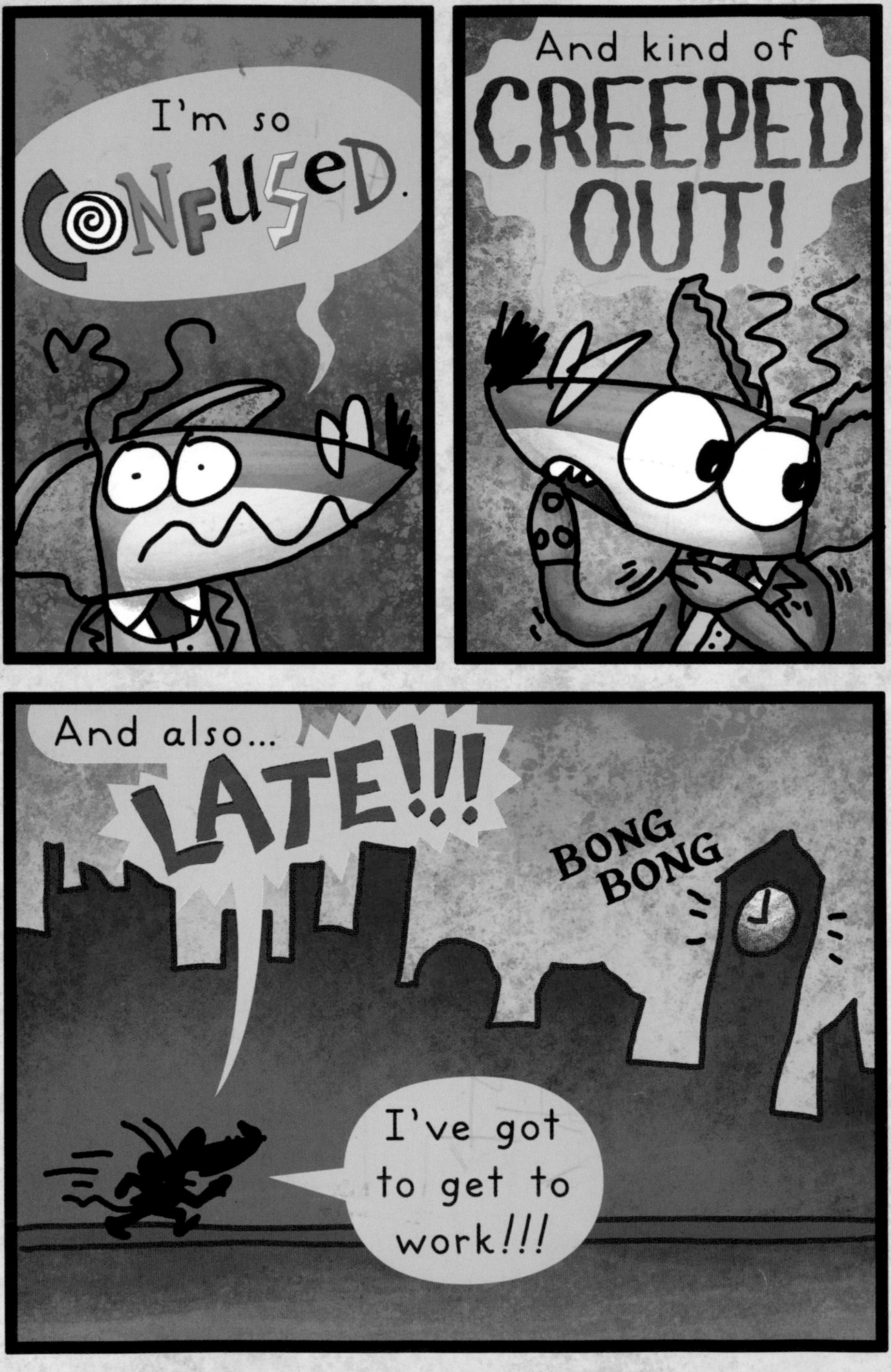
I'm so
CONFUSED.
And kind of
CREEPED OUT!
And also...
LATE!!!
BONG
BONG
I've got to get to work!!!

CHAPTER THREE

Pretty Please?

I ran through the streets of New Mouse City,
all the way to the offices of
THE RODENT'S GAZETTE: my newspaper!

OUR FOUNDER

Well, it's not exactly MY newspaper.
I'm the publisher, but it's owned by my
grandfather, William Shortpaws. And he
HATES it when anyone is late to work!

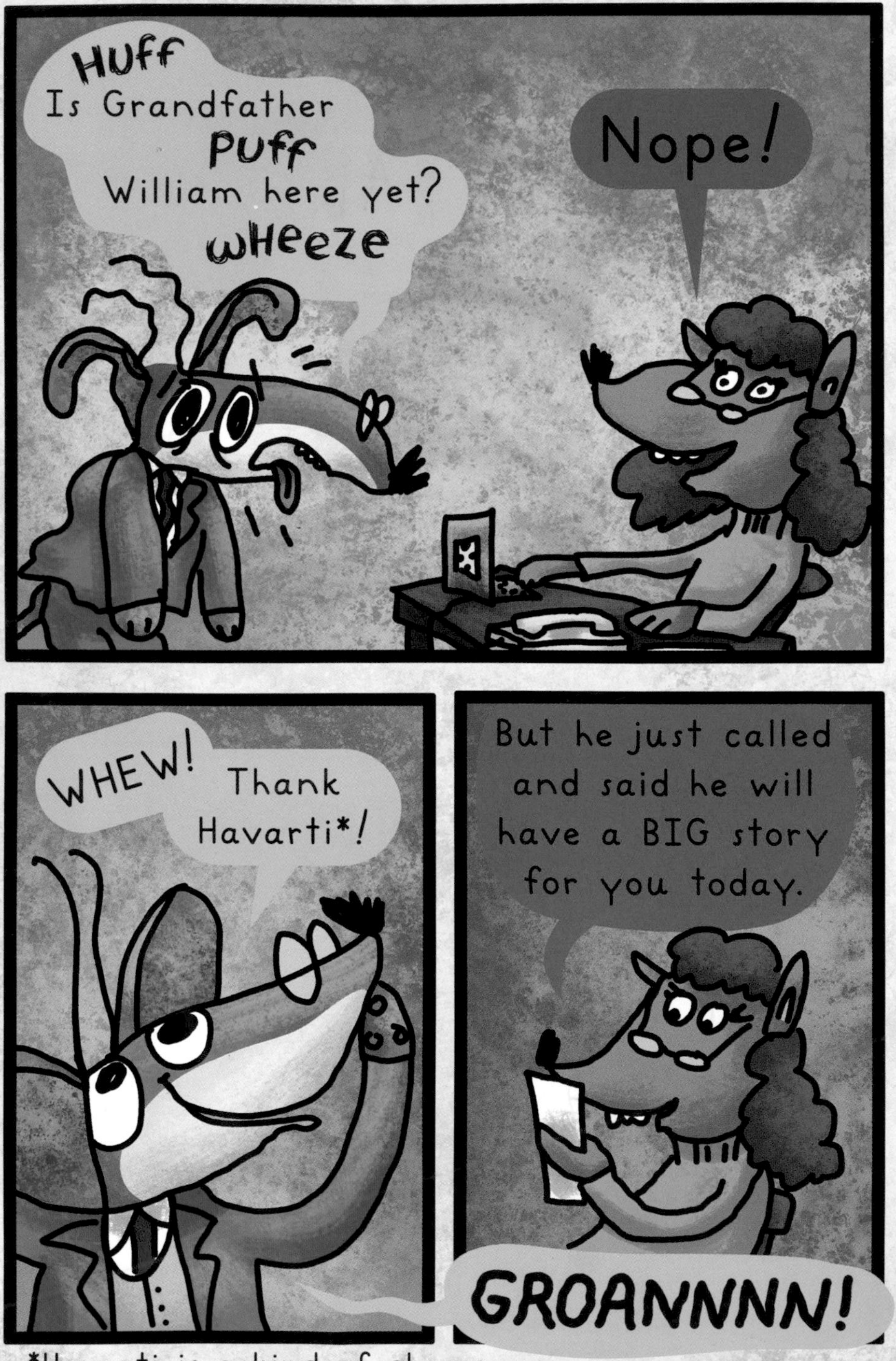
HUFF Is Grandfather PUFF William here yet? WHEEZE
Nope!
WHEW! Thank Havarti*!
But he just called and said he will have a BIG story for you today.
GROANNNN!

*Havarti is a kind of cheese.

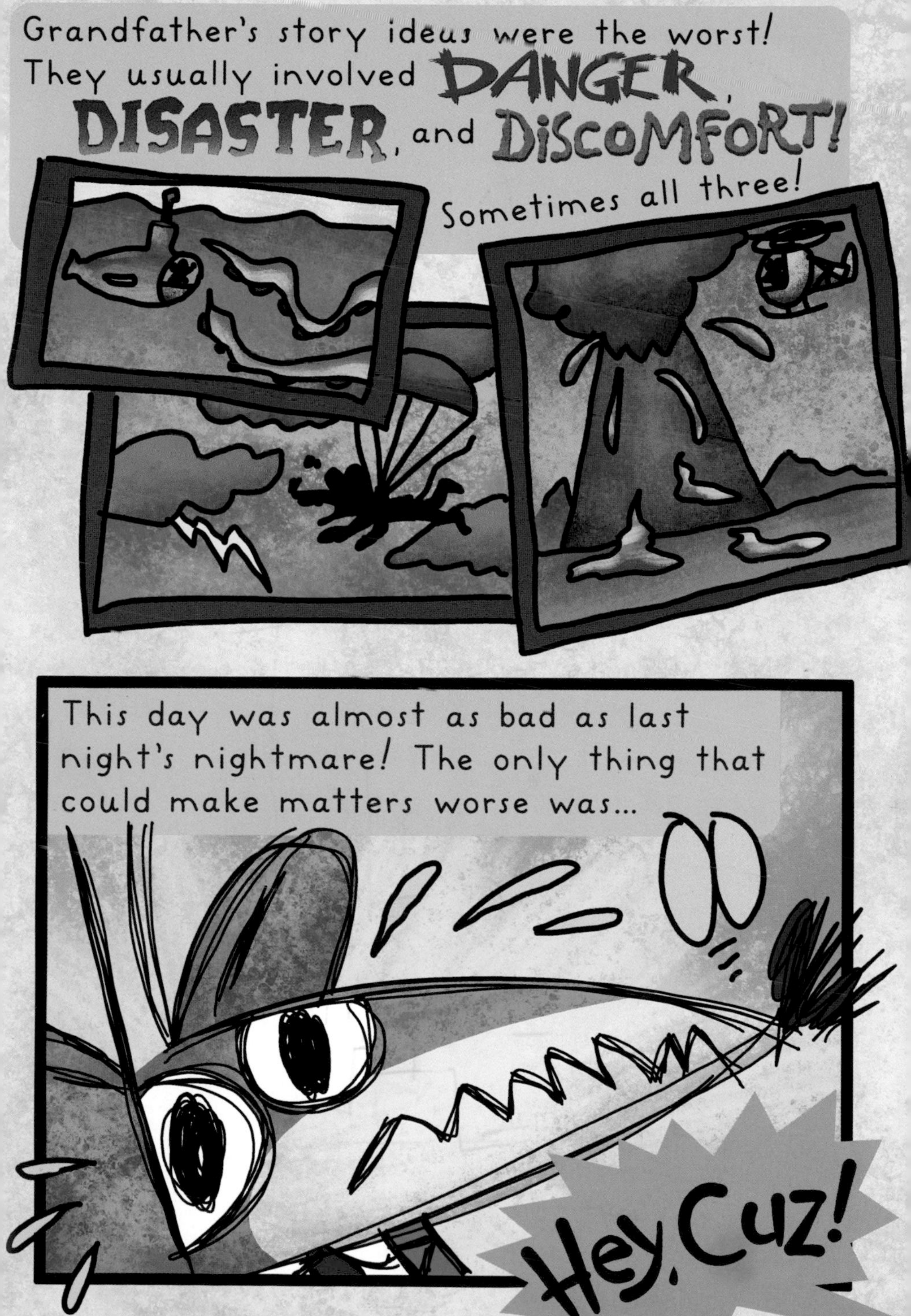
Grandfather's story ideas were the worst! They usually involved DANGER, DISASTER, and DISCOMFORT!
Sometimes all three!
This day was almost as bad as last night's nightmare! The only thing that could make matters worse was...
Hey, Cuz!

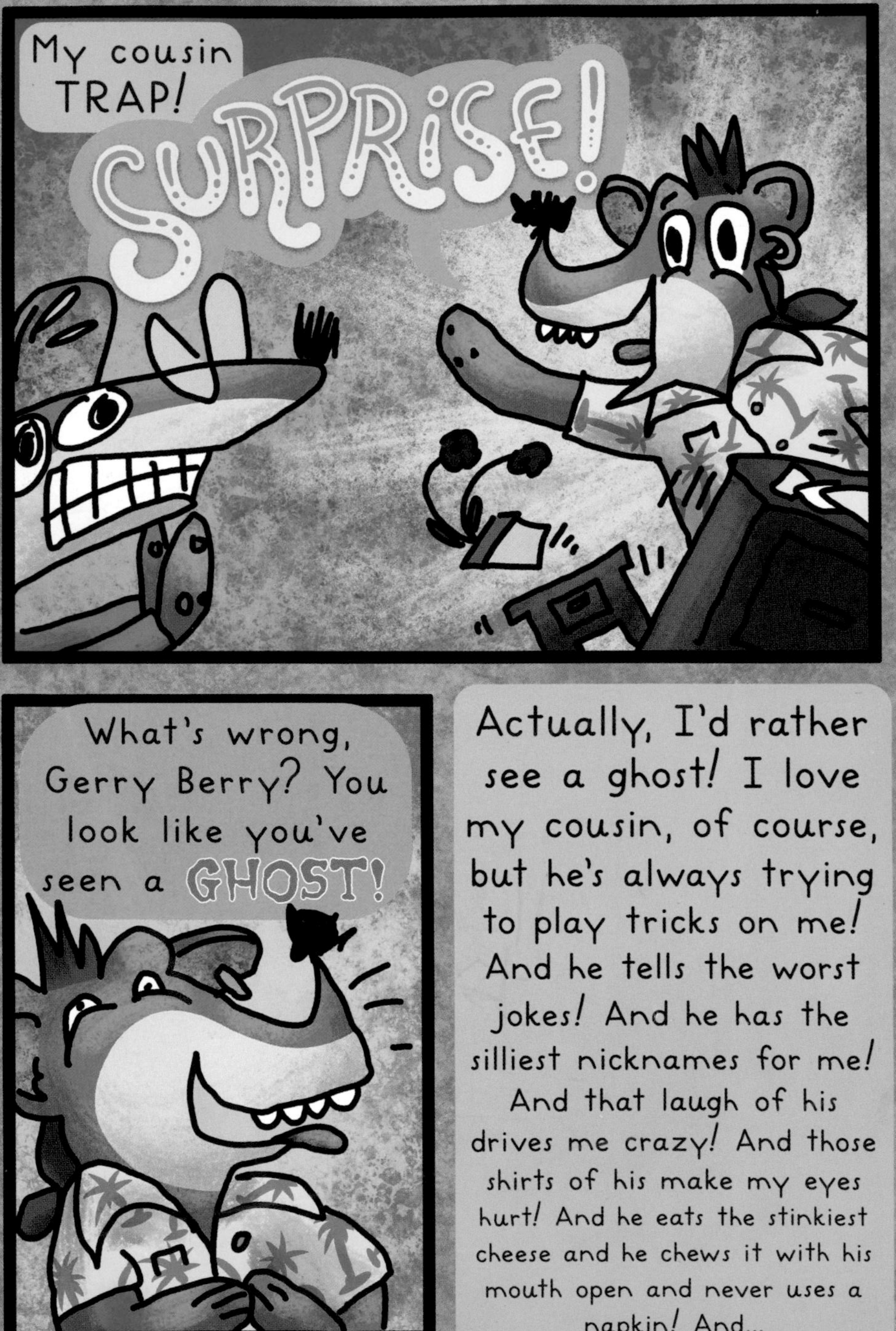
My cousin TRAP!
SURPRISE!
What's wrong, Gerry Berry? You look like you've seen a GHOST!
Actually, I'd rather see a ghost! I love my cousin, of course, but he's always trying to play tricks on me! And he tells the worst jokes! And he has the silliest nicknames for me! And that laugh of his drives me crazy! And those shirts of his make my eyes hurt! And he eats the stinkiest cheese and he chews it with his mouth open and never uses a napkin! And...

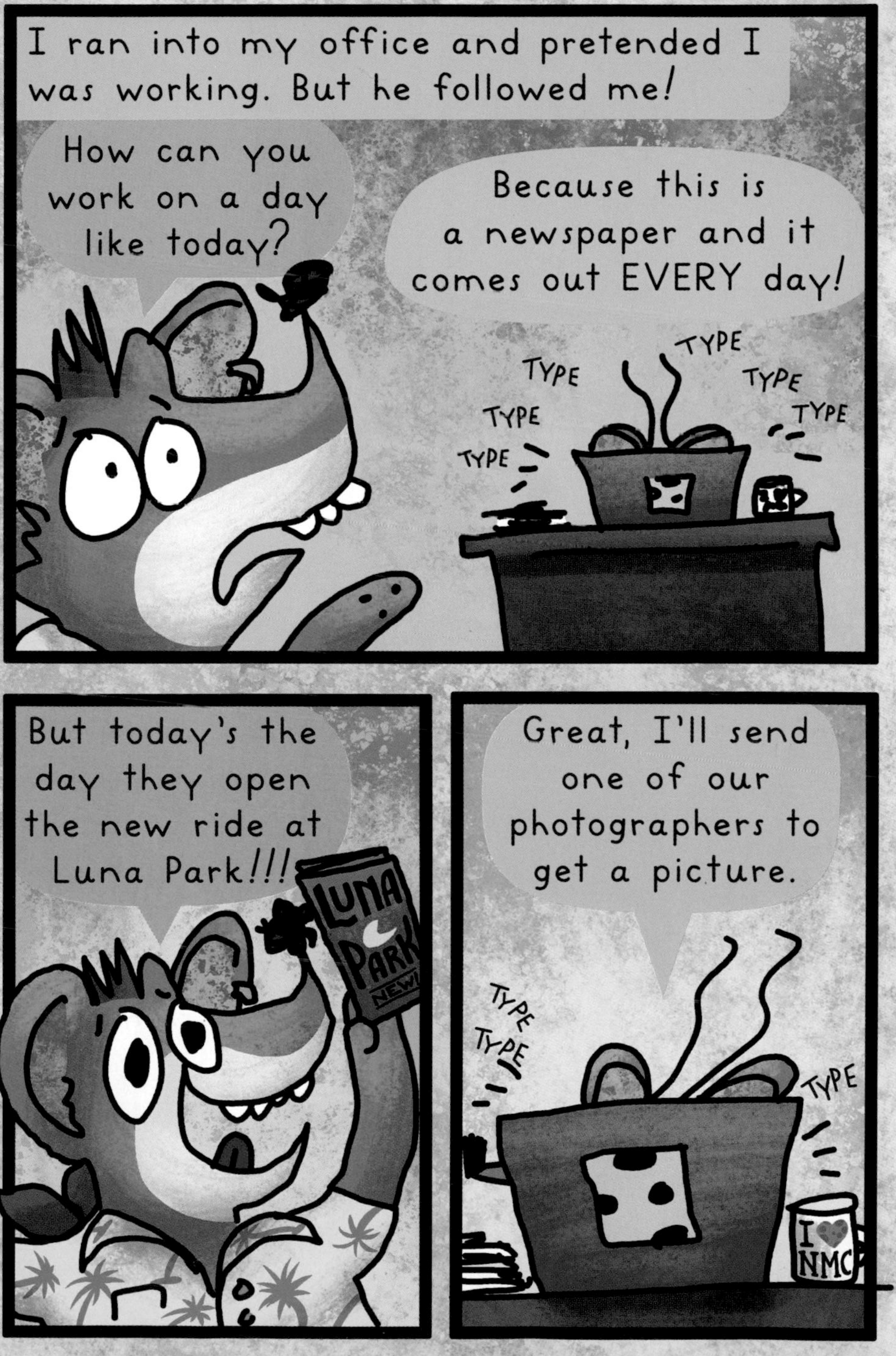
I ran into my office and pretended I was working. But he followed me!
How can you work on a day like today?
Because this is a newspaper and it comes out EVERY day!
TYPE TYPE TYPE TYPE TYPE TYPE
But today's the day they open the new ride at Luna Park!!!
LUNA PARK NEWS
Great, I'll send one of our photographers to get a picture.
TYPE TYPE TYPE
I ♥ NMC

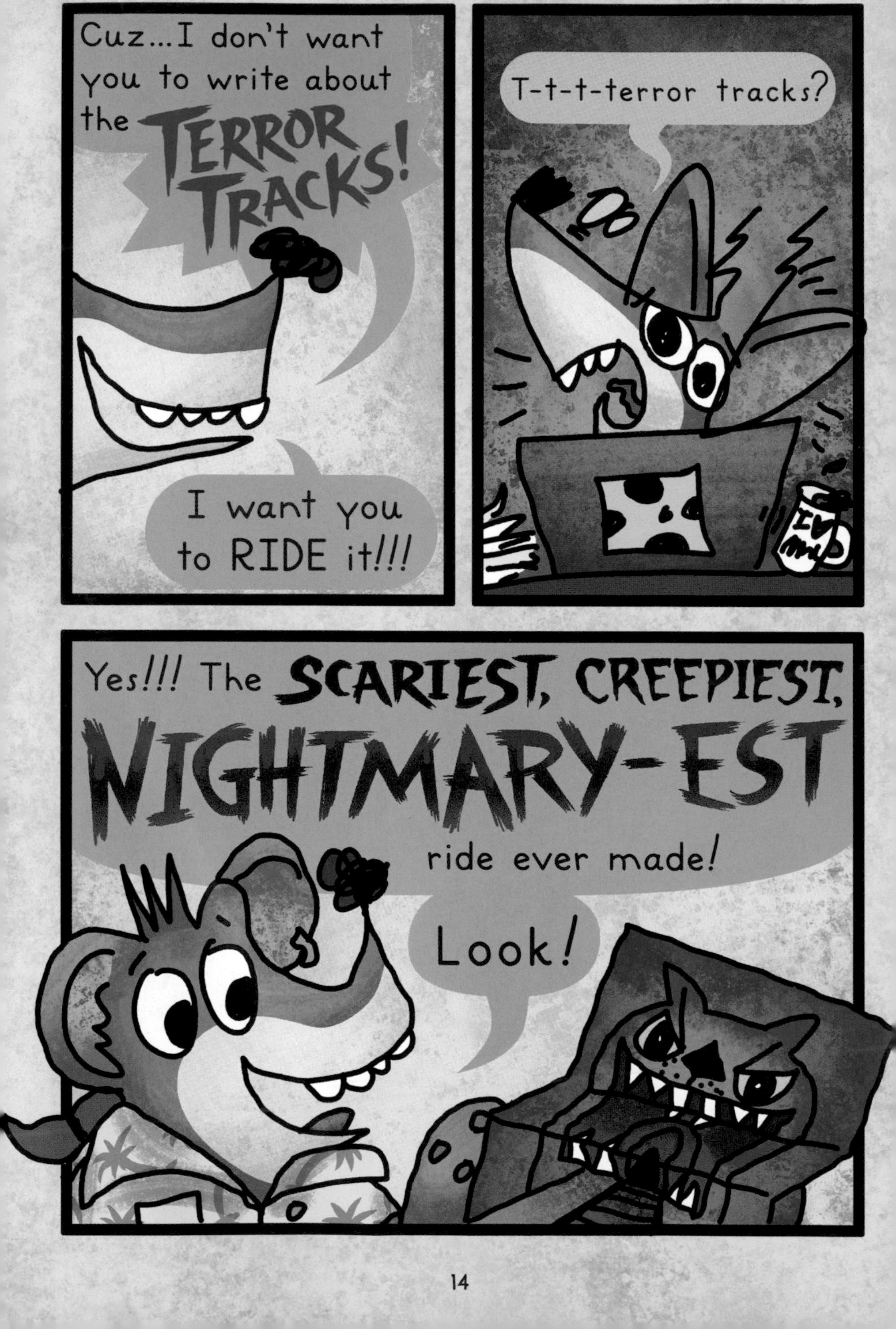
Cuz...I don't want you to write about the TERROR TRACKS!
I want you to RIDE it!!!
T-t-t-terror tracks?
Yes!!! The SCARIEST, CREEPIEST, NIGHTMARY-EST ride ever made!
Look!

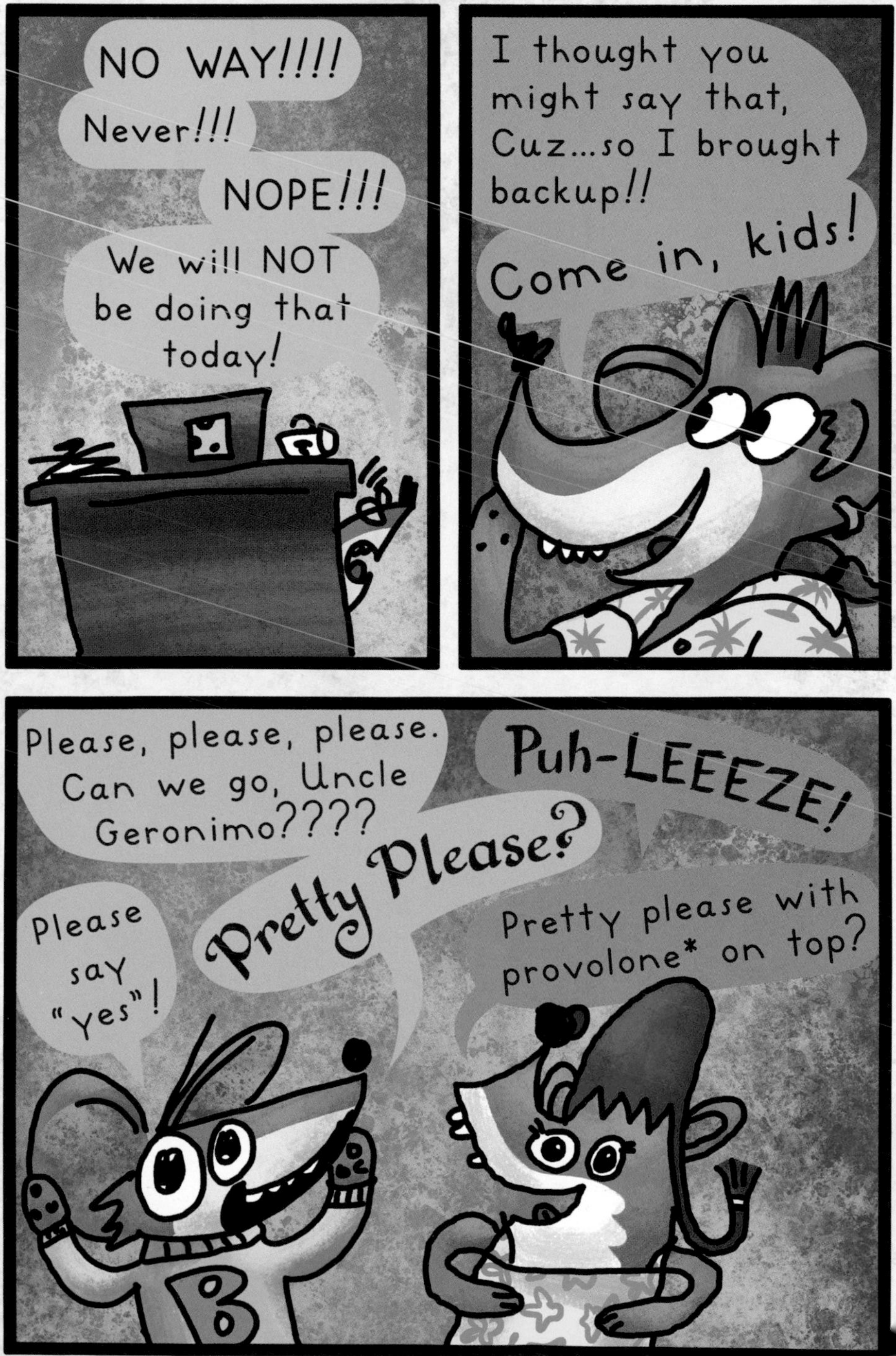
NO WAY!!!!
Never!!!
NOPE!!!
We will NOT be doing that today!
I thought you might say that, Cuz...so I brought backup!!
Come in, kids!
Please, please, please. Can we go, Uncle Geronimo????
Puh-LEEEEZE!
Pretty Please?
Please say "yes"!
Pretty please with provolone* on top?

*Provolone is a type of cheese.

CHAPTER FOUR

THE PERFECT EXCUSE!

It was my sweet little nephew Benjamin!
And my sweet little niece Trappy!!!
How could I possibly say no to such
adorable little rodents???

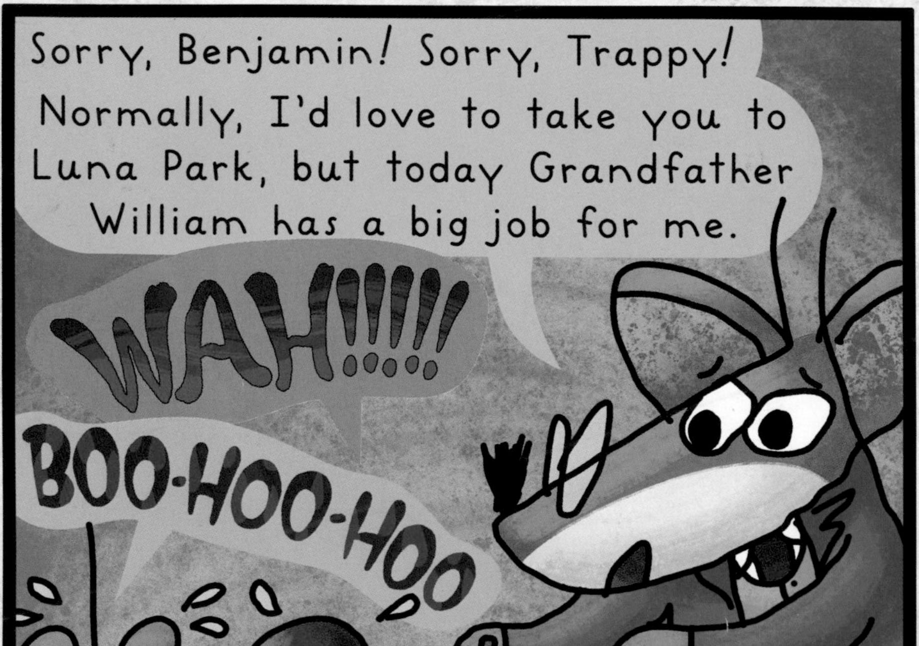
Sorry, Benjamin! Sorry, Trappy! Normally, I'd love to take you to Luna Park, but today Grandfather William has a big job for me.
WAH!!!!!
BOO-HOO-HOO-HOO

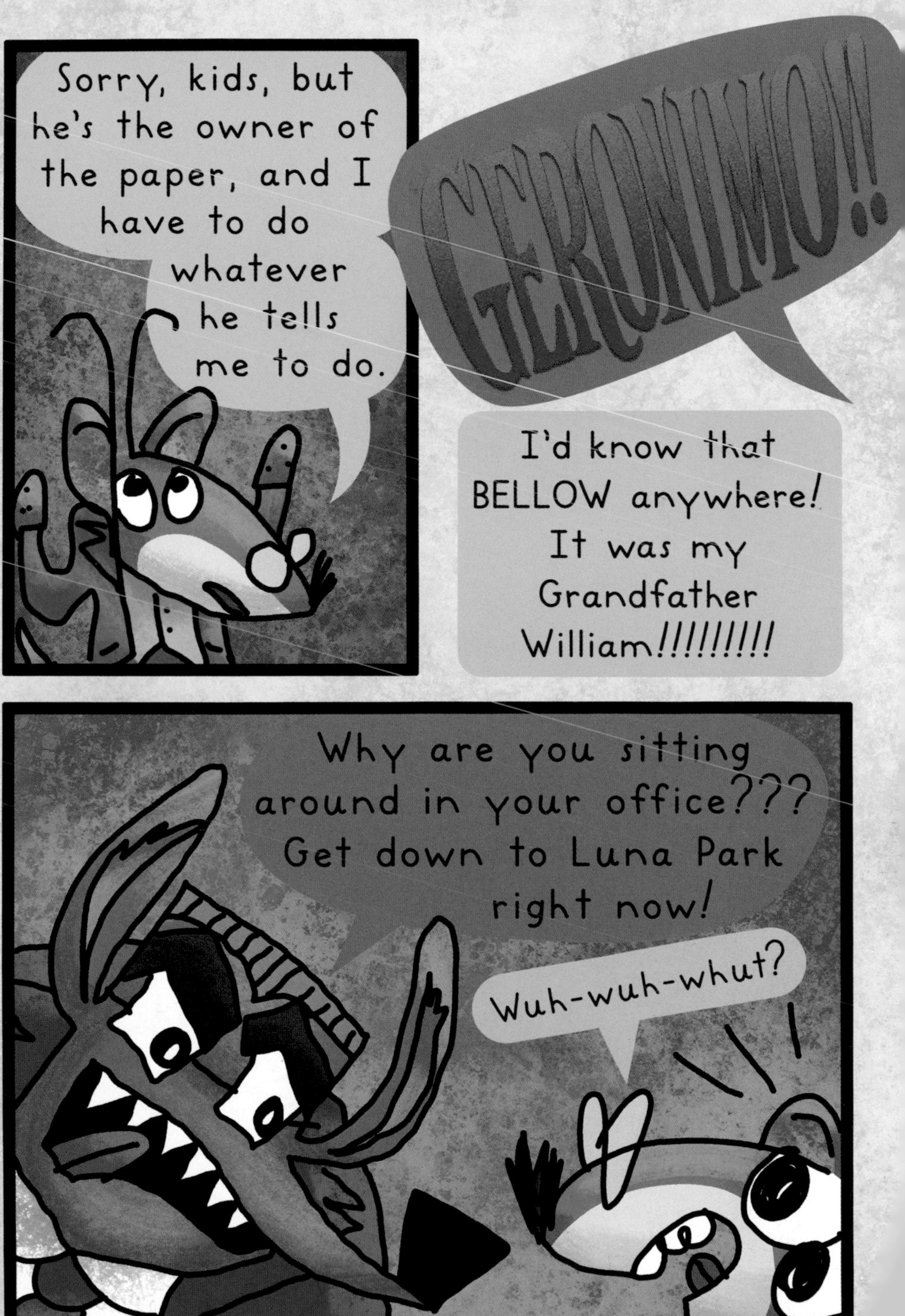
Sorry, kids, but he's the owner of the paper, and I have to do whatever he tells me to do.
GERONIMO!!
I'd know that BELLOW anywhere! It was my Grandfather William!!!!!!!!!
Why are you sitting around in your office??? Get down to Luna Park right now!
Wuh-wuh-whut?

Luna Park*!!!* They're opening a new ride today! It's **BIG NEWS!**

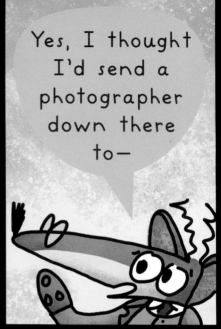

Yes, I thought I'd send a photographer down there to—

Send a photographer? While you loaf around the office? NO, SIR! This story is too big for that! You need to get the story yourself!

But WHY is it so—

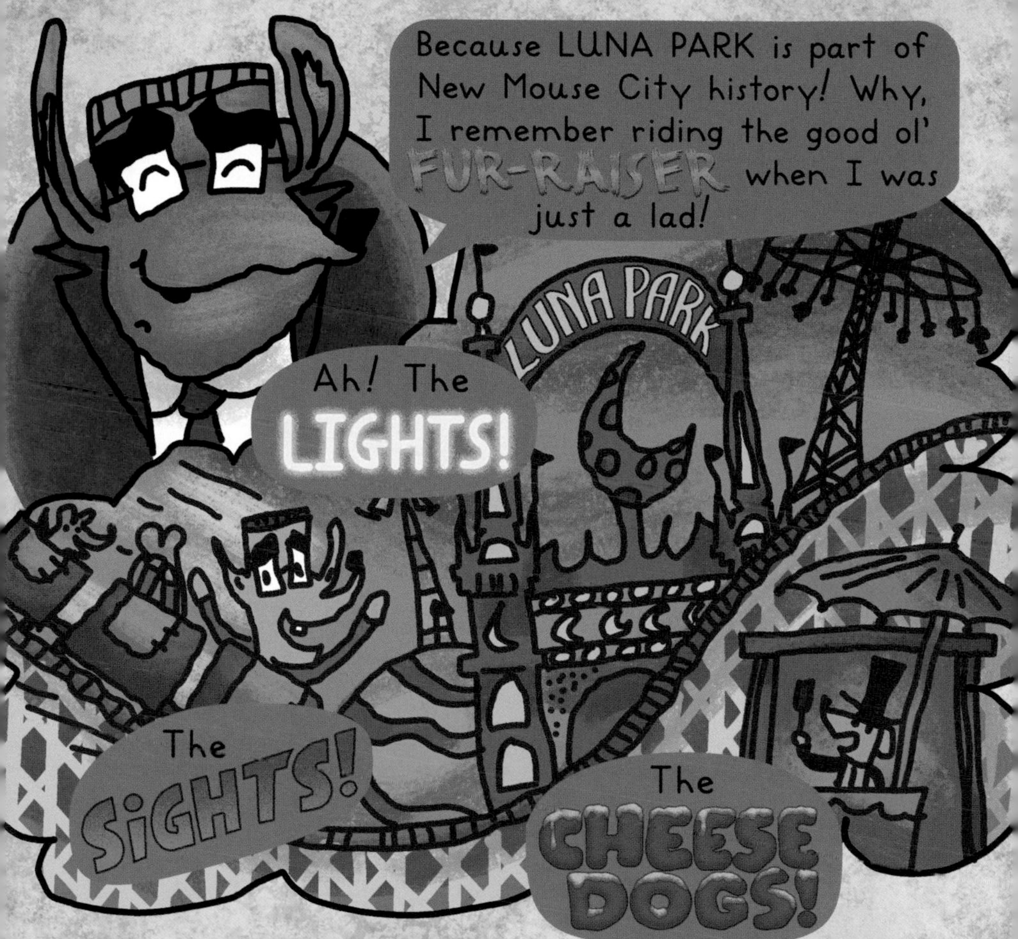
Because LUNA PARK is part of New Mouse City history! Why, I remember riding the good ol' FUR-RAISER when I was just a lad!
LUNA PARK
Ah! The LIGHTS!
The SIGHTS!
The CHEESE DOGS!

Once Grandfather William starts talking about the **GOOD OL' DAYS**, you know you've lost!

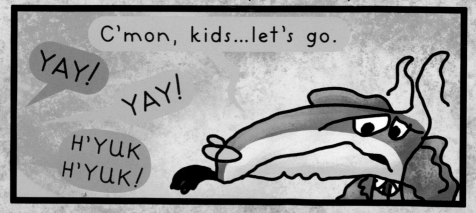

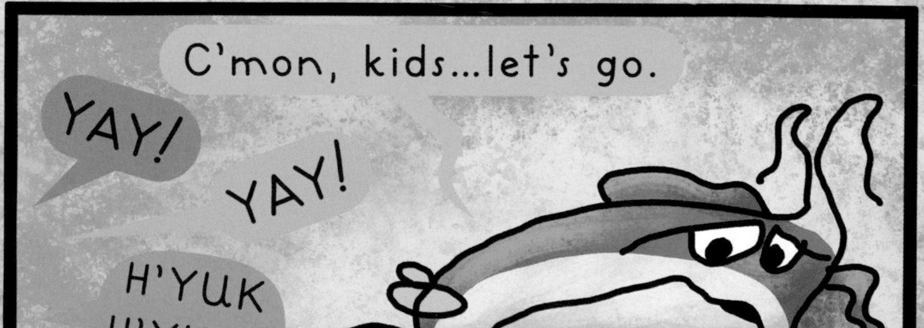
C'mon, kids...let's go.
YAY!
YAY!
H'YUK H'YUK!

CHAPTER FIVE

ONE QUICK RIDE!

When we got to Luna Park, I saw that Grandfather William was right. There was a big crowd, and **BIG CROWDS** mean **BIG NEWS!**

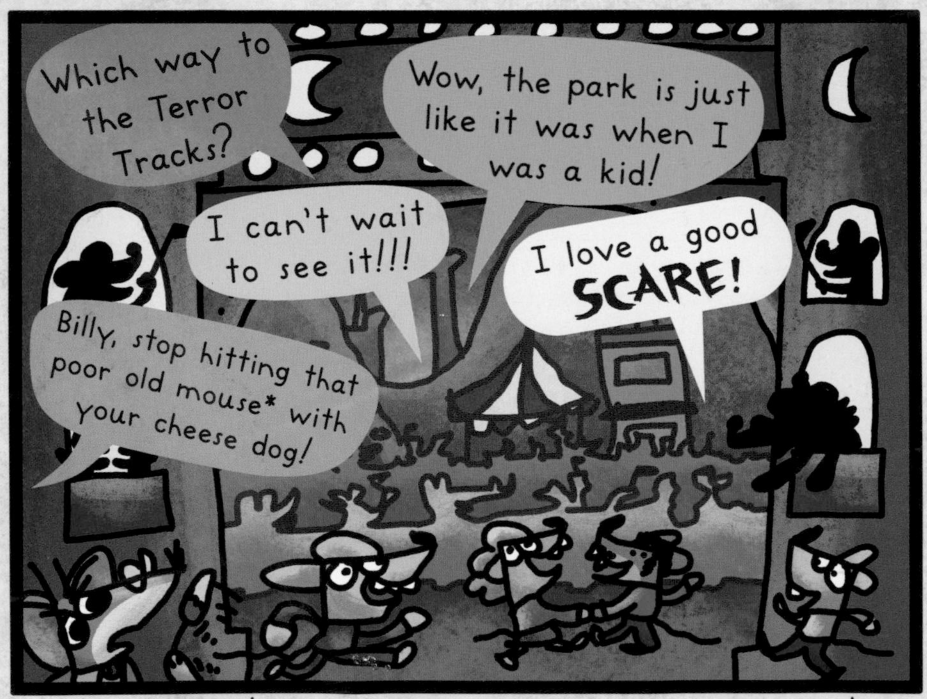

Which way to the Terror Tracks?
Wow, the park is just like it was when I was a kid!
I can't wait to see it!!!
I love a good SCARE!
Billy, stop hitting that poor old mouse* with your cheese dog!

*That was me! I still have cheese stains on my suit!

We were swept along with the crowd all the way to...a big yellow **TARP.**

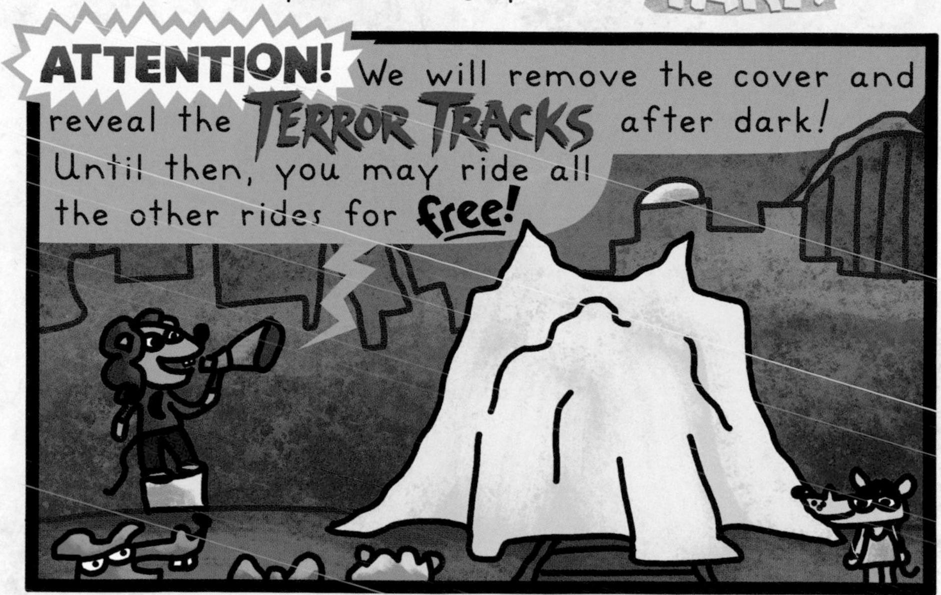
ATTENTION! We will remove the cover and reveal the TERROR TRACKS after dark! Until then, you may ride all the other rides for free!

Other rides?? Not for all the cheddar in **Cheese Valley.** It was bad enough I had to ride the Terror Tracks; there was no way I—

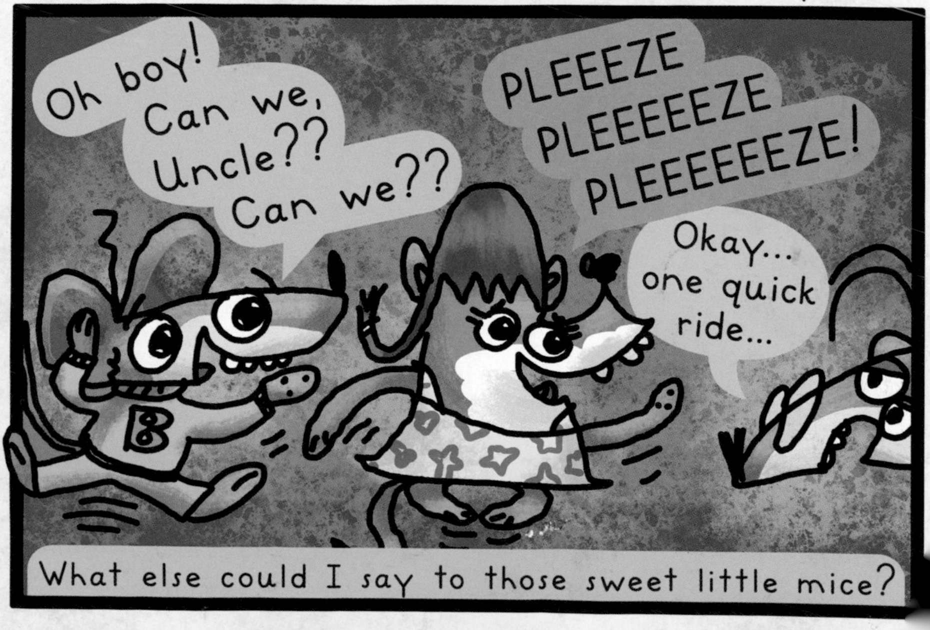
Oh boy! Can we, Uncle?? Can we??
PLEEEZE PLEEEEEZE PLEEEEEEEZE!
Okay... one quick ride...
What else could I say to those sweet little mice?

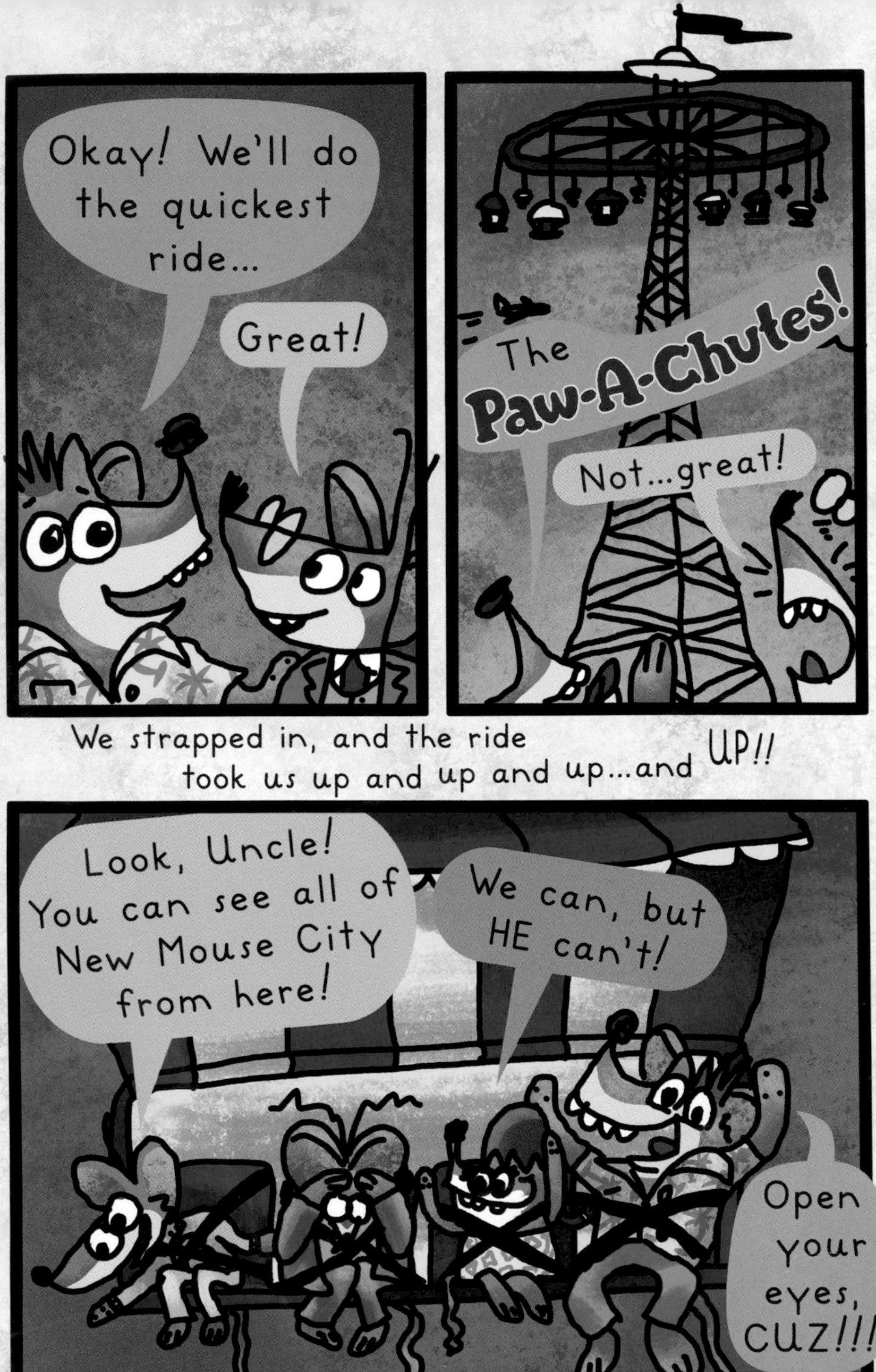
Okay! We'll do the quickest ride...
Great!
The Paw-A-Chutes!
Not...great!
We strapped in, and the ride took us up and up and up...and UP!!
Look, Uncle! You can see all of New Mouse City from here!
We can, but HE can't!
Open your eyes, CUZ!!!

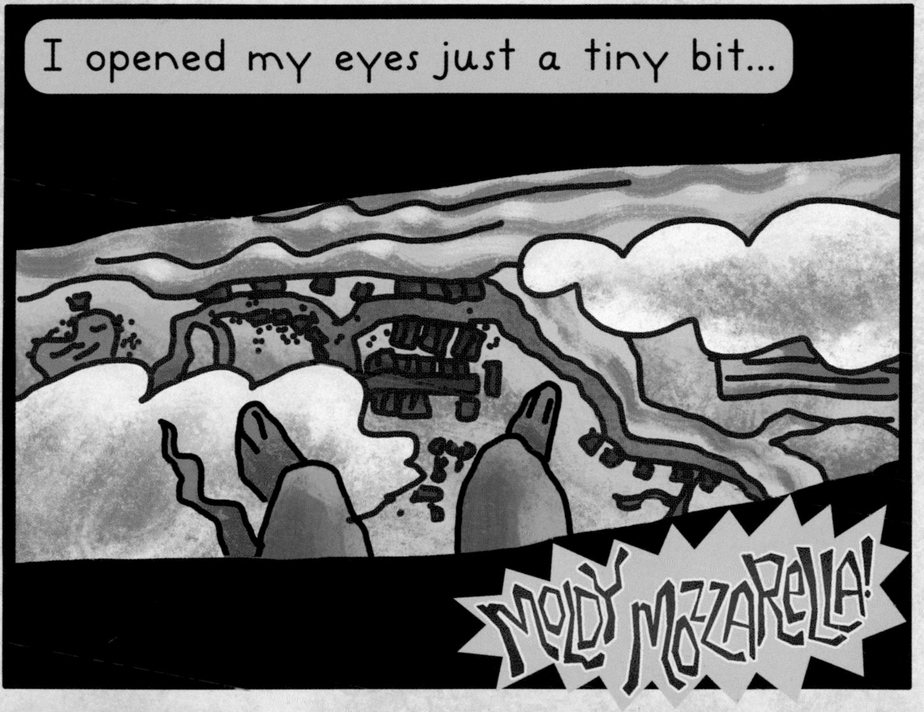
I opened my eyes just a tiny bit...
MOLDY MOZZARELLA!

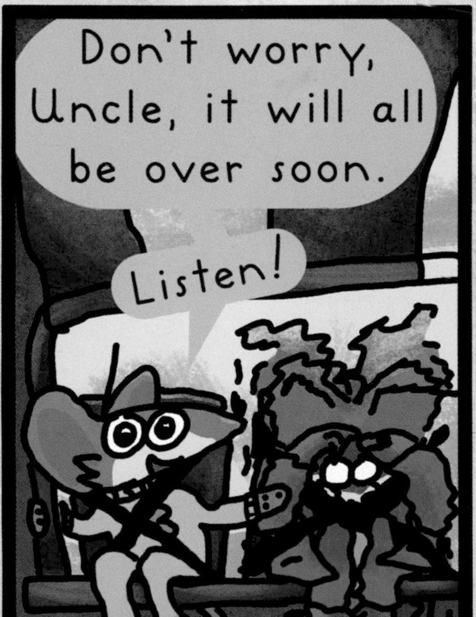
Don't worry, Uncle, it will all be over soon.
Listen!

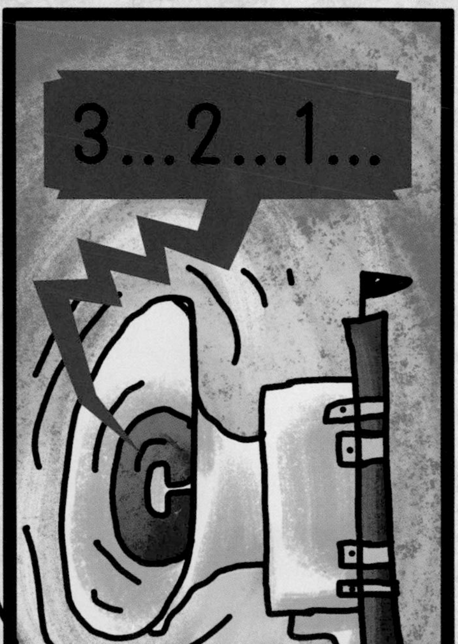
3...2...1...

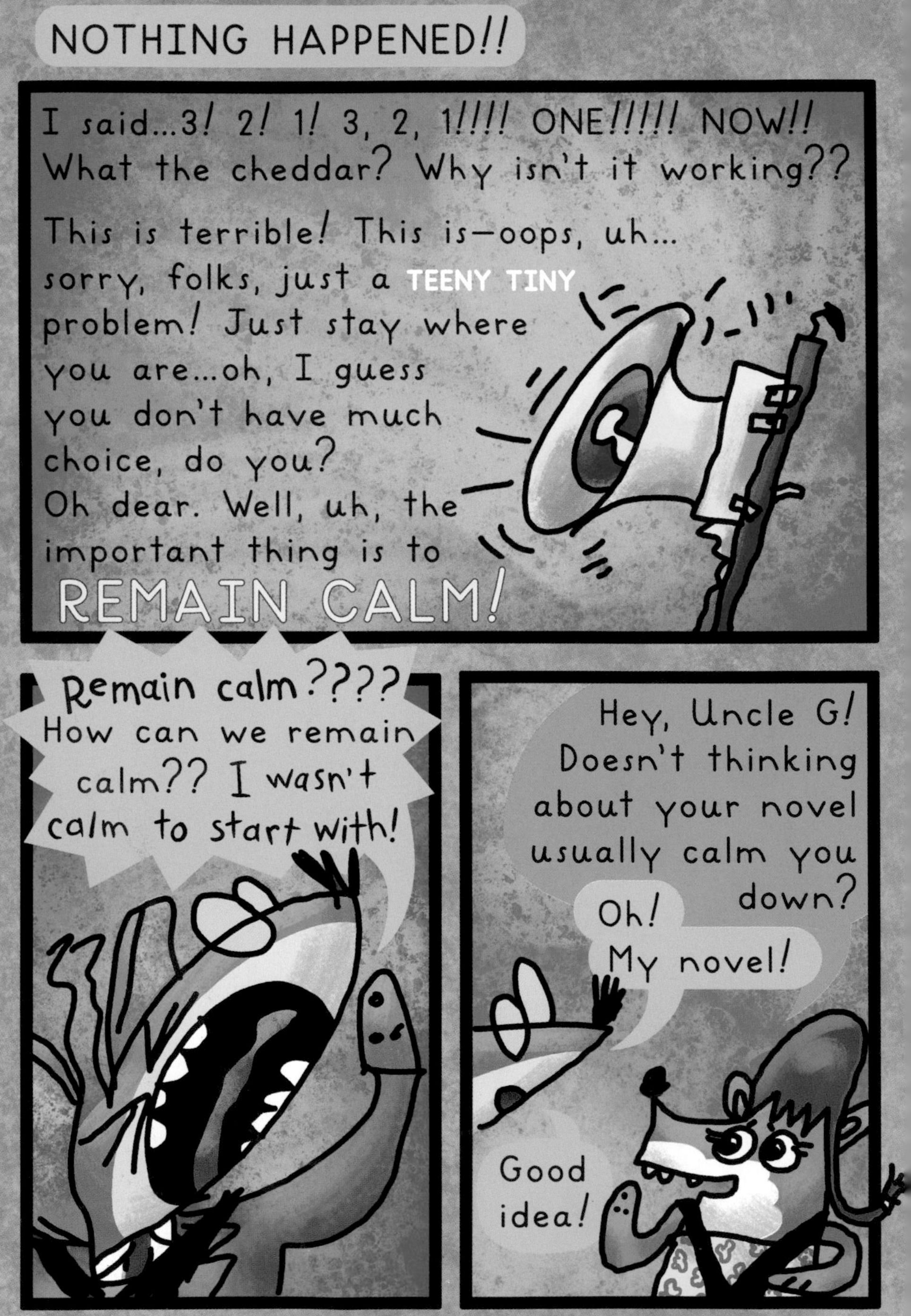
NOTHING HAPPENED!!
I said...3! 2! 1! 3, 2, 1!!!! ONE!!!!! NOW!!
What the cheddar? Why isn't it working??
This is terrible! This is—oops, uh... sorry, folks, just a TEENY TINY problem! Just stay where you are...oh, I guess you don't have much choice, do you?
Oh dear. Well, uh, the important thing is to REMAIN CALM!
Remain calm???? How can we remain calm?? I wasn't calm to start with!
Hey, Uncle G! Doesn't thinking about your novel usually calm you down?
Oh! My novel!
Good idea!

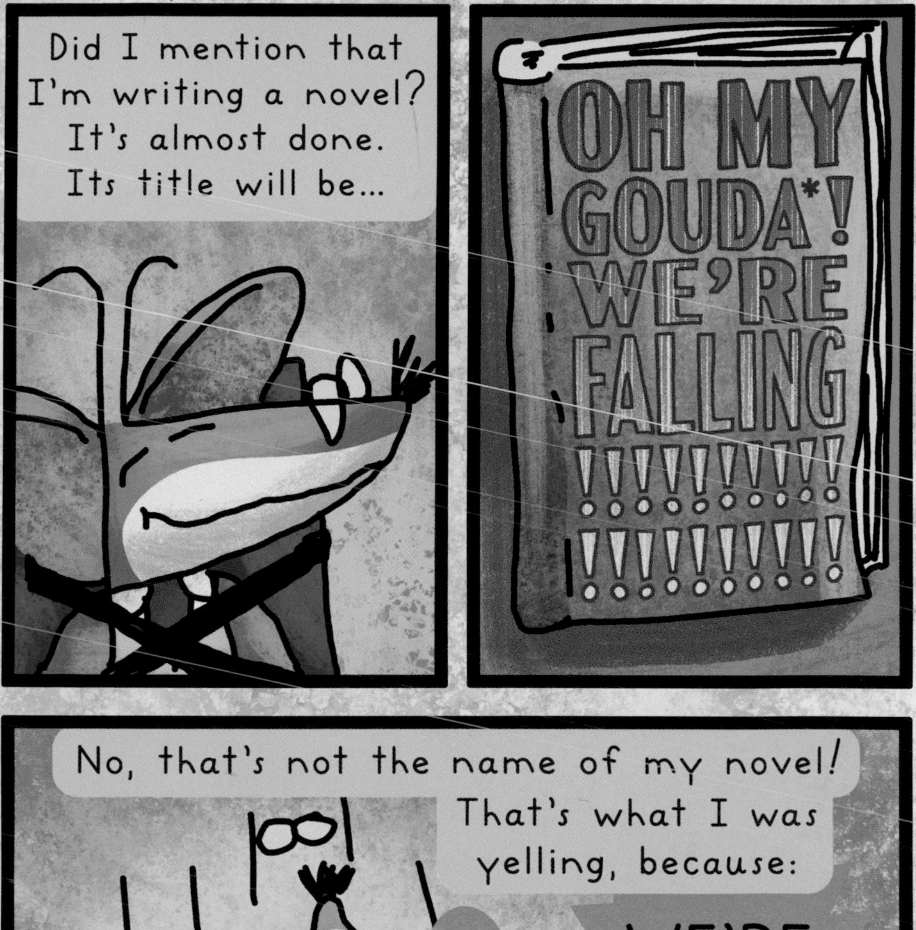
Did I mention that I'm writing a novel? It's almost done. Its title will be...
OH MY GOUDA*! WE'RE FALLING !!!!!!!!!! !!!!!!!!!!
No, that's not the name of my novel!
That's what I was yelling, because:
WE'RE FALLING
!!!!!!!!!!
!!!!!!!!!!
!!!!!!!!!!
!!!!!!!!!!

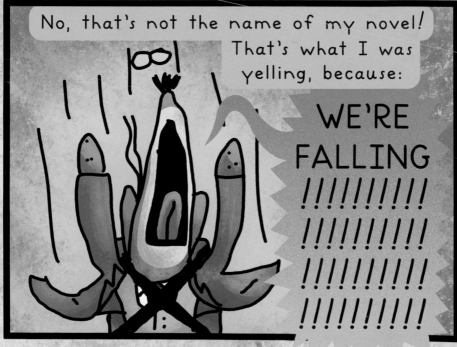

*Gouda is a kind of cheese.

CHAPTER SIX

OH NO! NOT THE CHEESELOGS!

We fell a looooong way, but just before we hit the ground, we stopped with a **TEETH-RATTLING** jerk! I was shaken, I was *shaking*, I was...so glad my niece and nephew (and my cousin) were safe!

Oh, Trappy! Benjamin!!! Thank Havarti you're okay!!!

Well, Cuz, you gotta admit...it was a quick ride!

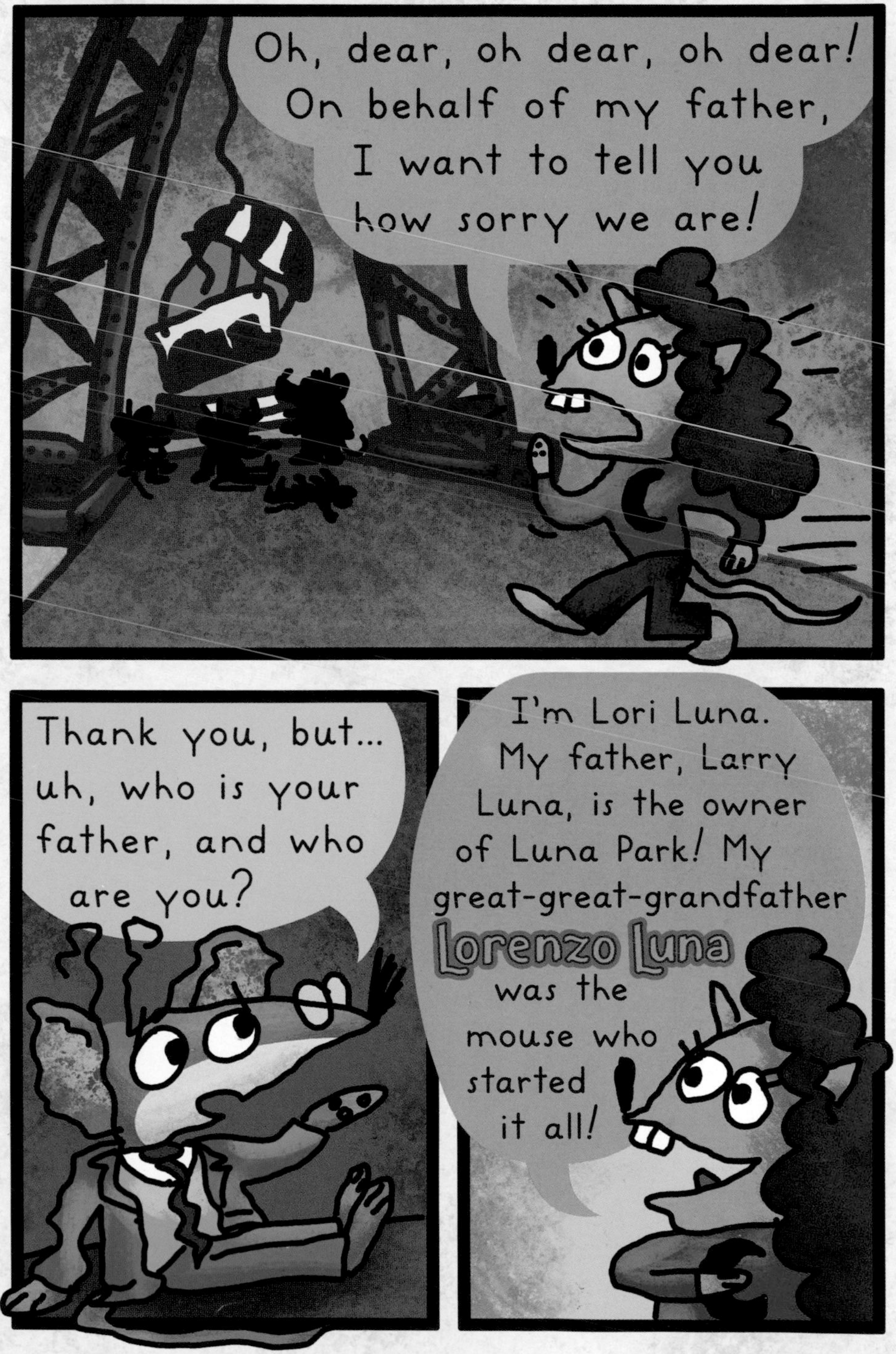
Oh, dear, oh dear, oh dear! On behalf of my father, I want to tell you how sorry we are!
Thank you, but... uh, who is your father, and who are you?
I'm Lori Luna. My father, Larry Luna, is the owner of Luna Park! My great-great-grandfather Lorenzo Luna was the mouse who started it all!

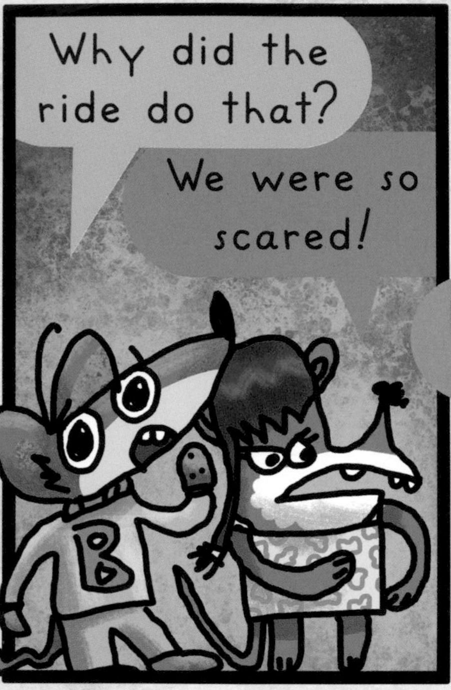
Why did the ride do that?
We were so scared!

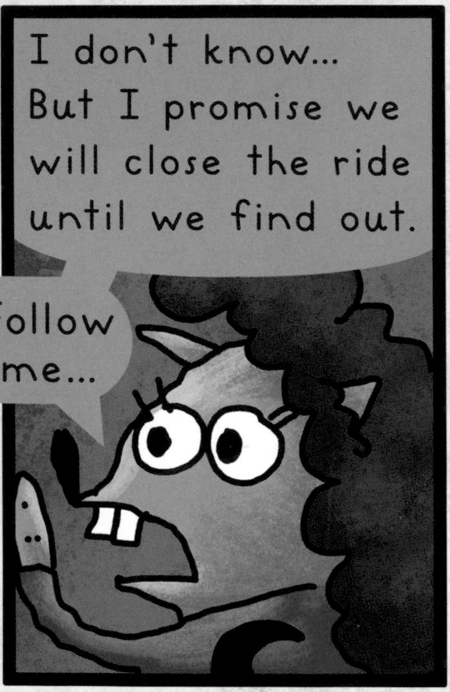
I don't know... But I promise we will close the ride until we find out.
Follow me...

We followed Miss Luna to a small building under the Paw-A-Chutes tower. Several workers were there working on a **BIG** motor.

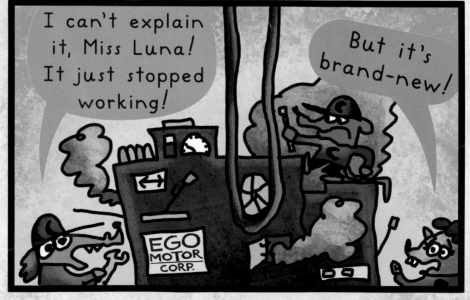

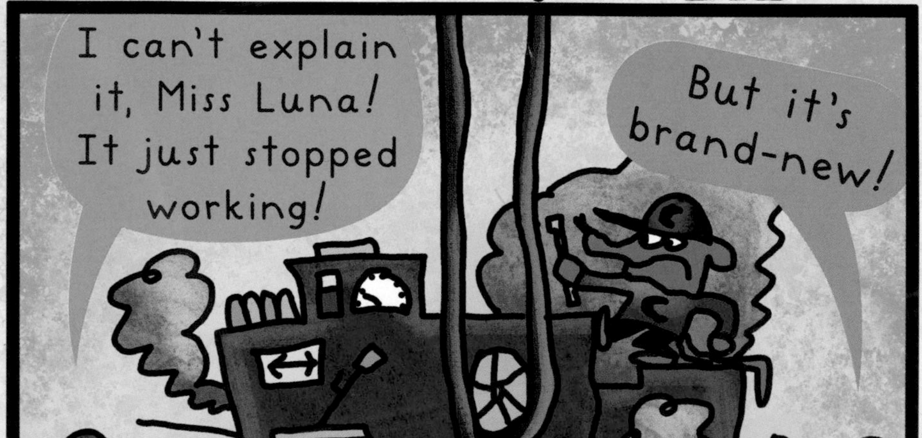
I can't explain it, Miss Luna! It just stopped working!
But it's brand-new!
EGO MOTOR CORP.

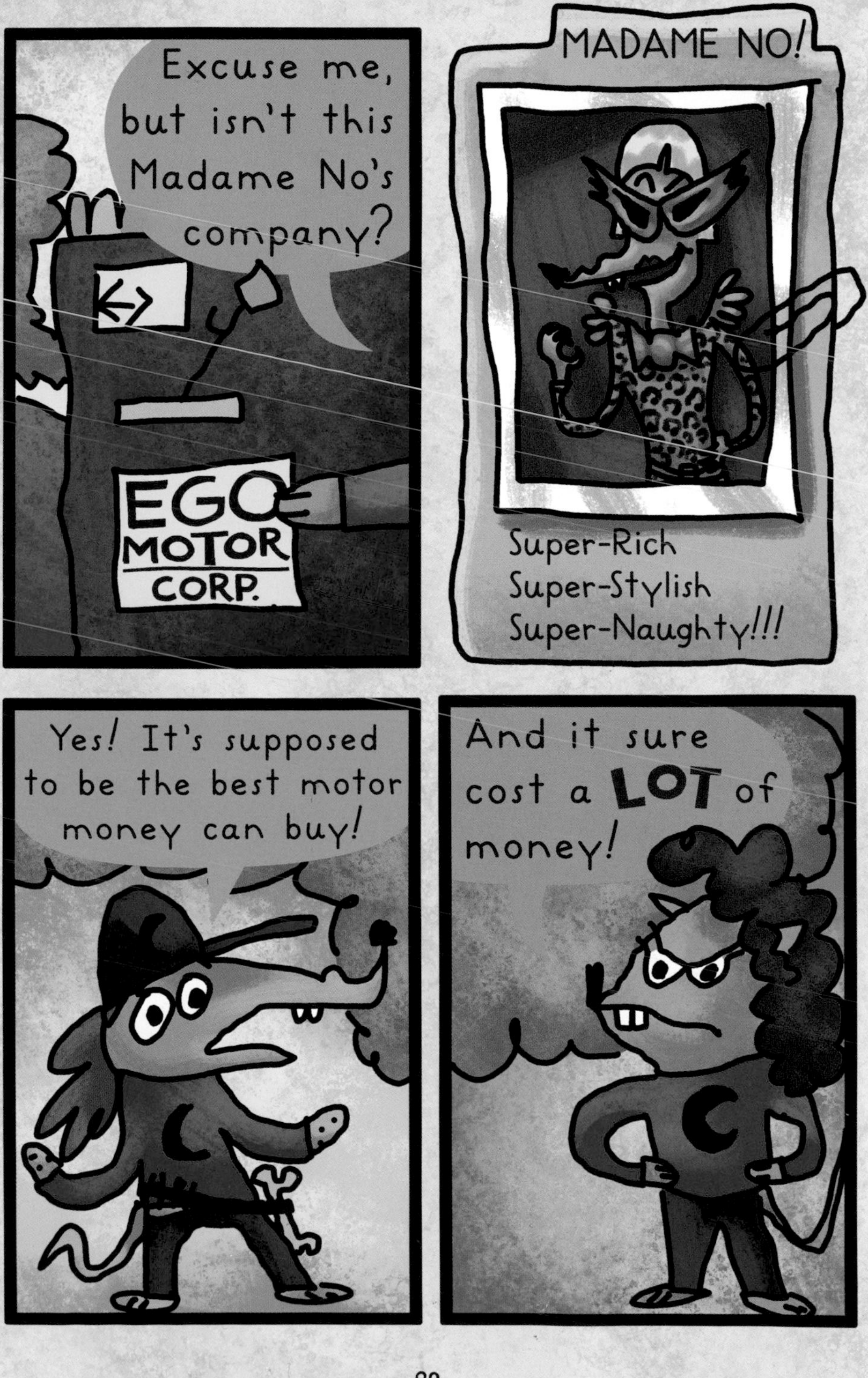
Excuse me, but isn't this Madame No's company?
EGO MOTOR CORP.
MADAME NO!
Super-Rich
Super-Stylish
Super-Naughty!!!
Yes! It's supposed to be the best motor money can buy!
And it sure cost a LOT of money!

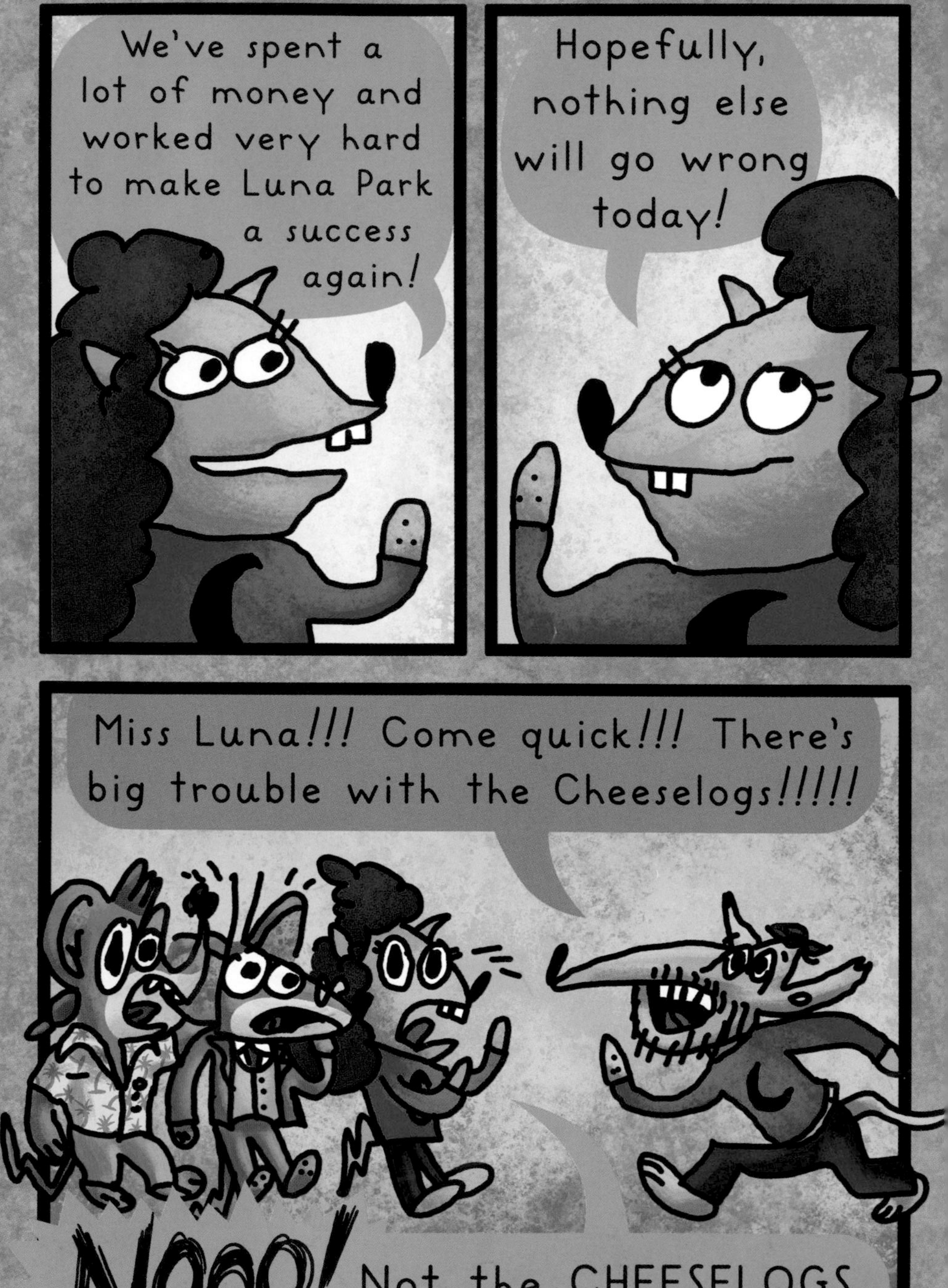
We've spent a lot of money and worked very hard to make Luna Park a success again!
Hopefully, nothing else will go wrong today!
Miss Luna!!! Come quick!!! There's big trouble with the Cheeselogs!!!!!
NOOO!
Not the CHEESELOGS.

CHAPTER SEVEN

CHEESELOG LOGJAM

As we ran across the park with Lori Luna, I was expecting to see some kind of problem with the famouse FLOATING CHEESELOG ride. But I was NOT expecting to see:

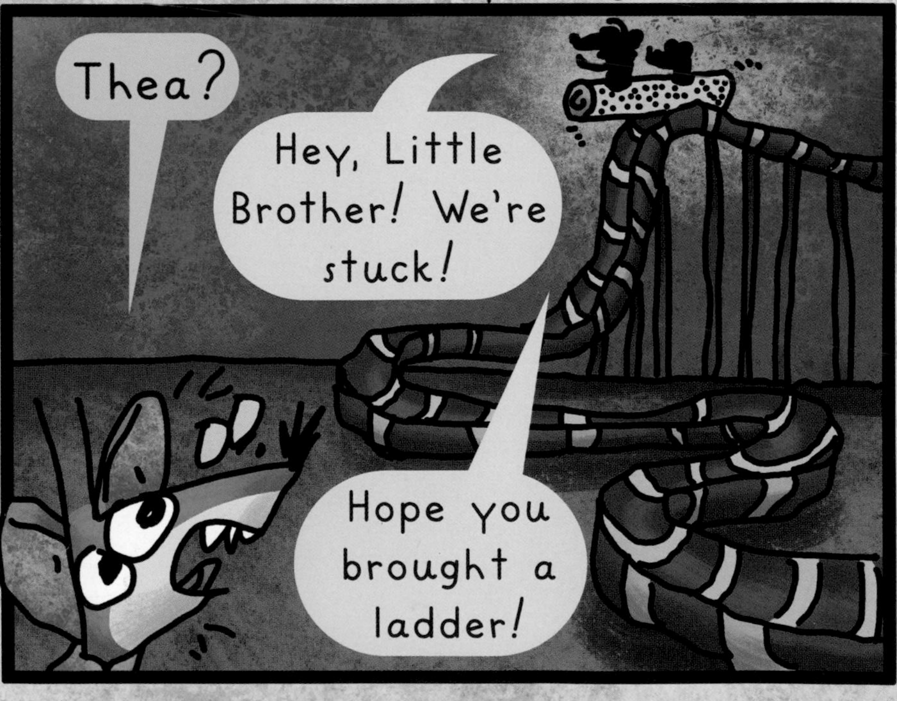
Thea?
Hey, Little Brother! We're stuck!
Hope you brought a ladder!

I didn't have a ladder, of course, but Lori called some workmice to bring one. And soon we were rescuing Thea and Bob.

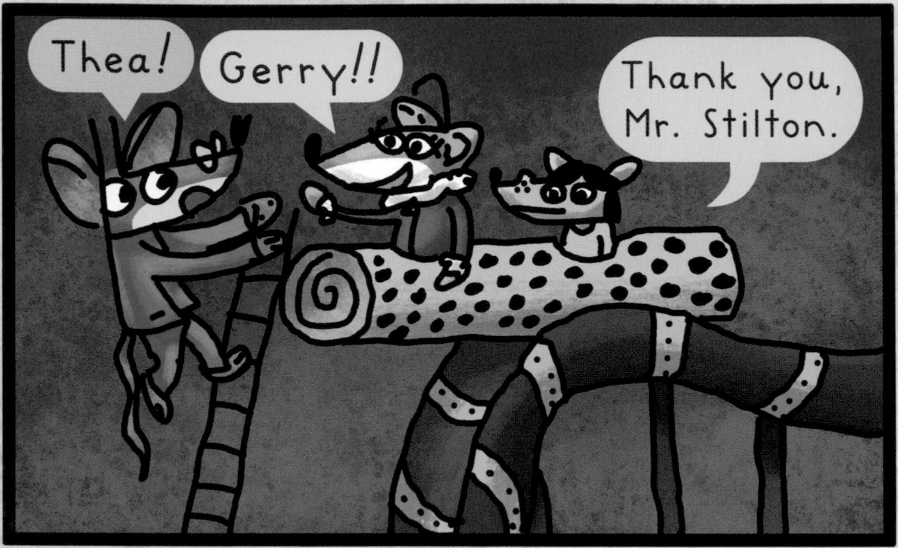

Thea!
Gerry!!
Thank you, Mr. Stilton.

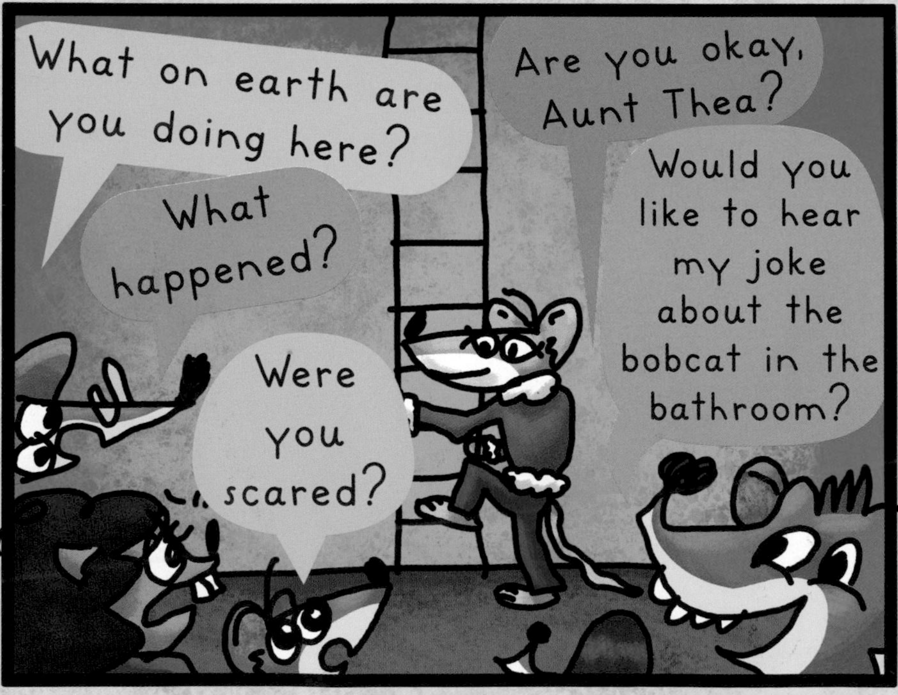

What on earth are you doing here?
What happened?
Were you scared?
Are you okay, Aunt Thea?
Would you like to hear my joke about the bobcat in the bathroom?

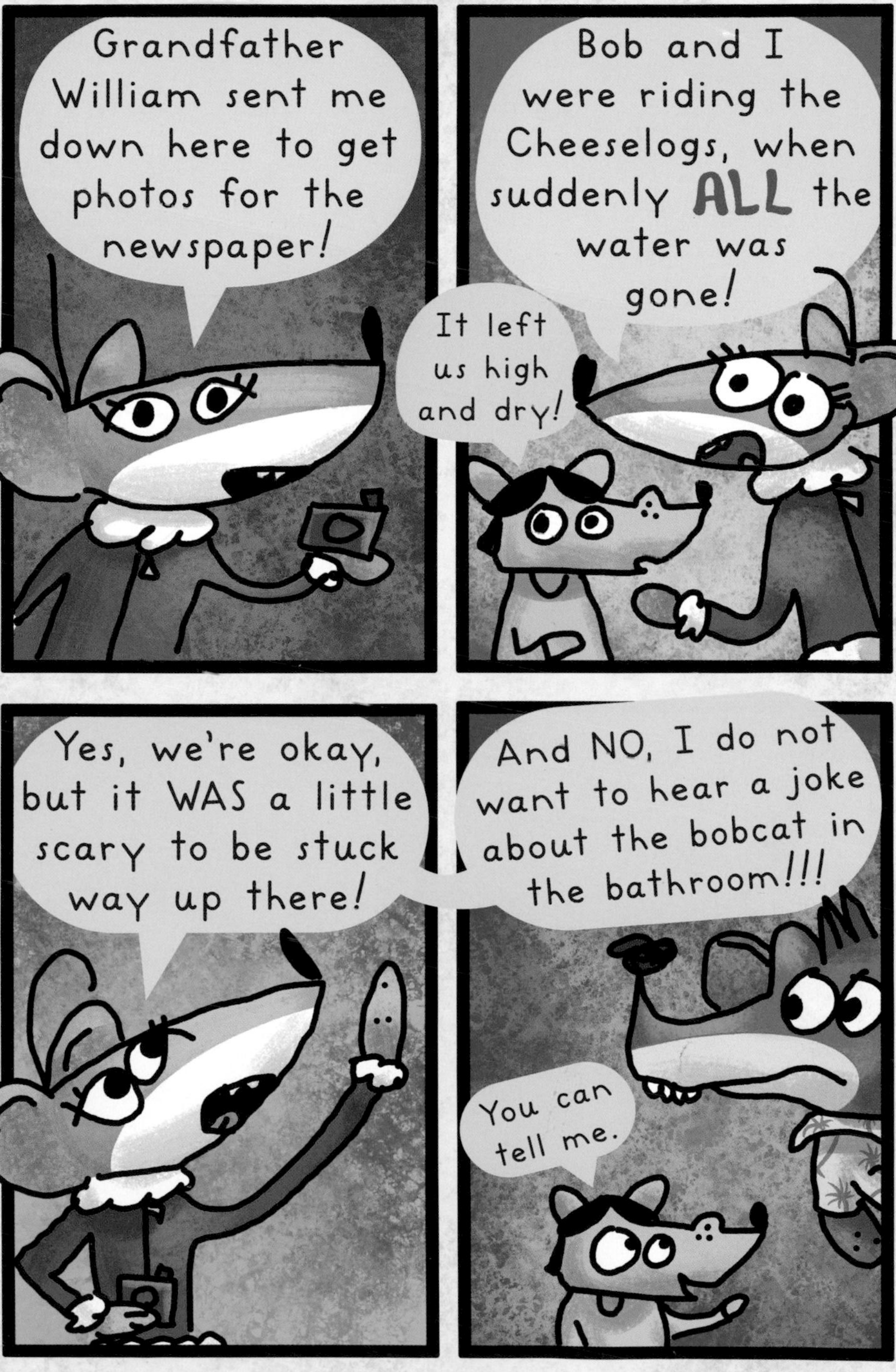
Grandfather William sent me down here to get photos for the newspaper!
Bob and I were riding the Cheeselogs, when suddenly ALL the water was gone!
It left us high and dry!
Yes, we're okay, but it WAS a little scary to be stuck way up there!
And NO, I do not want to hear a joke about the bobcat in the bathroom!!!
You can tell me.

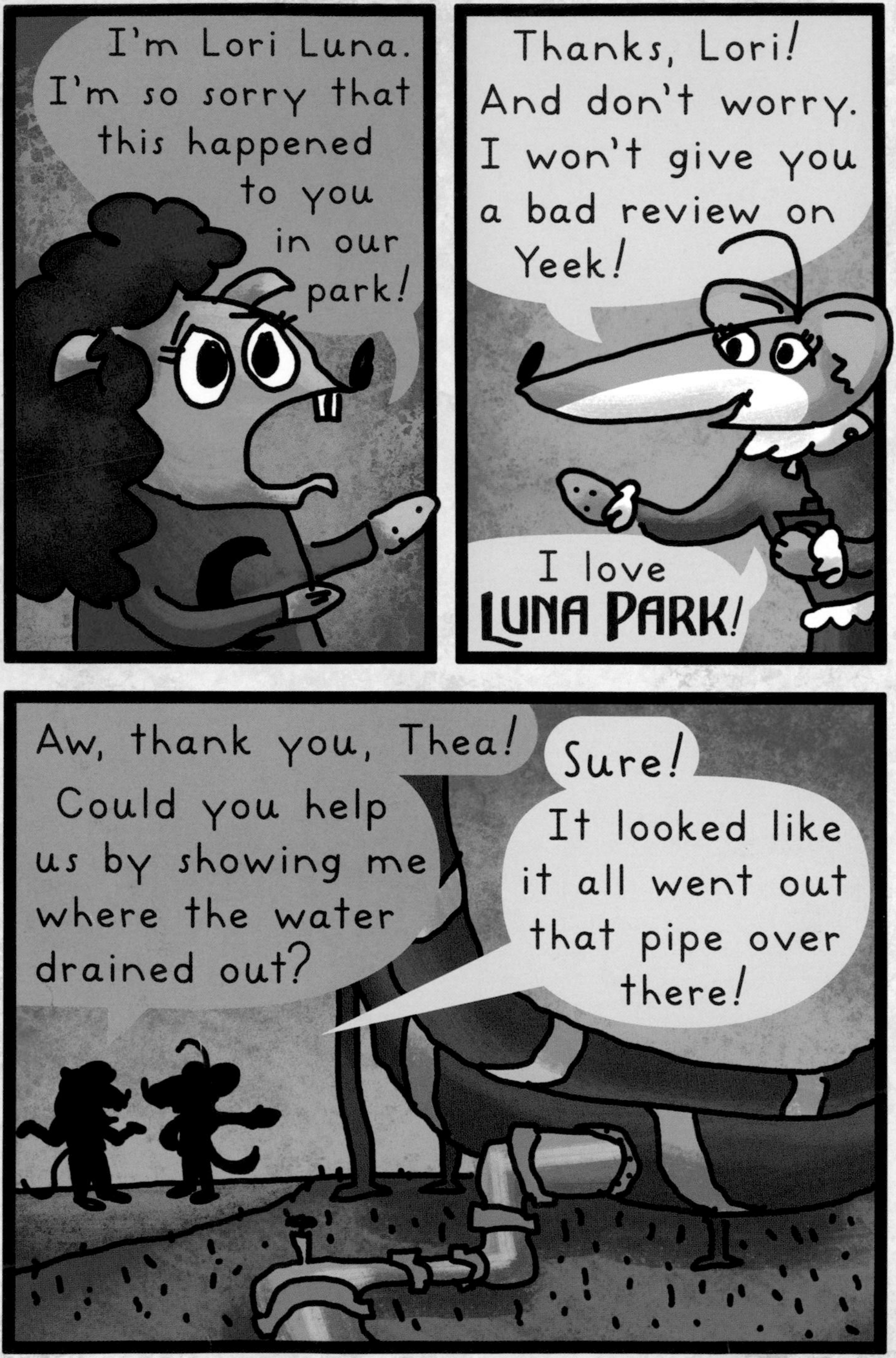

I'm Lori Luna. I'm so sorry that this happened to you in our park!
Thanks, Lori! And don't worry. I won't give you a bad review on Yeek!
I love LUNA PARK!
Aw, thank you, Thea!
Could you help us by showing me where the water drained out?
Sure!
It looked like it all went out that pipe over there!

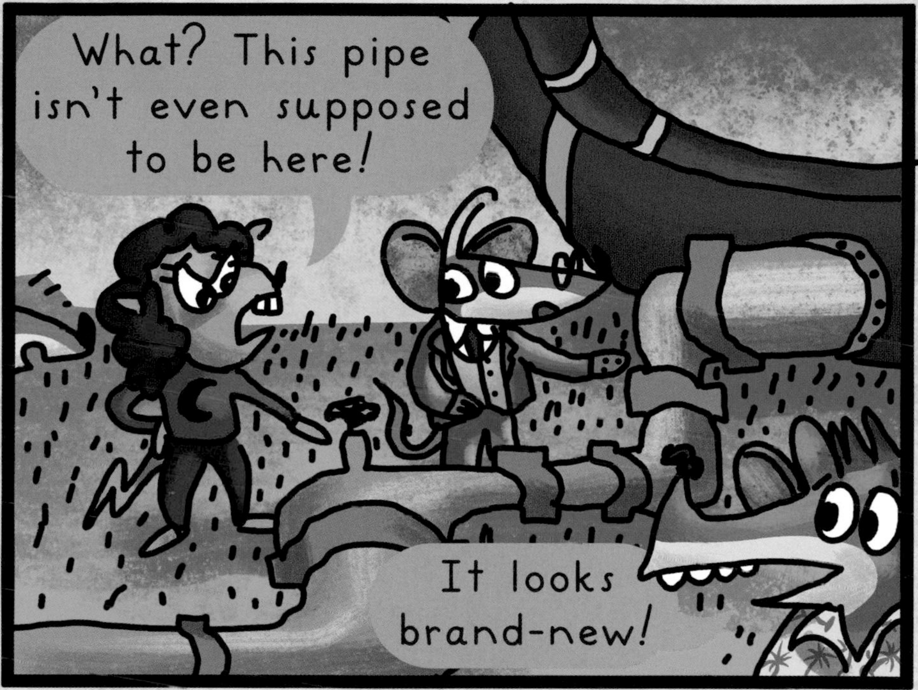
What? This pipe isn't even supposed to be here!
It looks brand-new!

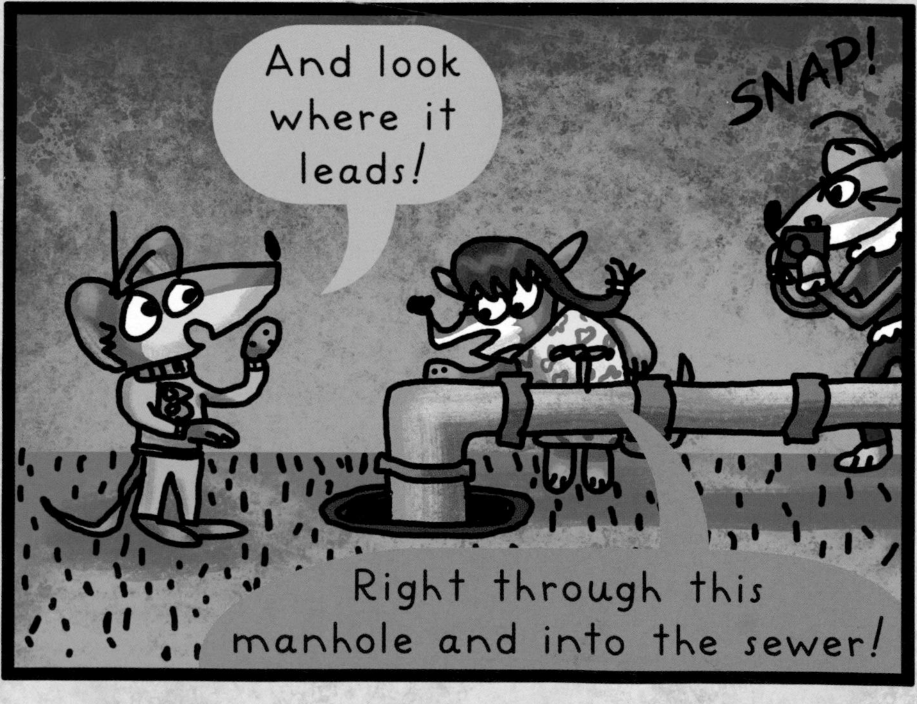
And look where it leads!
SNAP!
Right through this manhole and into the sewer!

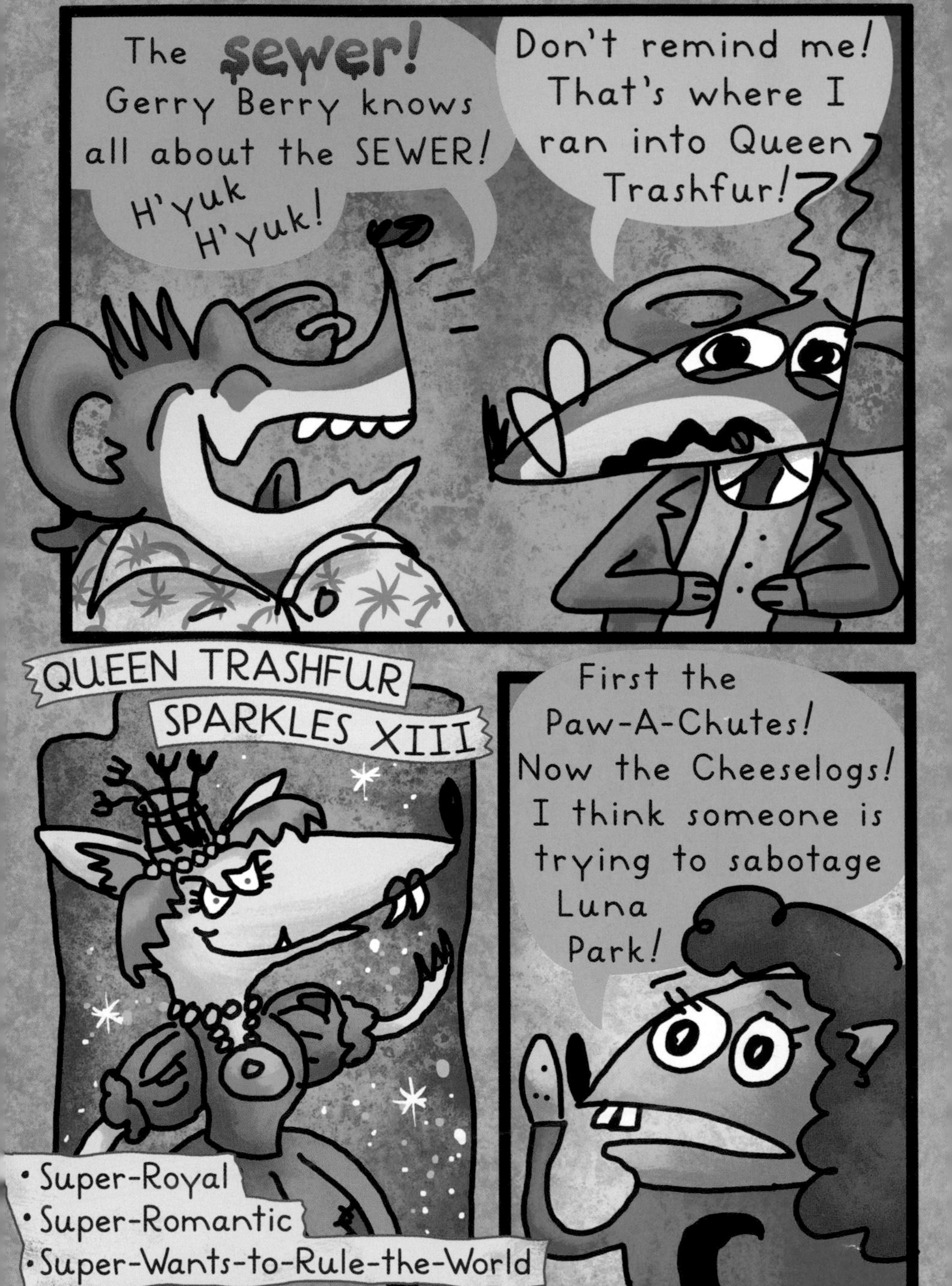
The sewer! Gerry Berry knows all about the SEWER!
H'yuk H'yuk!
Don't remind me! That's where I ran into Queen Trashfur!
QUEEN TRASHFUR SPARKLES XIII
• Super-Royal
• Super-Romantic
• Super-Wants-to-Rule-the-World
First the Paw-A-Chutes! Now the Cheeselogs! I think someone is trying to sabotage Luna Park!

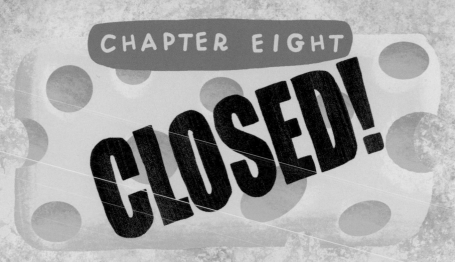

CHAPTER EIGHT

CLOSED!

Lori thanked us many times. Then, she went to help her staff put up **RIDE CLOSED** signs. Soon they were all over the park!

RIDE CLOSED
RIDE CLOSED
RIDE CLOSED
B

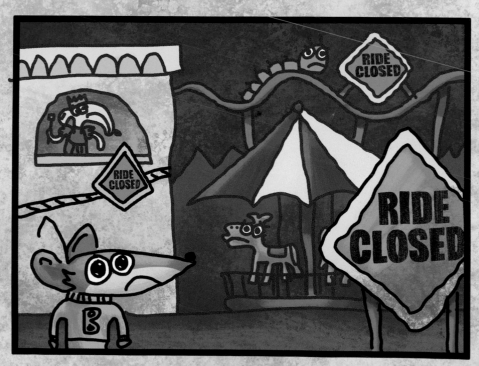

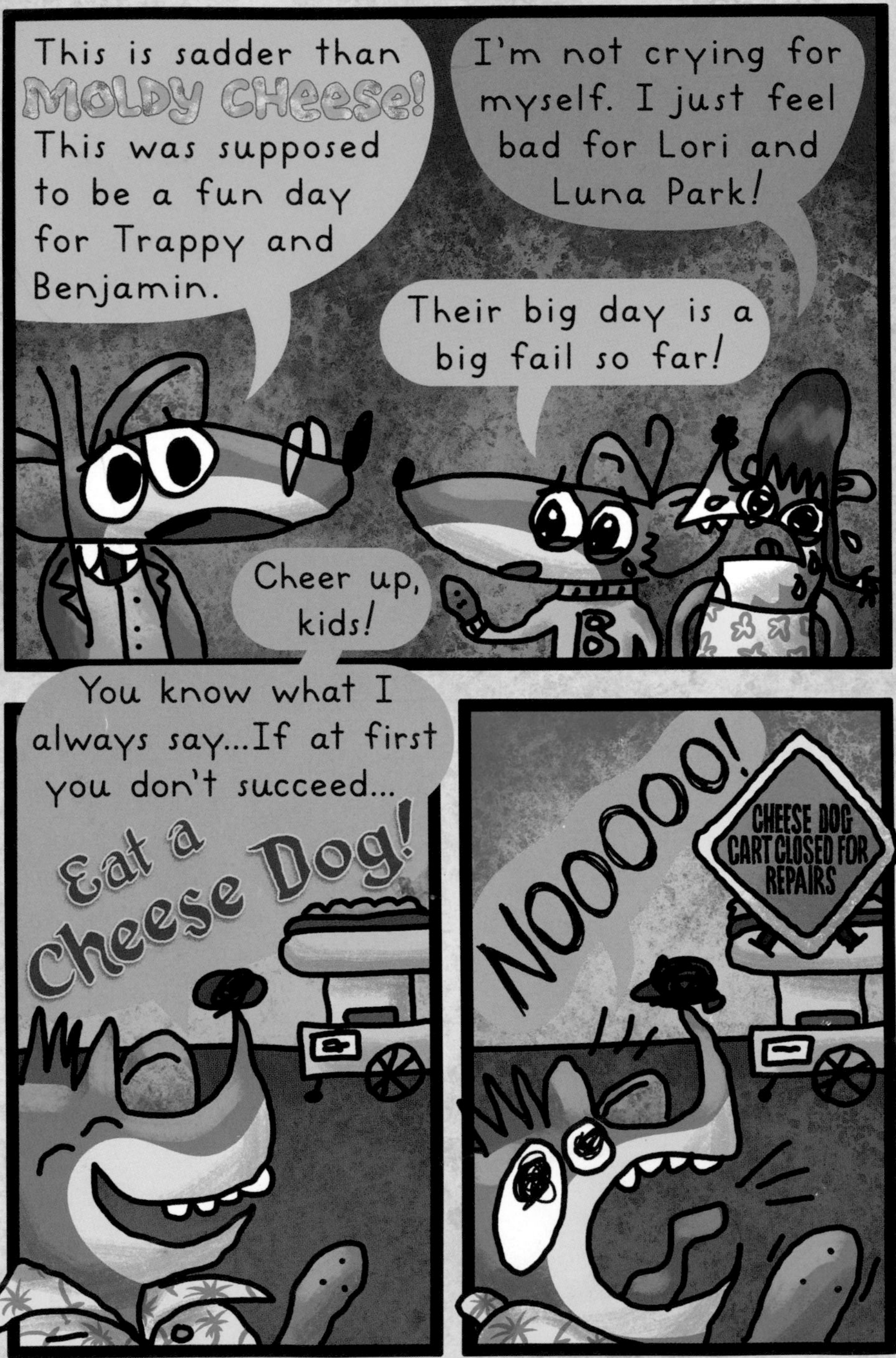
This is sadder than MOLDY CHEESE! This was supposed to be a fun day for Trappy and Benjamin.
I'm not crying for myself. I just feel bad for Lori and Luna Park!
Their big day is a big fail so far!
Cheer up, kids!
You know what I always say...If at first you don't succeed...
Eat a Cheese Dog!
NOOOOOO!
CHEESE DOG CART CLOSED FOR REPAIRS

We weren't the only ones having a bad time; a lot of other mice were grumbling, too.

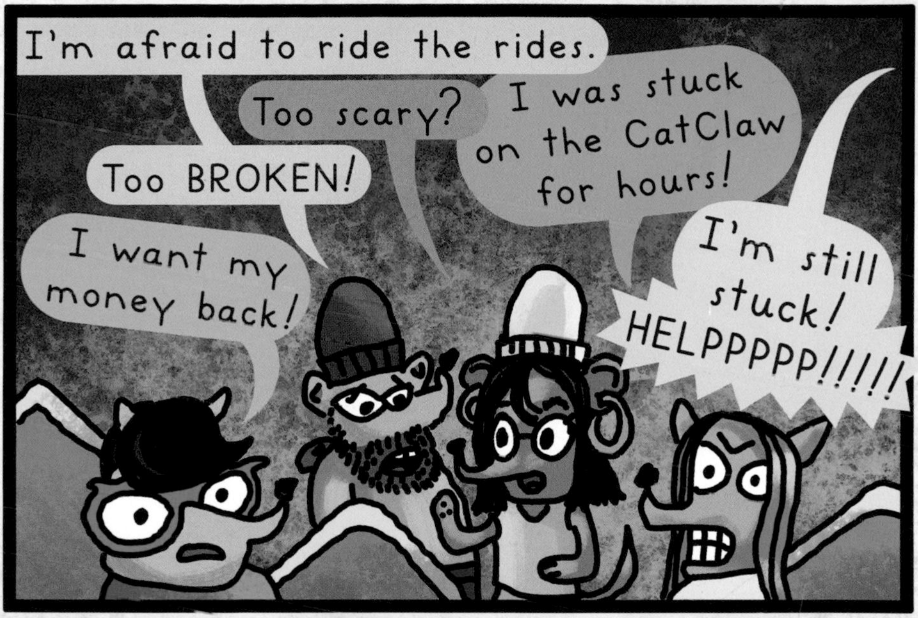
I'm afraid to ride the rides.
Too scary?
I was stuck on the CatClaw for hours!
Too BROKEN!
I want my money back!
I'm still stuck! HELPPPPP!!!!!

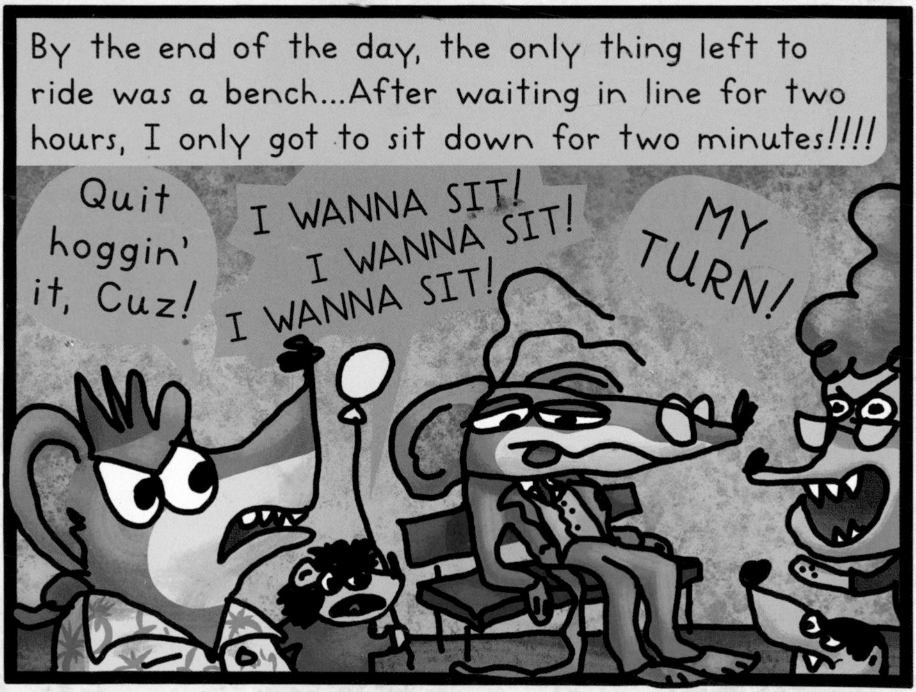
By the end of the day, the only thing left to ride was a bench...After waiting in line for two hours, I only got to sit down for two minutes!!!!
Quit hoggin' it, Cuz!
I WANNA SIT! I WANNA SIT! I WANNA SIT!
MY TURN!

FINALLY, it was time for the big ceremony to show off the new ride.

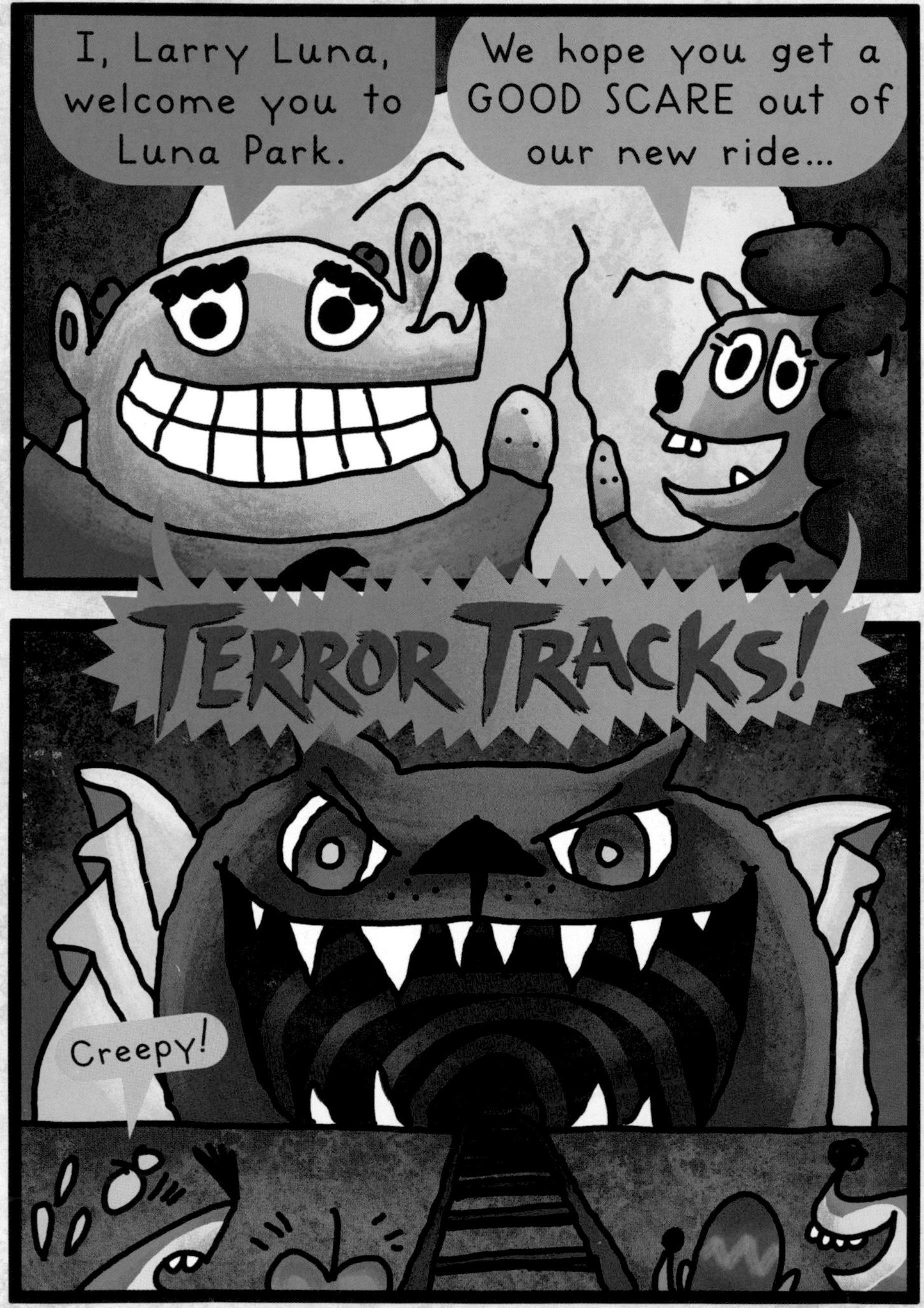
I, Larry Luna, welcome you to Luna Park.
We hope you get a GOOD SCARE out of our new ride...
TERROR TRACKS!
Creepy!

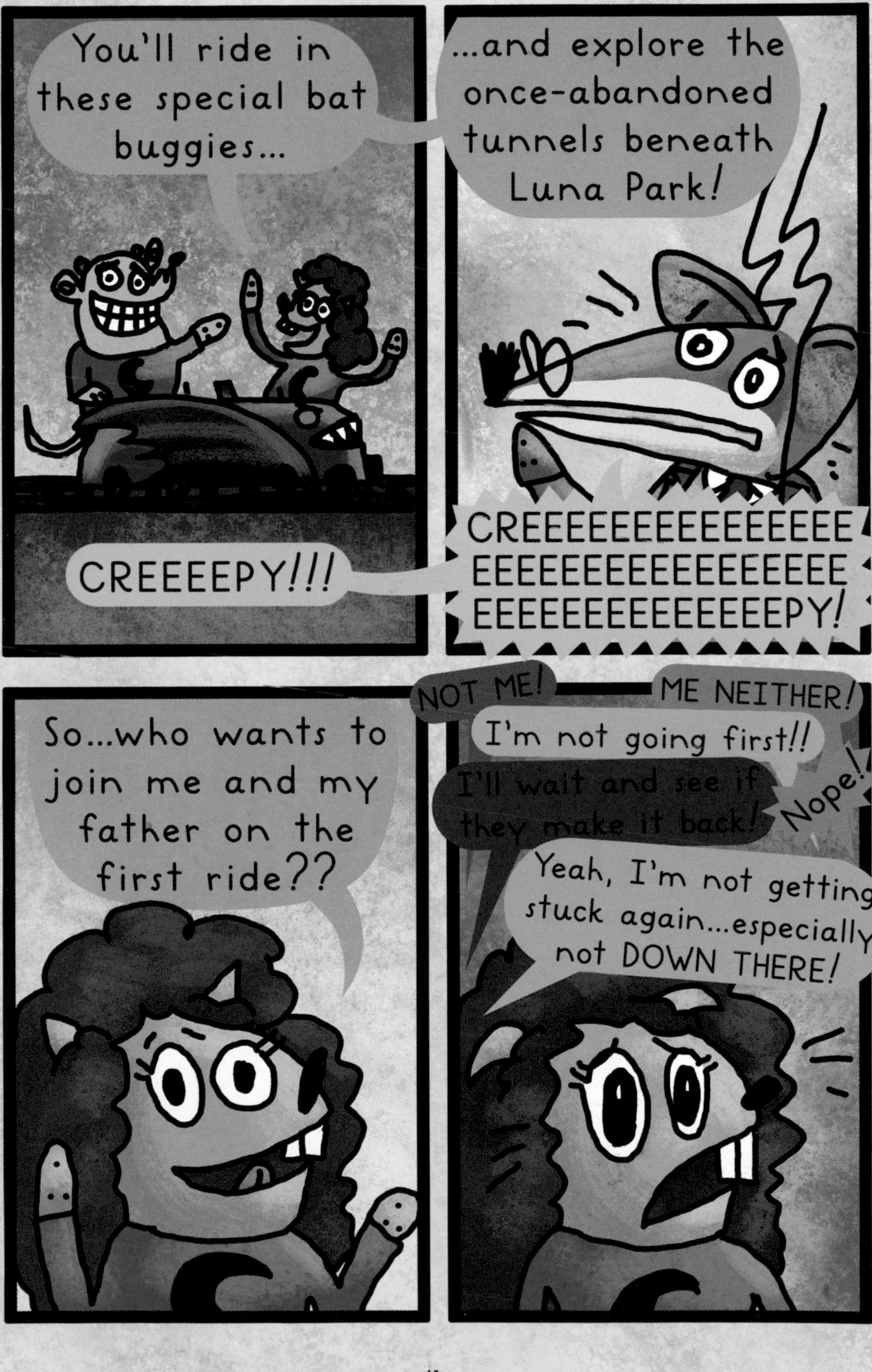
You'll ride in these special bat buggies...
...and explore the once-abandoned tunnels beneath Luna Park!
CREEEEPY!!!
CREEEEEEEEEEEEEEEE EEEEEEEEEEEEEEEEEE EEEEEEEEEEEEEEEPY!
So...who wants to join me and my father on the first ride??
NOT ME!
ME NEITHER!
I'm not going first!!
I'll wait and see if they make it back!
Nope!
Yeah, I'm not getting stuck again...especially not DOWN THERE!

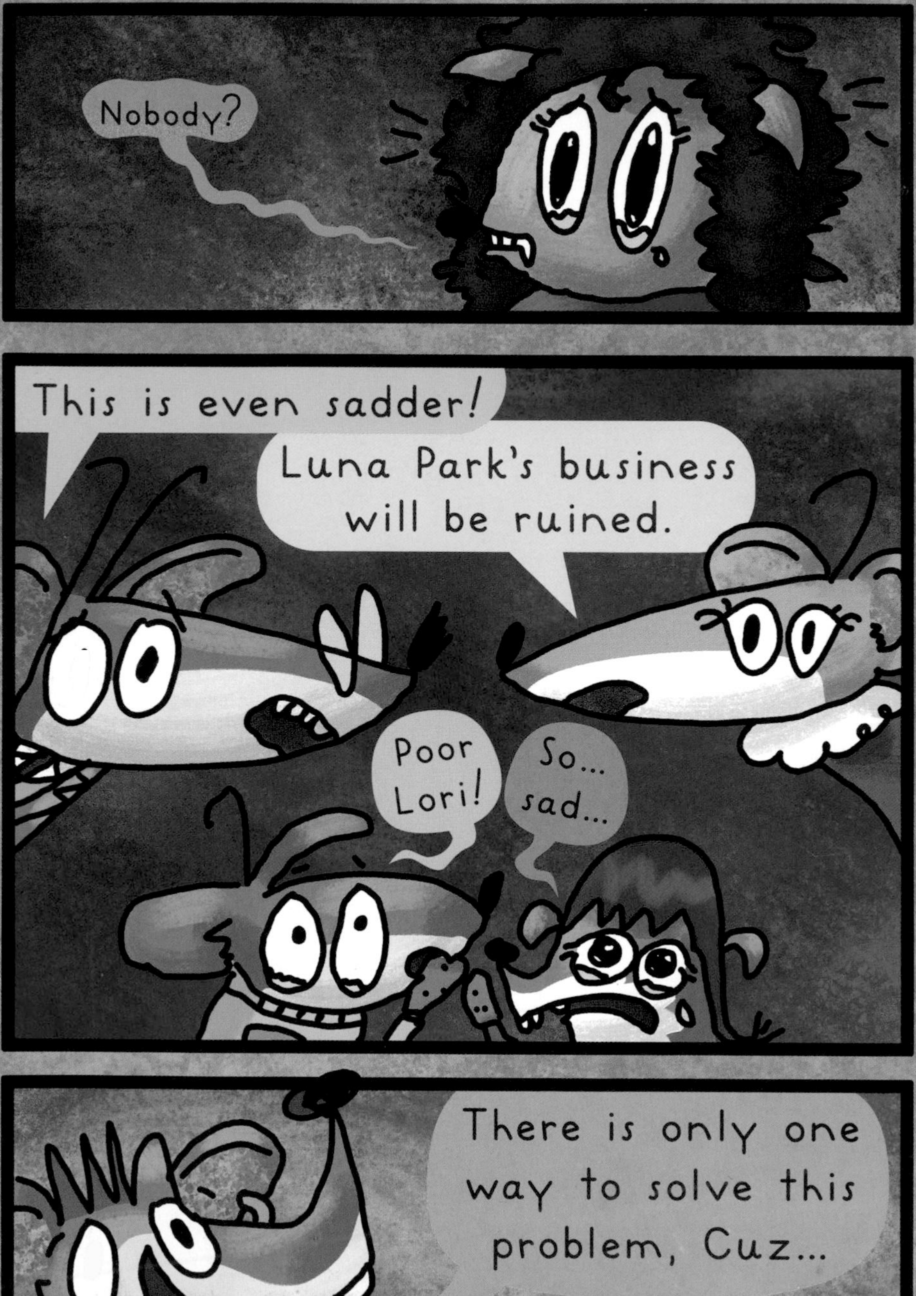
Nobody?
This is even sadder!
Luna Park's business will be ruined.
Poor Lori!
So... sad...
There is only one way to solve this problem, Cuz...

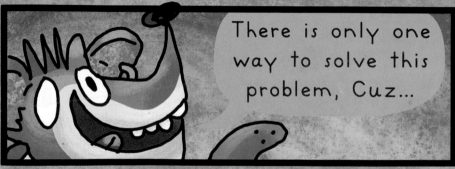

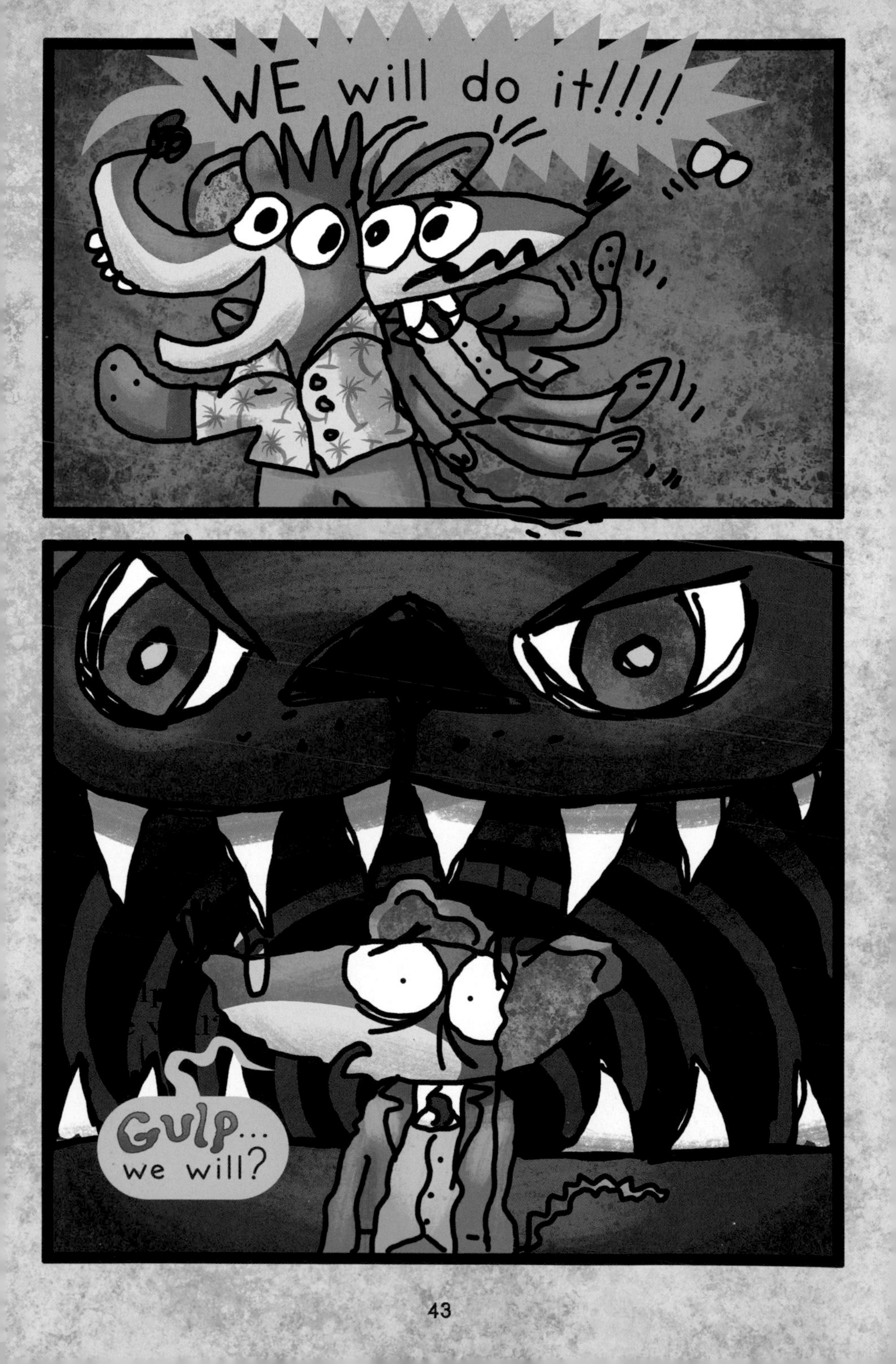
WE will do it!!!!
Gulp... we will?

CHAPTER NINE

IT ALMOST SEEMS REAL...

I was **SCARED!** I was **TERRIFIED!** I was being shoved into the bat buggy by my cousin before I could think of a way out!

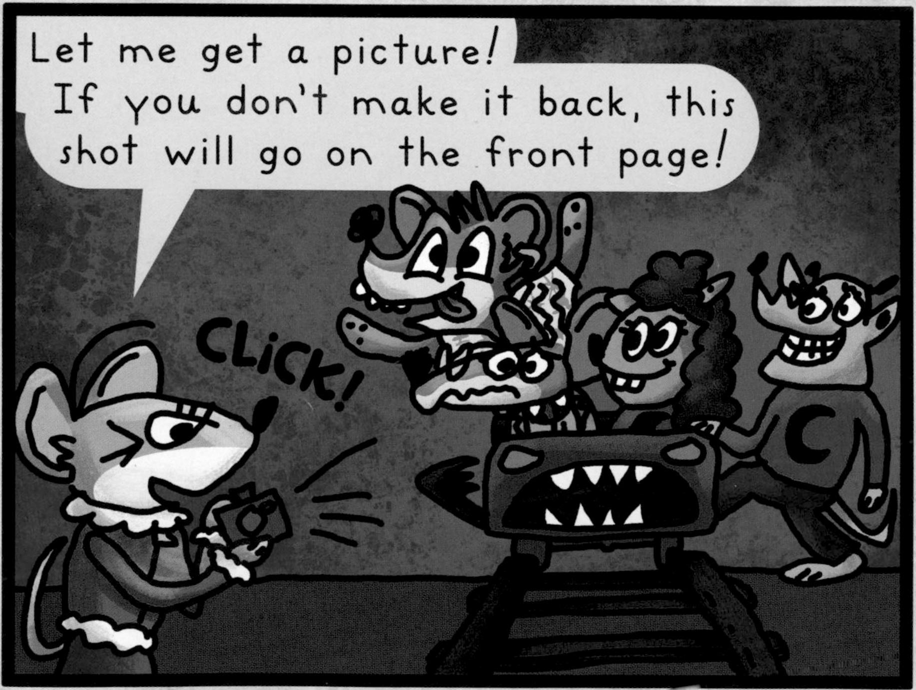

Let me get a picture! If you don't make it back, this shot will go on the front page!
CLICK!

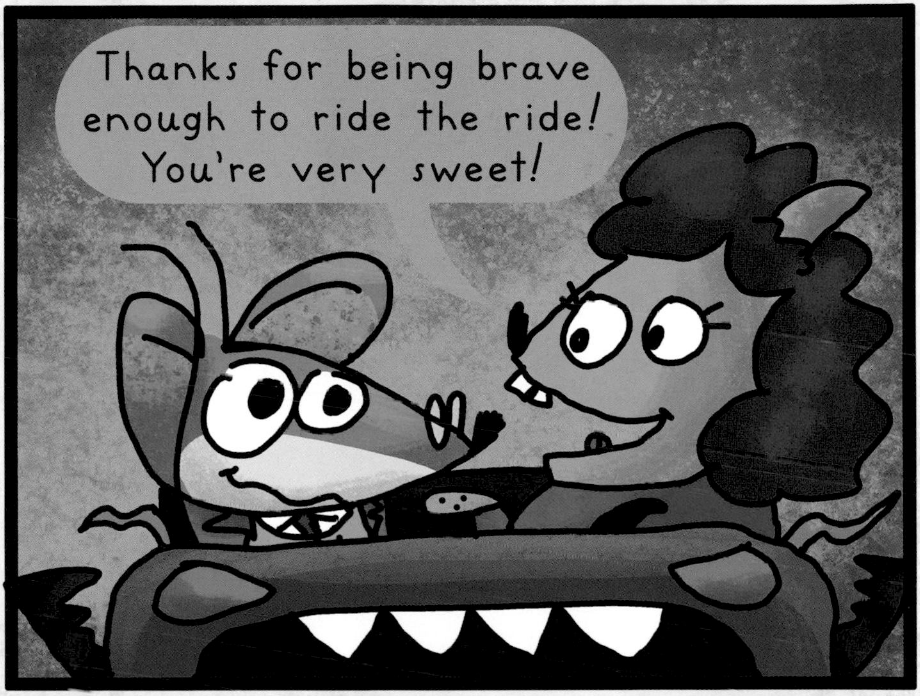
Thanks for being brave enough to ride the ride! You're very sweet!

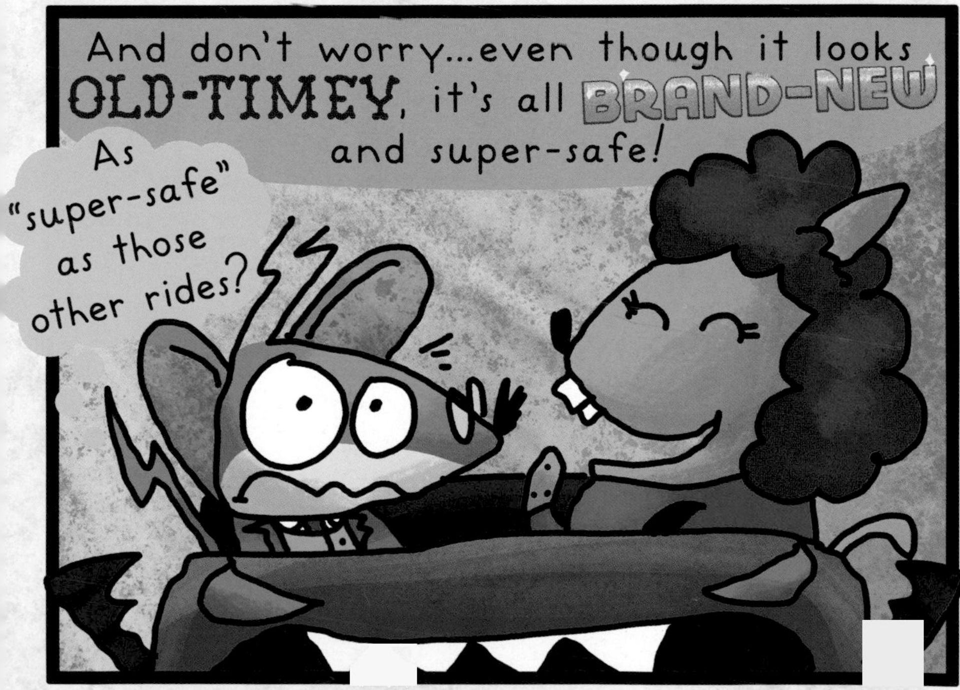
And don't worry...even though it looks OLD-TIMEY, it's all BRAND-NEW and super-safe!
As "super-safe" as those other rides?

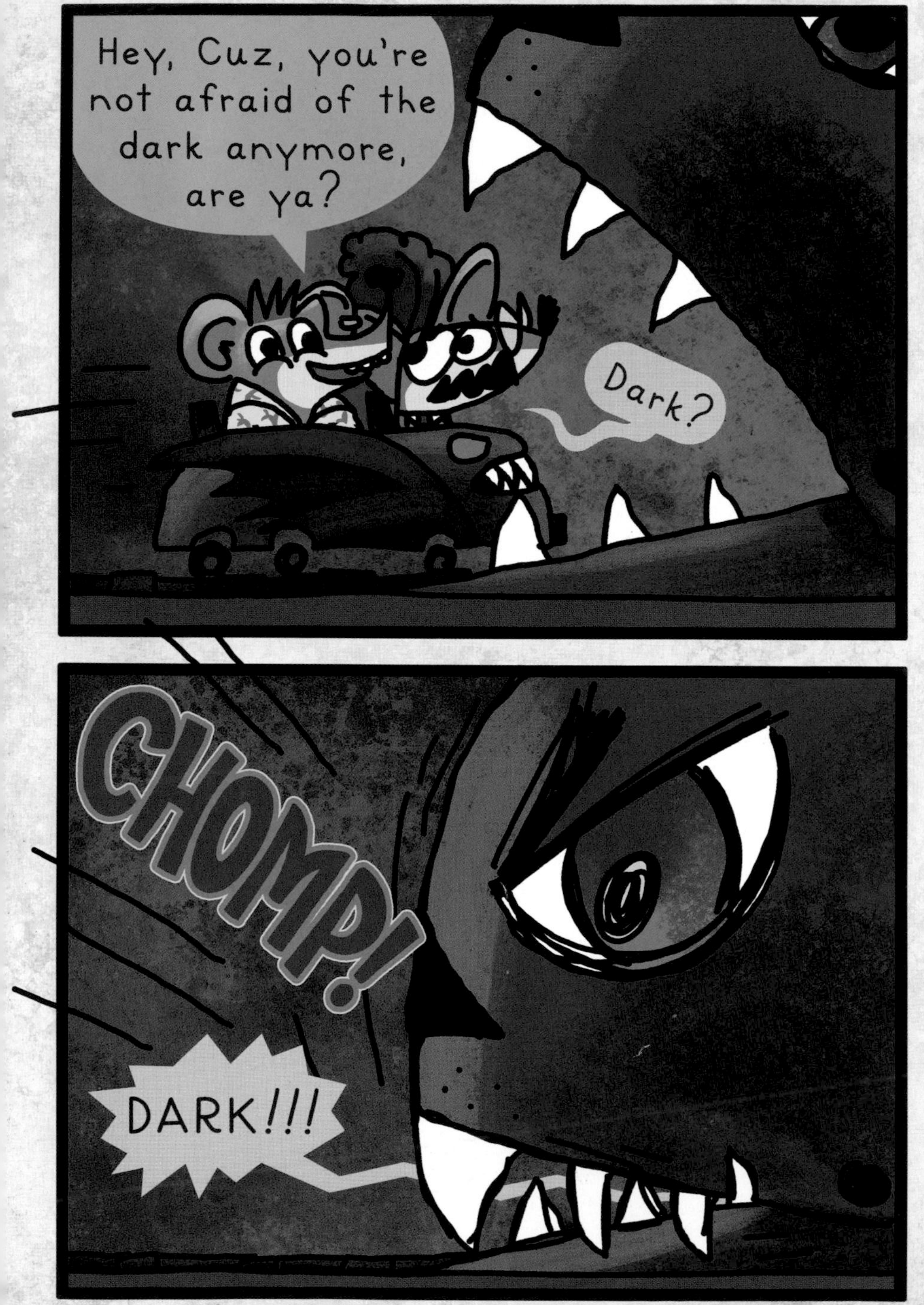
Hey, Cuz, you're not afraid of the dark anymore, are ya?
Dark?
CHOMP!
DARK!!!

In seconds we were *ZOOMING* through the dark with **HORRIBLE** monsters jumping out at us!

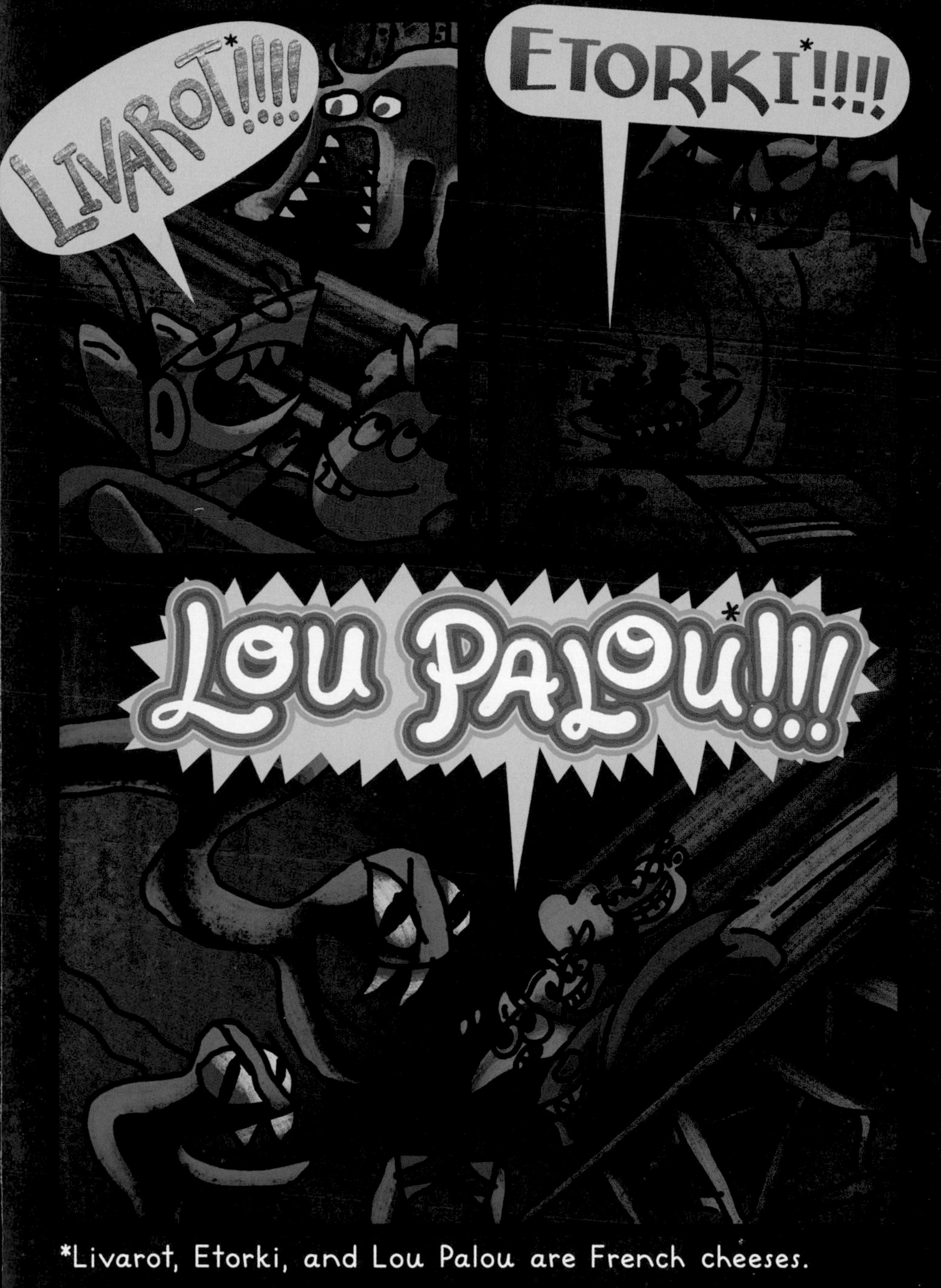

LIVAROT*!!!!
ETORKI*!!!!
LOU PALOU*!!!

*Livarot, Etorki, and Lou Palou are French cheeses.

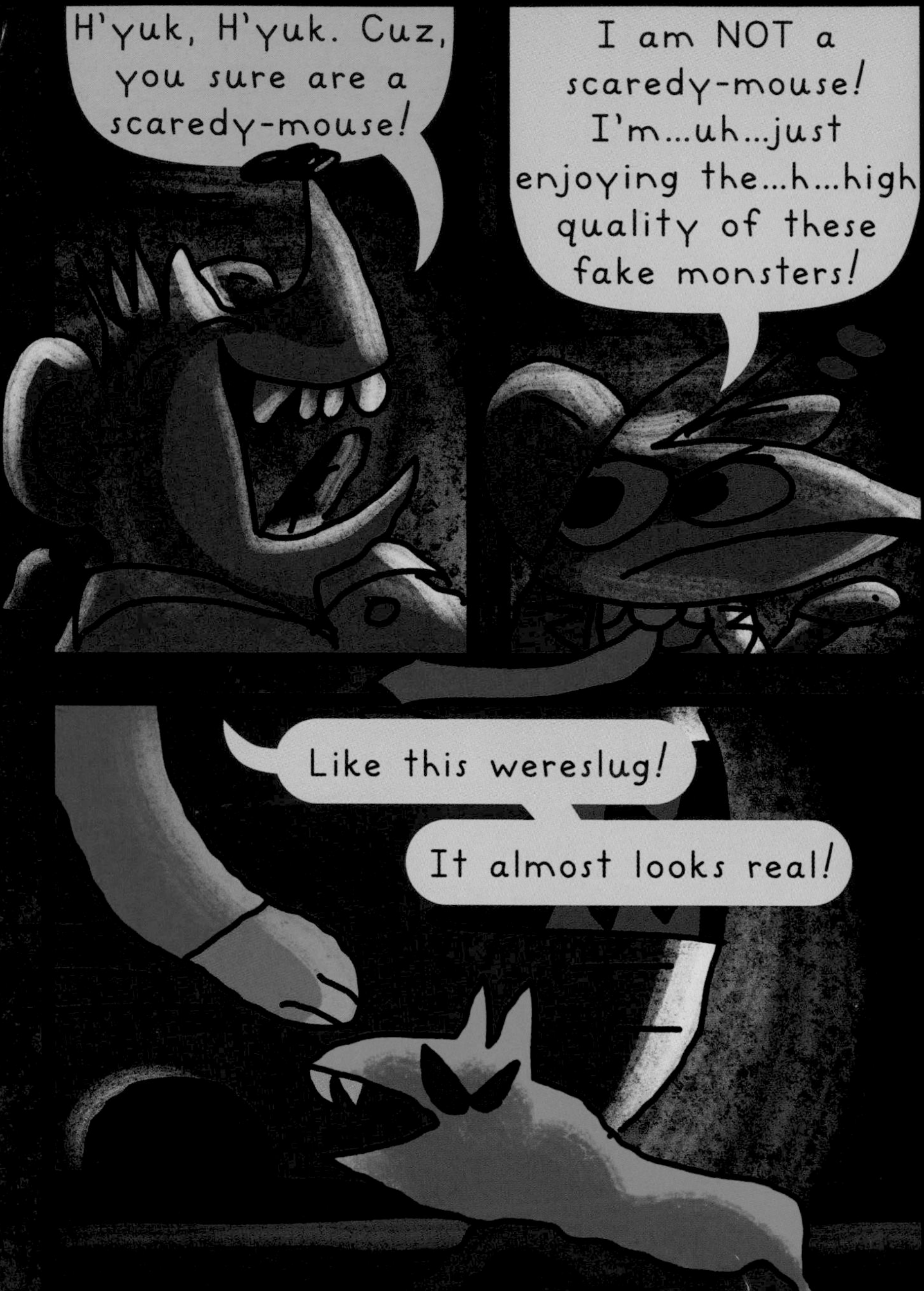
H'yuk, H'yuk. Cuz, you sure are a scaredy-mouse!
I am NOT a scaredy-mouse! I'm...uh...just enjoying the...h...high quality of these fake monsters!
Like this wereslug!
It almost looks real!

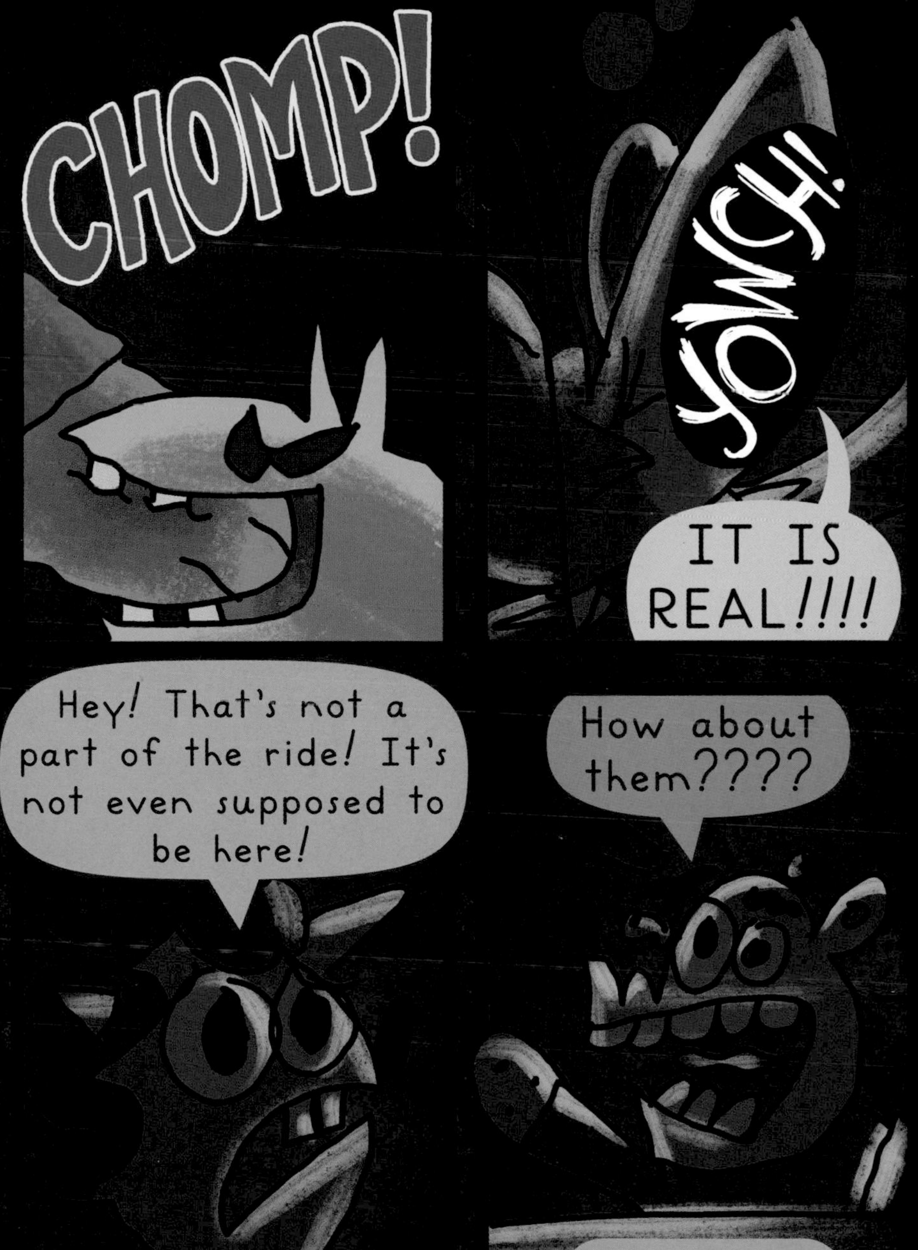
CHOMP!
YOWCH!
IT IS REAL!!!!
Hey! That's not a part of the ride! It's not even supposed to be here!
How about them????
Them???

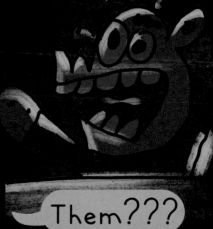

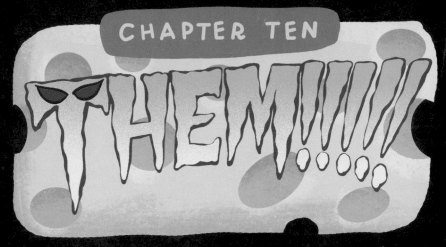

CHAPTER TEN
THEM!!!!!

The wereslug wasn't alone!
There was a whole swarm of them!!!
They were **oozing** from
all directions!

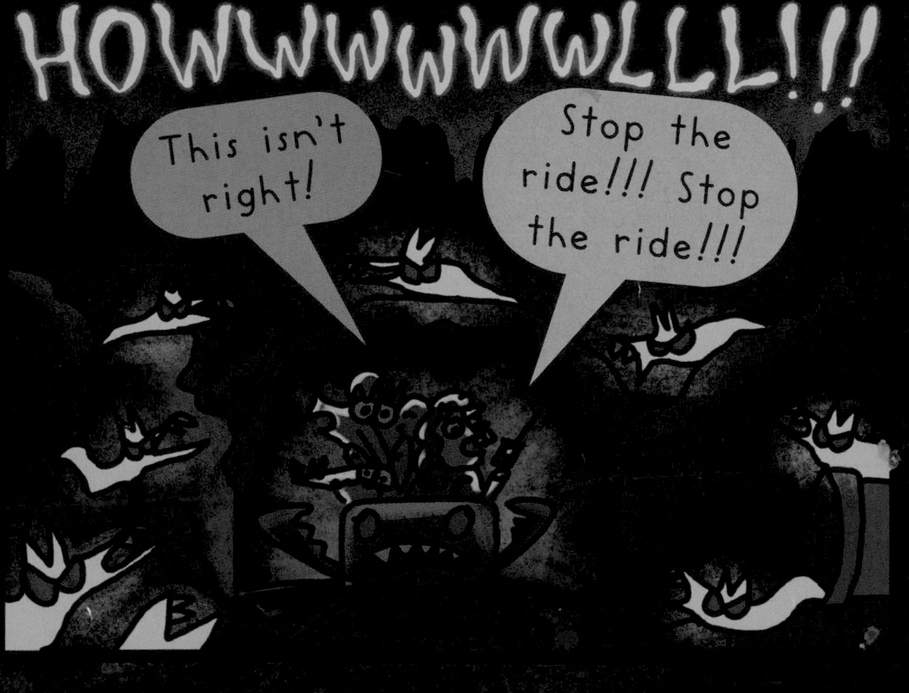
HOWWWWWLLL!!!
This isn't right!
Stop the ride!!! Stop the ride!!!

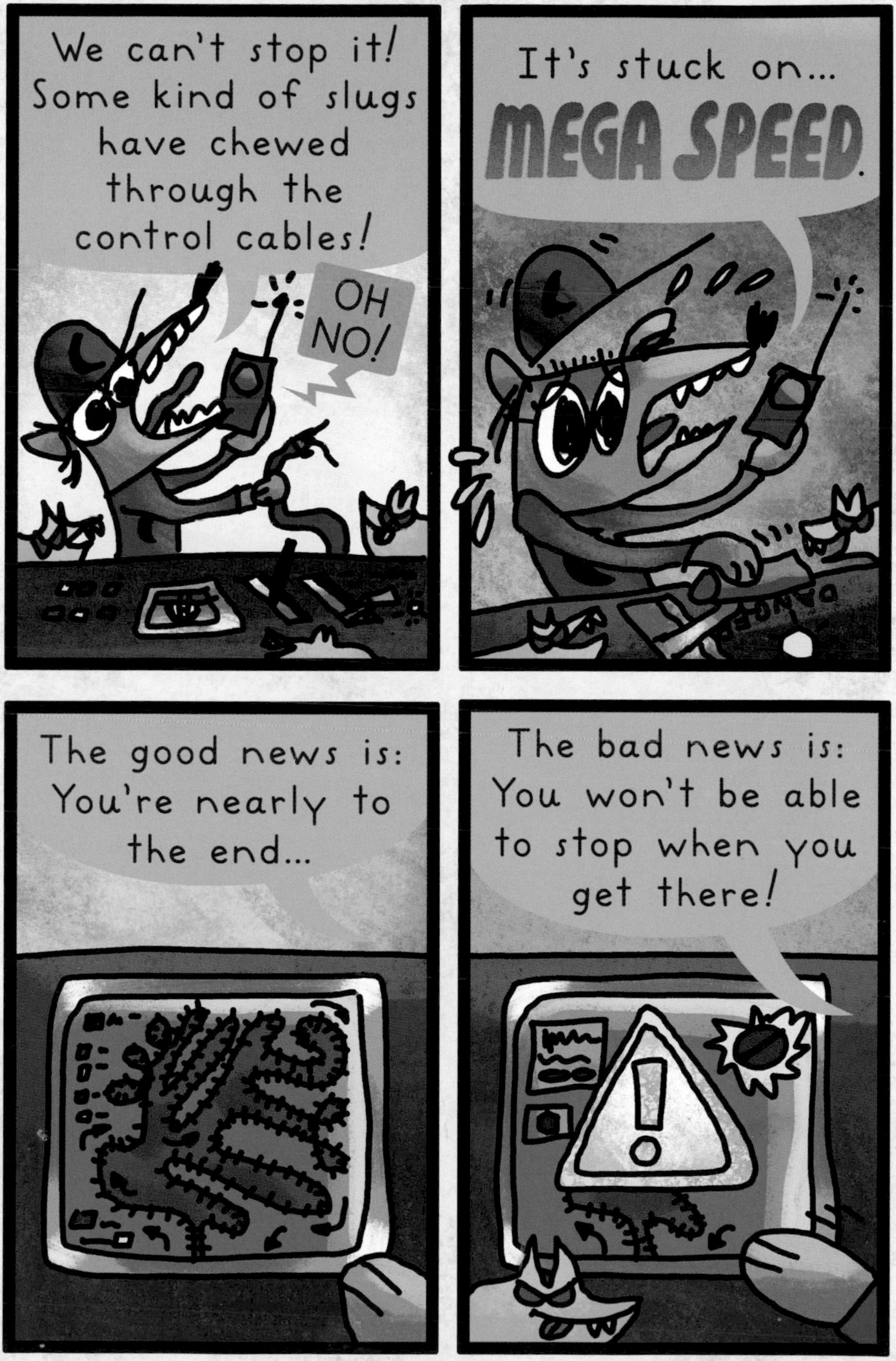
We can't stop it! Some kind of slugs have chewed through the control cables!
OH NO!
It's stuck on...
MEGA SPEED.
The good news is: You're nearly to the end...
The bad news is: You won't be able to stop when you get there!

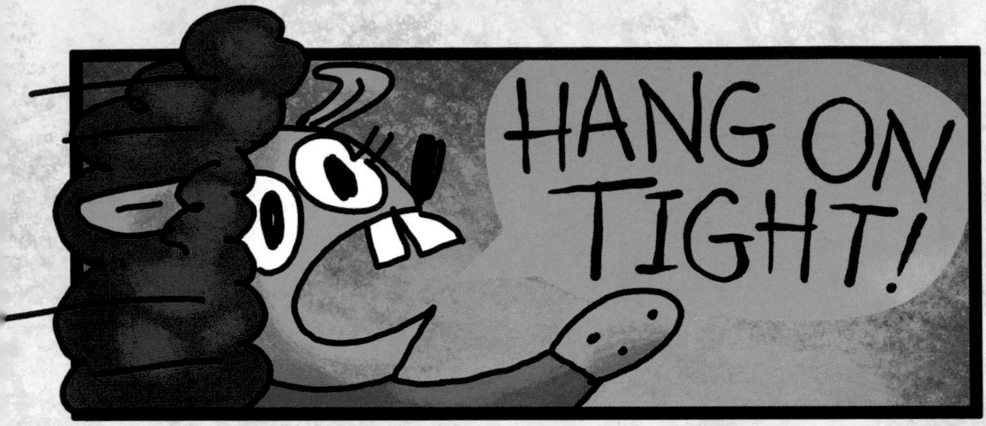
HANG ON TIGHT!

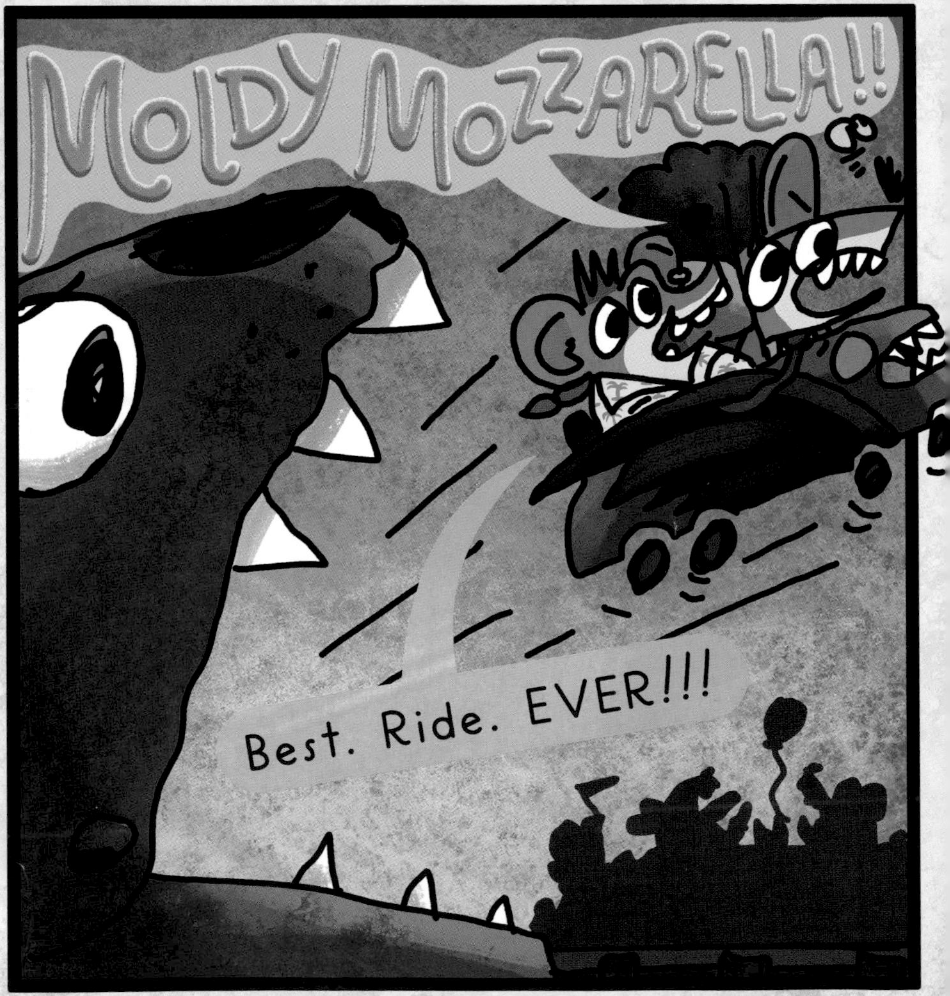
MOLDY MOZZARELLA!!
Best. Ride. EVER!!!

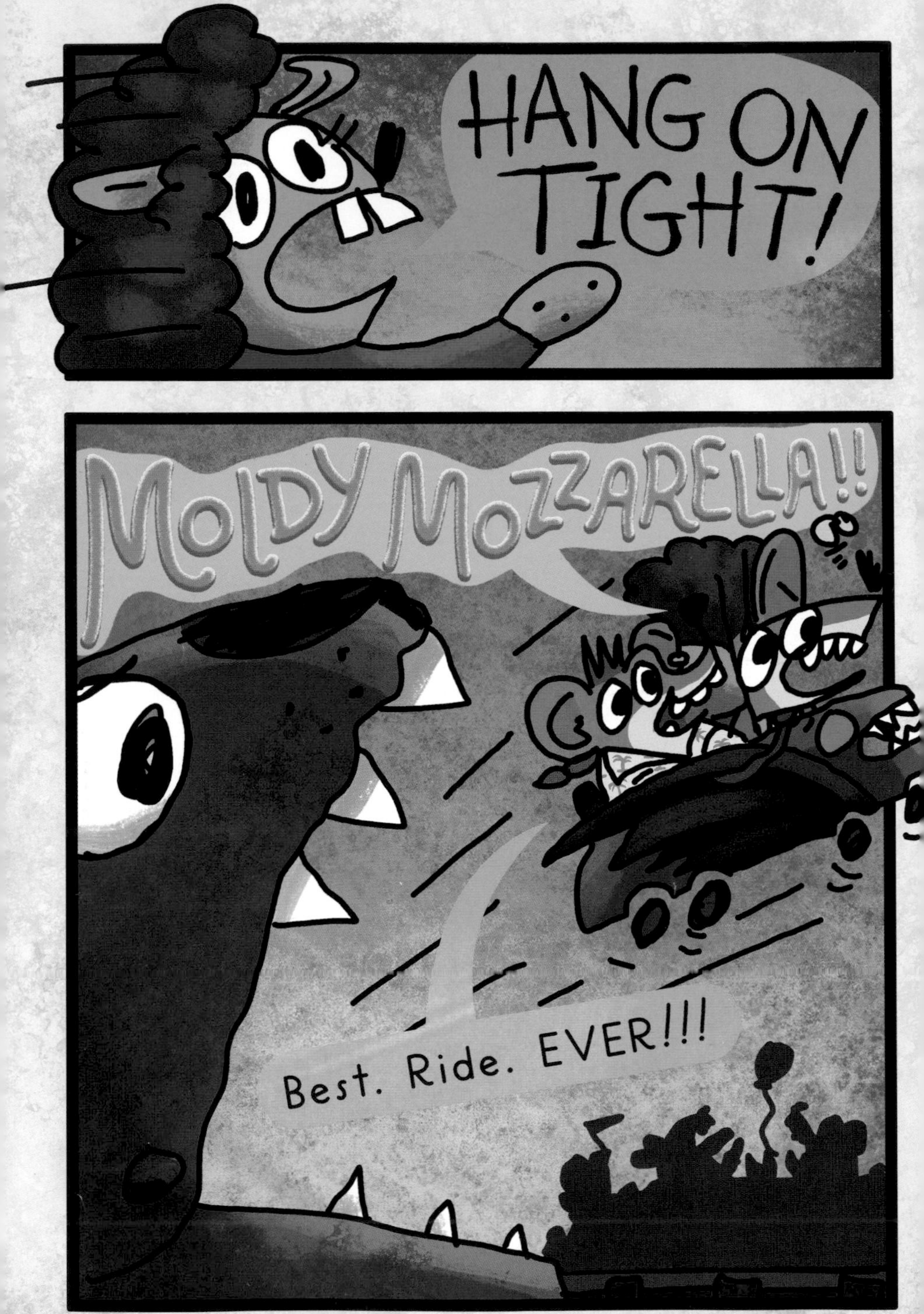
HANG ON TIGHT!
MOLDY MOZZARELLA!!
Best. Ride. EVER!!!

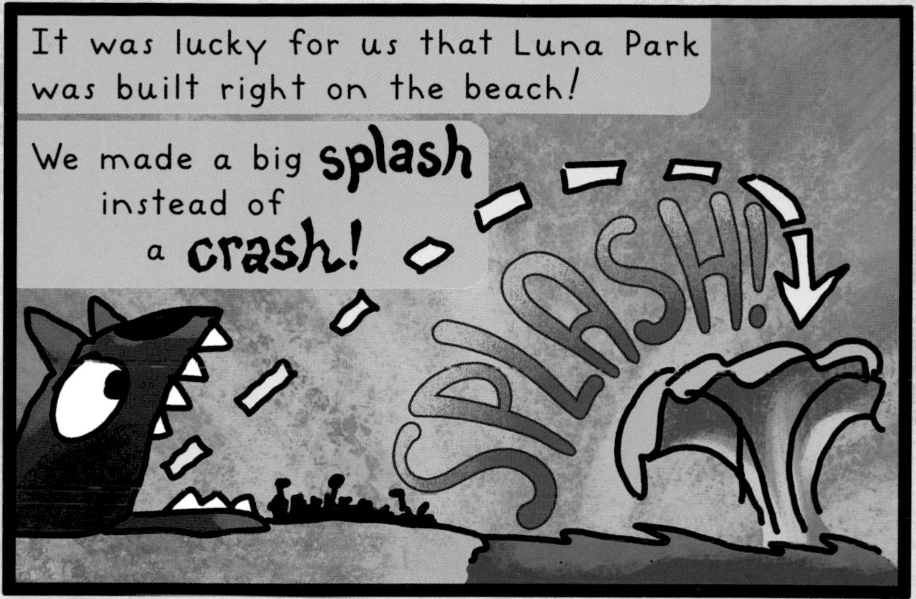
It was lucky for us that Luna Park was built right on the beach!
We made a big splash instead of a crash!
SPLASH!

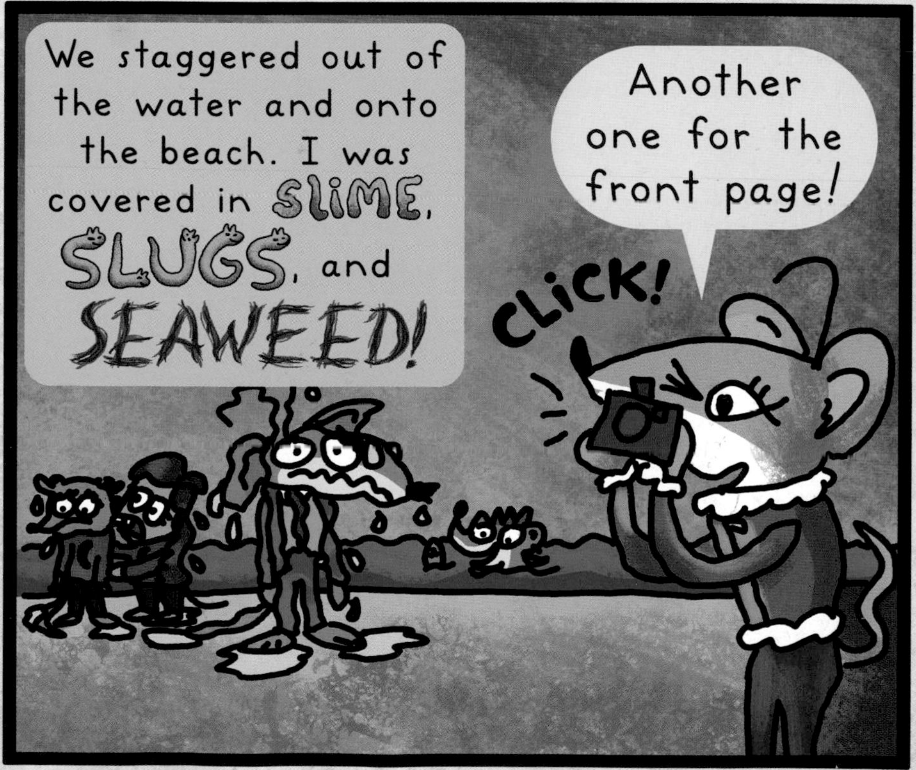
We staggered out of the water and onto the beach. I was covered in SLIME, SLUGS, and SEAWEED!
Another one for the front page!
CLICK!

CHAPTER ELEVEN

RUN FOR YOUR LIVES!!!

Thea wasn't too worried about us. But Trappy and Benjamin were! They raced over and gave us big hugs, even though we were wet and slimy! Then they started asking us questions...

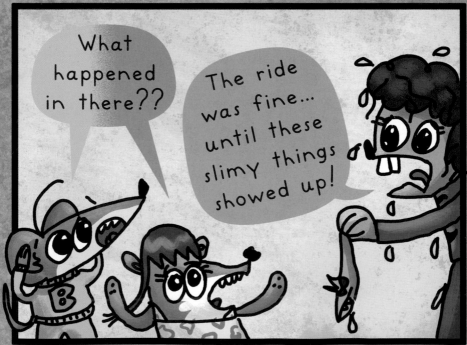

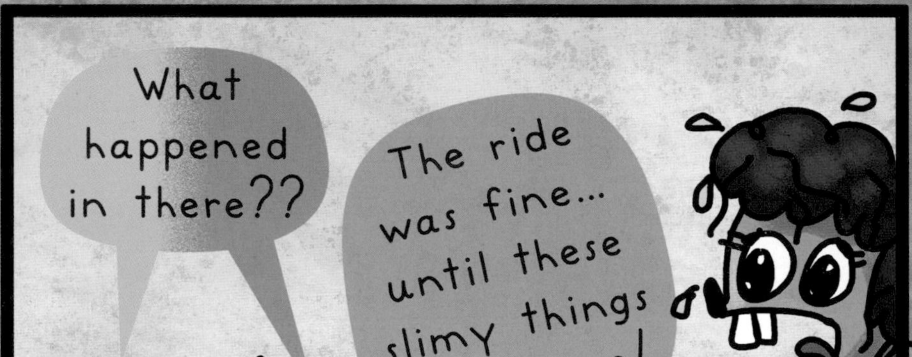
What happened in there??
The ride was fine... until these slimy things showed up!

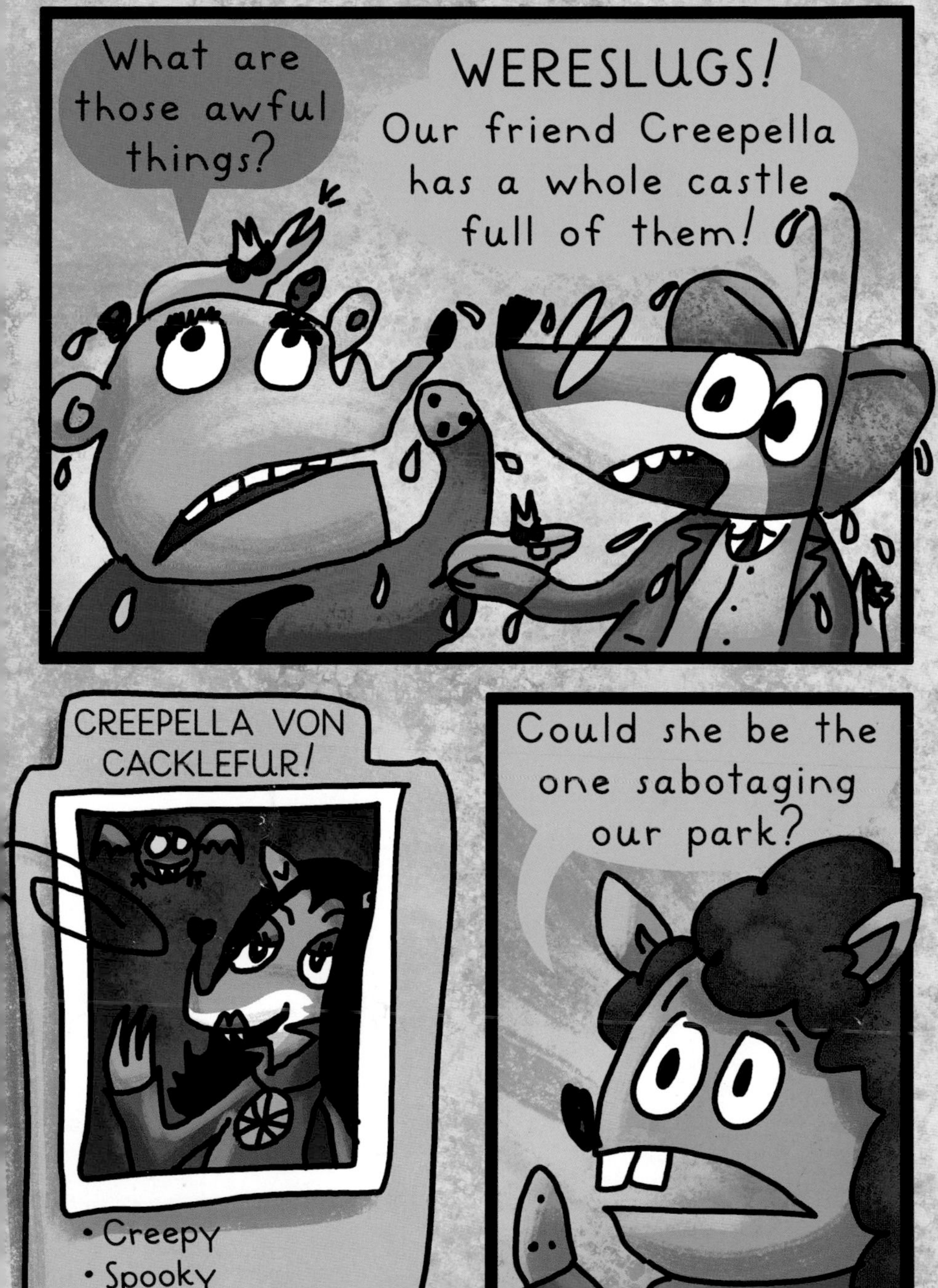
What are those awful things?
WERESLUGS! Our friend Creepella has a whole castle full of them!
CREEPELLA VON CACKLEFUR!
• Creepy
• Spooky
• Loves slimy slugs
Could she be the one sabotaging our park?

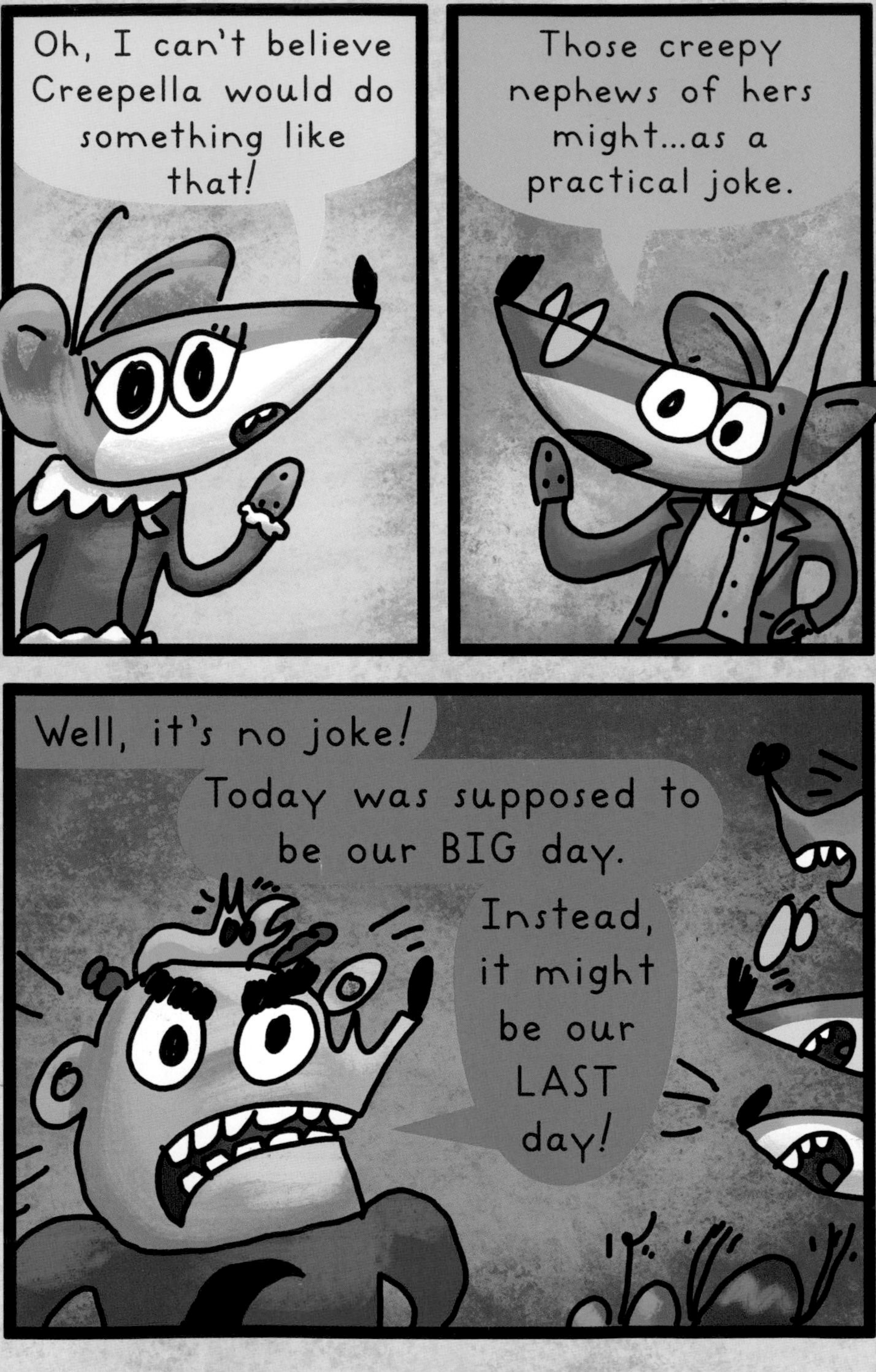
Oh, I can't believe Creepella would do something like that!
Those creepy nephews of hers might...as a practical joke.
Well, it's no joke!
Today was supposed to be our BIG day.
Instead, it might be our LAST day!

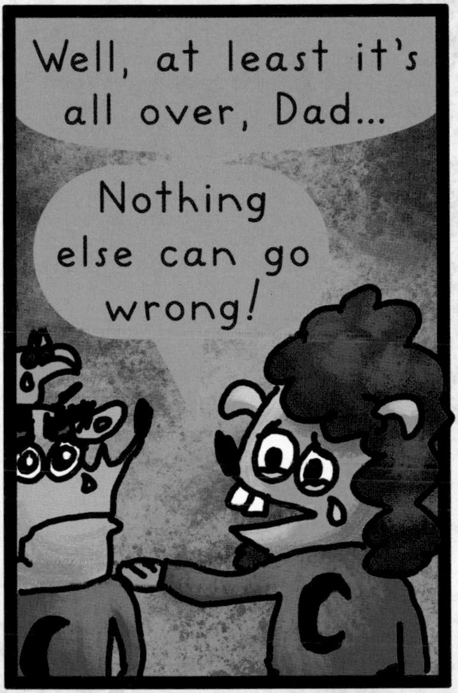
Well, at least it's all over, Dad...
Nothing else can go wrong!

I'm not a su-paw-stitious mouse, but I wished she hadn't said that!

Anytime somebody says that, you just know that somebody else is about to yell something like...

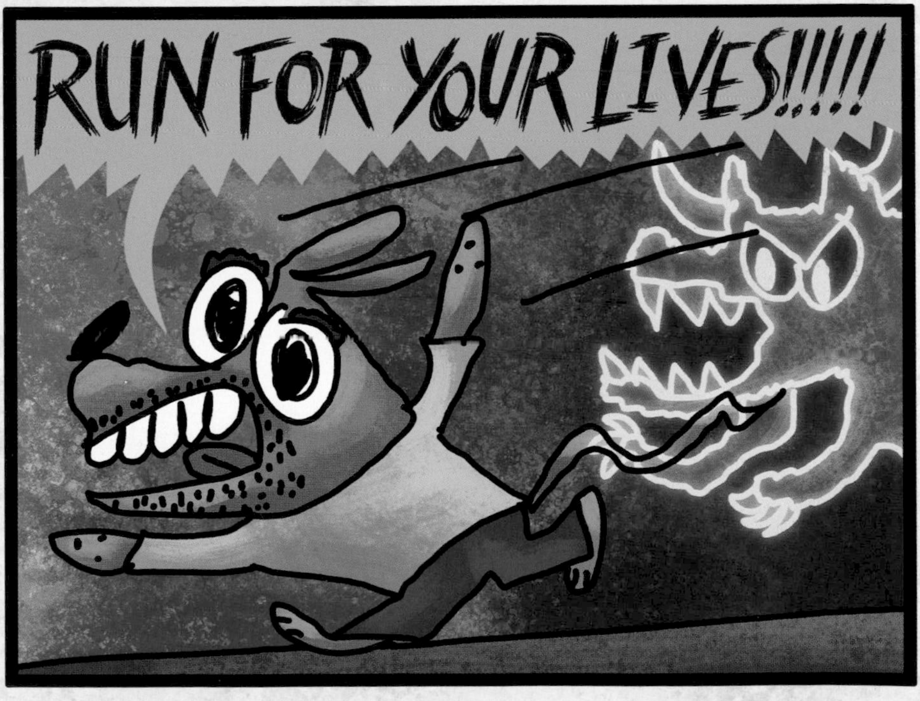
RUN FOR YOUR LIVES!!!!!

CHAPTER TWELVE
GHOSTS!!!
(AND WORSE)

It was **PANIC** at the park!
It was a **Freak Out** at the fair!
It was **CHAOS** at the carnival!!!
All around us, mice were scampering away
from **SCARRRRY** ghosts (and worse)!

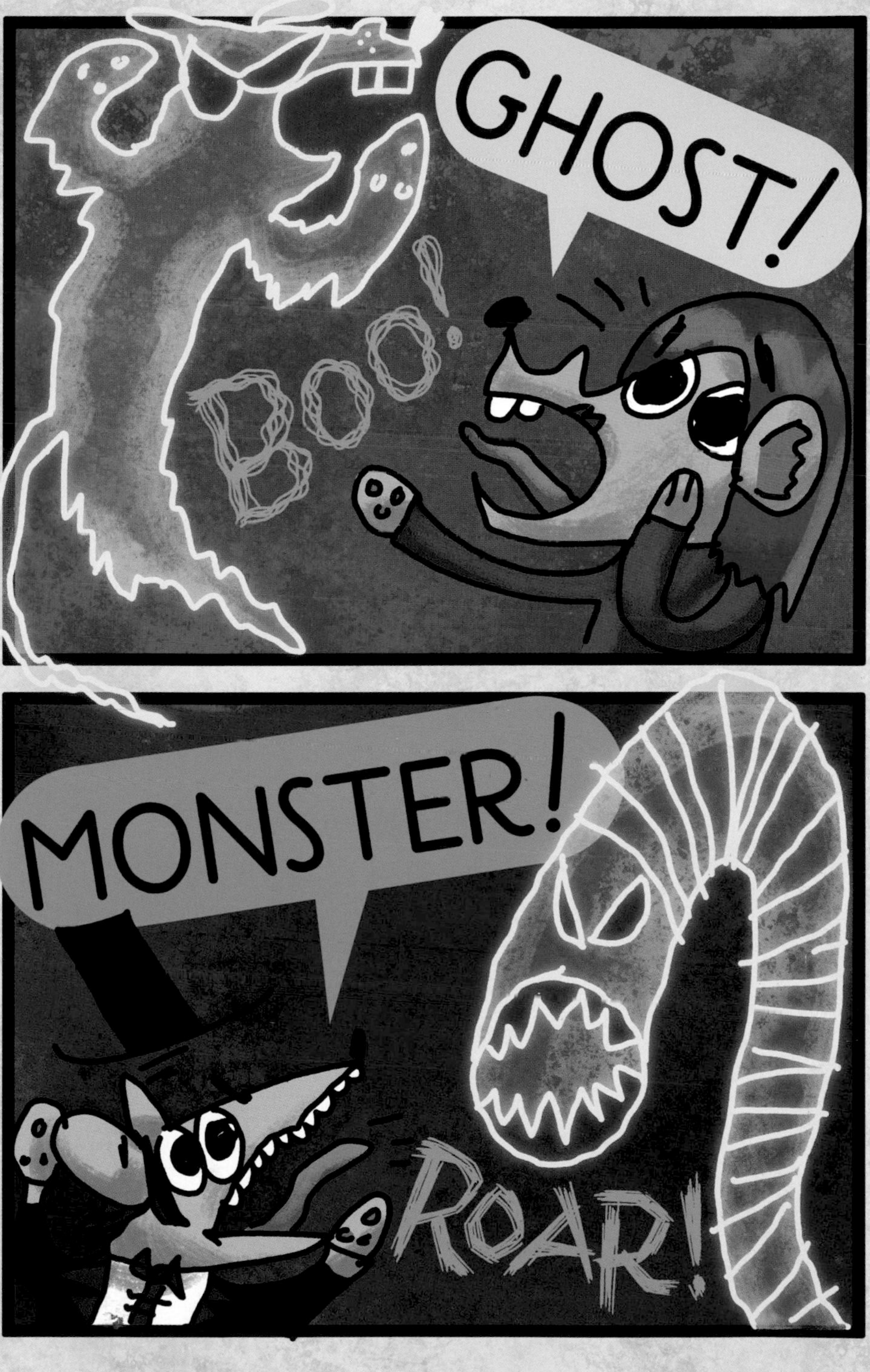
GHOST!
BOO!
MONSTER!
ROAR!

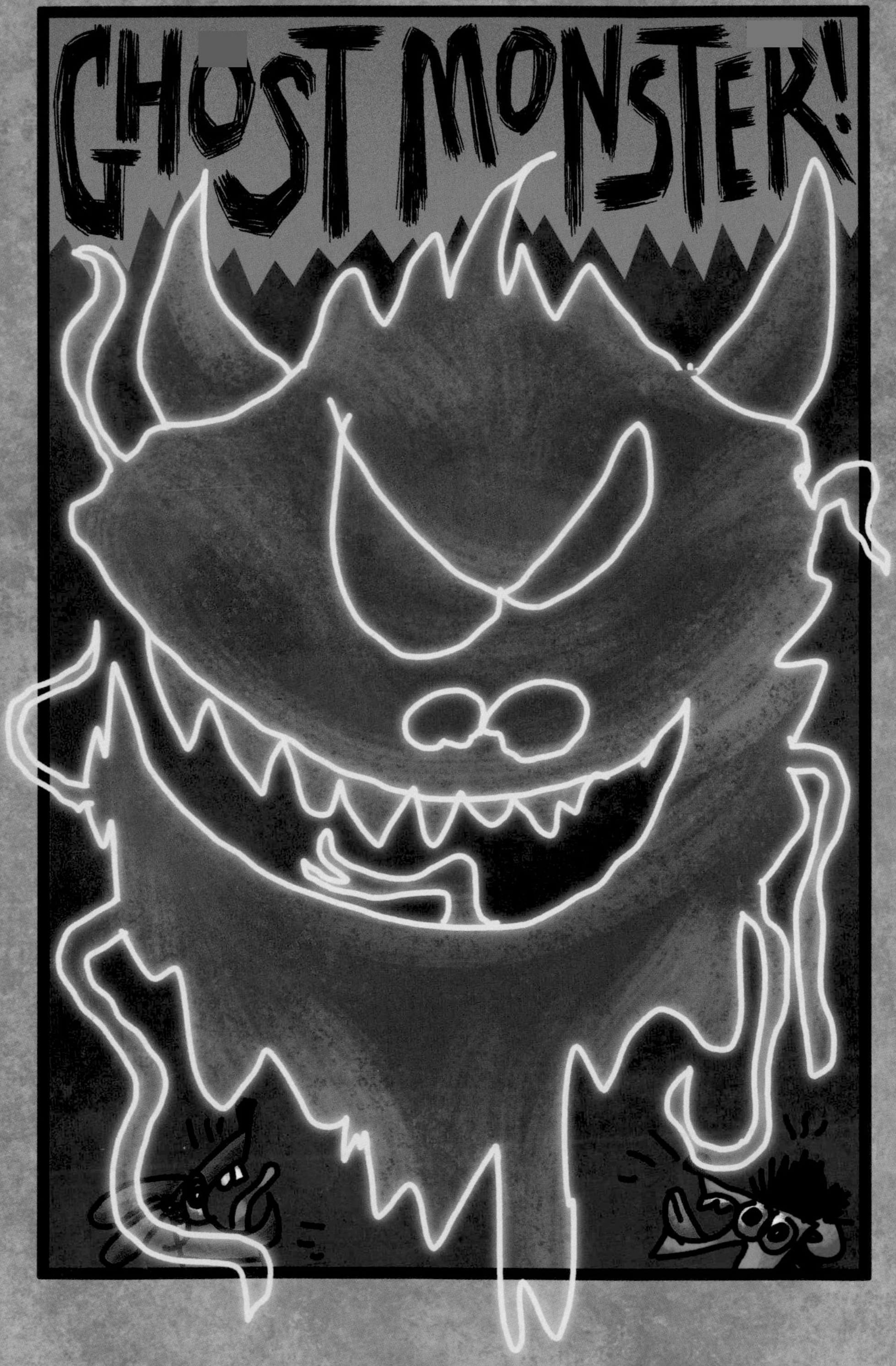
GHOST MONSTER!

Mice were running every which way...
but mostly for the **EXIT!**

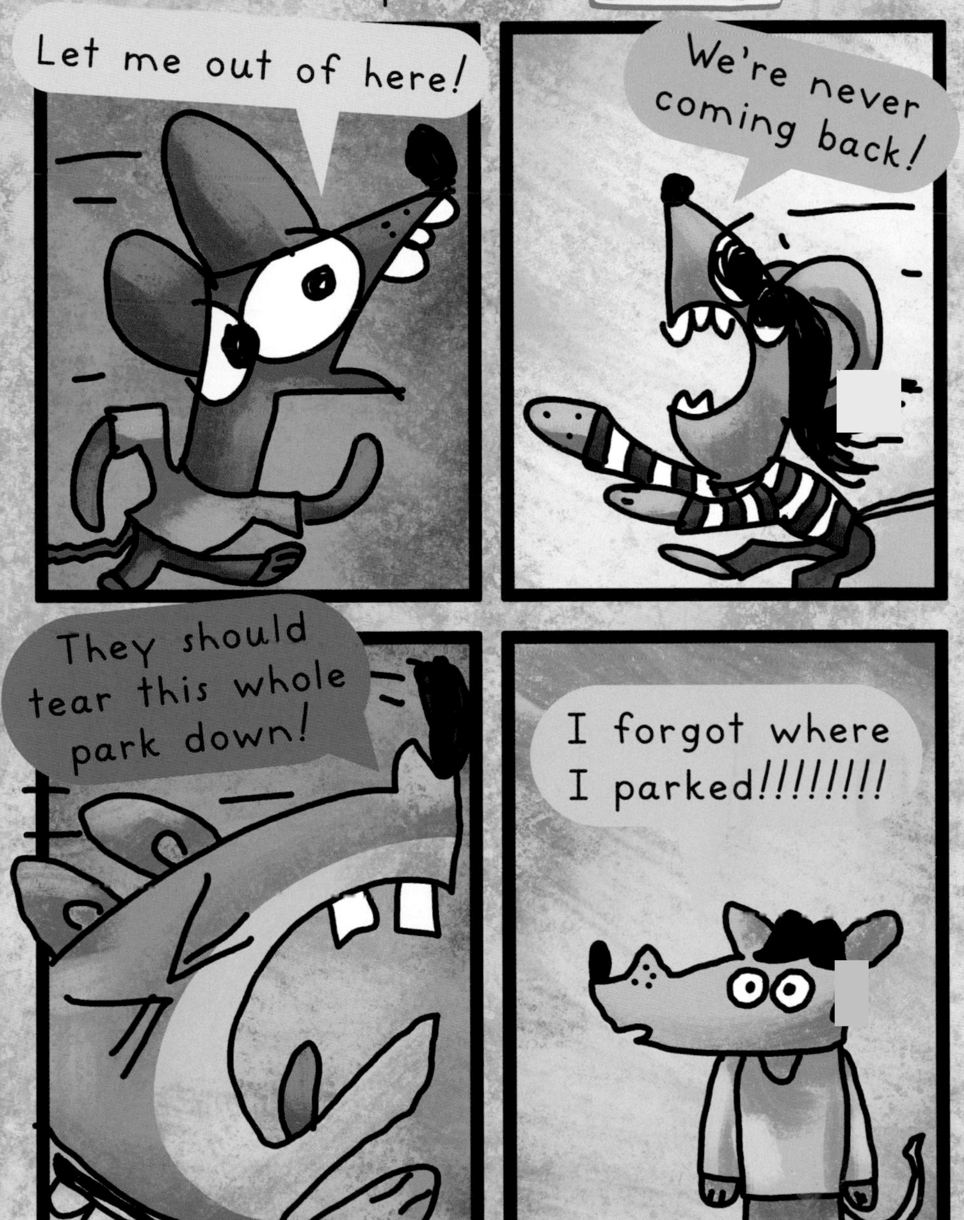
Let me out of here!
We're never coming back!
They should tear this whole park down!
I forgot where I parked!!!!!!!!

And soon it was EMPTY! Even the ghosts and MONSTERS were gone.

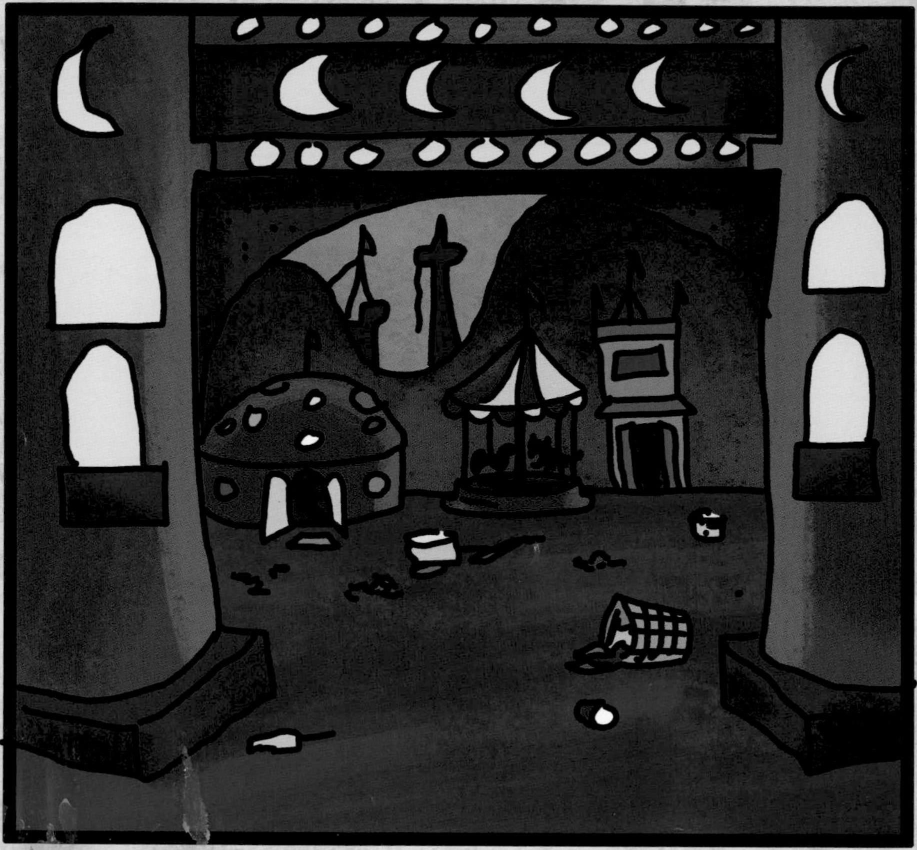

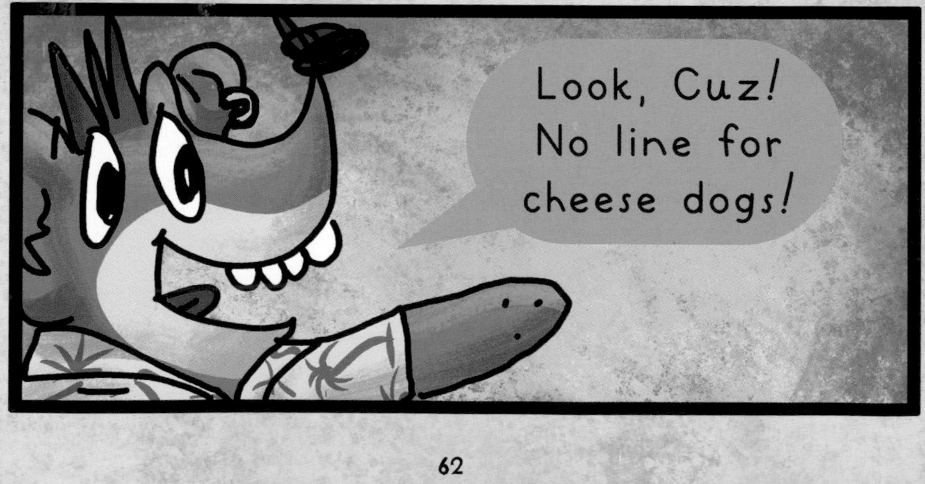
Look, Cuz! No line for cheese dogs!

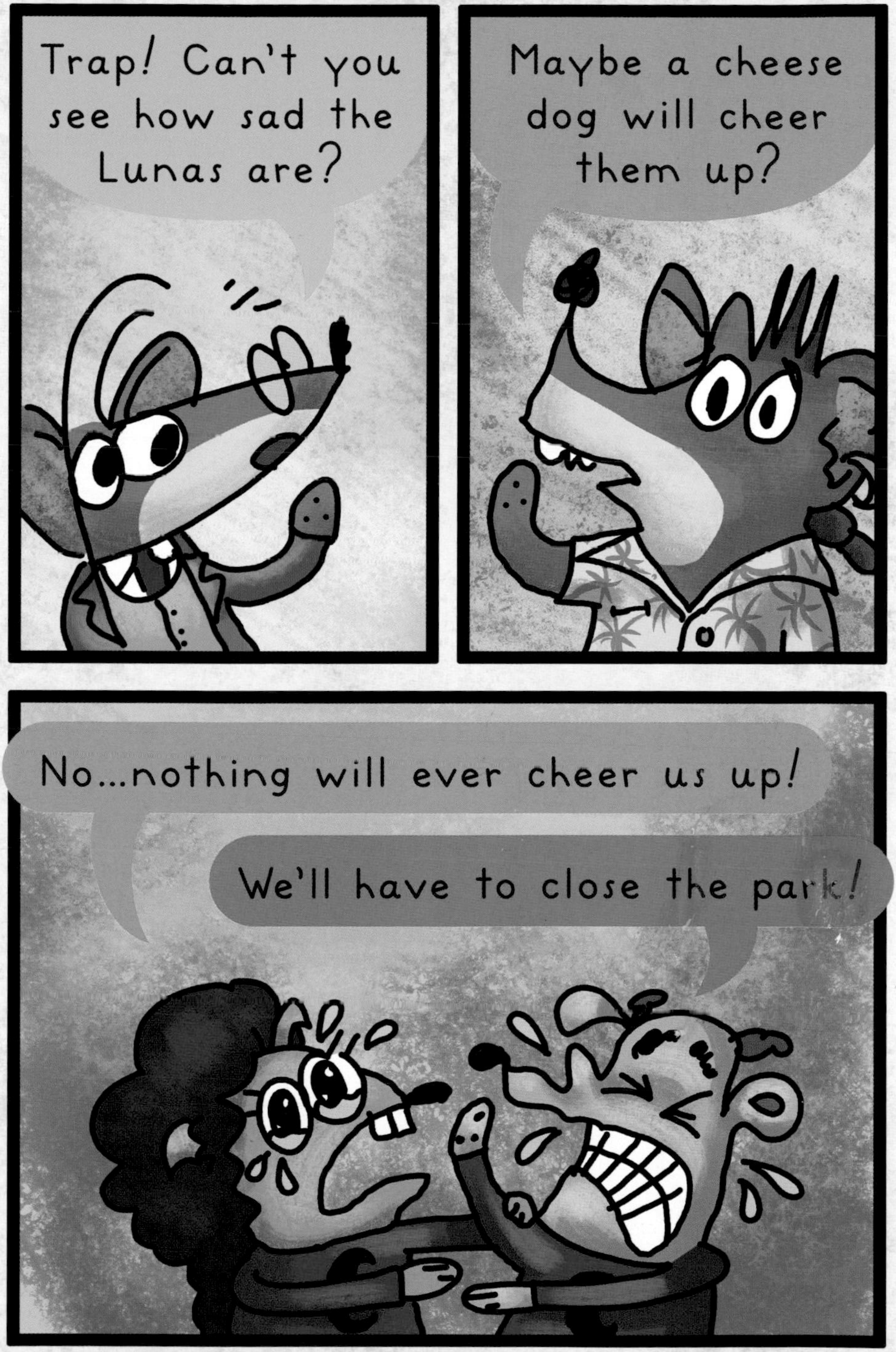
Trap! Can't you see how sad the Lunas are?
Maybe a cheese dog will cheer them up?
No...nothing will ever cheer us up!
We'll have to close the park!

CHAPTER THIRTEEN

IT'S A MYSTERY!

Everyone was so **sad** for the Lunas!
We couldn't just go home and forget it.
We all agreed to stay up **LATE** and try
to help them figure out what happened.

I think it was sabotage!
Someone wanted to ruin
our big day!

But who would do
something that awful?

And where would
they get ghosts?

And monsters?

And wereslugs?

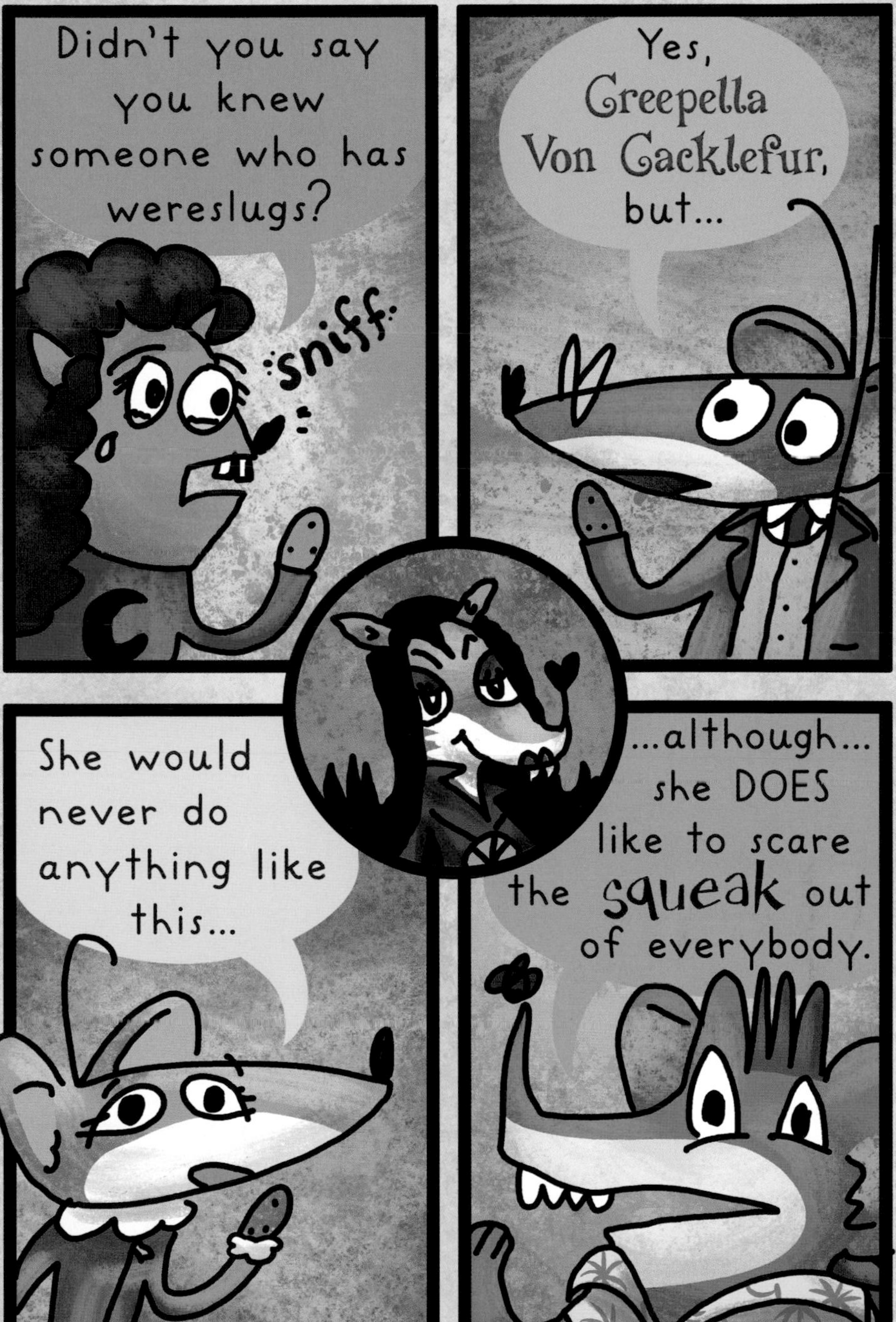
Didn't you say you knew someone who has wereslugs?
sniff.
Yes, Creepella Von Cacklefur, but...
She would never do anything like this...
...although... she DOES like to scare the squeak out of everybody.

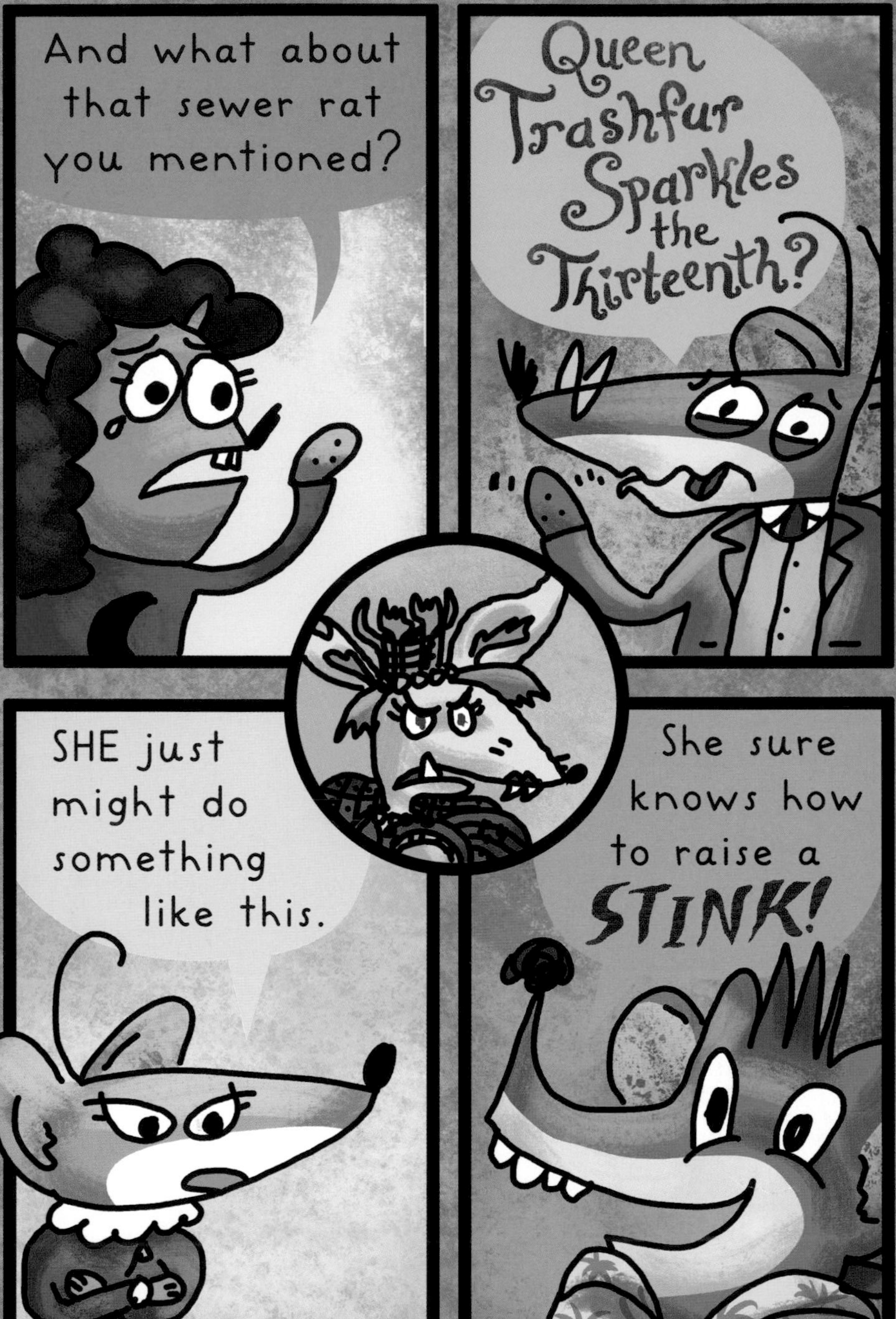
And what about that sewer rat you mentioned?
Queen Trashfur Sparkles the Thirteenth?
SHE just might do something like this.
She sure knows how to raise a STINK!

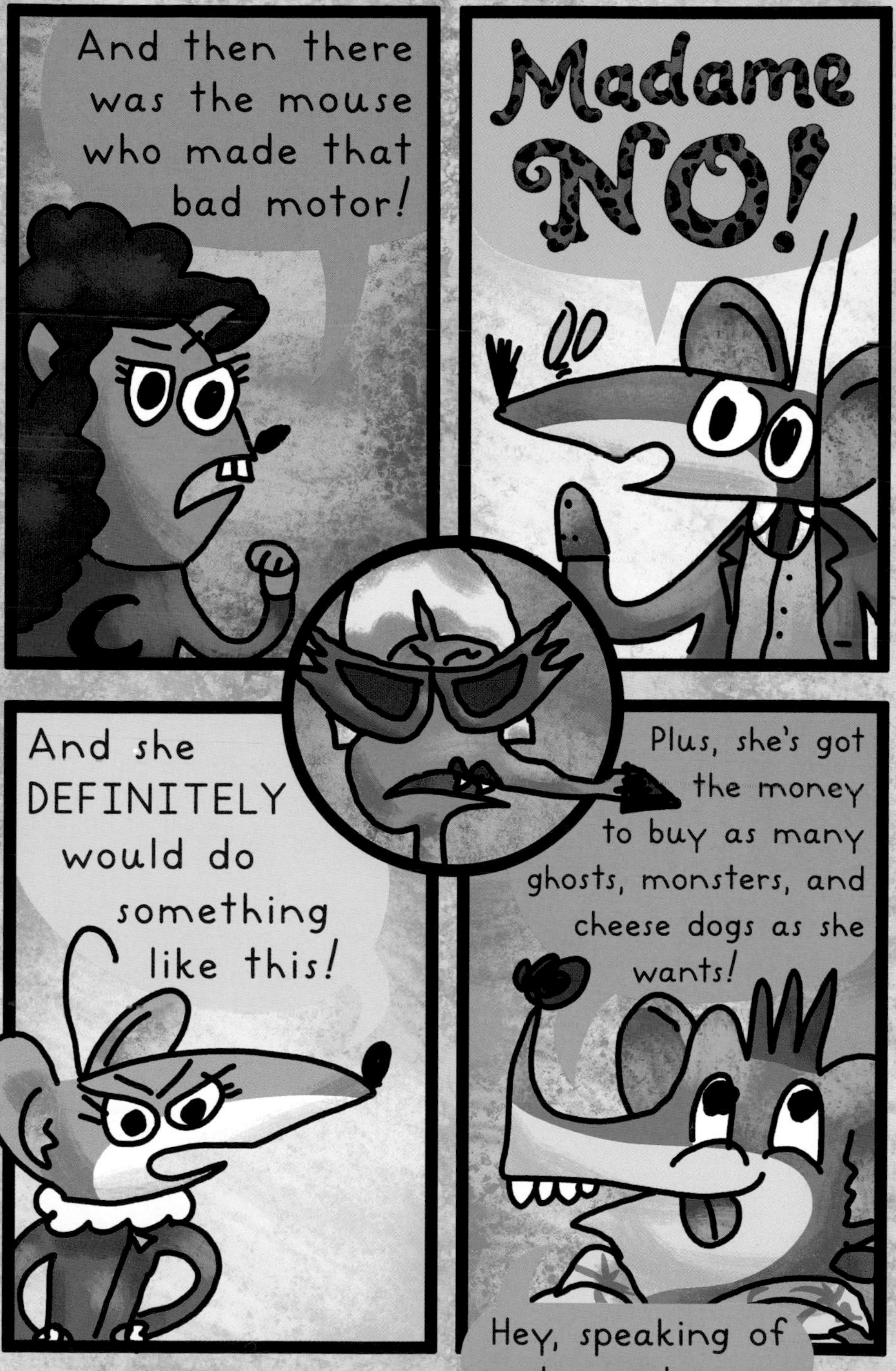
And then there was the mouse who made that bad motor!
Madame NO!
And she DEFINITELY would do something like this!
Plus, she's got the money to buy as many ghosts, monsters, and cheese dogs as she wants!
Hey, speaking of cheese dogs...

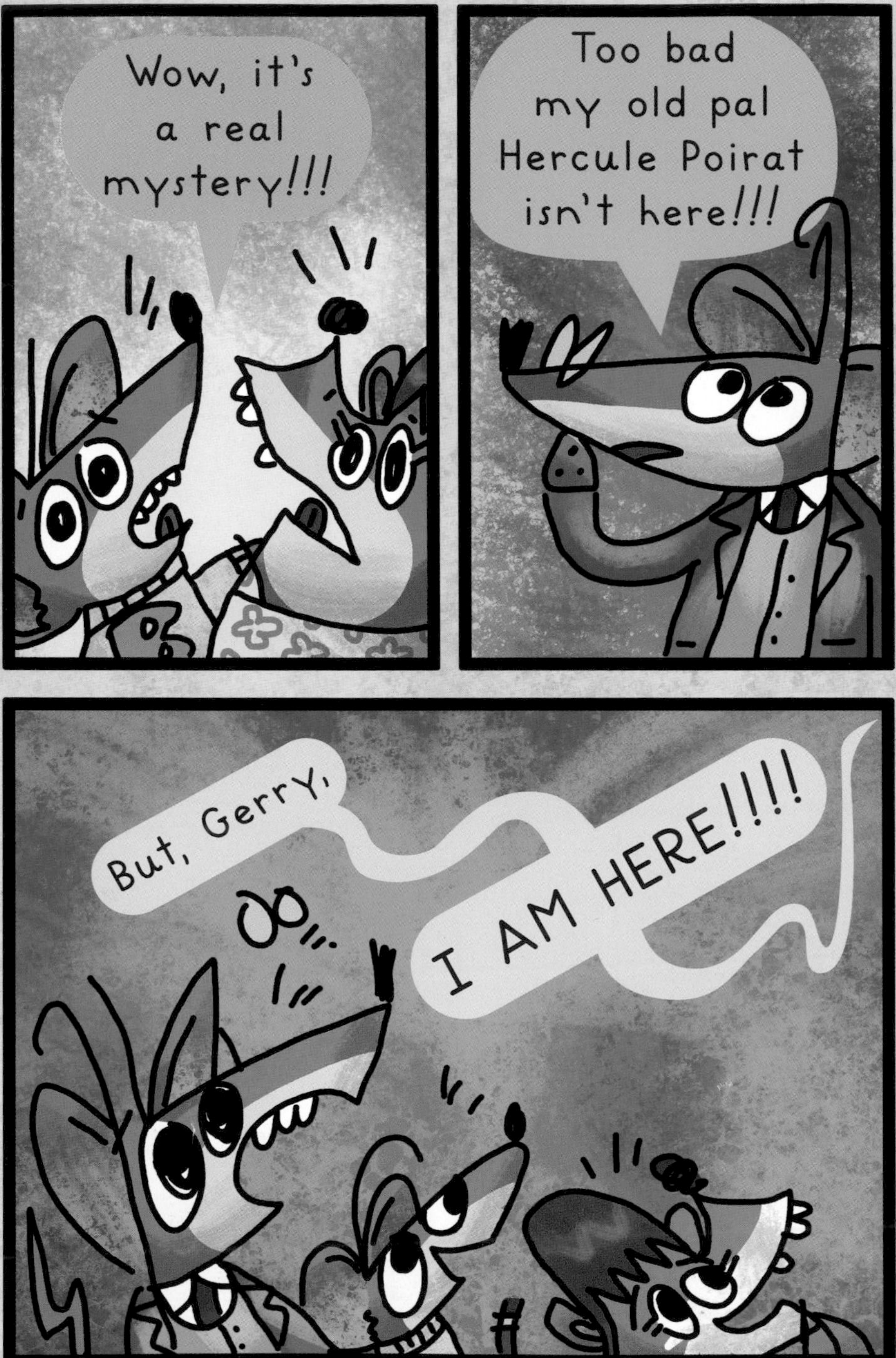
Wow, it's a real mystery!!!
Too bad my old pal Hercule Poirat isn't here!!!
But, Gerry,
I AM HERE!!!!

CHAPTER FOURTEEN

A CLOVER DISGUISE!

It sure sounded like the world-**famouse** detective Hercule Poirat! But none of us could see him anywhere!

I'm right here!!!!

Where?!?!

Where?
Right here!
WHERE?
Right here!
WHERE?!?!?!
RIGHT HERE!!!!

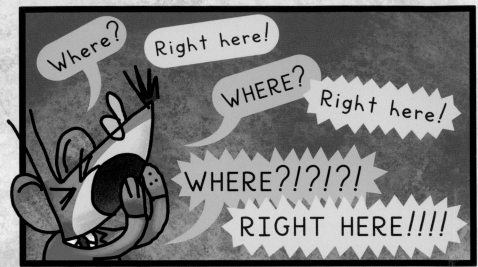

I was PUZZLED. I was PERPLEXED.
I was getting pretty TIRED of yelling WHERE!
Luckily, Hercule couldn't resist answering Thea!
(Who he has a little bit of a crush on.)

YOO-HOO!
Hercule!
Please come out!
Anything for you, Thea!

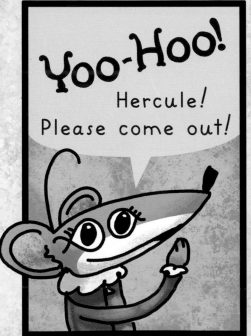

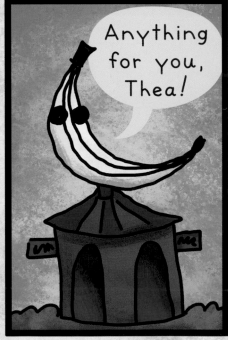

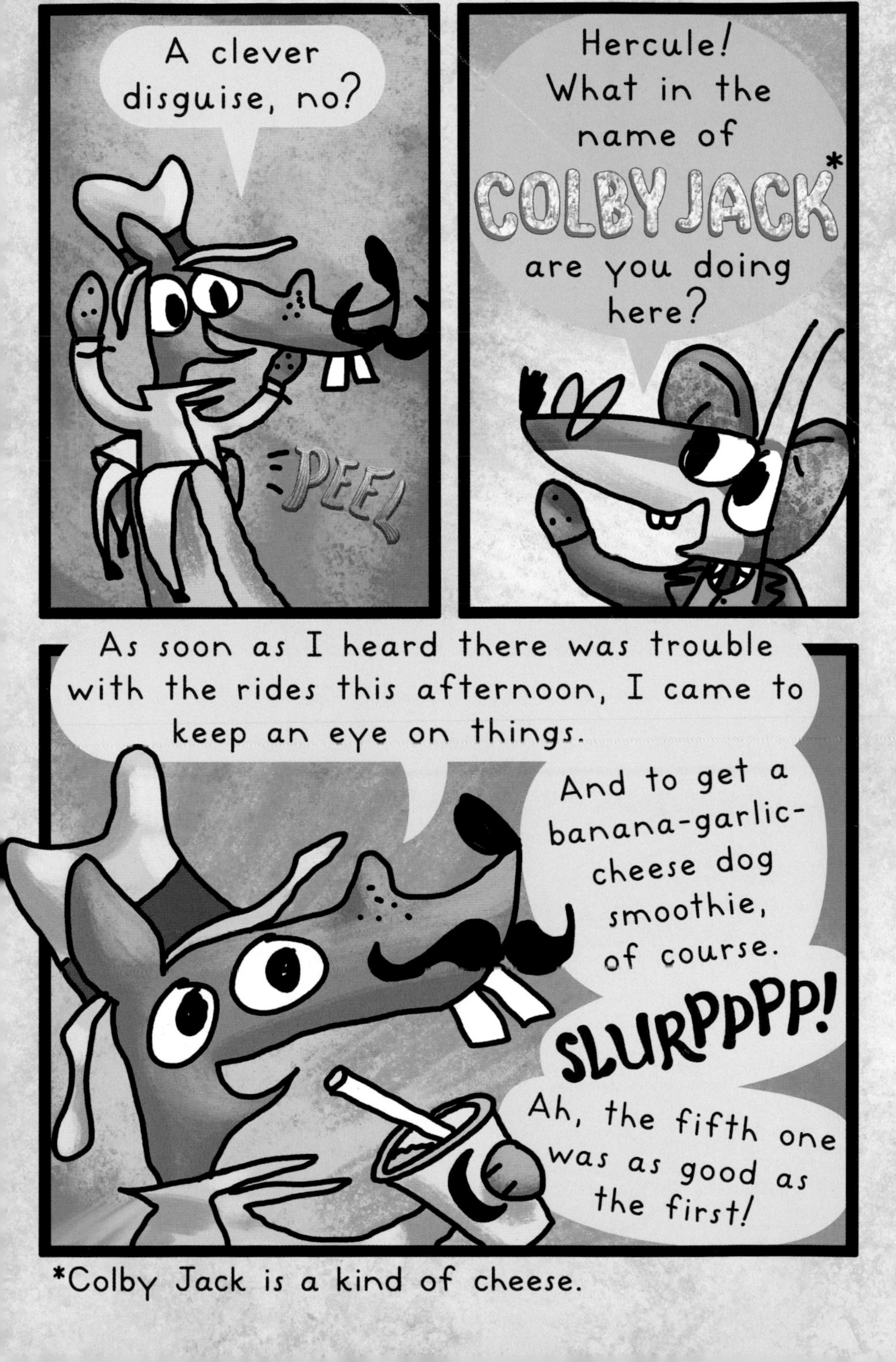
A clever disguise, no?
PEEL
Hercule! What in the name of COLBY JACK* are you doing here?
As soon as I heard there was trouble with the rides this afternoon, I came to keep an eye on things.
And to get a banana-garlic-cheese dog smoothie, of course.
SLURPPPP!
Ah, the fifth one was as good as the first!

*Colby Jack is a kind of cheese.

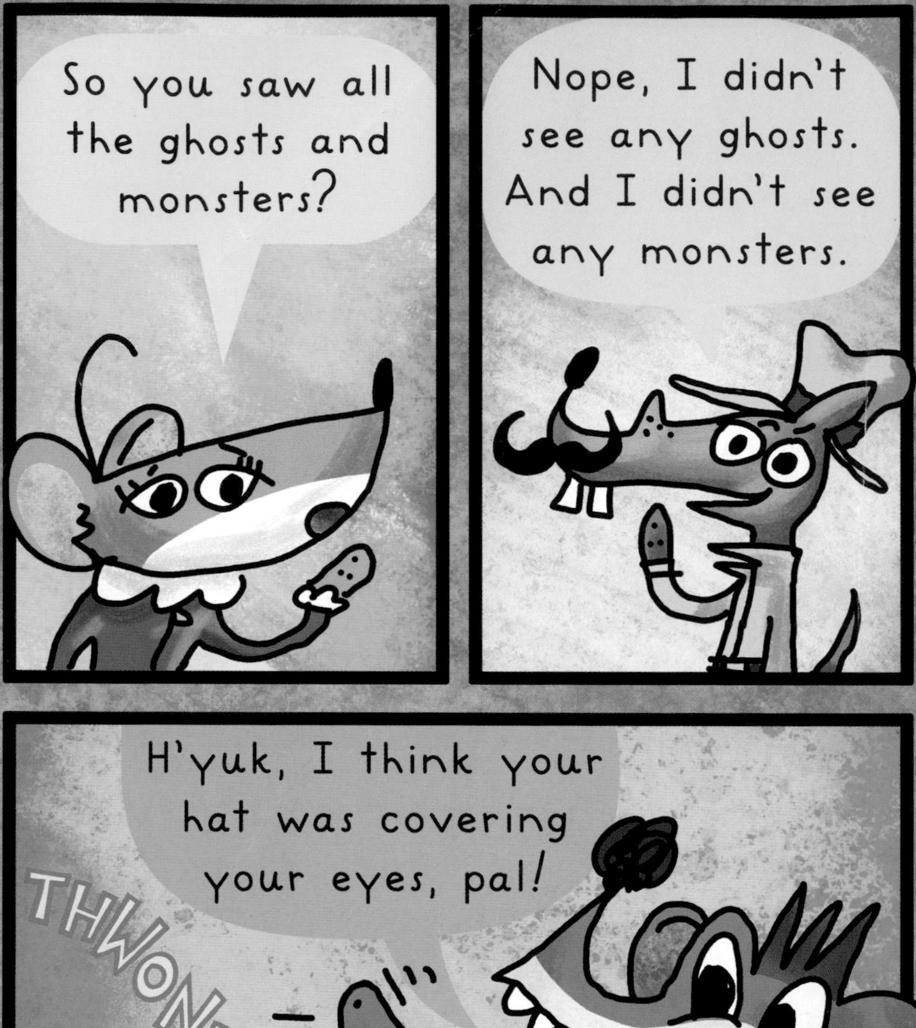
So you saw all the ghosts and monsters?
Nope, I didn't see any ghosts. And I didn't see any monsters.
H'yuk, I think your hat was covering your eyes, pal!
THWONK

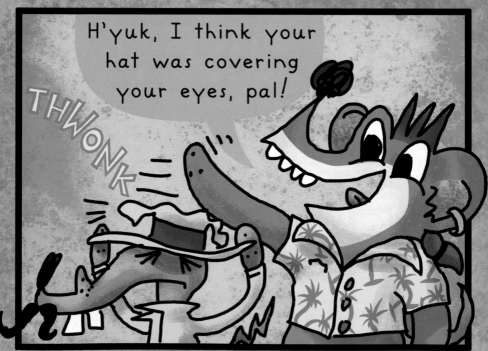

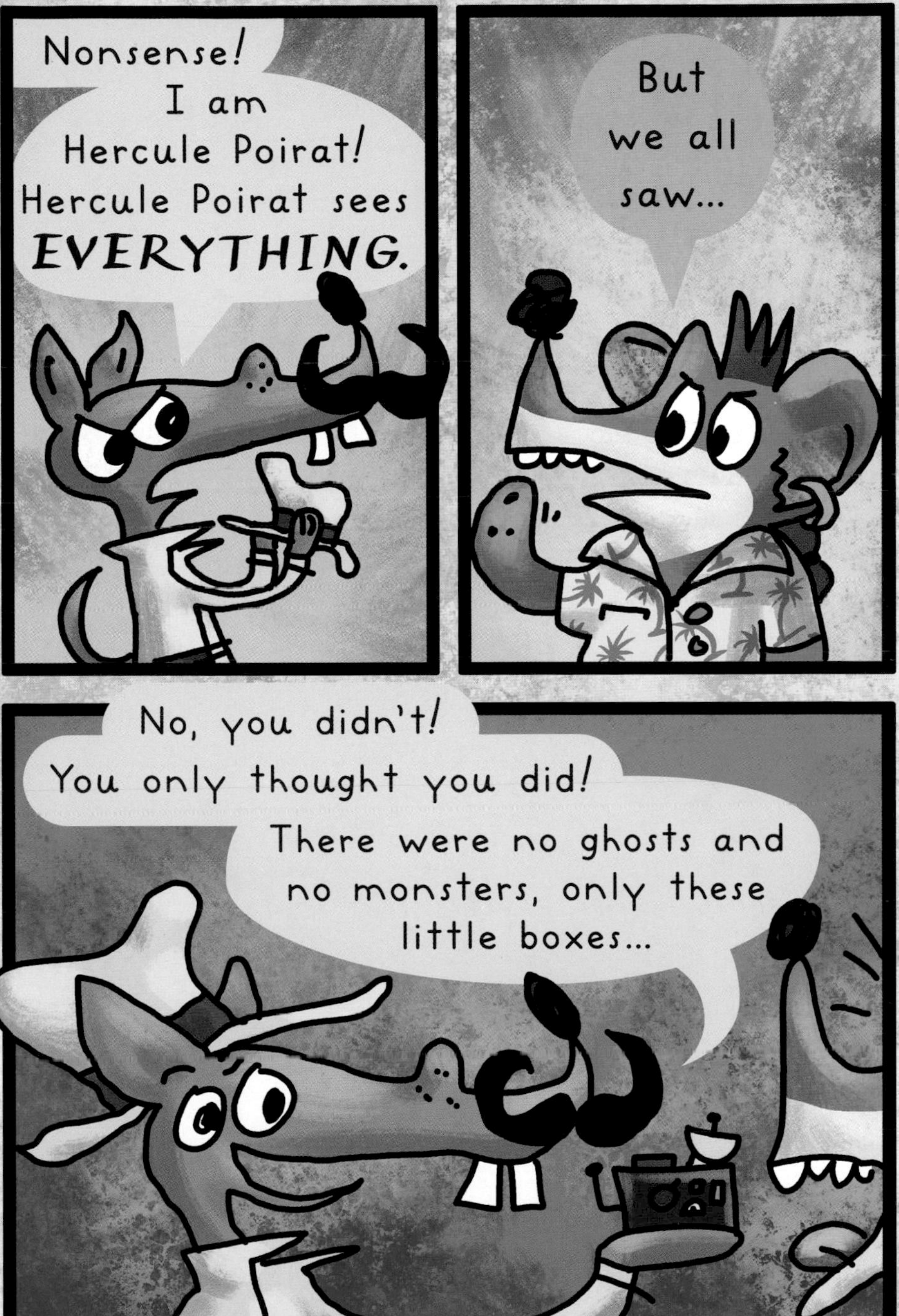
Nonsense! I am Hercule Poirat! Hercule Poirat sees EVERYTHING.
But we all saw...
No, you didn't!
You only thought you did!
There were no ghosts and no monsters, only these little boxes...

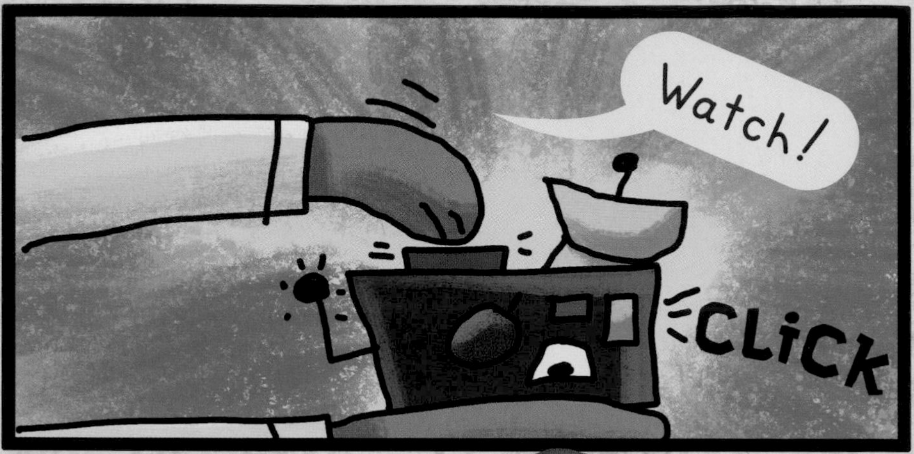
Watch!
CLICK

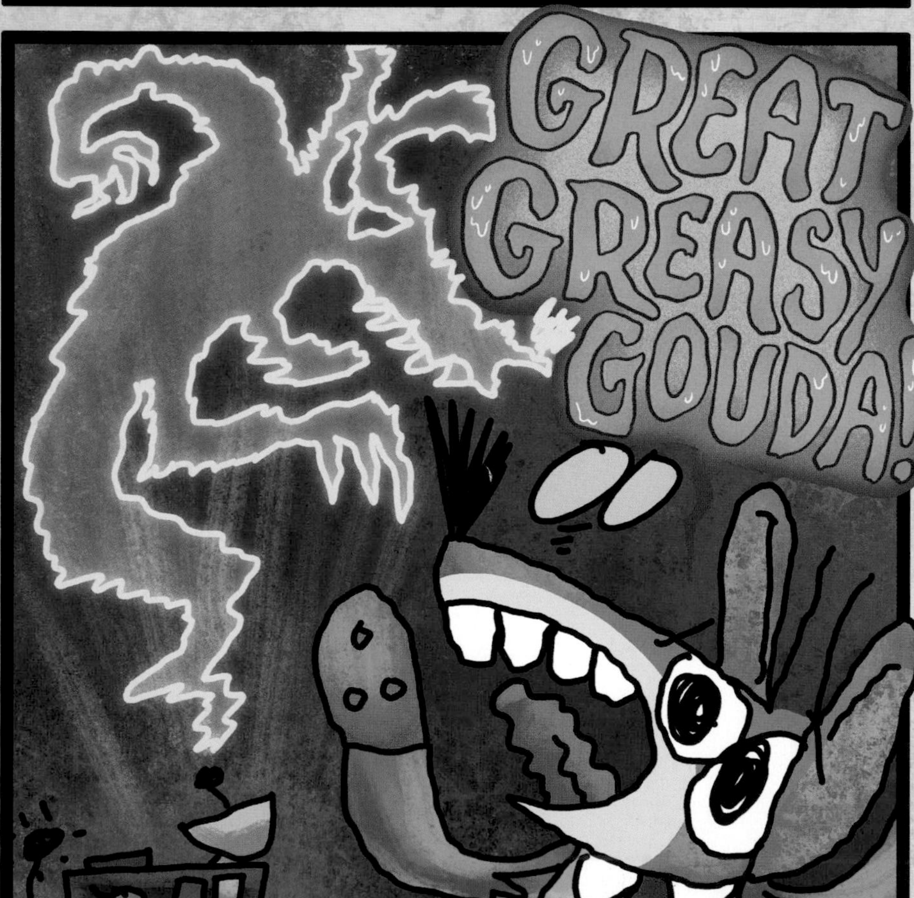
GREAT GREASY GOUDA!

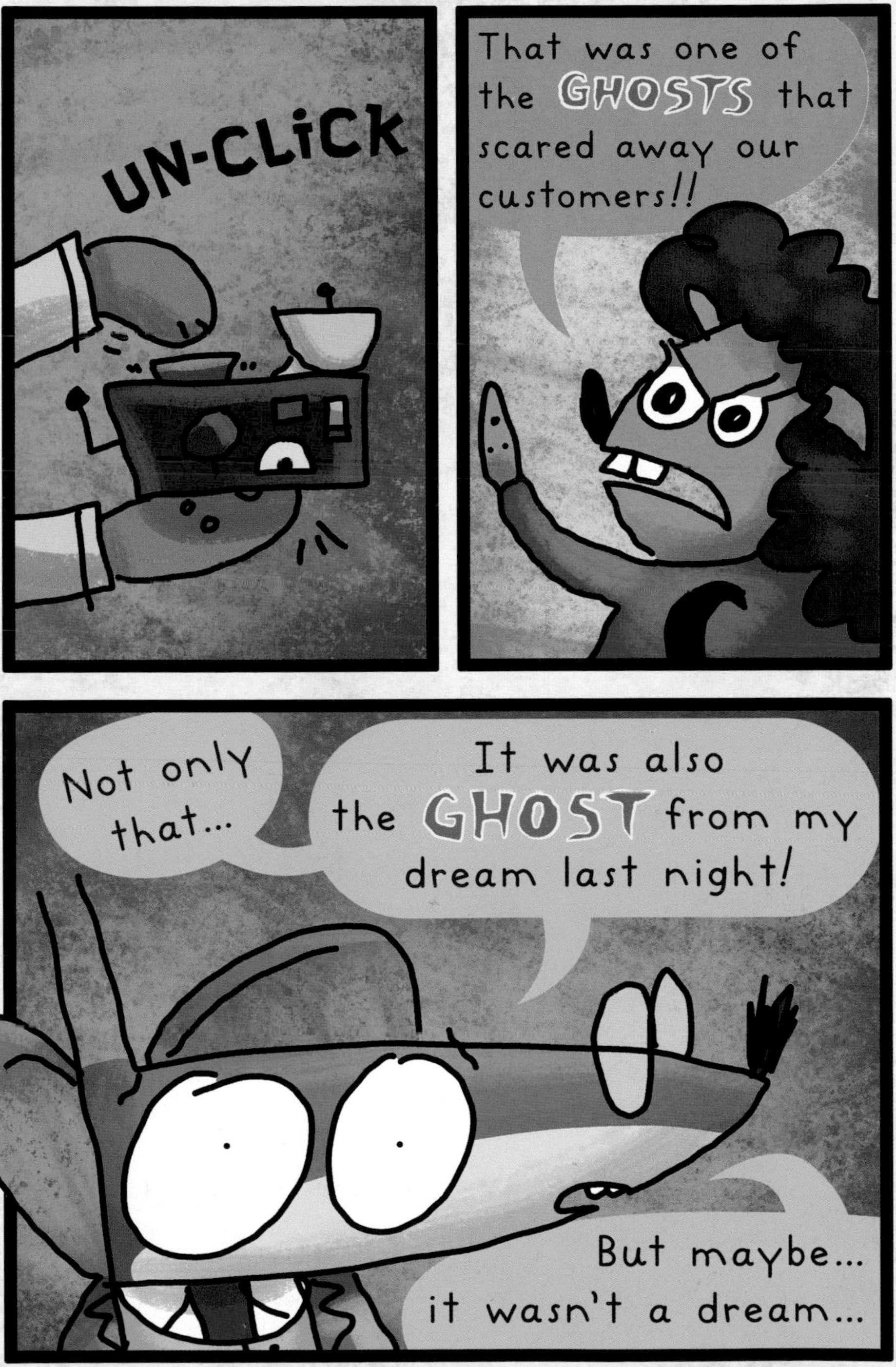
UN-CLiCK
That was one of the GHOSTS that scared away our customers!!
Not only that...
It was also the GHOST from my dream last night!
But maybe... it wasn't a dream...

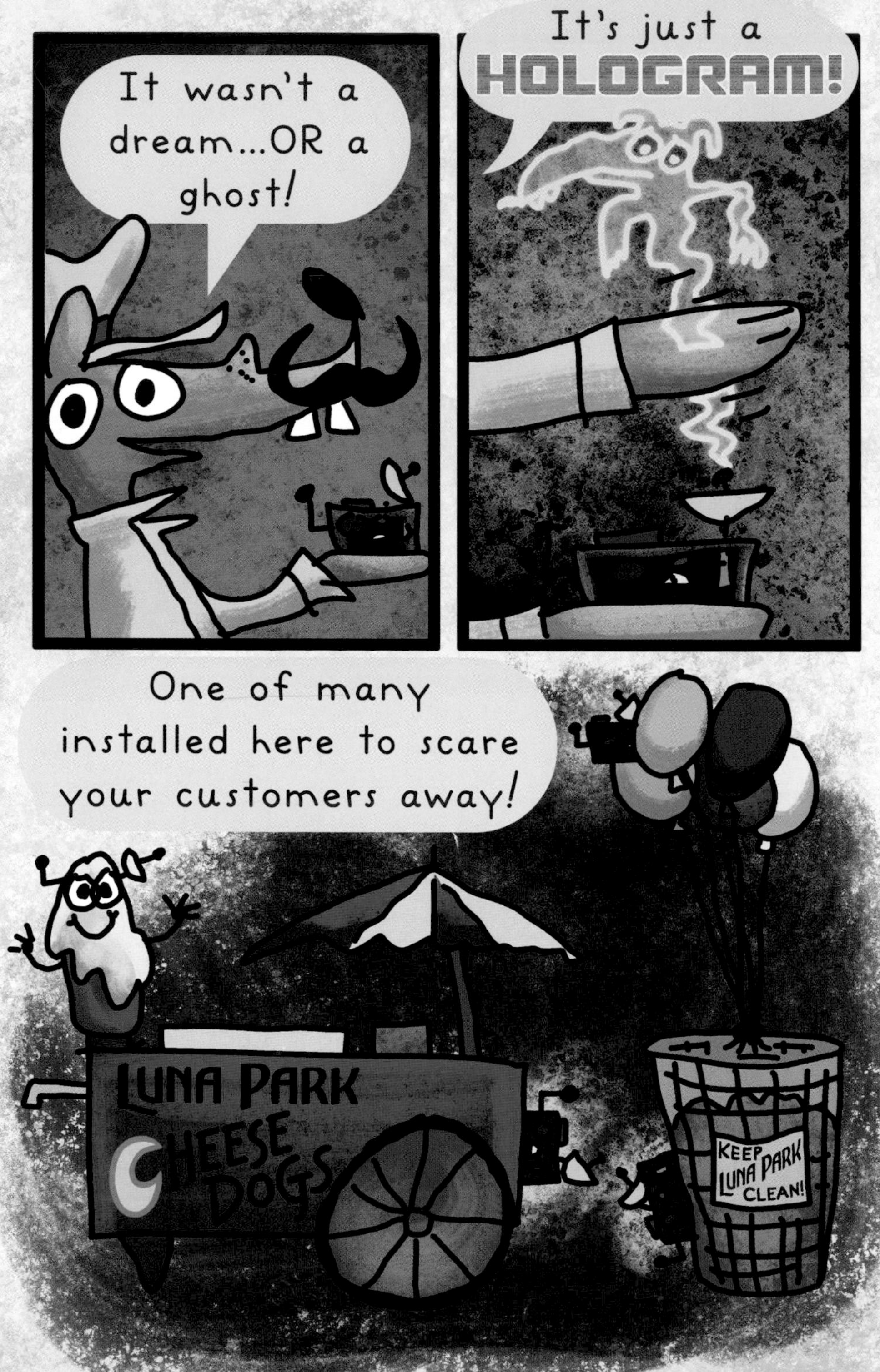
It wasn't a dream...OR a ghost!
It's just a HOLOGRAM!
One of many installed here to scare your customers away!
LUNA PARK CHEESE DOGS
KEEP LUNA PARK CLEAN!

CHAPTER FIFTEEN

LET'S SPLIT UP!

Trap claimed he knew the ghosts were FAKE all along. But they sure fooled me! I decided to be a lot more skeptical and not fall for more tricks...

So these WERESLUGS are just holograms, too?

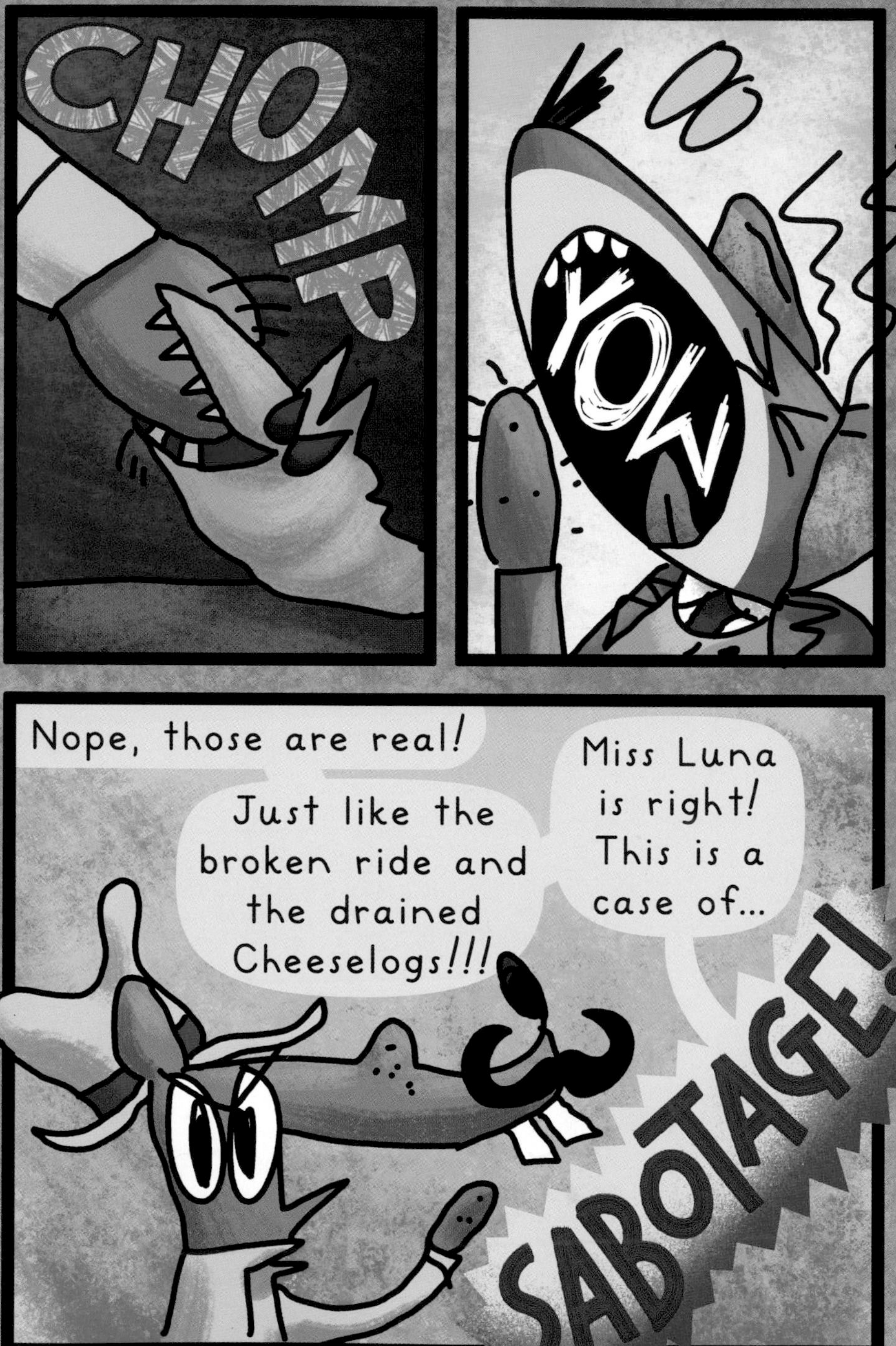
CHOMP
YOW
Nope, those are real!
Just like the broken ride and the drained Cheeselogs!!!
Miss Luna is right! This is a case of...
SABOTAGE!

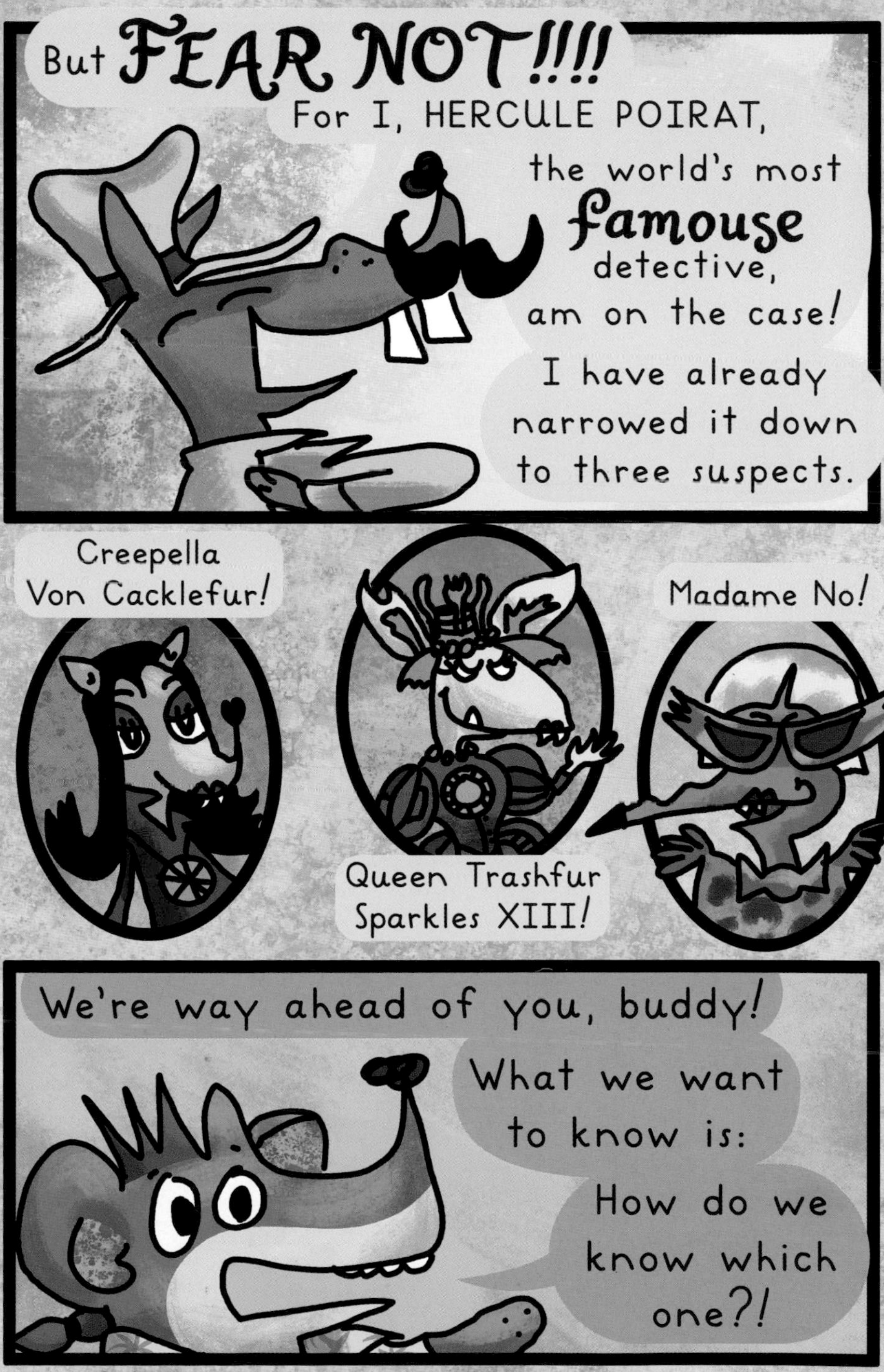
But FEAR NOT!!!!
For I, HERCULE POIRAT,
the world's most famouse detective, am on the case!
I have already narrowed it down to three suspects.
Creepella Von Cacklefur!
Queen Trashfur Sparkles XIII!
Madame No!
We're way ahead of you, buddy!
What we want to know is:
How do we know which one?!

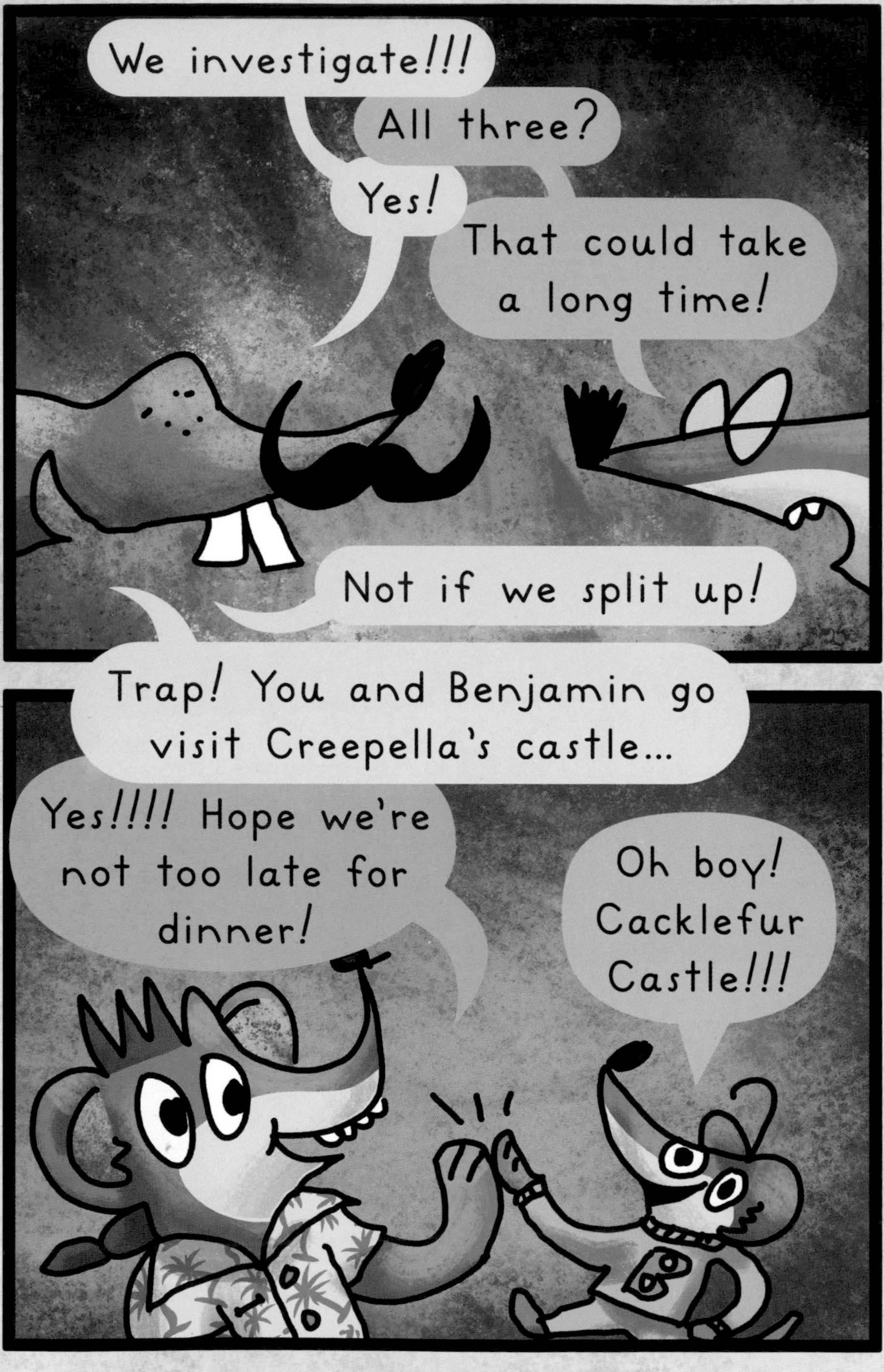
We investigate!!!
All three?
Yes!
That could take a long time!
Not if we split up!
Trap! You and Benjamin go visit Creepella's castle...
Yes!!!! Hope we're not too late for dinner!
Oh boy! Cacklefur Castle!!!

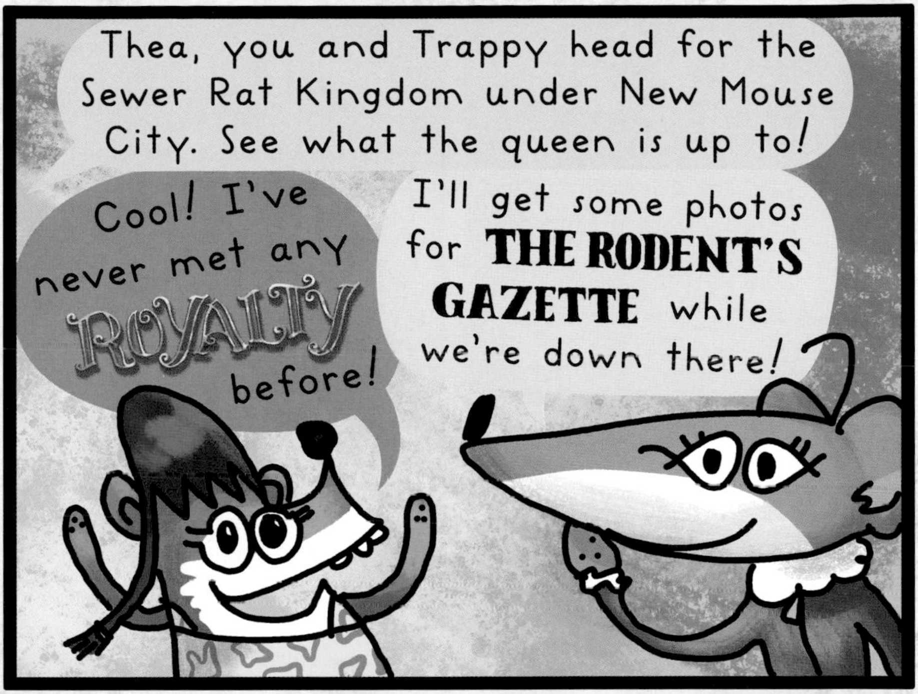
Thea, you and Trappy head for the Sewer Rat Kingdom under New Mouse City. See what the queen is up to!
Cool! I've never met any ROYALTY before!
I'll get some photos for THE RODENT'S GAZETTE while we're down there!

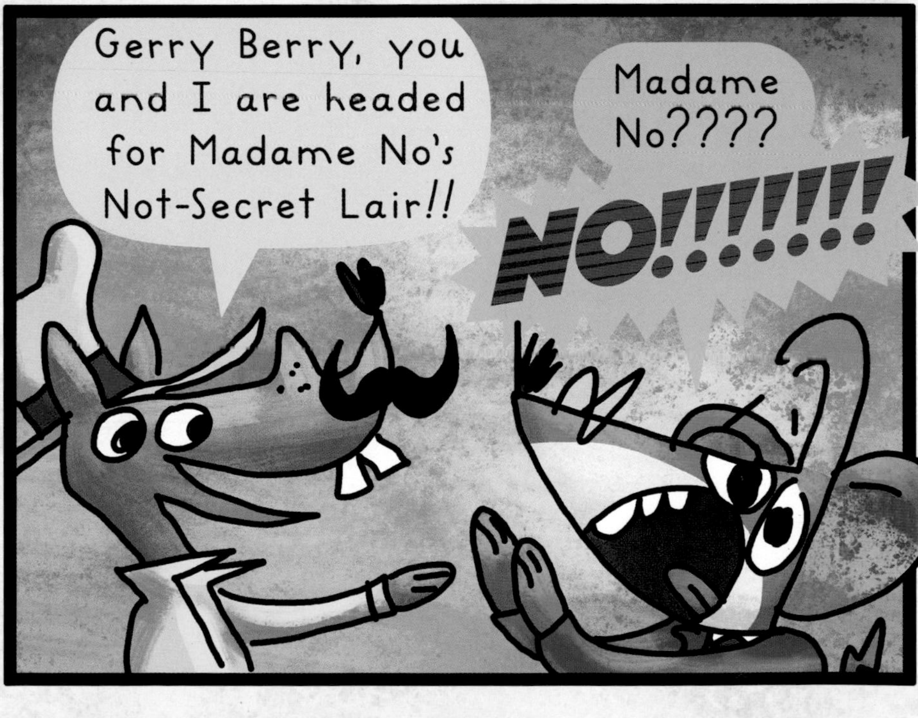
Gerry Berry, you and I are headed for Madame No's Not-Secret Lair!!
Madame No????
NO!!!!!!!

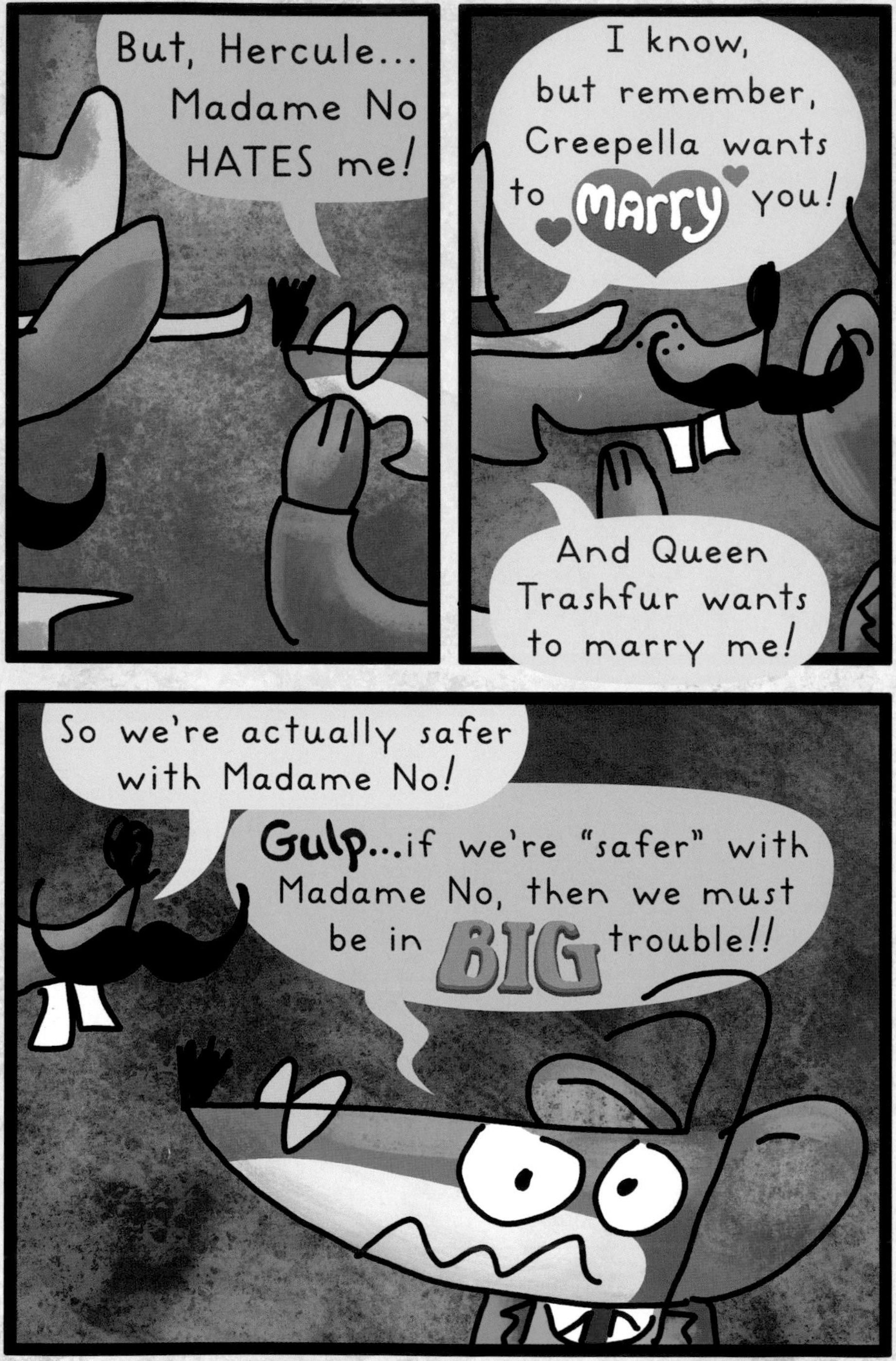
But, Hercule... Madame No HATES me!
I know, but remember, Creepella wants to MARRY you!
And Queen Trashfur wants to marry me!
So we're actually safer with Madame No!
Gulp...if we're "safer" with Madame No, then we must be in BIG trouble!!

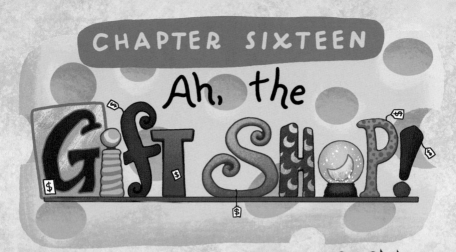

CHAPTER SIXTEEN

Ah, the GIFT SHOP!

Trap and Benjamin hurried off to CACKLEFUR CASTLE while Thea and Trappy headed for Manhole 13, the entrance to the SEWER KINGDOM. But Hercule wasn't ready for us to go yet...

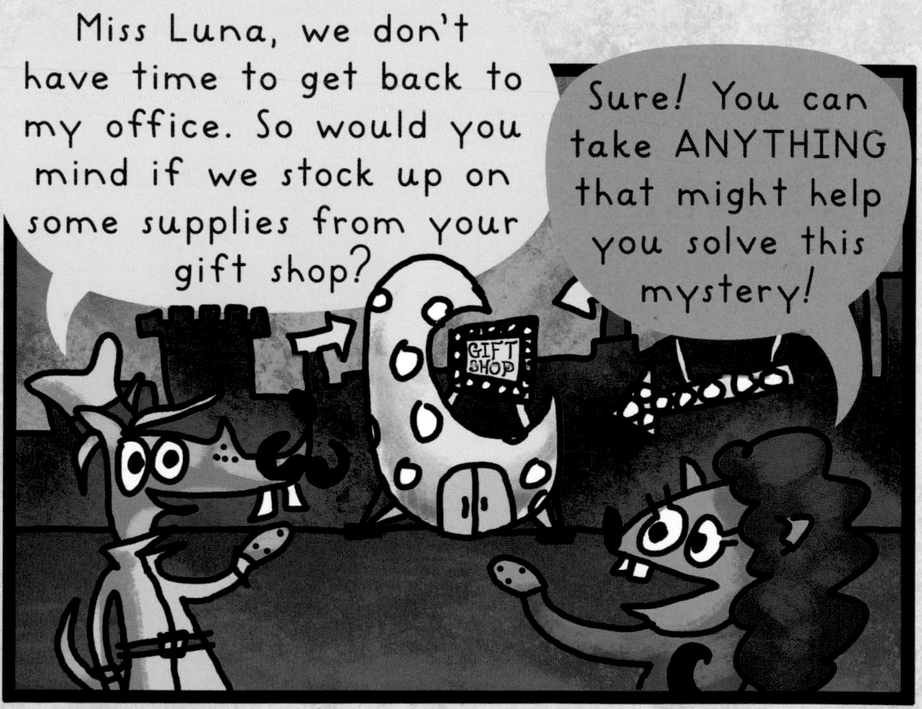
Miss Luna, we don't have time to get back to my office. So would you mind if we stock up on some supplies from your gift shop?
Sure! You can take ANYTHING that might help you solve this mystery!
GIFT SHOP

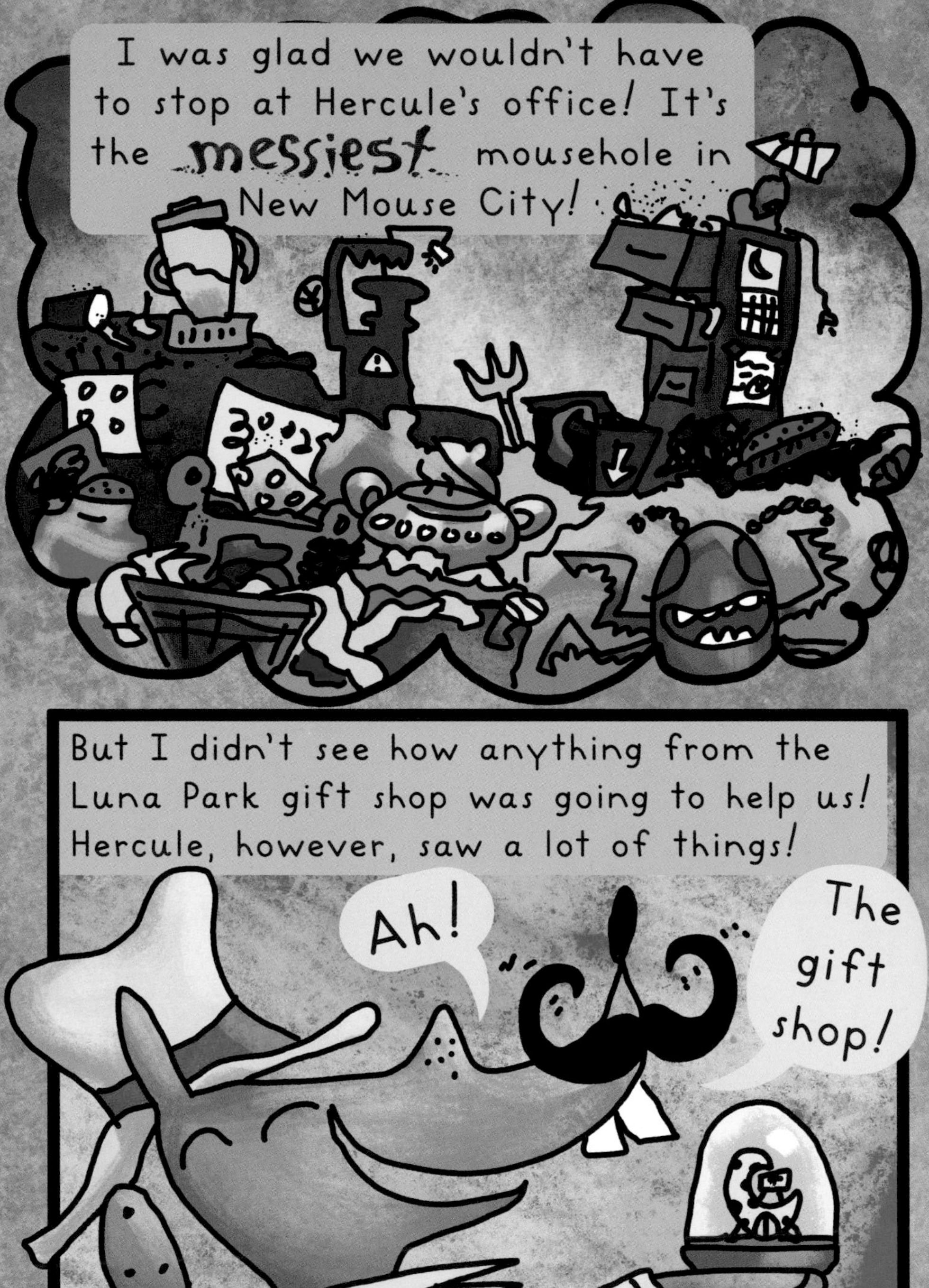
I was glad we wouldn't have to stop at Hercule's office! It's the messiest mousehole in New Mouse City!
But I didn't see how anything from the Luna Park gift shop was going to help us! Hercule, however, saw a lot of things!
Ah!
The gift shop!

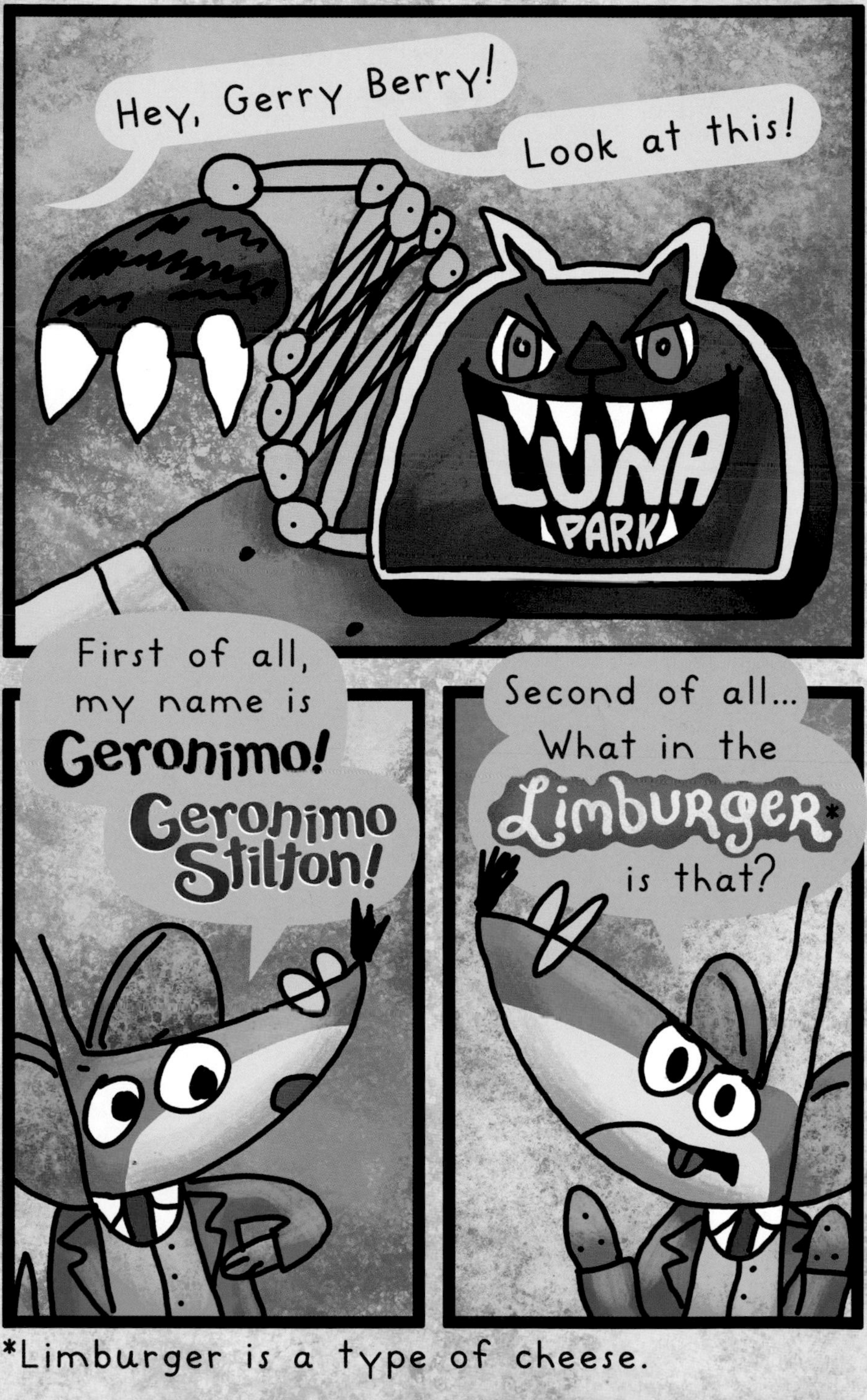
Hey, Gerry Berry!
Look at this!
LUNA PARK
First of all, my name is Geronimo!
Geronimo Stilton!
Second of all... What in the Limburger* is that?

*Limburger is a type of cheese.

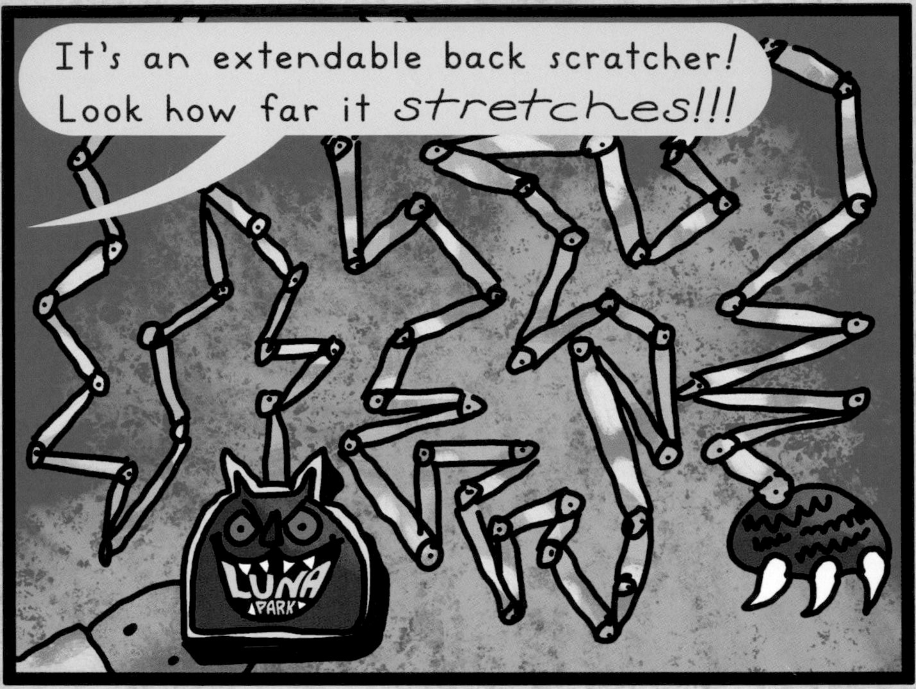
It's an extendable back scratcher! Look how far it stretches!!!
LUNA PARK

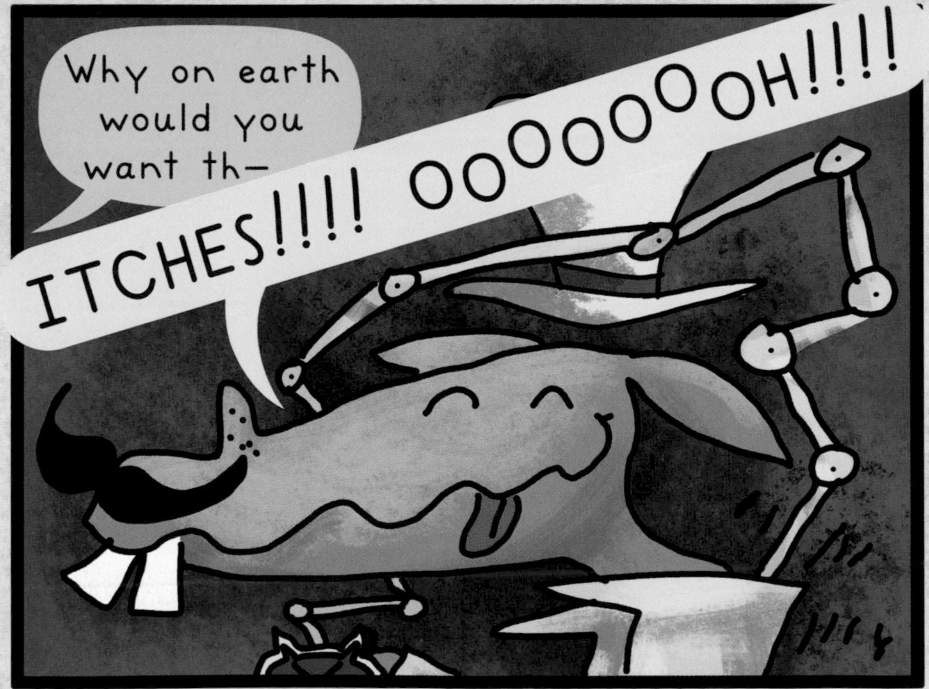
Why on earth would you want th—
ITCHES!!!! OOOOOOOOH!!!!

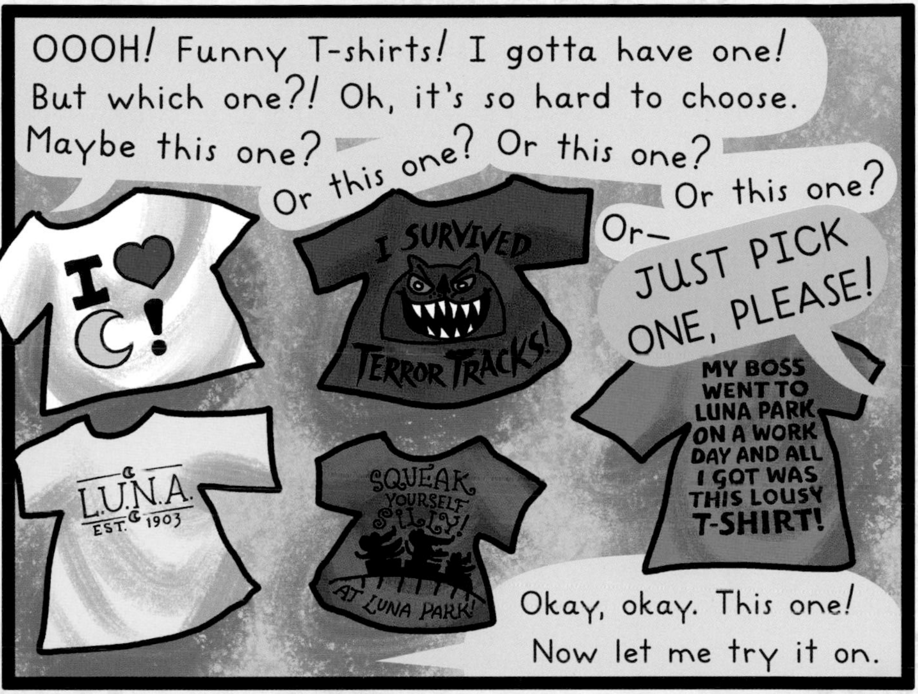
OOOH! Funny T-shirts! I gotta have one! But which one?! Oh, it's so hard to choose. Maybe this one?
Or this one? Or this one?
Or this one?
Or—
JUST PICK ONE, PLEASE!
I ♥ ☾!
I SURVIVED TERROR TRACKS!
MY BOSS WENT TO LUNA PARK ON A WORK DAY AND ALL I GOT WAS THIS LOUSY T-SHIRT!
L.U.N.A. EST. 1903
SQUEAK YOURSELF SILLY! AT LUNA PARK!
Okay, okay. This one! Now let me try it on.

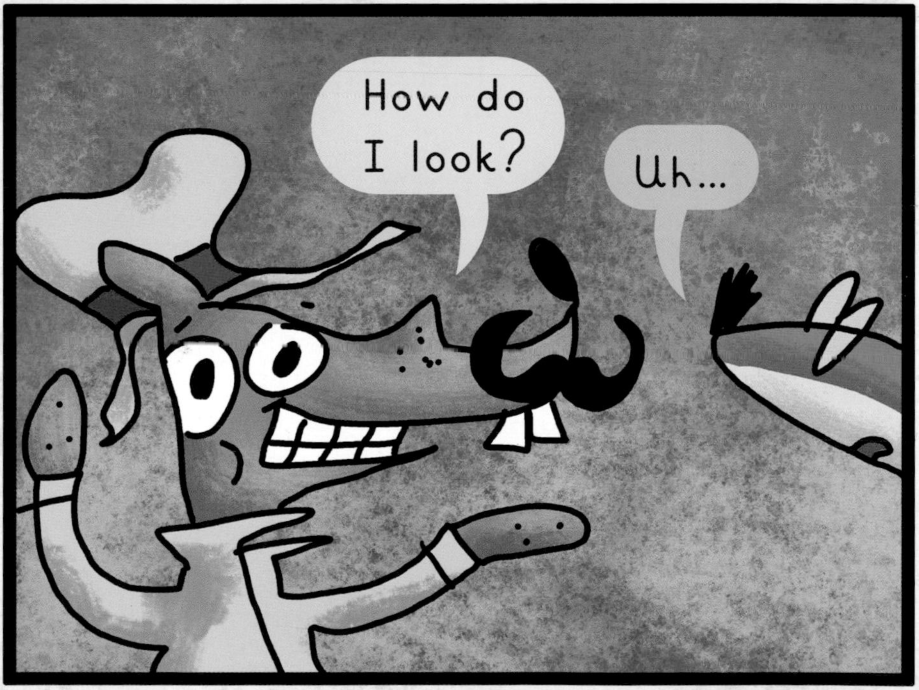
How do I look?
Uh...

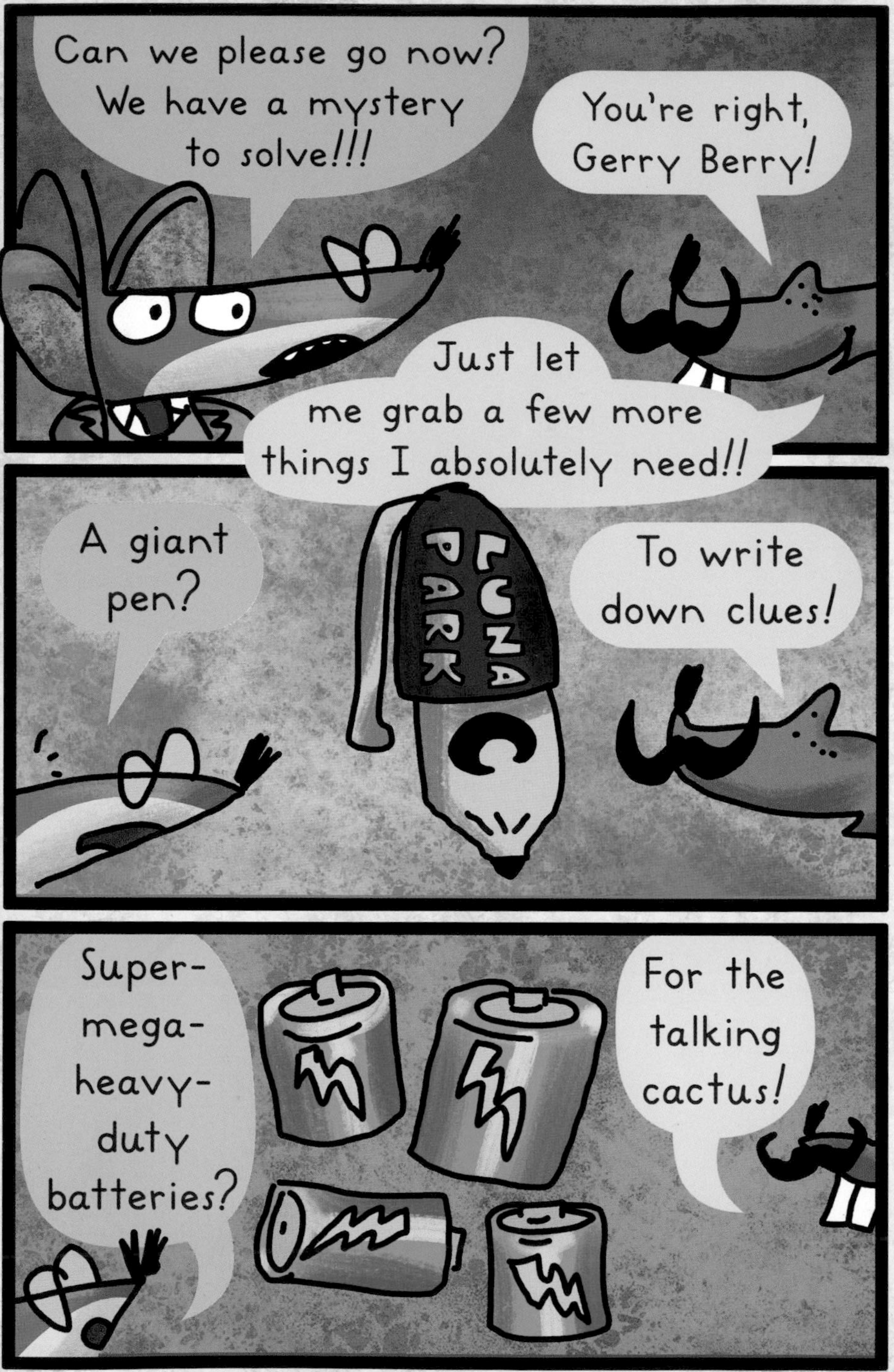
Can we please go now? We have a mystery to solve!!!
You're right, Gerry Berry!
Just let me grab a few more things I absolutely need!!
A giant pen?
LUNA PARK
To write down clues!
Super-mega-heavy-duty batteries?
For the talking cactus!

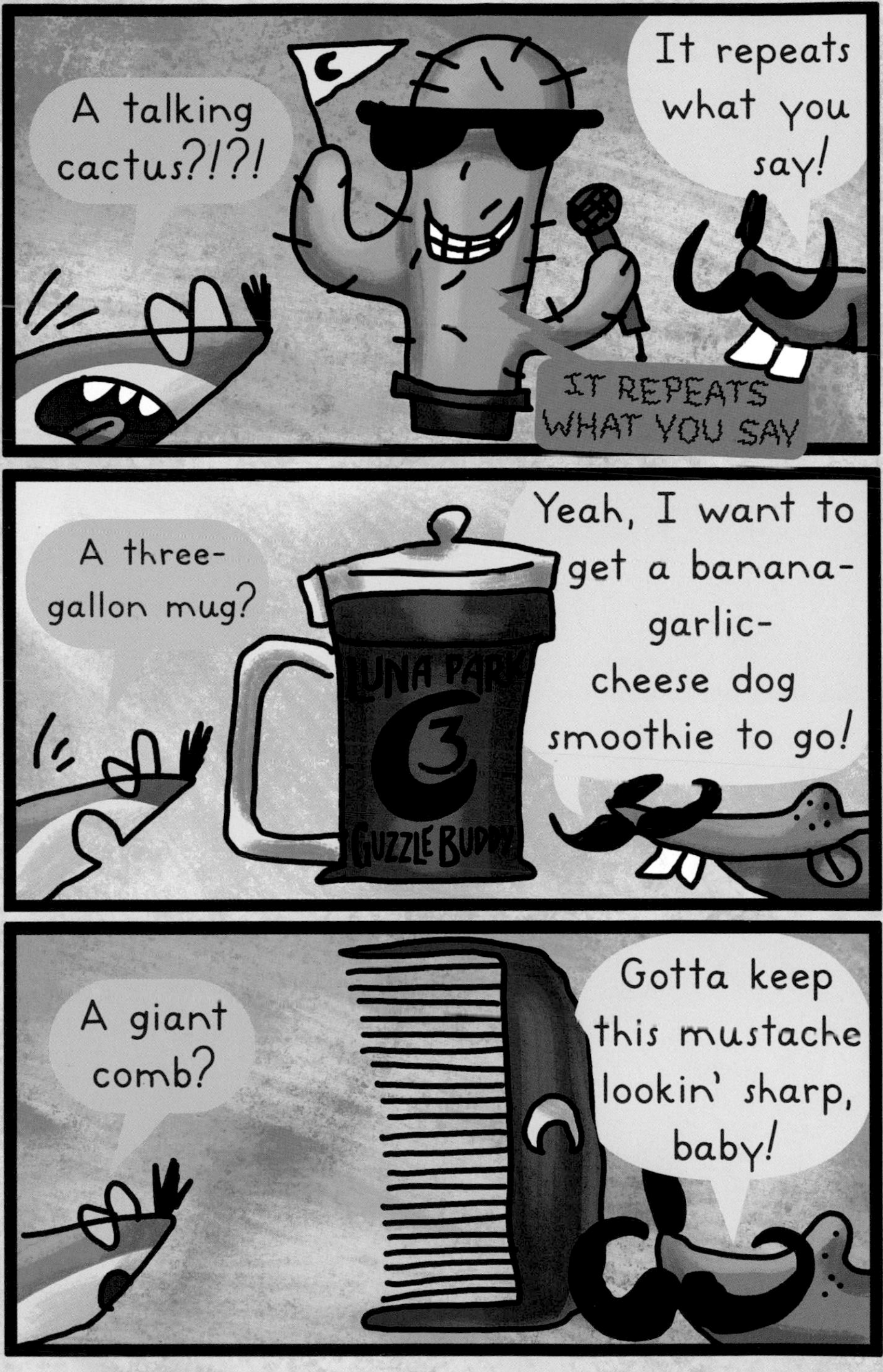
A talking cactus?!?!
It repeats what you say!
IT REPEATS WHAT YOU SAY
A three-gallon mug?
Yeah, I want to get a banana-garlic-cheese dog smoothie to go!
LUNA PARK
GUZZLE BUDDY
A giant comb?
Gotta keep this mustache lookin' sharp, baby!

CHAPTER SEVENTEEN

BAT BUGGY!

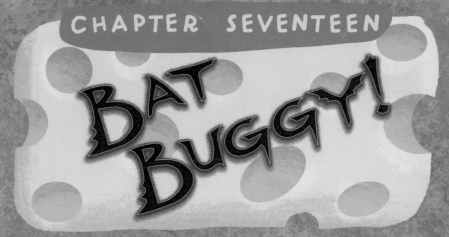

Finally, after Hercule had loaded a huge **LUNA PARK** tote bag with **LUNA PARK** stuff, we were ready to leave the **LUNA PARK** gift shop and head for Madame No's Not-Secret Lair.

Okay, Gerry, where's your car?
I don't have a car! We'll have to use yours.

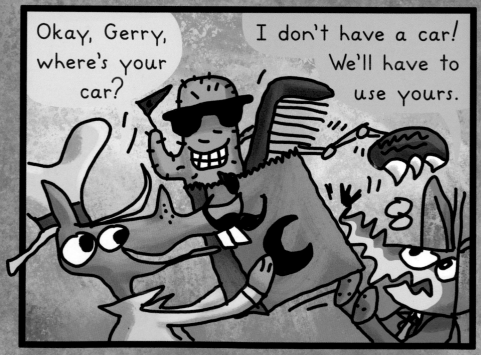

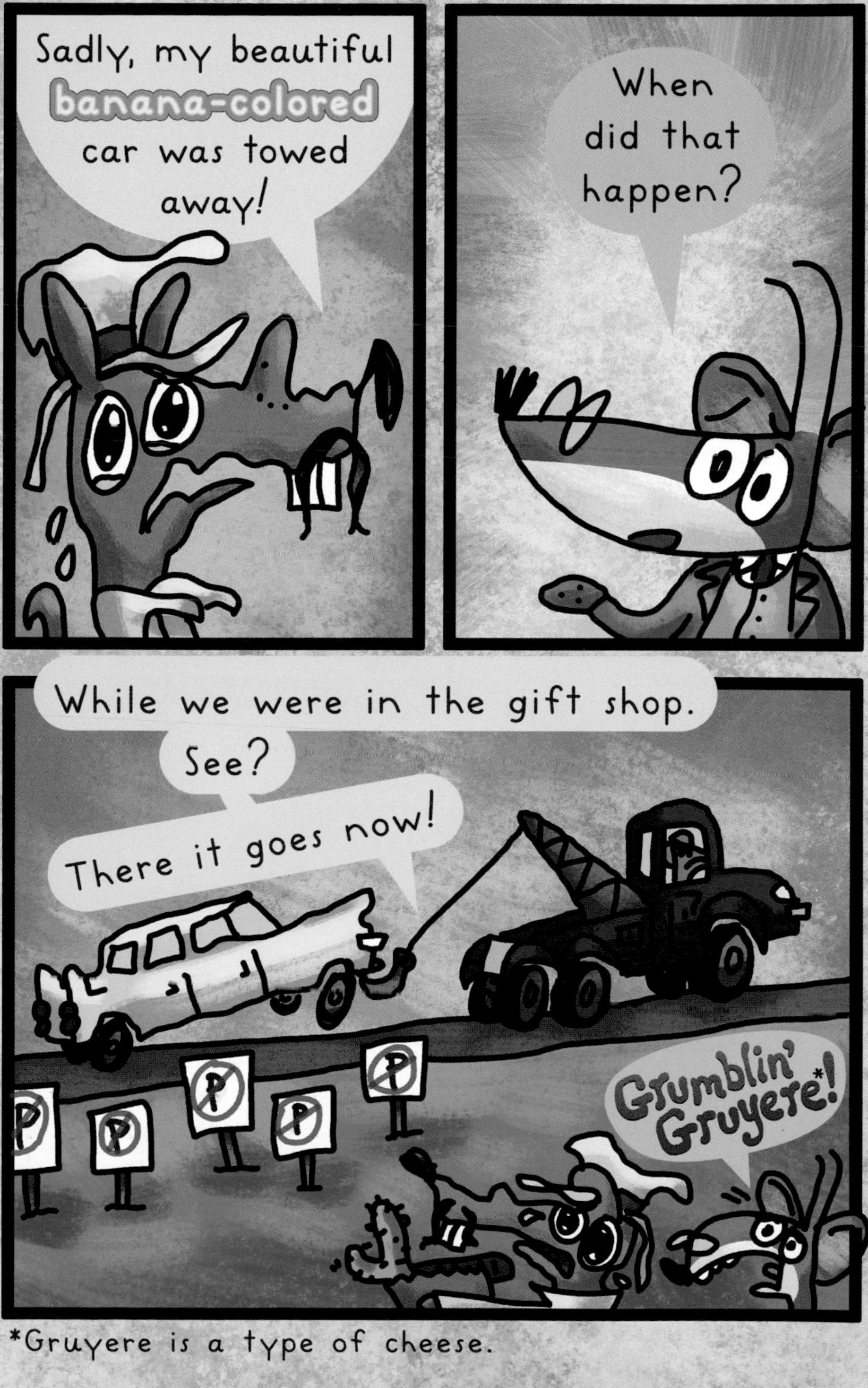
Sadly, my beautiful banana-colored car was towed away!
When did that happen?
While we were in the gift shop.
See?
There it goes now!
Grumblin' Gruyere*!

*Gruyere is a type of cheese.

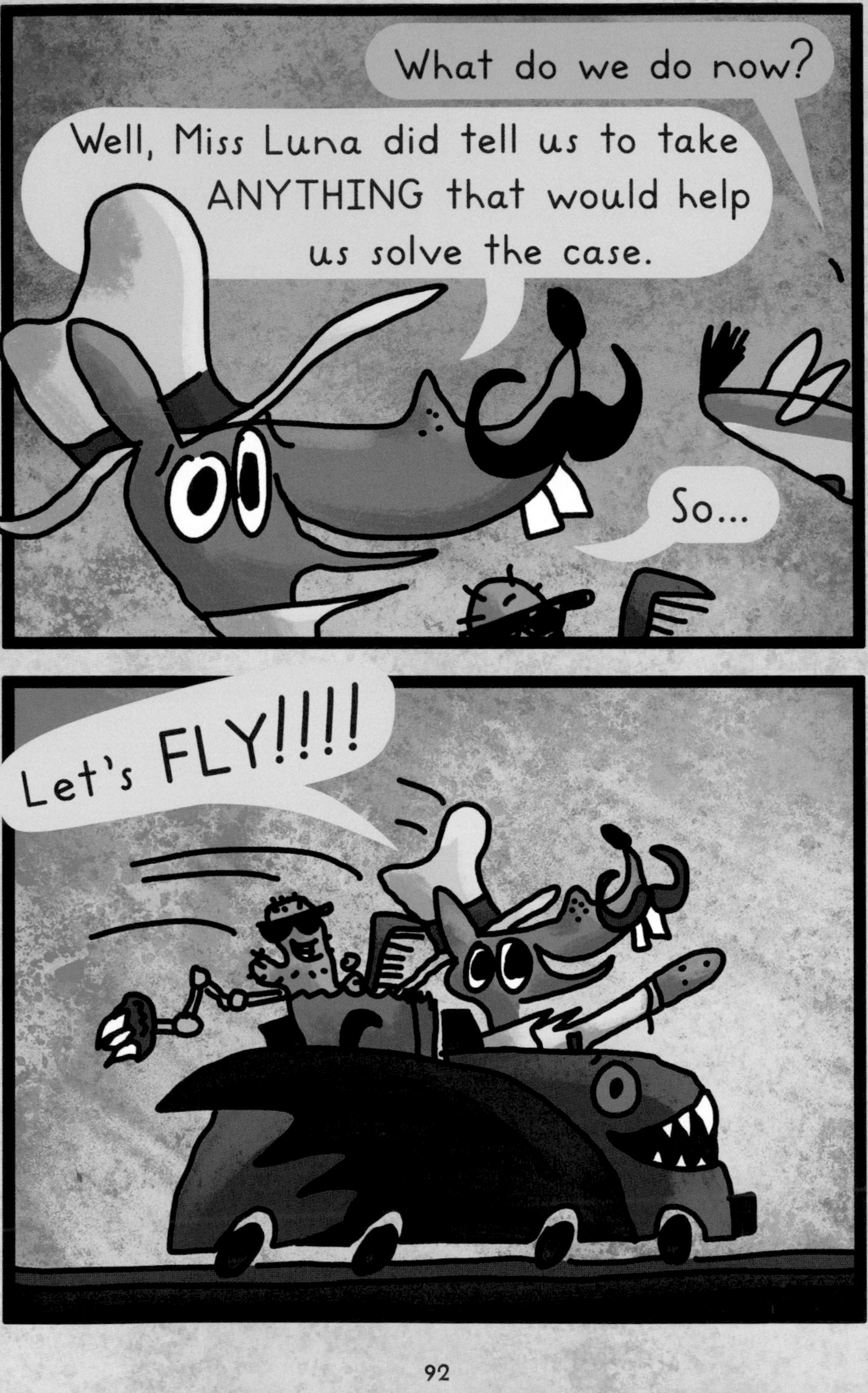
What do we do now?
Well, Miss Luna did tell us to take ANYTHING that would help us solve the case.
So...
Let's FLY!!!!

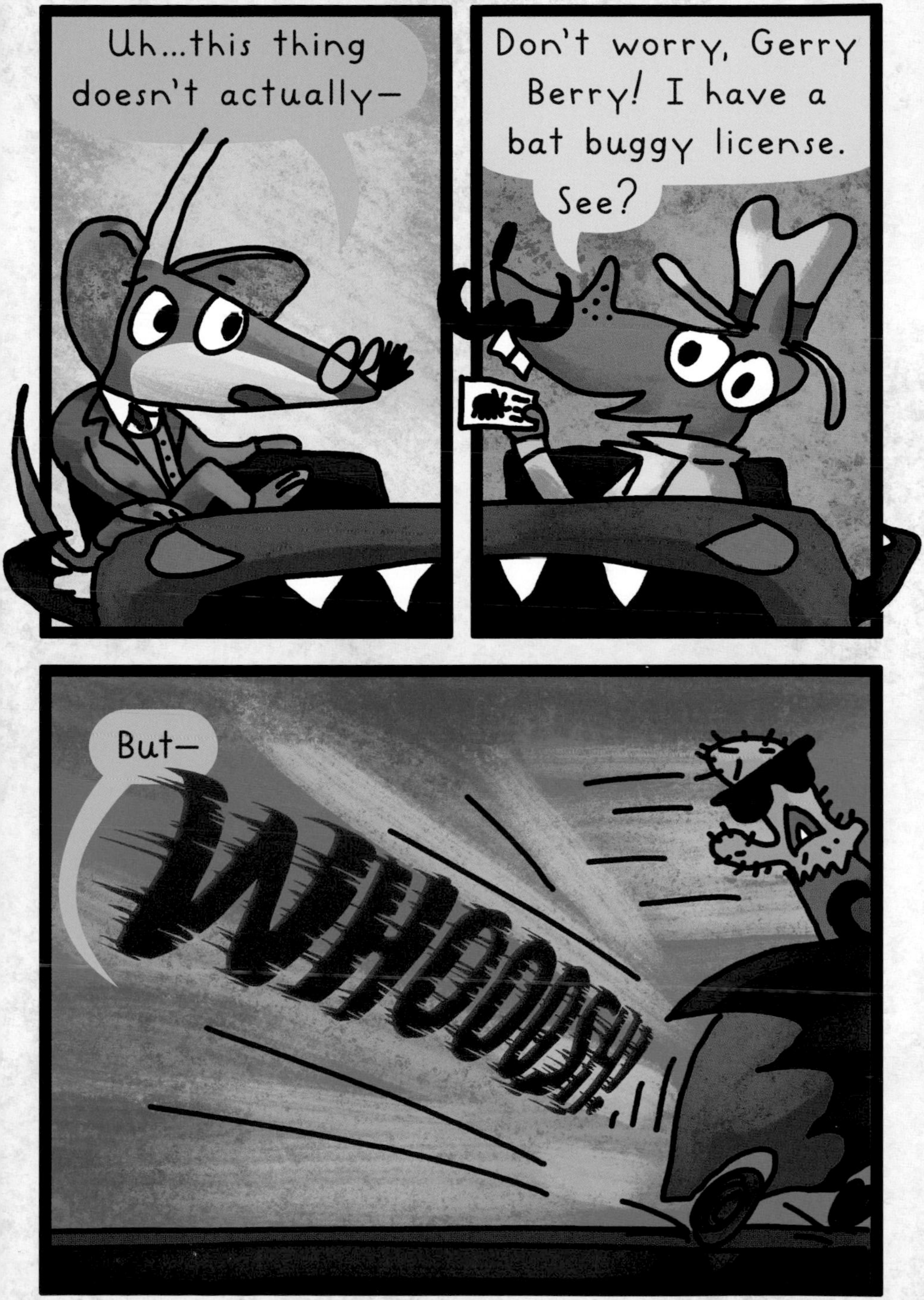
Uh...this thing doesn't actually—
Don't worry, Gerry Berry! I have a bat buggy license. See?
But—
WHOOOSH!

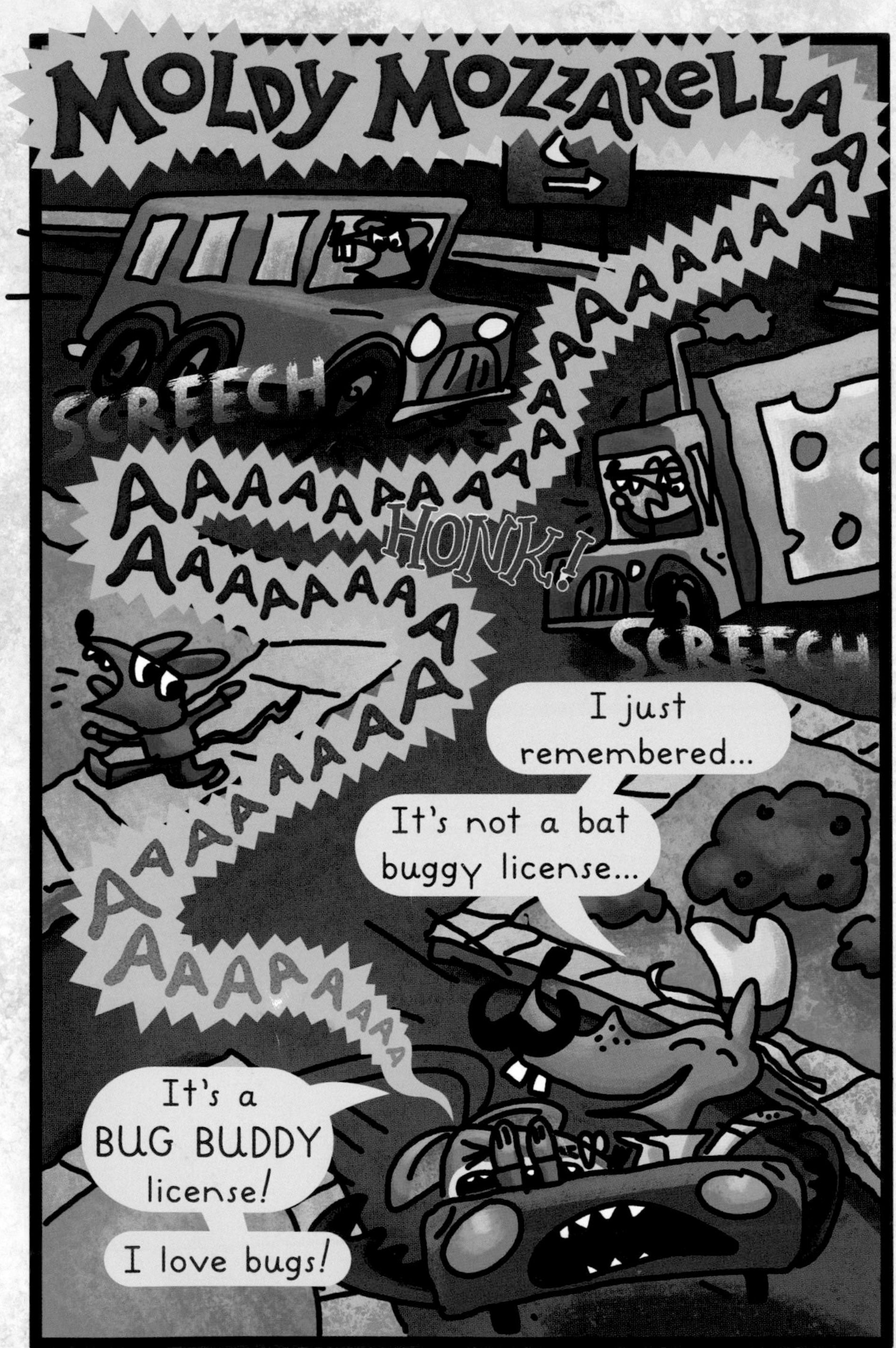
MOLDY MOZZARELLA
SCREECH
AAAAAAAAAAAAAAAAAAAAAAAAAAAAAAAAAAAAAAAAAAAAAAAAAAAAAAAAAAAAAA
HONK!
SCREECH
I just remembered...
It's not a bat buggy license...
It's a BUG BUDDY license!
I love bugs!

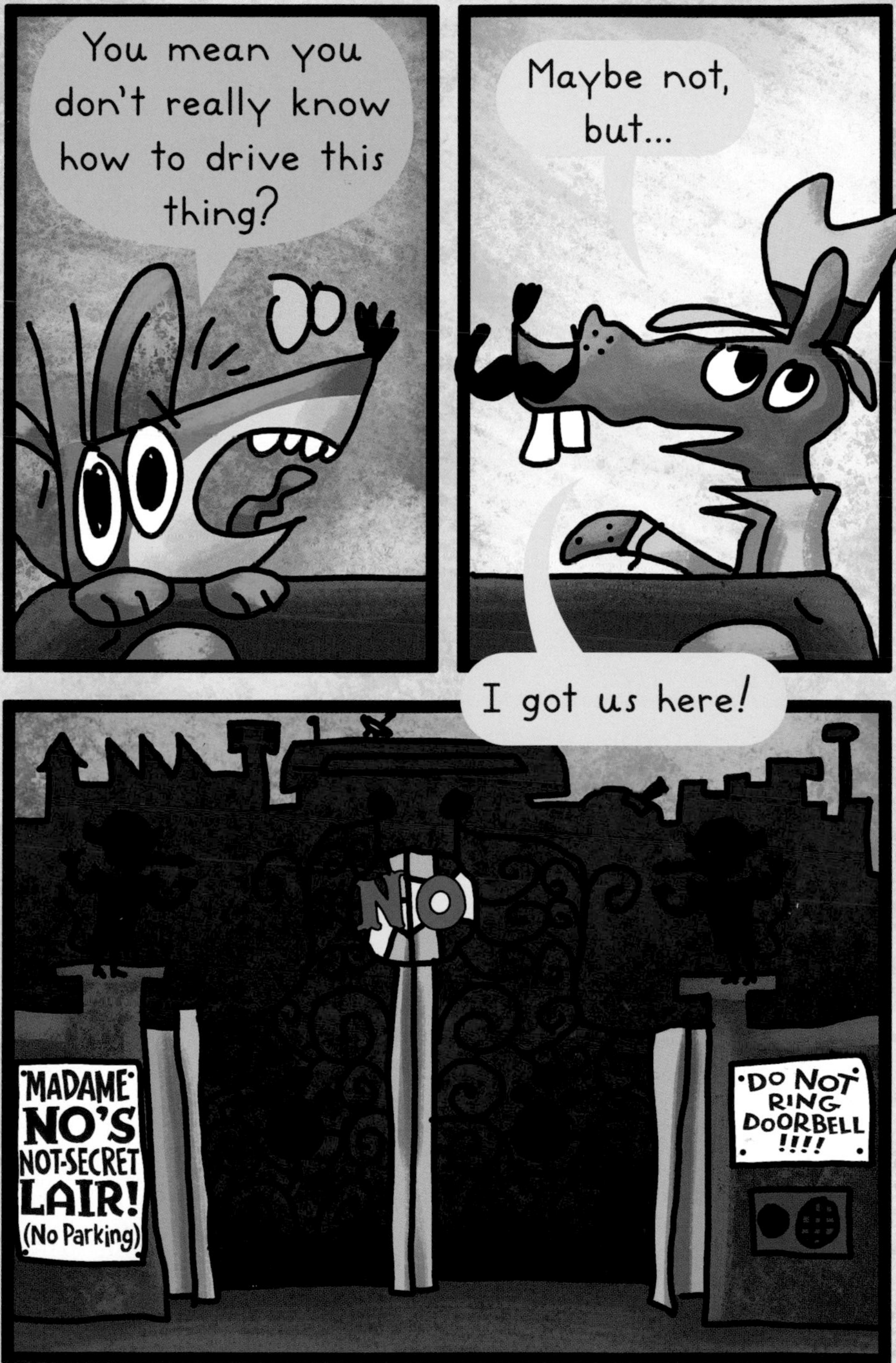
You mean you don't really know how to drive this thing?
Maybe not, but...
I got us here!
NO
MADAME NO'S NOT-SECRET LAIR! (No Parking)
DO NOT RING DOORBELL !!!!

CHAPTER EIGHTEEN
At the Gates of NO!

I'm still not sure how we got there, but we did! Next I had to face my most **DANGEROUS** rival: Madame No! If I could get through the huge **STEEL** gate, that is.

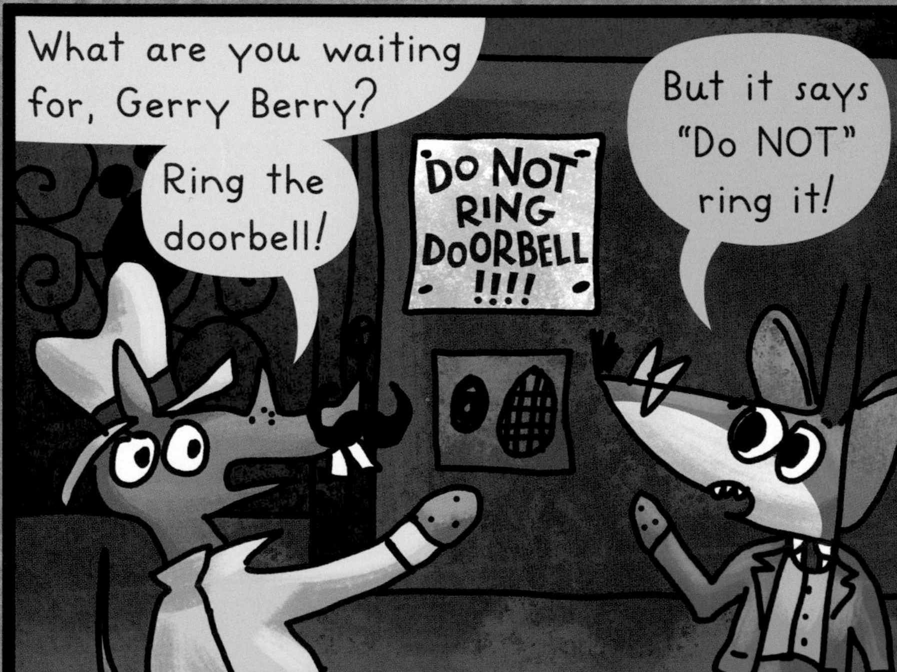
What are you waiting for, Gerry Berry?
Ring the doorbell!
DO NOT RING DOORBELL !!!!
But it says "Do NOT" ring it!

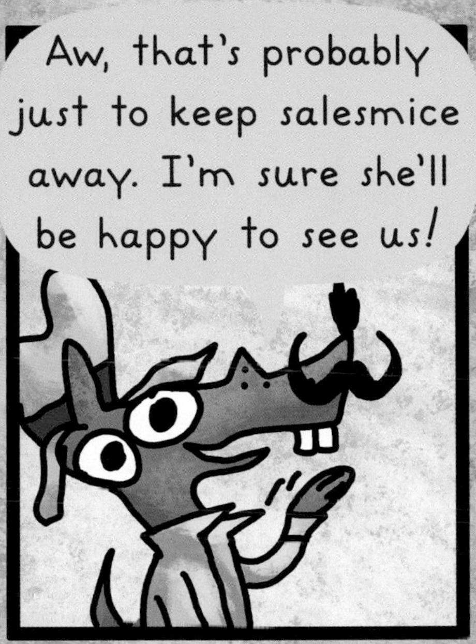
Aw, that's probably just to keep salesmice away. I'm sure she'll be happy to see us!

I was sure she would NOT be happy at all!!

But what choice did I have?

What if Luna Park closed, all because I was afraid to ring a **DOORBELL?**

Slowly, I reached out my paw and...

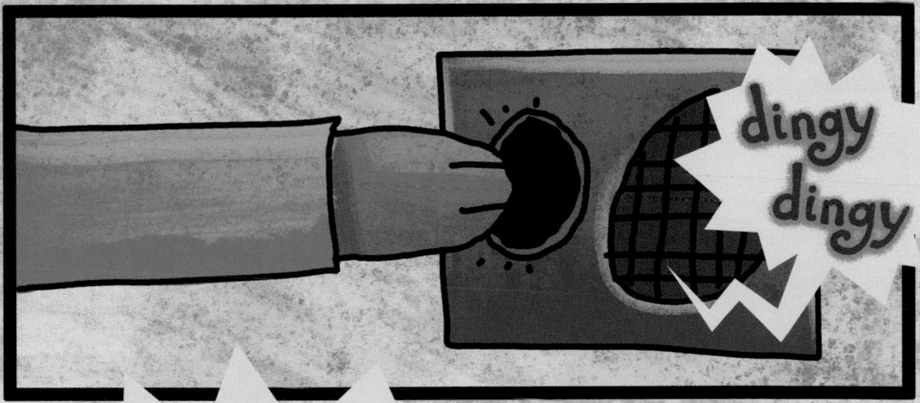
dingy
dingy

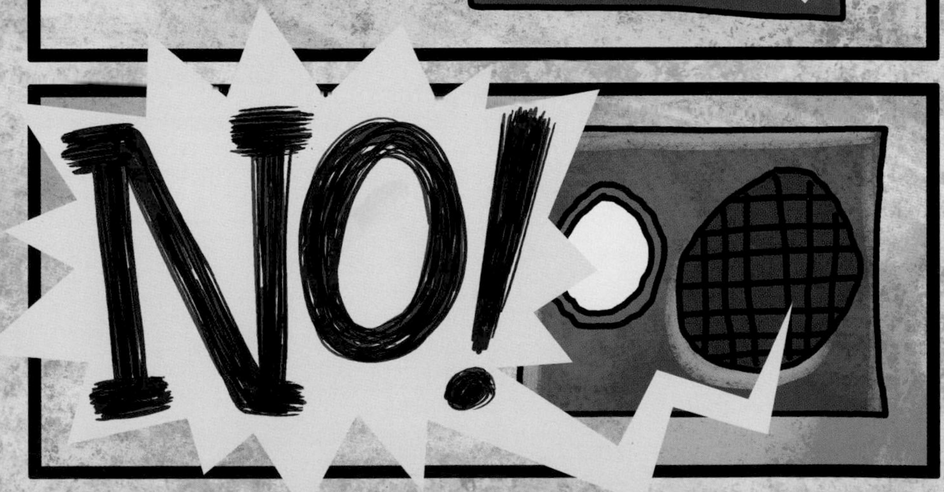
NO!

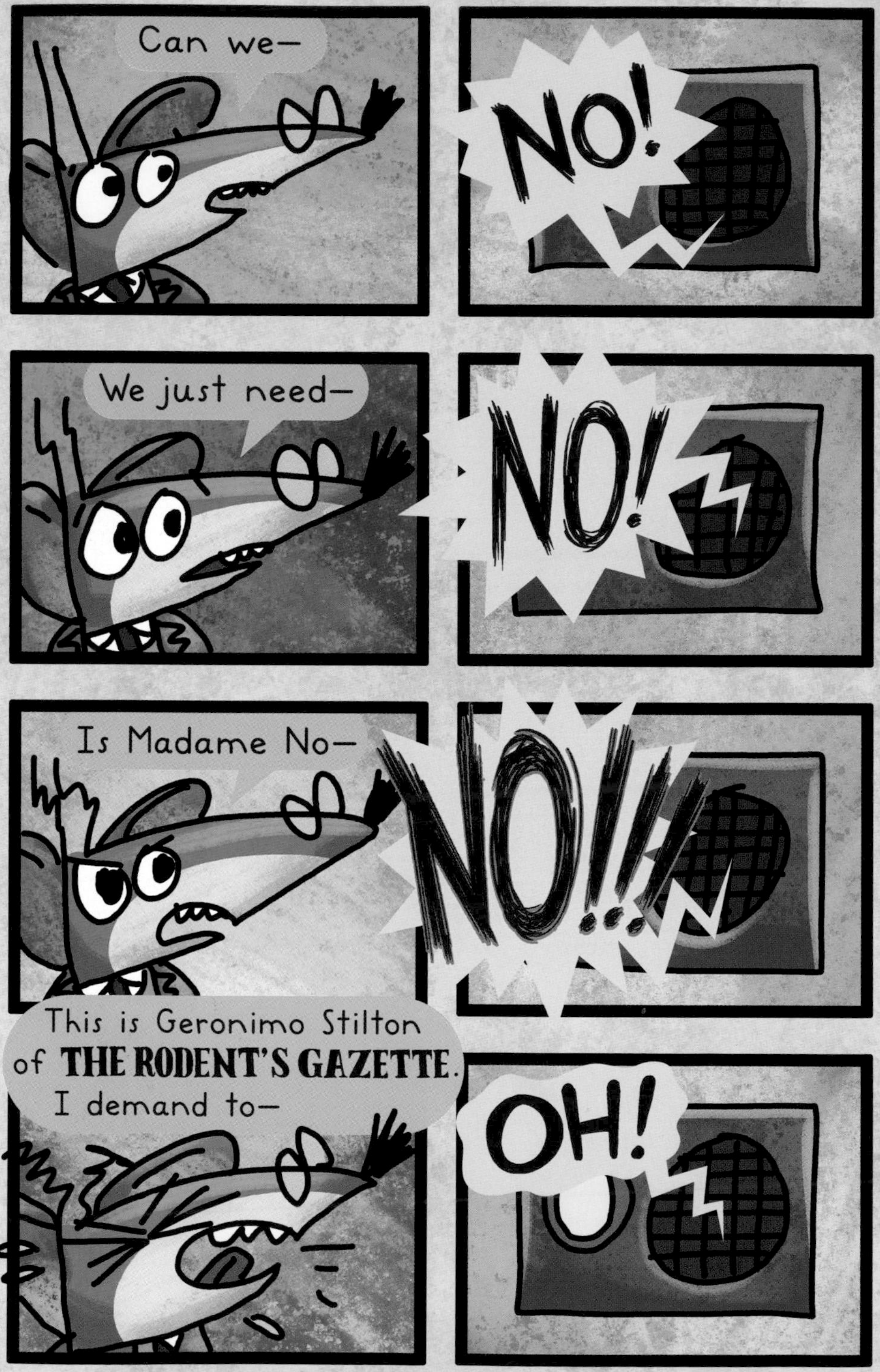

Can we–
NO!
We just need–
NO!
Is Madame No–
NO!!!
This is Geronimo Stilton of THE RODENT'S GAZETTE. I demand to–
OH!

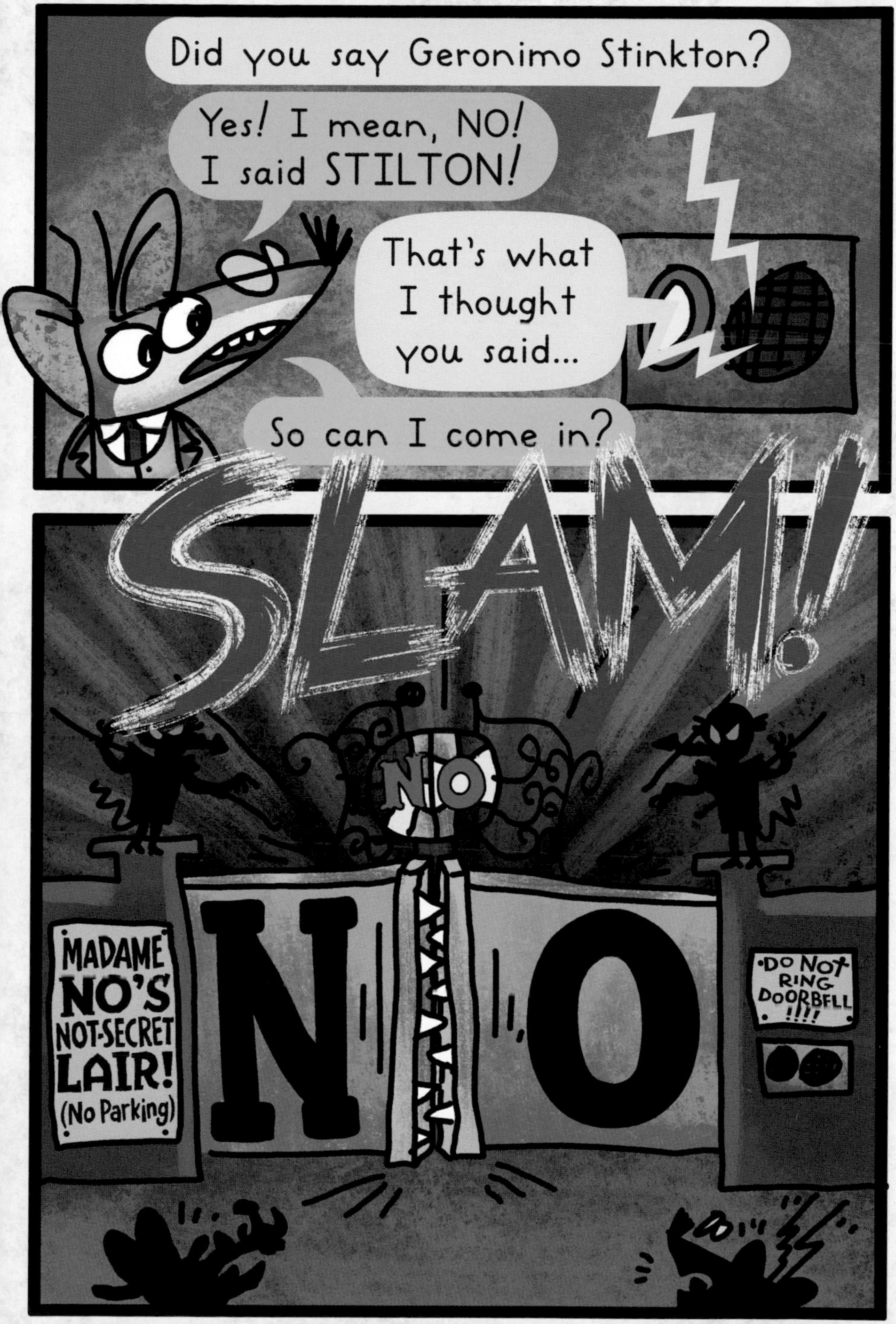
Did you say Geronimo Stinkton?
Yes! I mean, NO! I said STILTON!
That's what I thought you said...
So can I come in?
SLAM!!
NO
MADAME NO'S NOT-SECRET LAIR! (No Parking)
NO
DO NOT RING DOORBELL !!!!

CHAPTER NINETEEN

DIAL M FOR MOUSE-TERY!

Madame No's Not-Secret Lair may have been not-secret, but it WAS definitely well protected! There was no way of getting through that **GATE!**

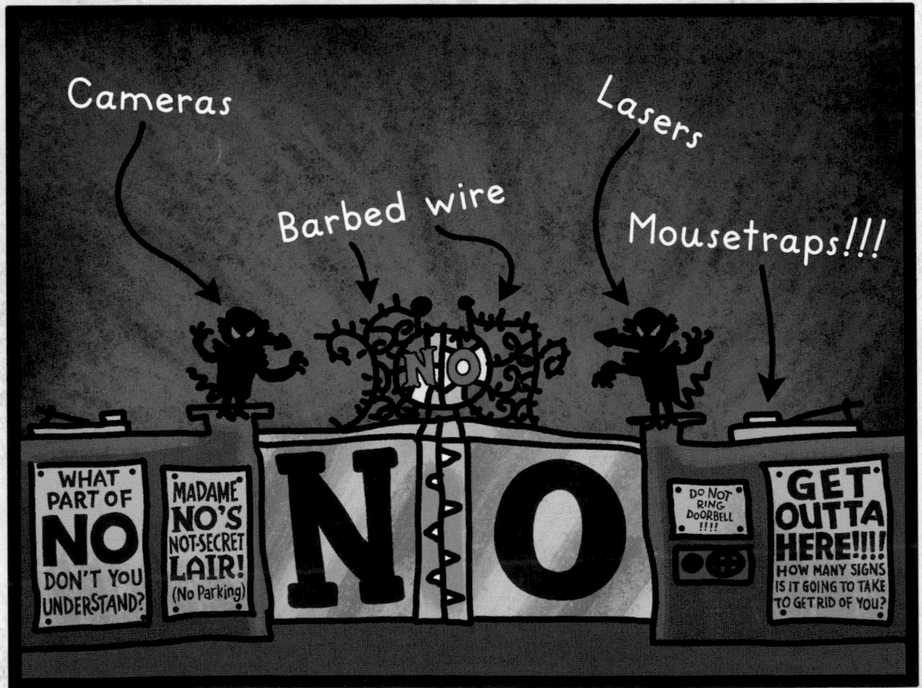

Cameras
Lasers
Barbed wire
Mousetraps!!!
WHAT PART OF NO DON'T YOU UNDERSTAND?
MADAME NO'S NOT-SECRET LAIR! (No Parking)
NO
NO
DO NOT RING DOORBELL !!!!
GET OUTTA HERE!!!! HOW MANY SIGNS IS IT GOING TO TAKE TO GET RID OF YOU?

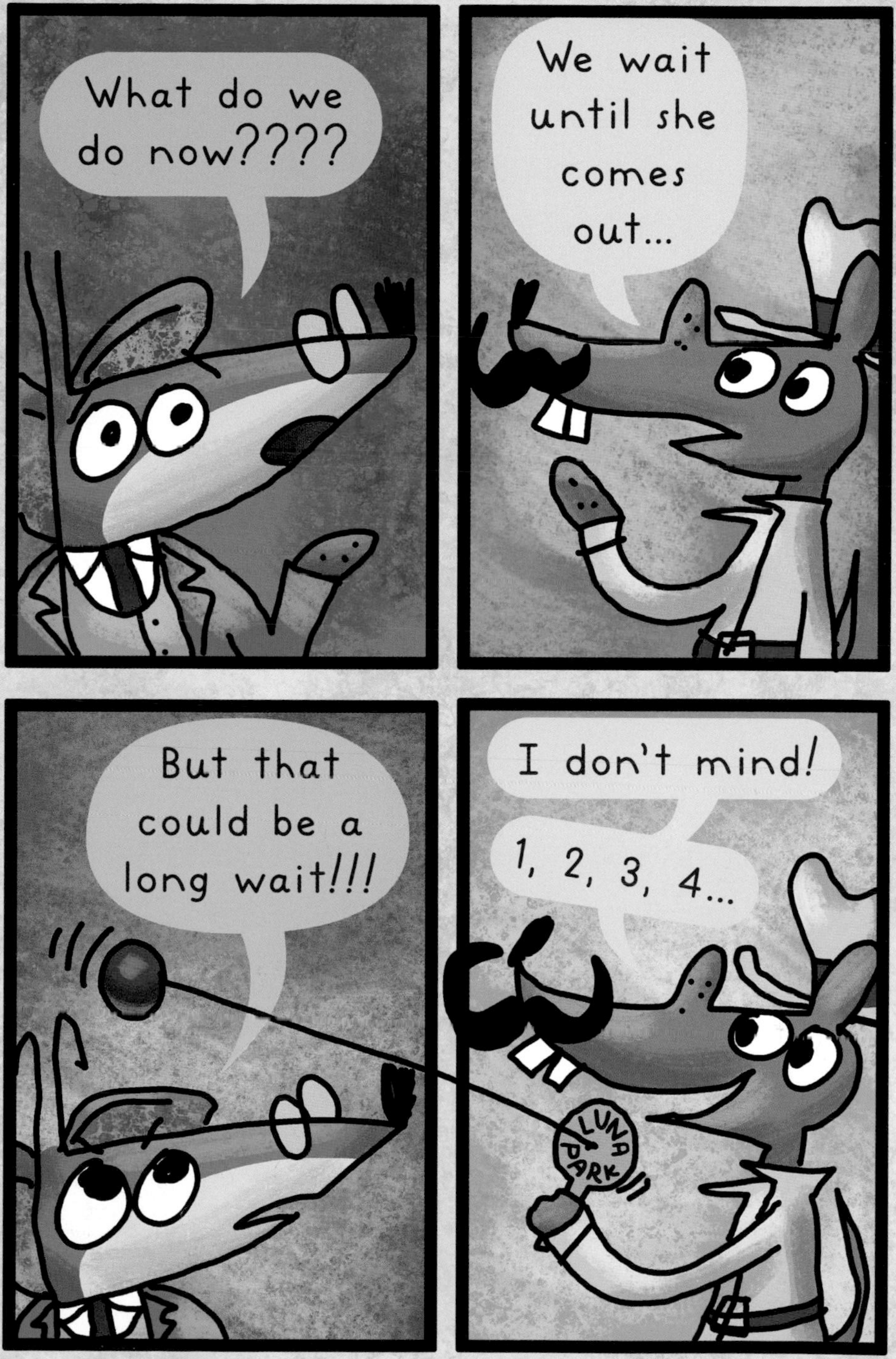
What do we do now????
We wait until she comes out...
But that could be a long wait!!!
I don't mind!
1, 2, 3, 4...
LUNA PARK

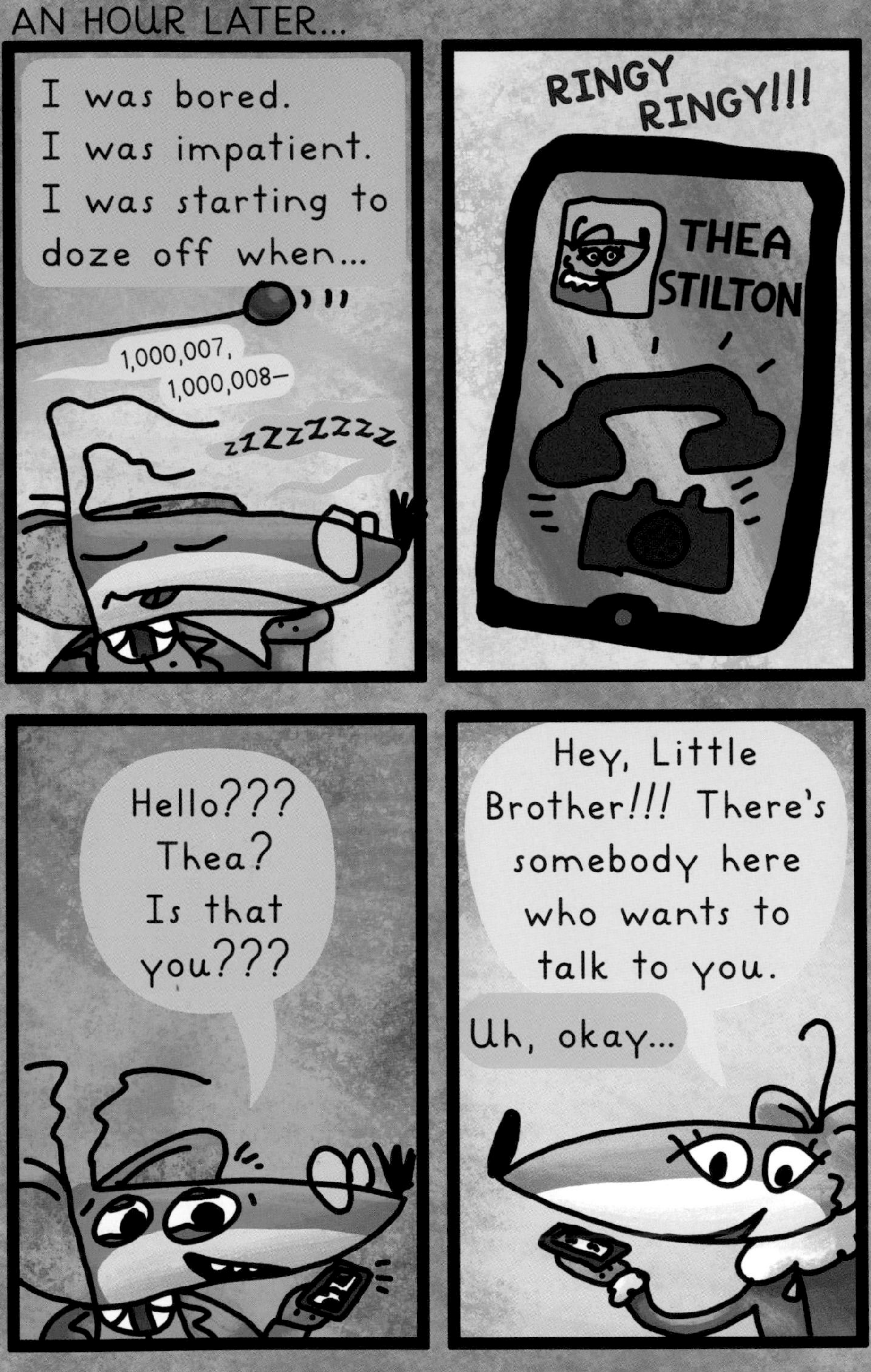
AN HOUR LATER...
I was bored. I was impatient. I was starting to doze off when...
1,000,007, 1,000,008–
zZZZZZZz
RINGY RINGY!!!
THEA STILTON
Hello??? Thea? Is that you???
Hey, Little Brother!!! There's somebody here who wants to talk to you.
Uh, okay...

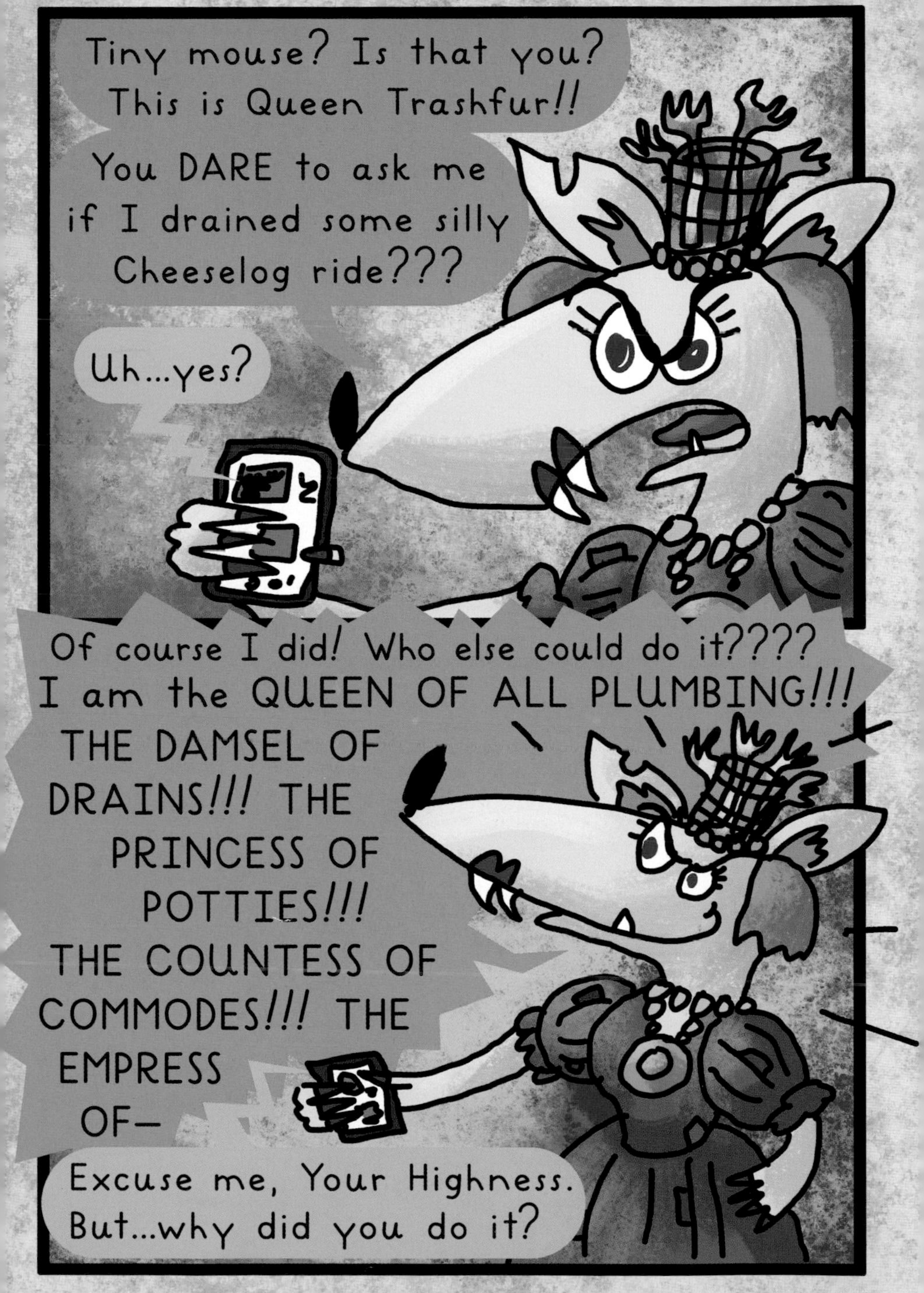
Tiny mouse? Is that you? This is Queen Trashfur!!
You DARE to ask me if I drained some silly Cheeselog ride???
Uh...yes?
Of course I did! Who else could do it???? I am the QUEEN OF ALL PLUMBING!!! THE DAMSEL OF DRAINS!!! THE PRINCESS OF POTTIES!!! THE COUNTESS OF COMMODES!!! THE EMPRESS OF—
Excuse me, Your Highness. But...why did you do it?

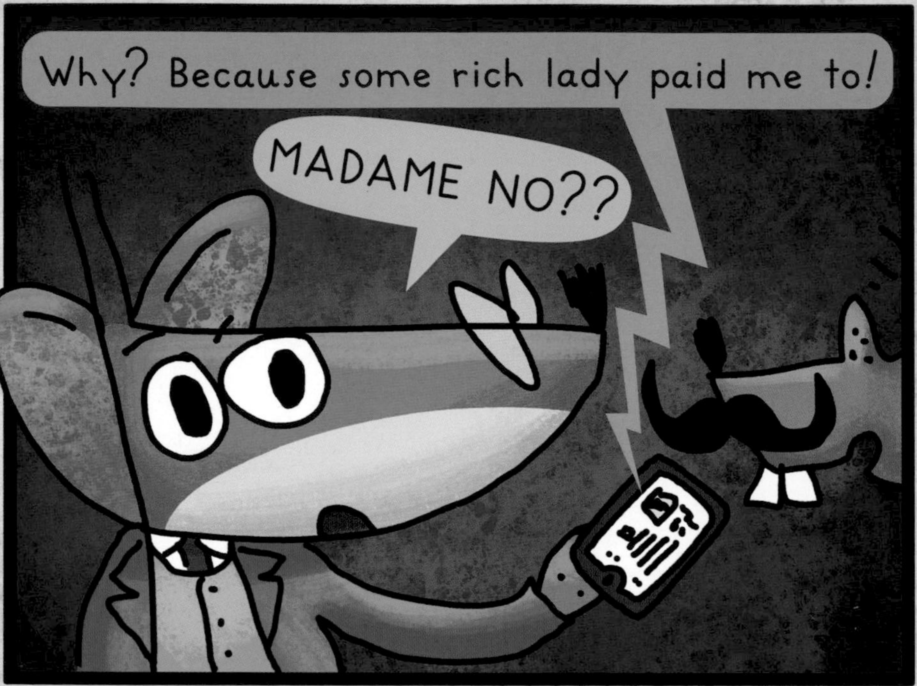
Why? Because some rich lady paid me to!
MADAME NO??

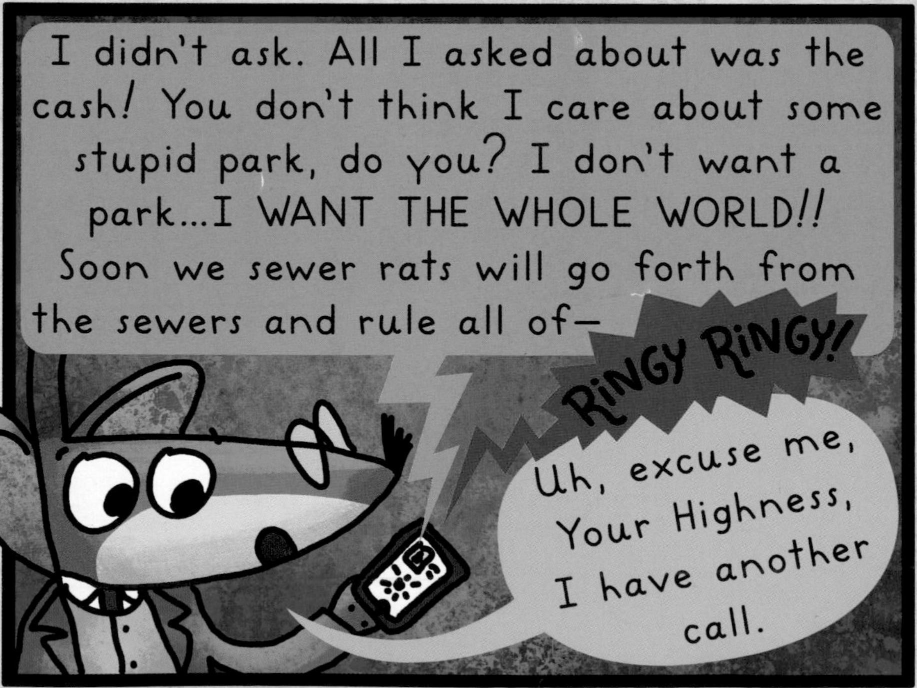
I didn't ask. All I asked about was the cash! You don't think I care about some stupid park, do you? I don't want a park...I WANT THE WHOLE WORLD!! Soon we sewer rats will go forth from the sewers and rule all of—
RINGY RINGY!
Uh, excuse me, Your Highness, I have another call.

I'm glad I wasn't there to see how **MAD** Queen Trashfur got when I hung up on her! But I really did have another call!!

TRAP STILTON
Trap? Is that you??
Who'd you think it was, Cheesehead? Grant Gentlemouse*?
H'YUK H'YUK

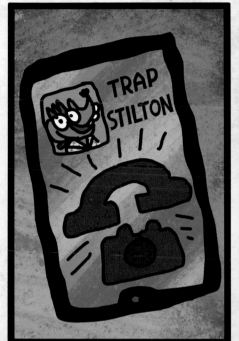

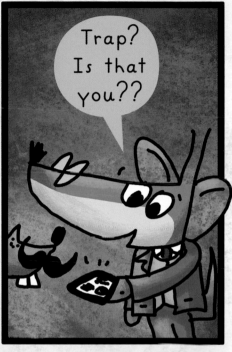

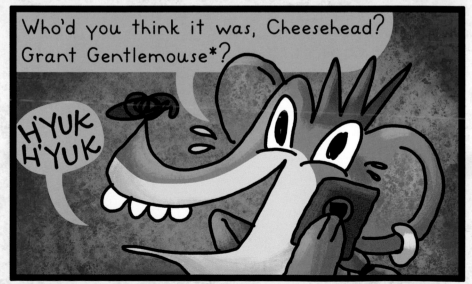

*The founder of New Mouse City...200 years ago!

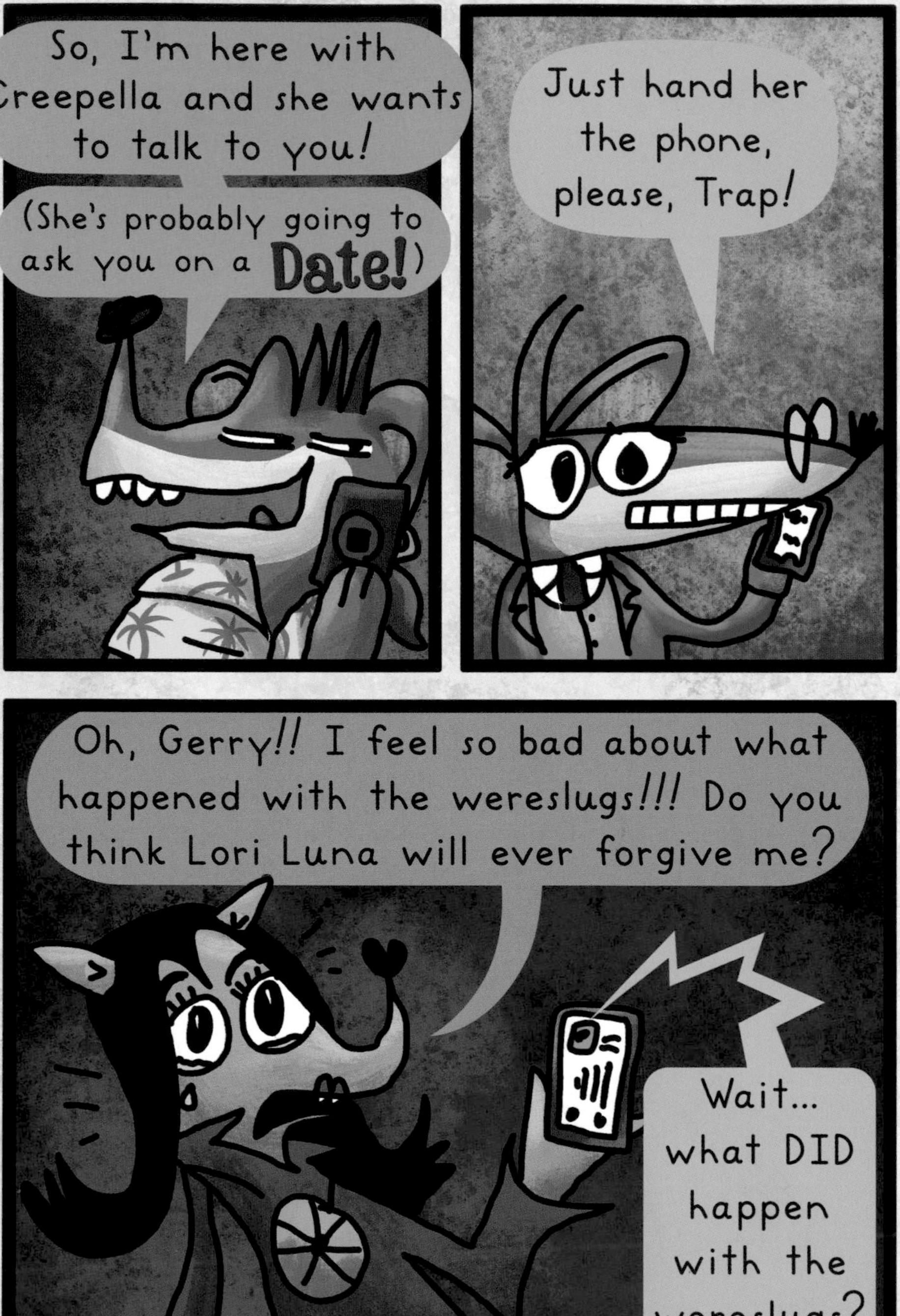
So, I'm here with Creepella and she wants to talk to you!
(She's probably going to ask you on a Date!)
Just hand her the phone, please, Trap!
Oh, Gerry!! I feel so bad about what happened with the wereslugs!!! Do you think Lori Luna will ever forgive me?
Wait... what DID happen with the wereslugs?

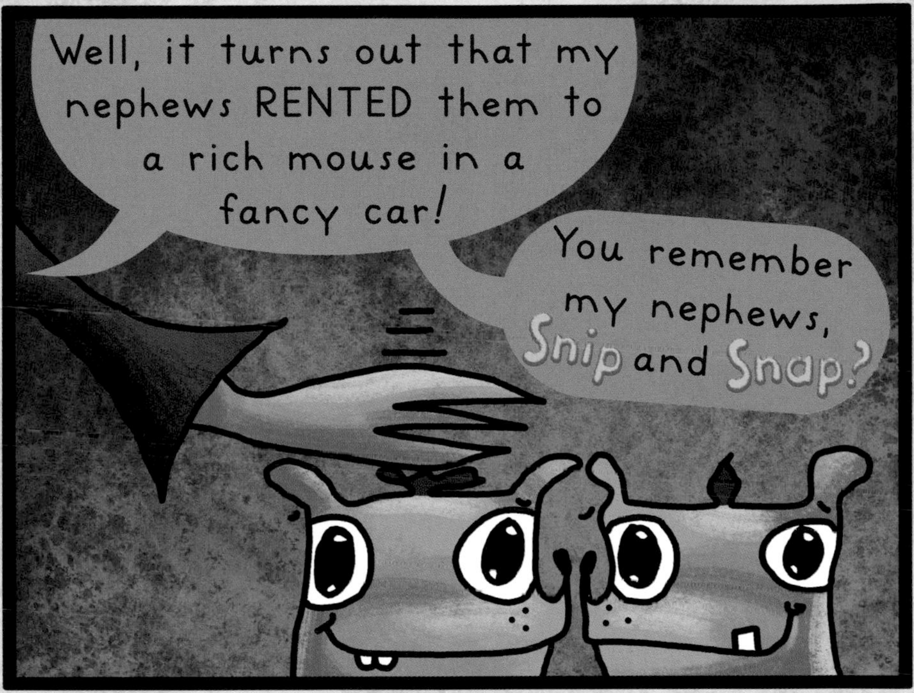
Well, it turns out that my nephews RENTED them to a rich mouse in a fancy car!
You remember my nephews, Snip and Snap?

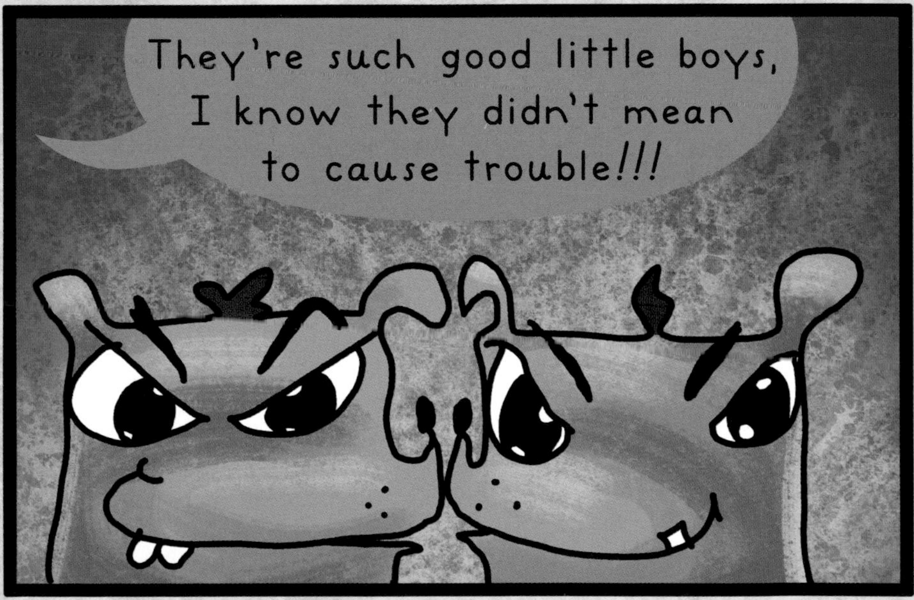
They're such good little boys, I know they didn't mean to cause trouble!!!

I sure did remember Snip and Snap!
And I was sure they DID mean to cause TROUBLE!

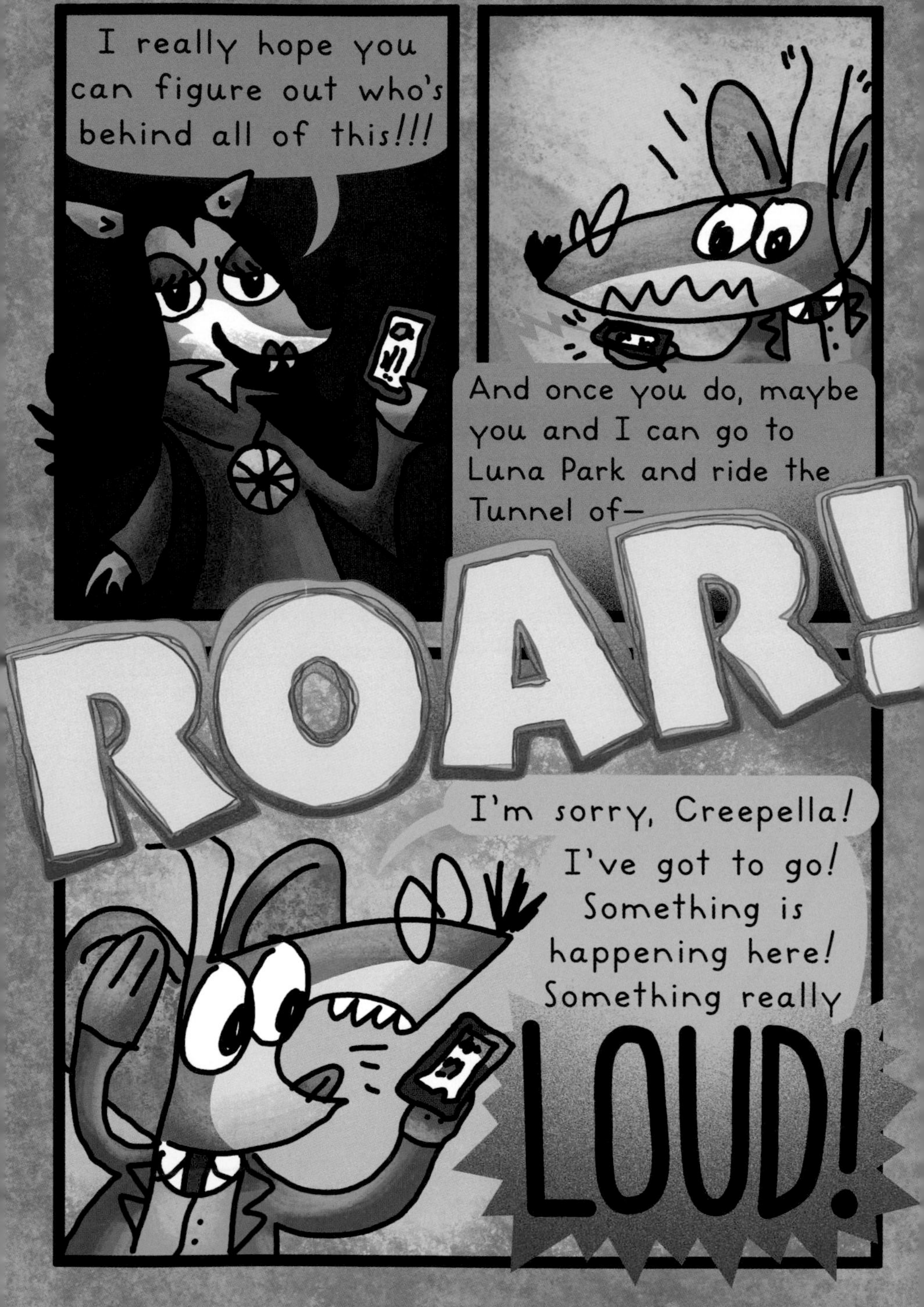

I really hope you can figure out who's behind all of this!!!
And once you do, maybe you and I can go to Luna Park and ride the Tunnel of—
ROAR!
I'm sorry, Creepella!
I've got to go! Something is happening here! Something really
LOUD!

CHAPTER TWENTY

ON THE TRAIL OF Madame No!

Behind the big gate, an engine was REVVING and ROARING! There's only one car that LOUD!! The SUPER NO!!! Madame No's company made them until they were OUTLAWED!

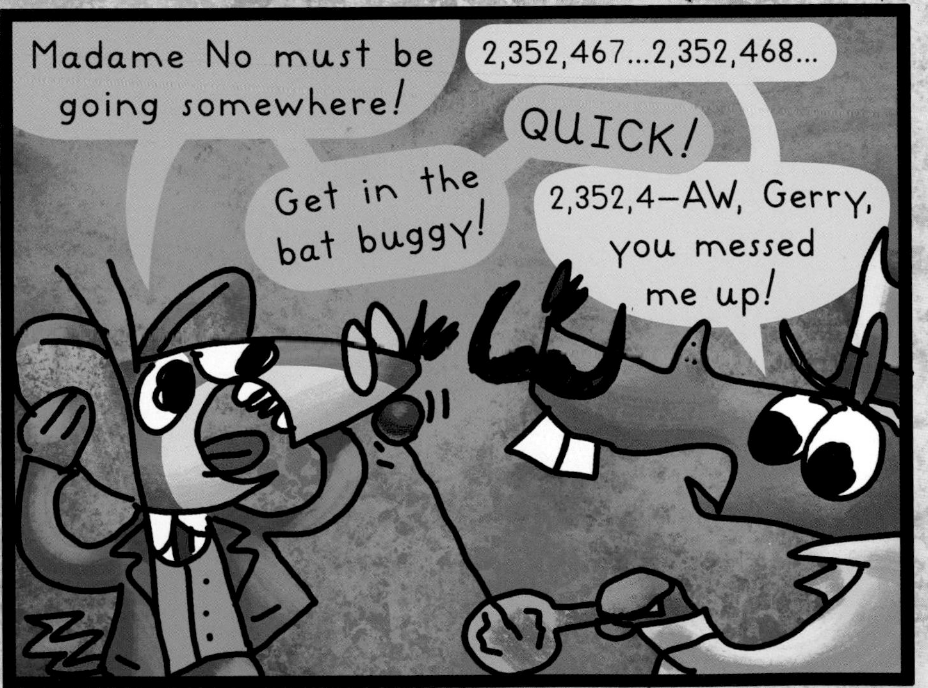

Madame No must be going somewhere!
2,352,467...2,352,468...
QUICK!
Get in the bat buggy!
2,352,4—AW, Gerry, you messed me up!

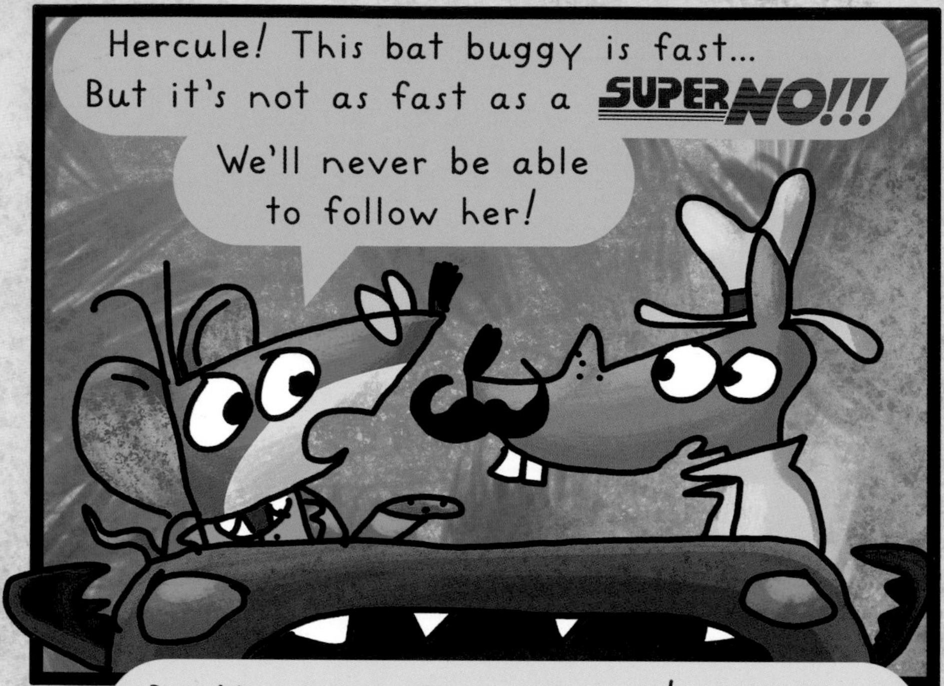
Hercule! This bat buggy is fast... But it's not as fast as a SUPER NO!!!
We'll never be able to follow her!

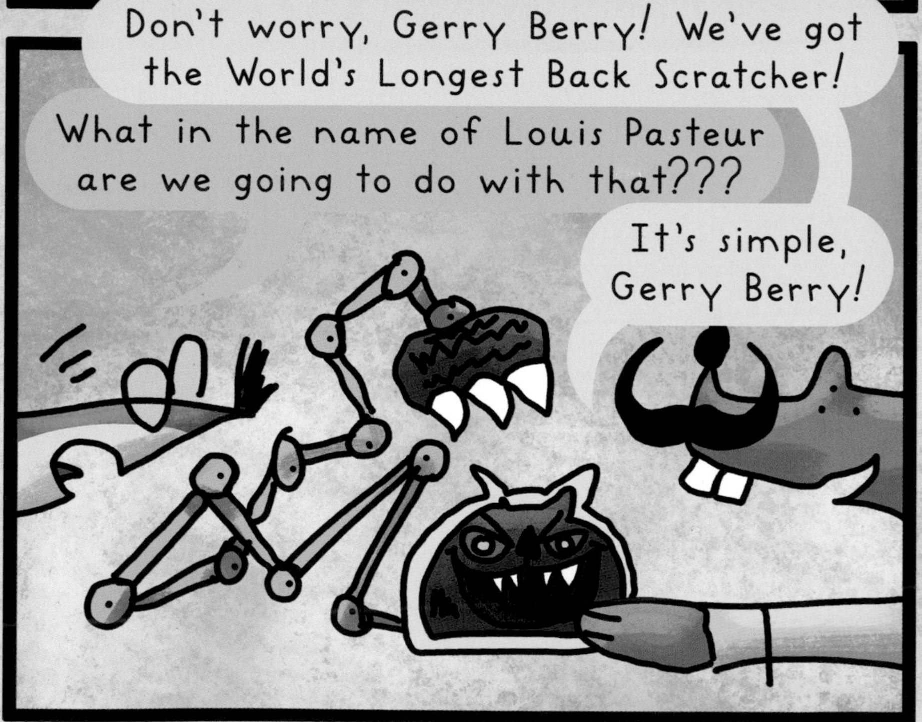
Don't worry, Gerry Berry! We've got the World's Longest Back Scratcher!
What in the name of Louis Pasteur are we going to do with that???
It's simple, Gerry Berry!

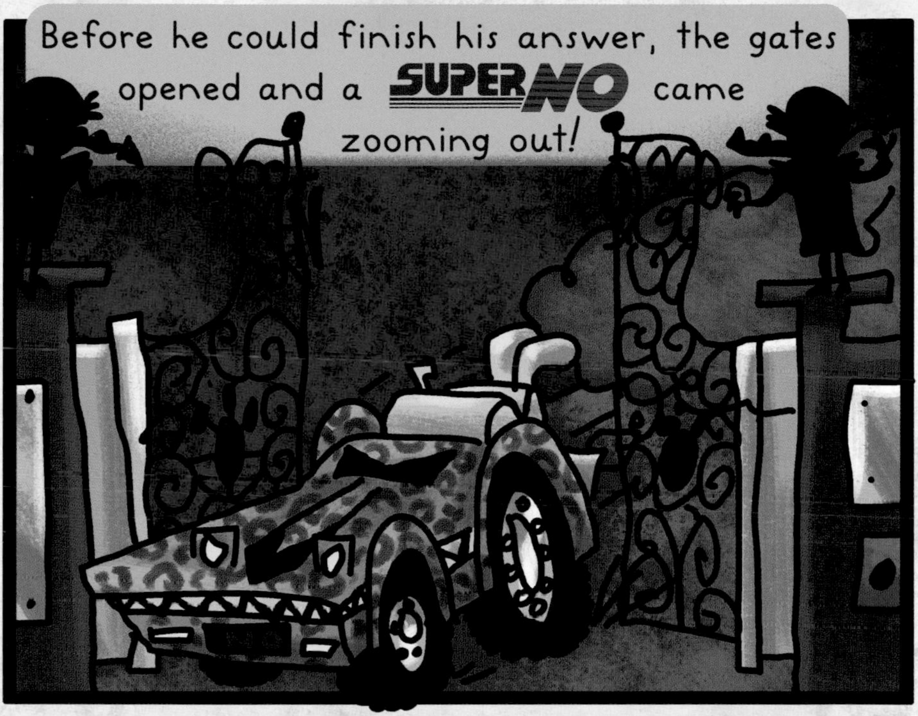
Before he could finish his answer, the gates opened and a SUPERNO came zooming out!

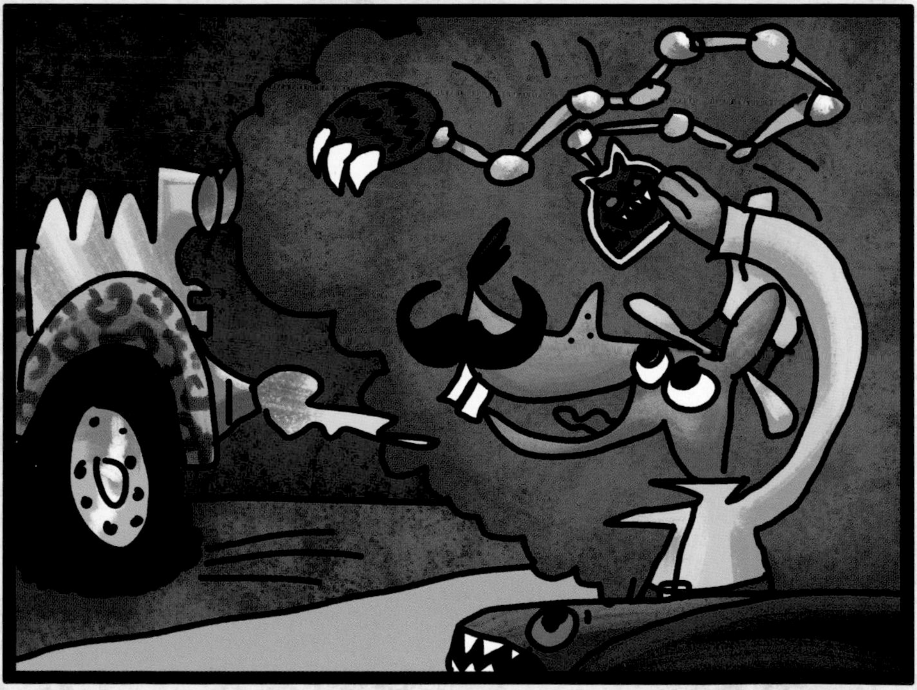

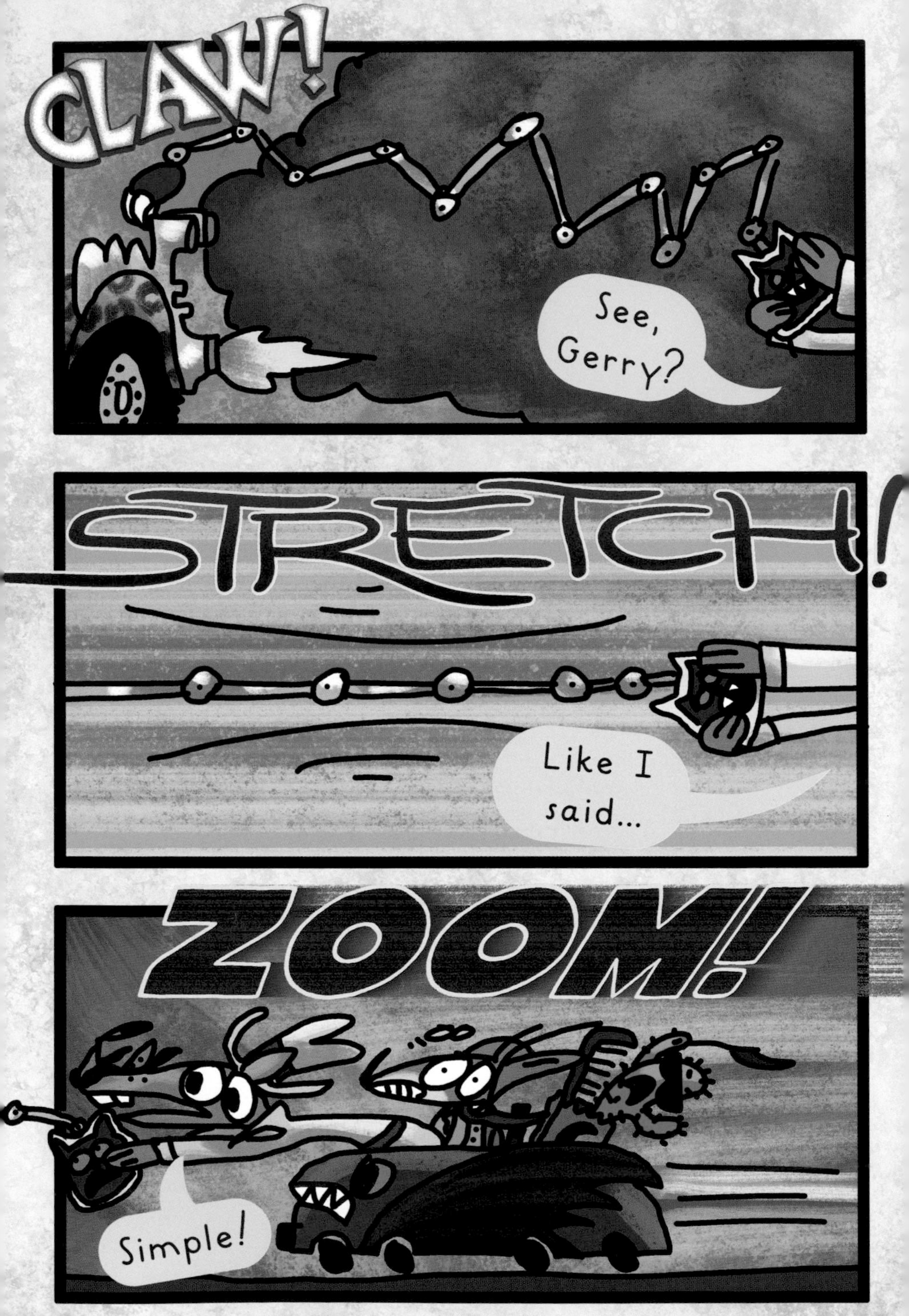
CLAW!
See, Gerry?
STRETCH!
Like I said...
ZOOM!
Simple!

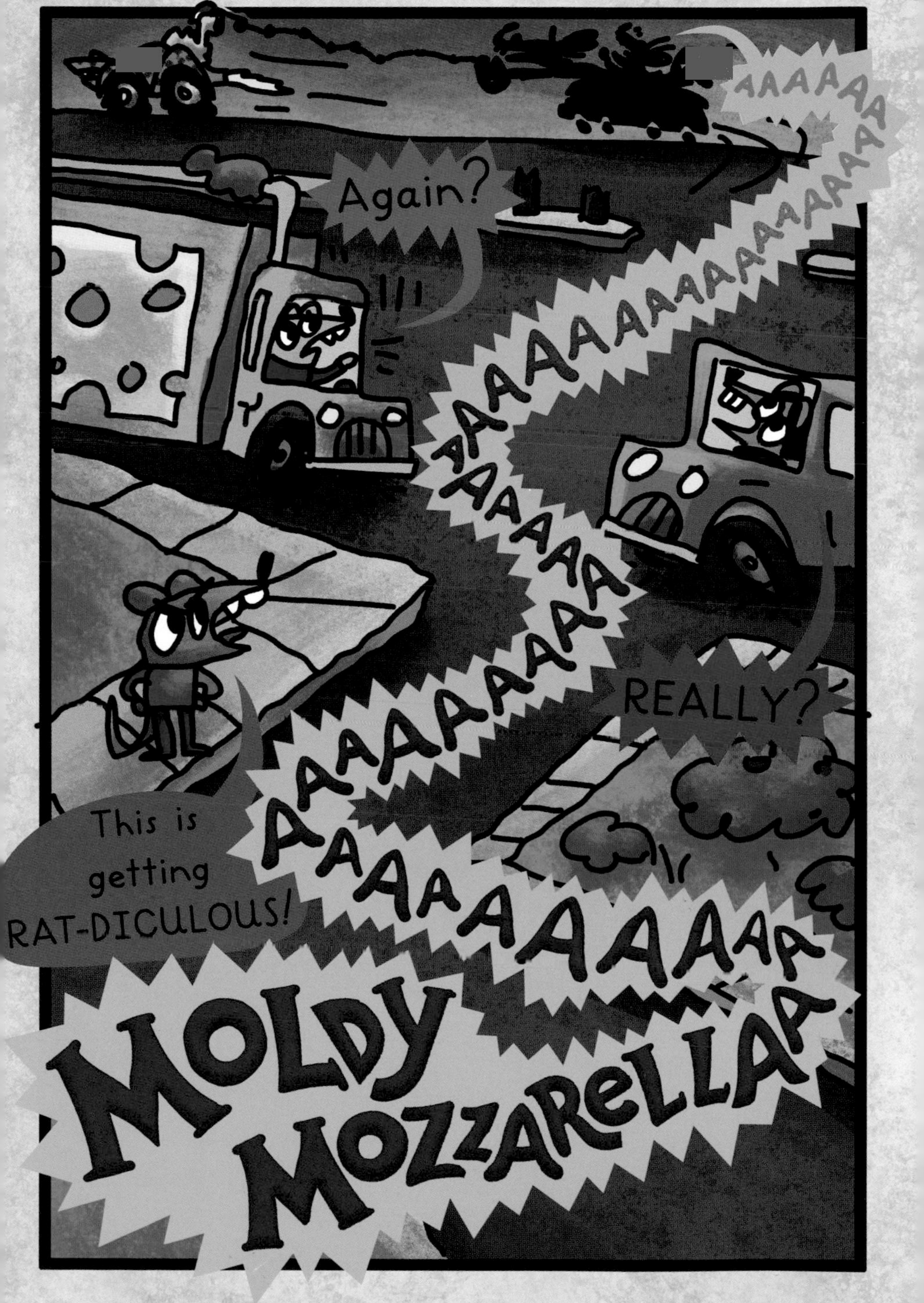
Again?
AAAAAAAAAAAAAAAAAAAAAAAAAAAAAAAAAAAAAAAAAAAAAAAAAA
REALLY?
This is getting RAT-DICULOUS!
MOLDY MOZZARELLAA

CHAPTER TWENTY-ONE

PLEASE REMAIN SEATED UNTIL THE RIDE COMES TO A COMPLETE STOP

We zoomed toward the edge of New Mouse City. There's a big *meadow* out there with nothing but *birds* and *butterflies* as far as you can see.

Oh, I mean there WAS a big meadow...

What in the **HAVARTI** is all this????

WELCOME TO NO NO LAND!

It looks like ANOTHER amousement park!

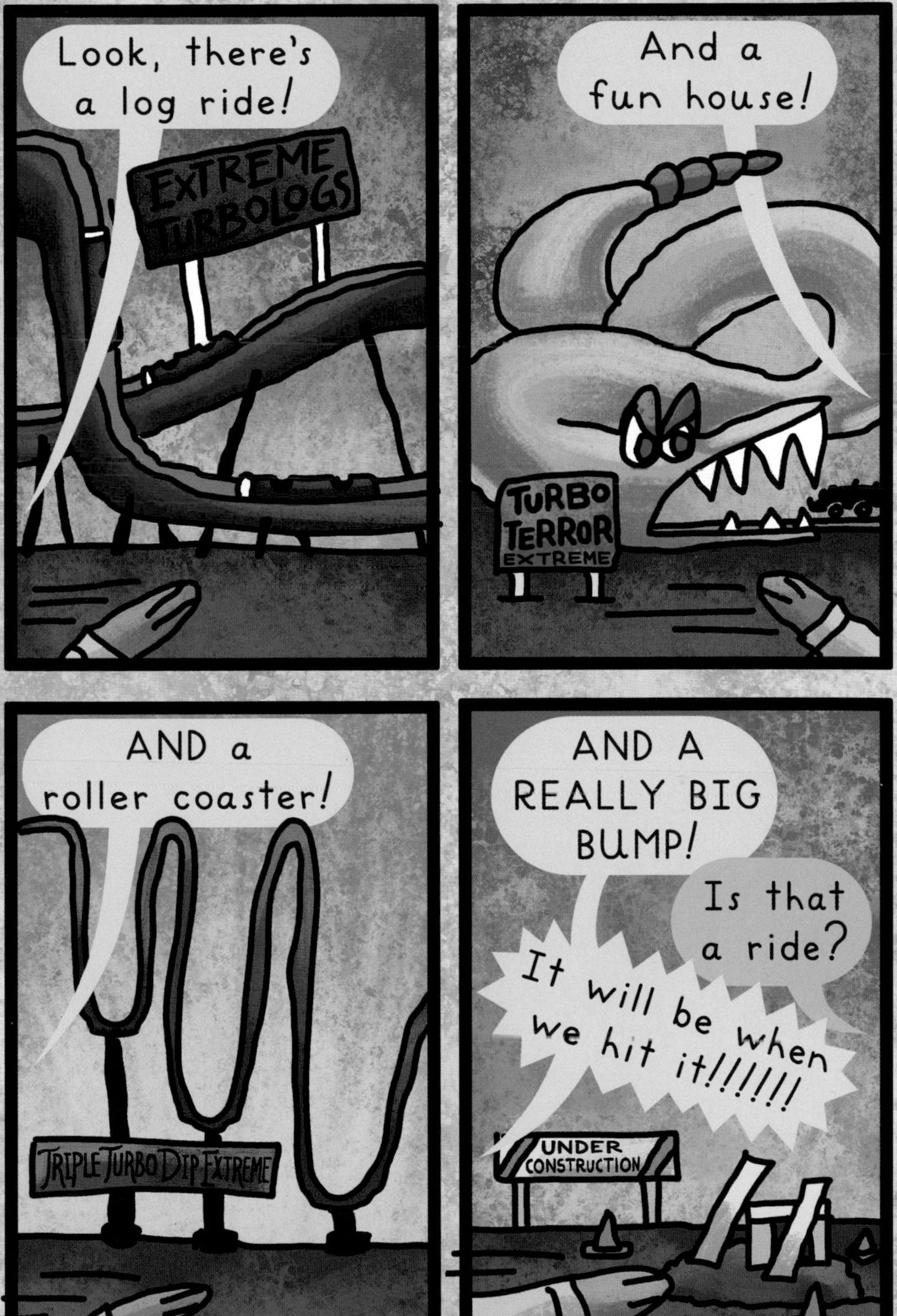
Look, there's a log ride!
EXTREME TURBOLOGS
And a fun house!
TURBO TERROR EXTREME
AND a roller coaster!
TRIPLE TURBO DIP EXTREME
AND A REALLY BIG BUMP!
Is that a ride?
It will be when we hit it!!!!!!
UNDER CONSTRUCTION

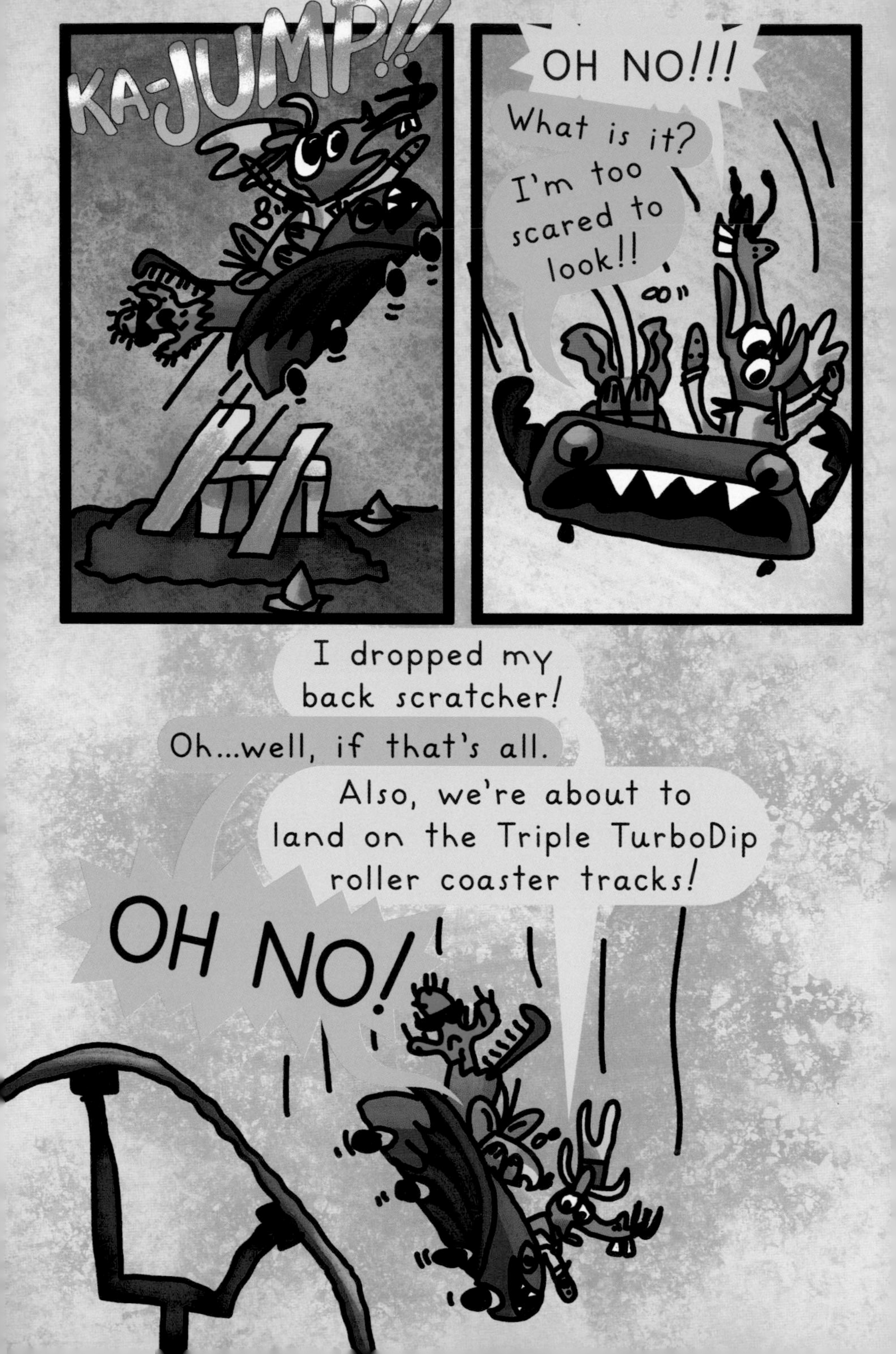
KA-JUMP!!
OH NO!!!
What is it? I'm too scared to look!!
I dropped my back scratcher!
Oh...well, if that's all.
Also, we're about to land on the Triple TurboDip roller coaster tracks!
OH NO!

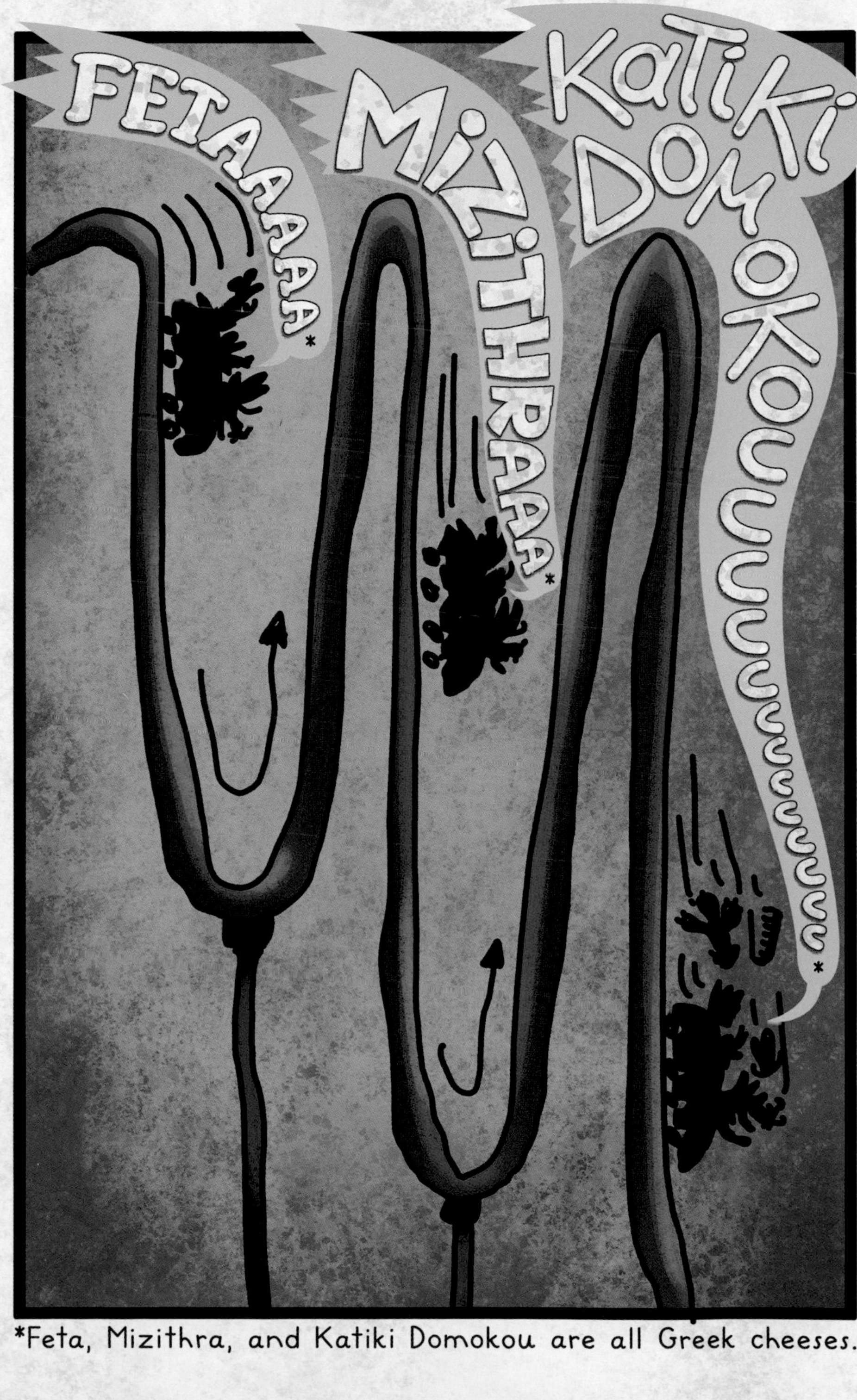
FETAAAAA*
MIZITHRAAA*
KATIKI DOMOKOUUUUUUUUUUU*

*Feta, Mizithra, and Katiki Domokou are all Greek cheeses.

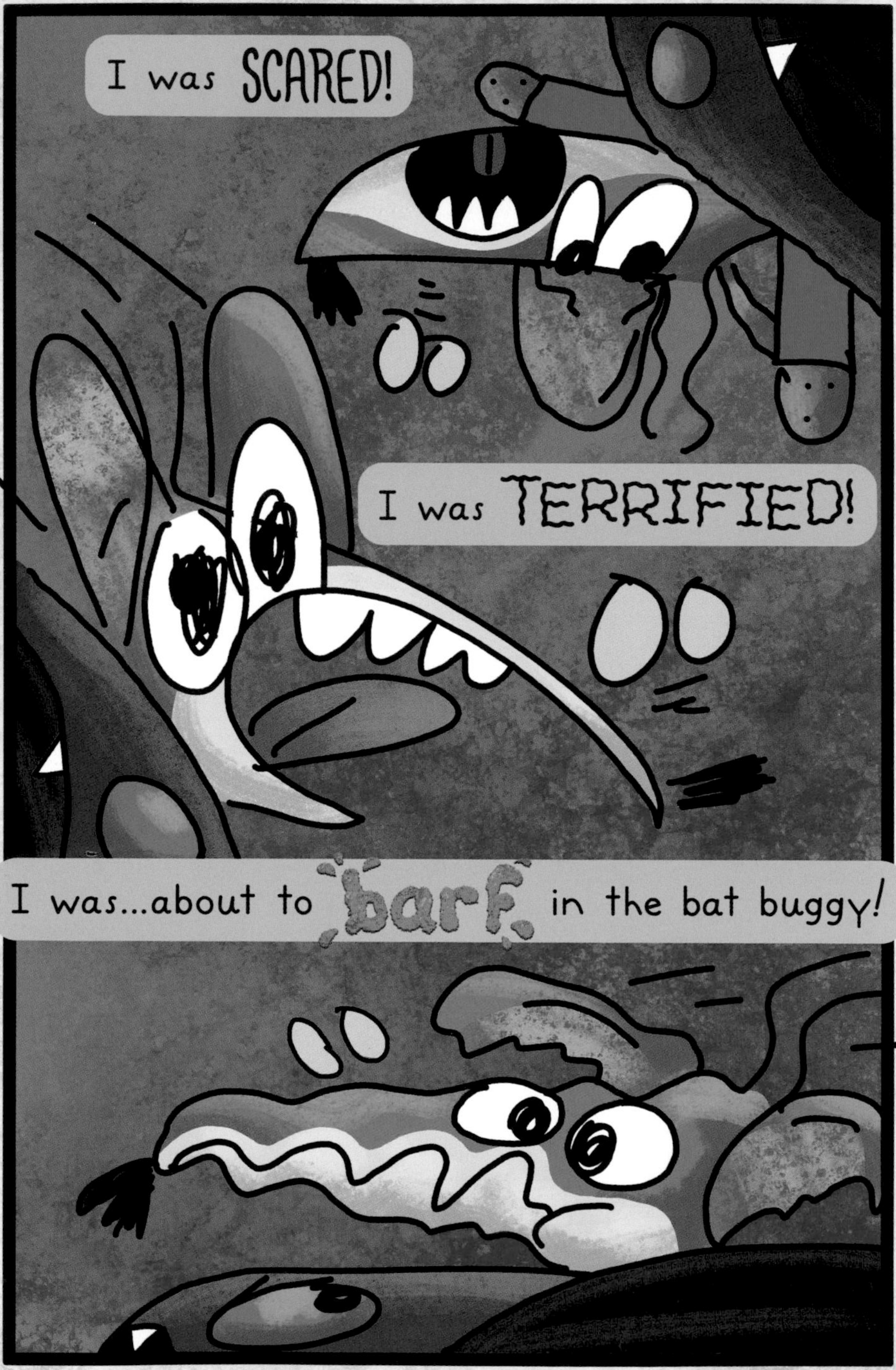
I was SCARED!
I was TERRIFIED!
I was...about to barf in the bat buggy!

CHAPTER TWENTY-TWO

NOT WITHOUT MY Cactus

I couldn't take anymore!
Somewhere around the tenth spiral *Loop*,
I fainted. When I started to wake up,
we weren't moving anymore.

What— what's happening?

Gerry Berry, I got good news, bad news, and REALLY bad news!

Give me the good news! PLEASE!

We've stopped!

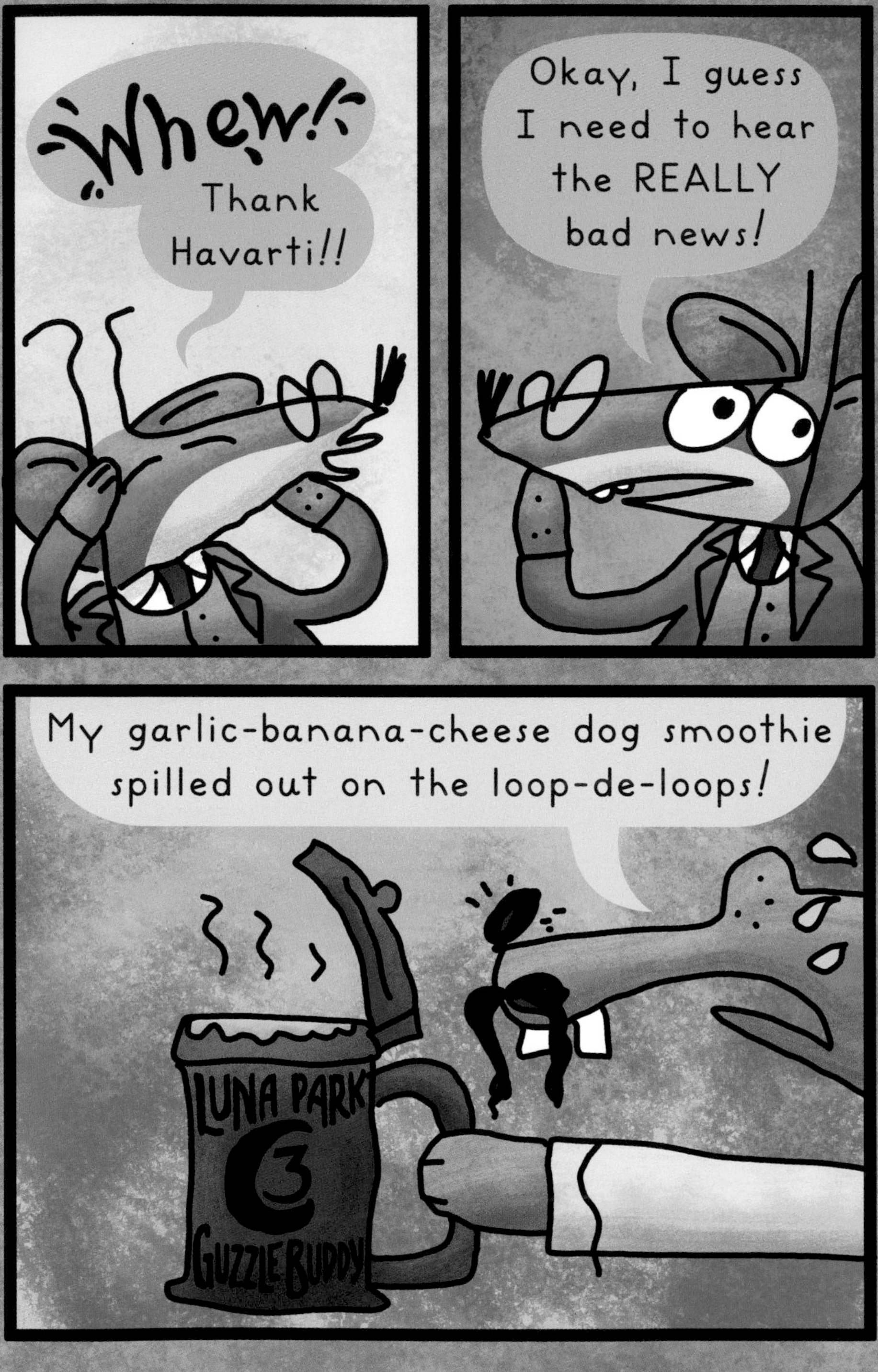
Whew!
Thank Havarti!!
Okay, I guess I need to hear the REALLY bad news!
My garlic-banana-cheese dog smoothie spilled out on the loop-de-loops!
LUNA PARK
3
GUZZLE BUDDY

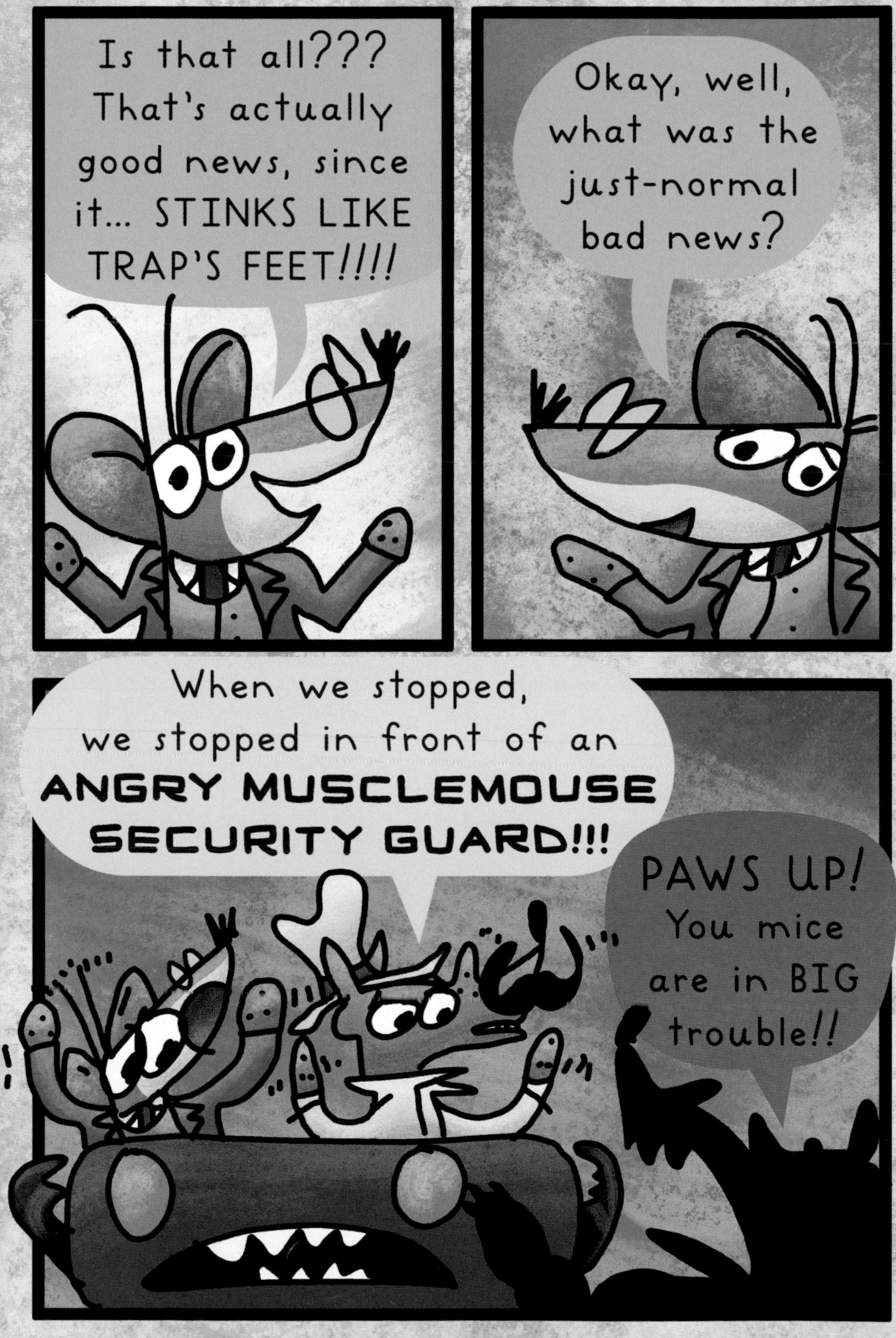
Is that all??? That's actually good news, since it... STINKS LIKE TRAP'S FEET!!!!
Okay, well, what was the just-normal bad news?
When we stopped, we stopped in front of an ANGRY MUSCLEMOUSE SECURITY GUARD!!!
PAWS UP! You mice are in BIG trouble!!

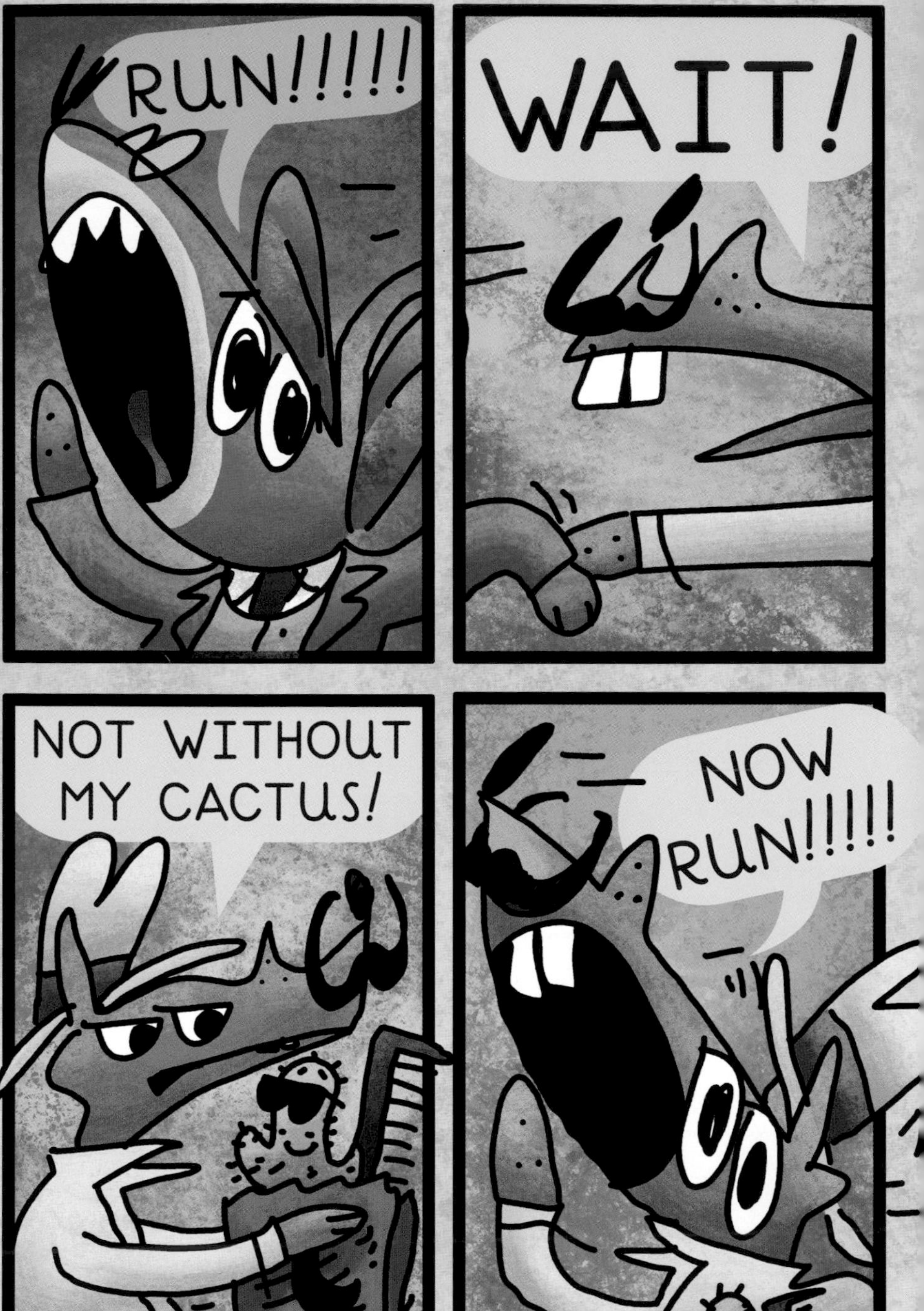
RUN!!!!!
WAIT!
NOT WITHOUT MY CACTUS!
NOW RUN!!!!!

CHAPTER TWENTY-THREE

AQUATIC GETAWAY!

We ran out the roller coaster exit, around a corner, and into the entrance of a big

BUBBLE-SHAPED

building called:

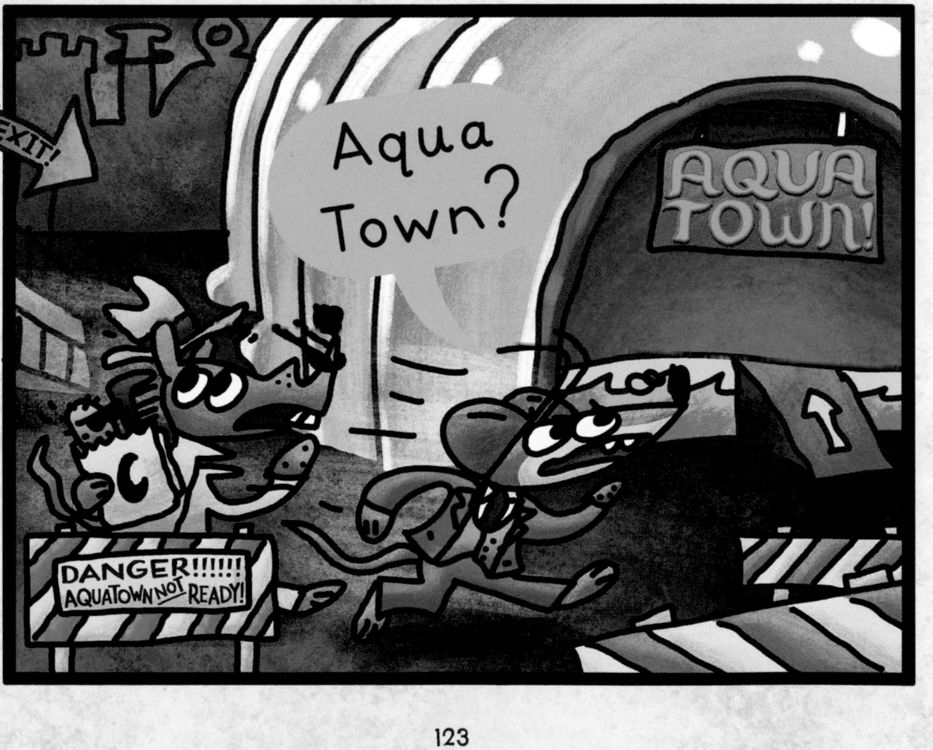
EXIT!
Aqua Town?
AQUA TOWN!
DANGER!!!!!!
AQUATOWN NOT READY!

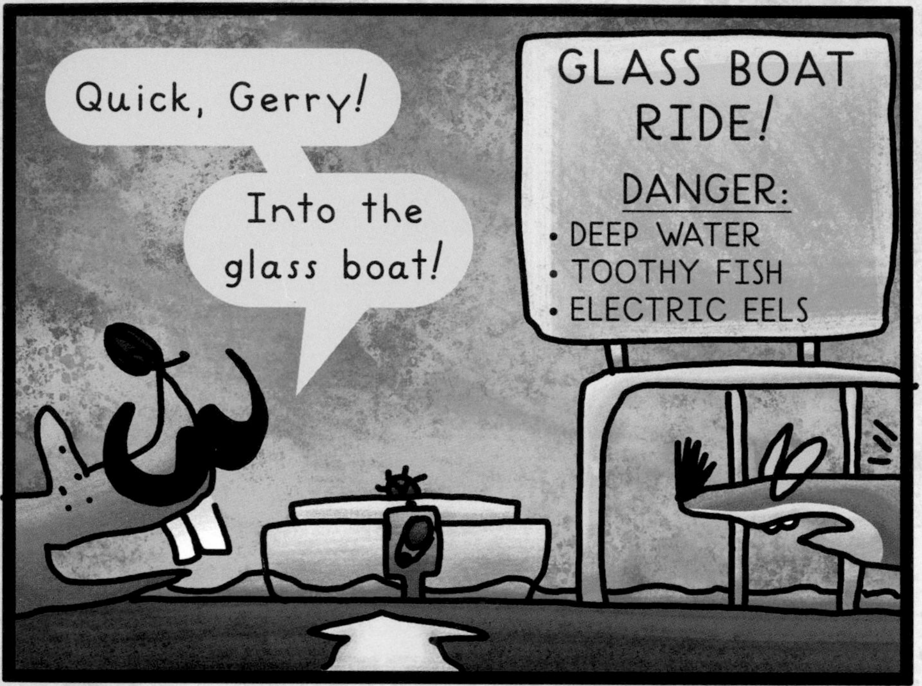
Quick, Gerry!
Into the glass boat!
GLASS BOAT RIDE!
DANGER:
• DEEP WATER
• TOOTHY FISH
• ELECTRIC EELS

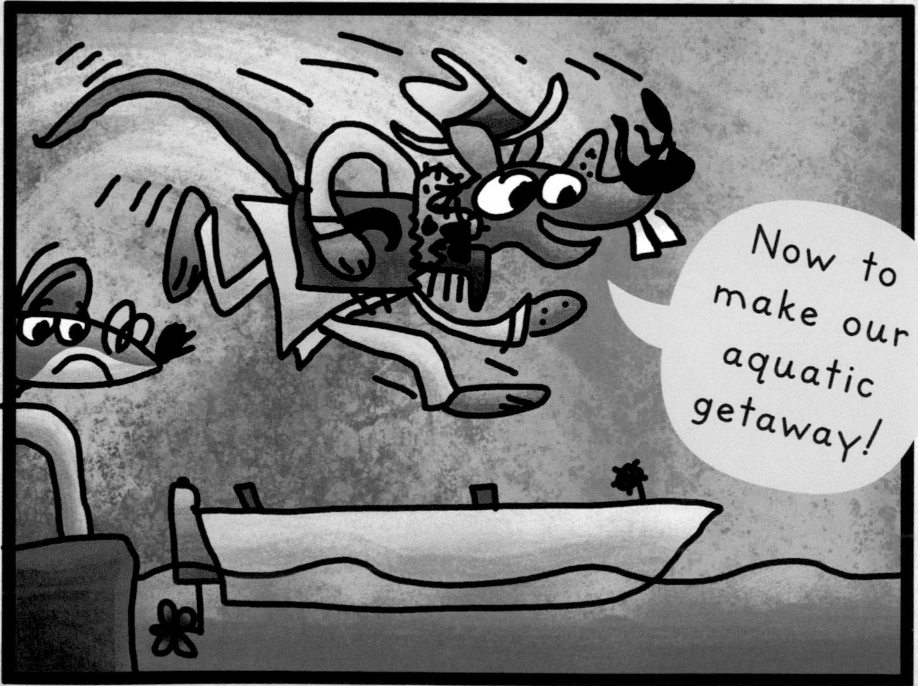
Now to make our aquatic getaway!

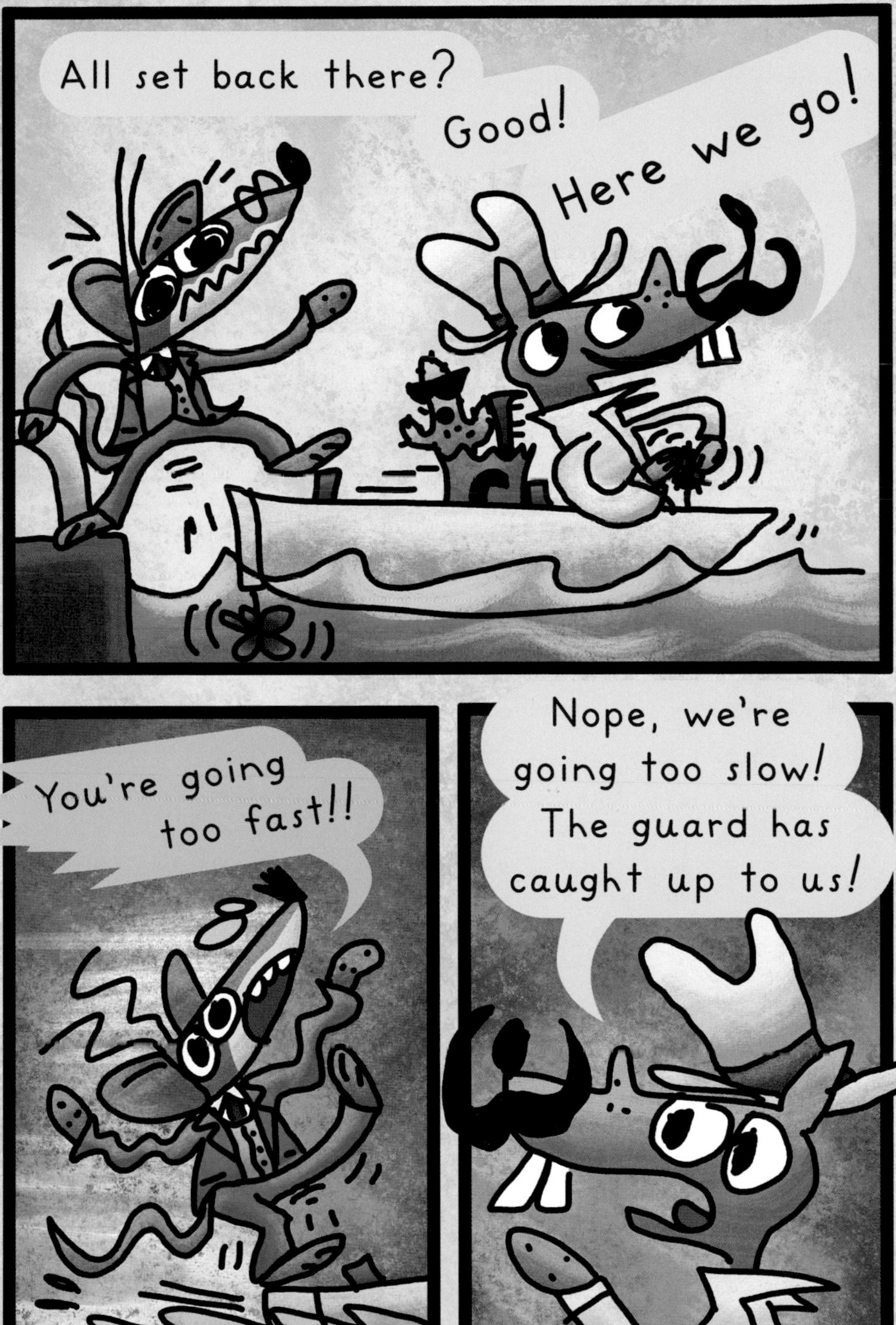
All set back there?
Good!
Here we go!
You're going too fast!!
Nope, we're going too slow!
The guard has caught up to us!

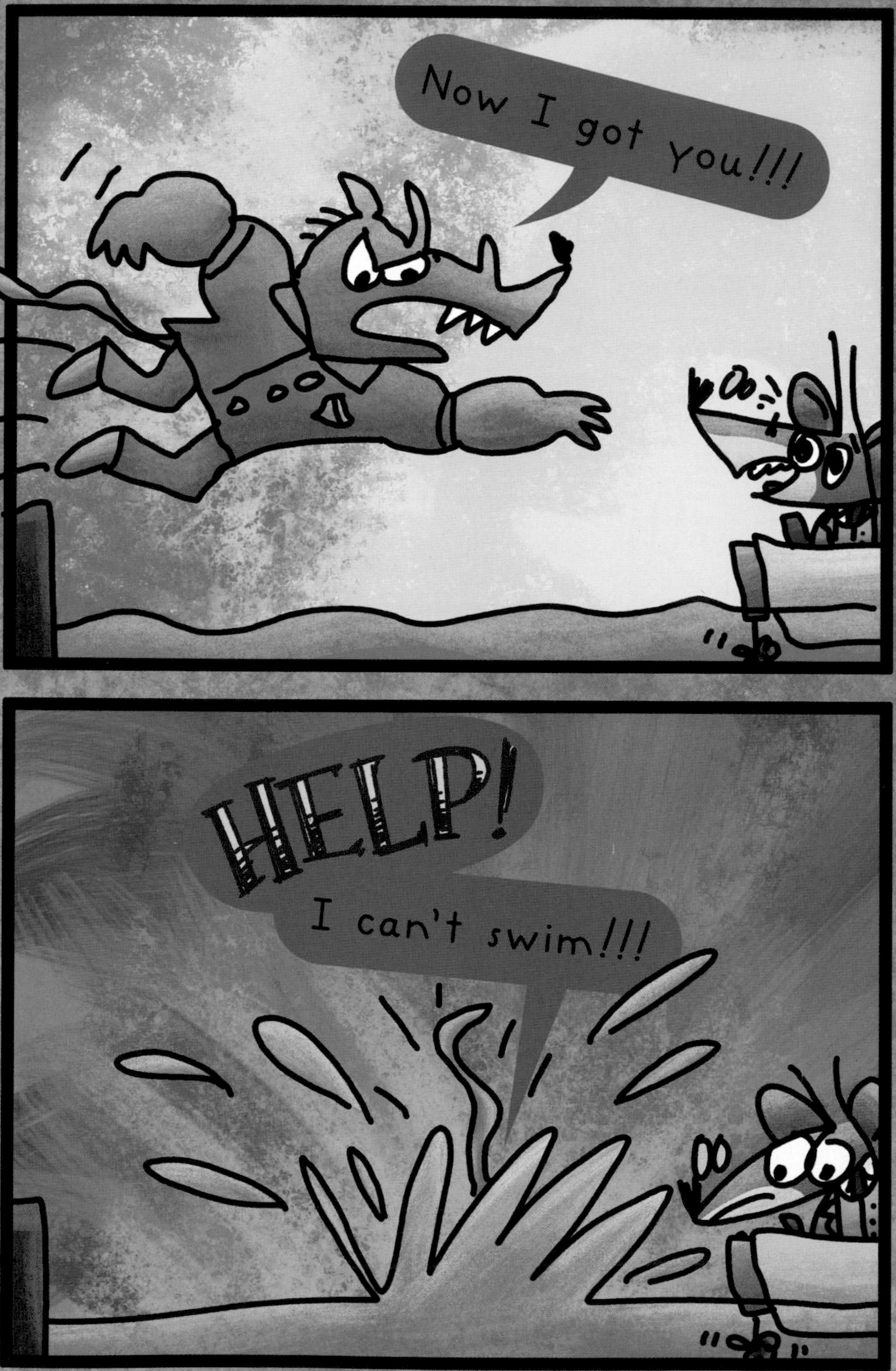

Now I got you!!!
HELP!
I can't swim!!!

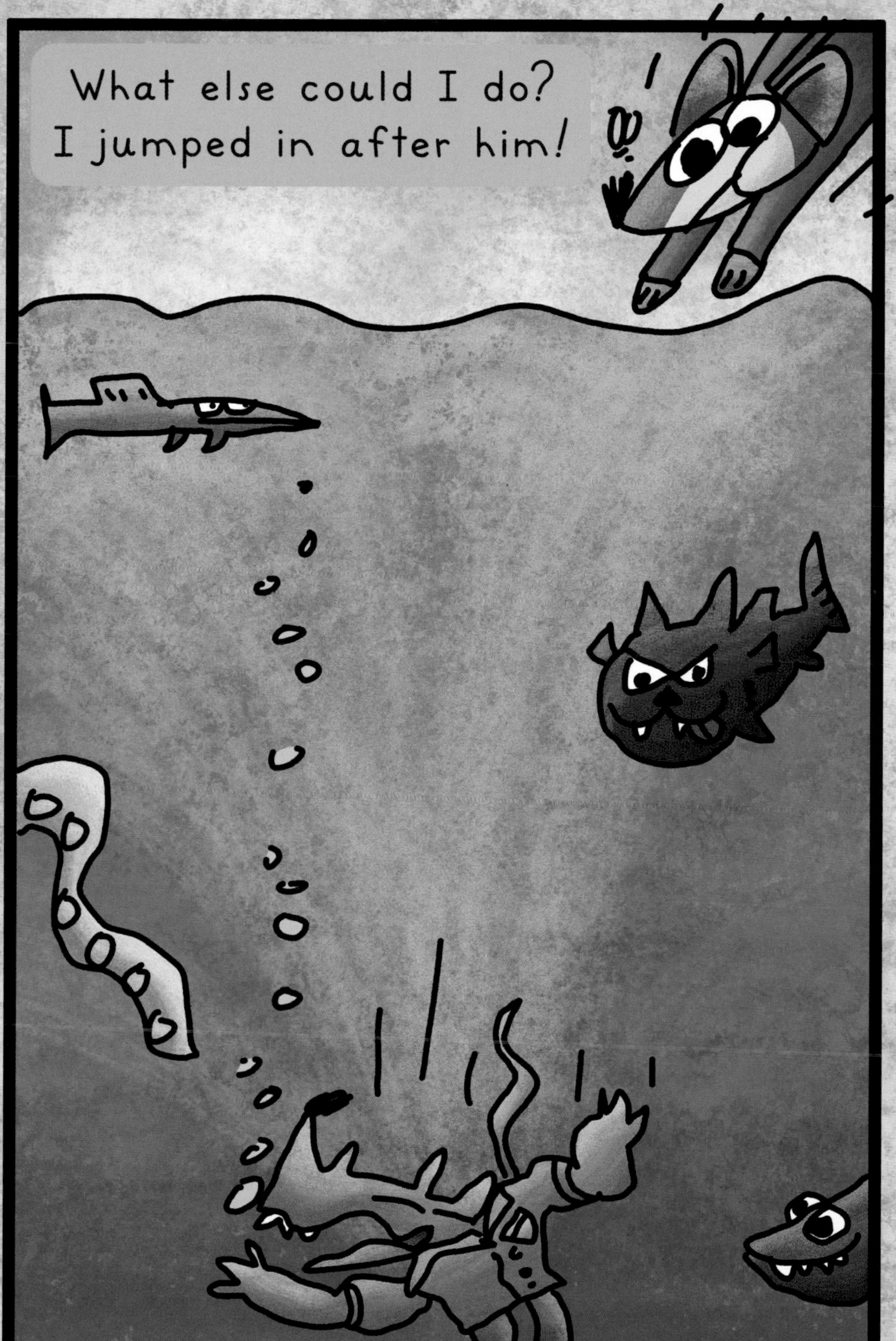
What else could I do? I jumped in after him!

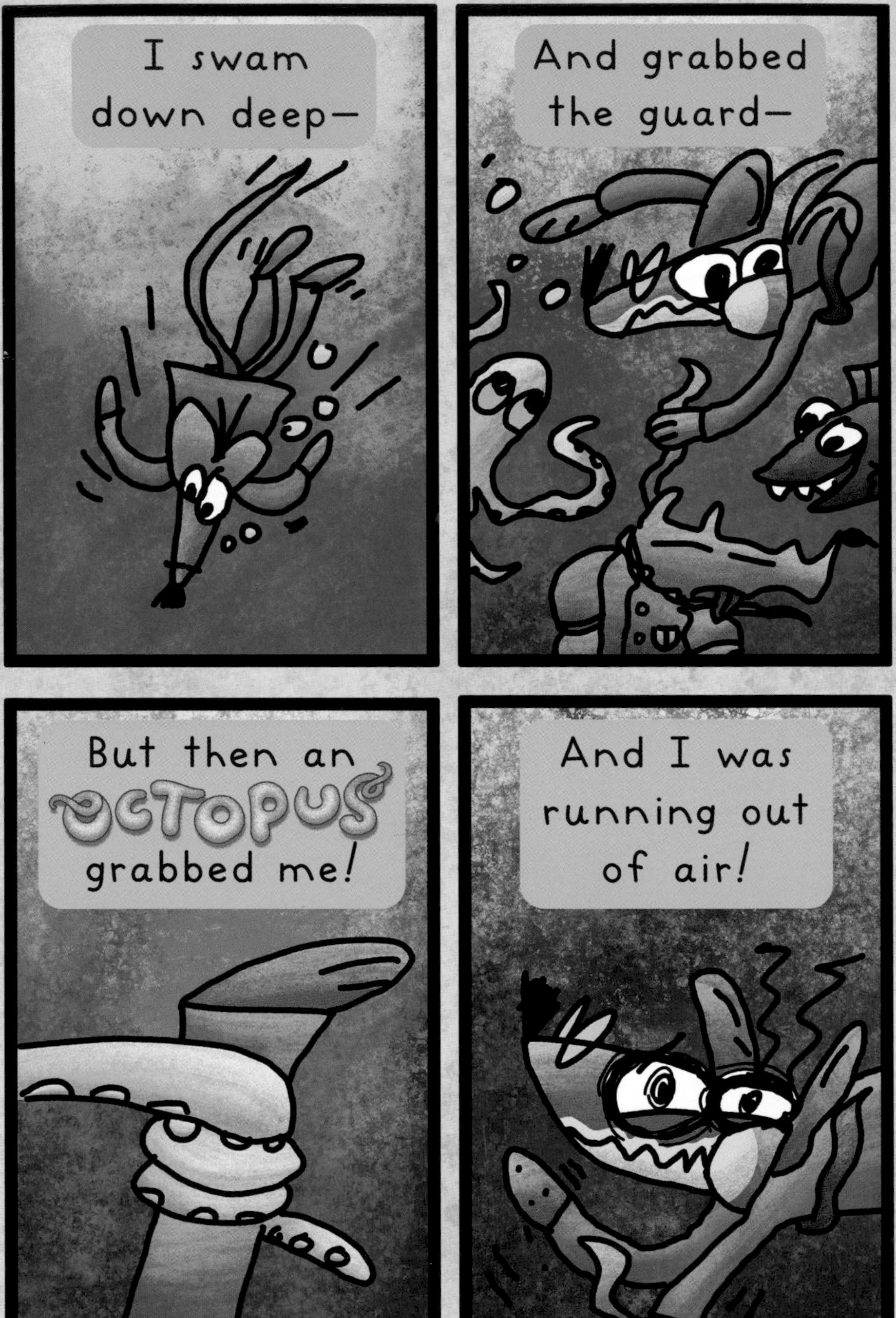
I swam down deep—
And grabbed the guard—
But then an OCTOPUS grabbed me!
And I was running out of air!

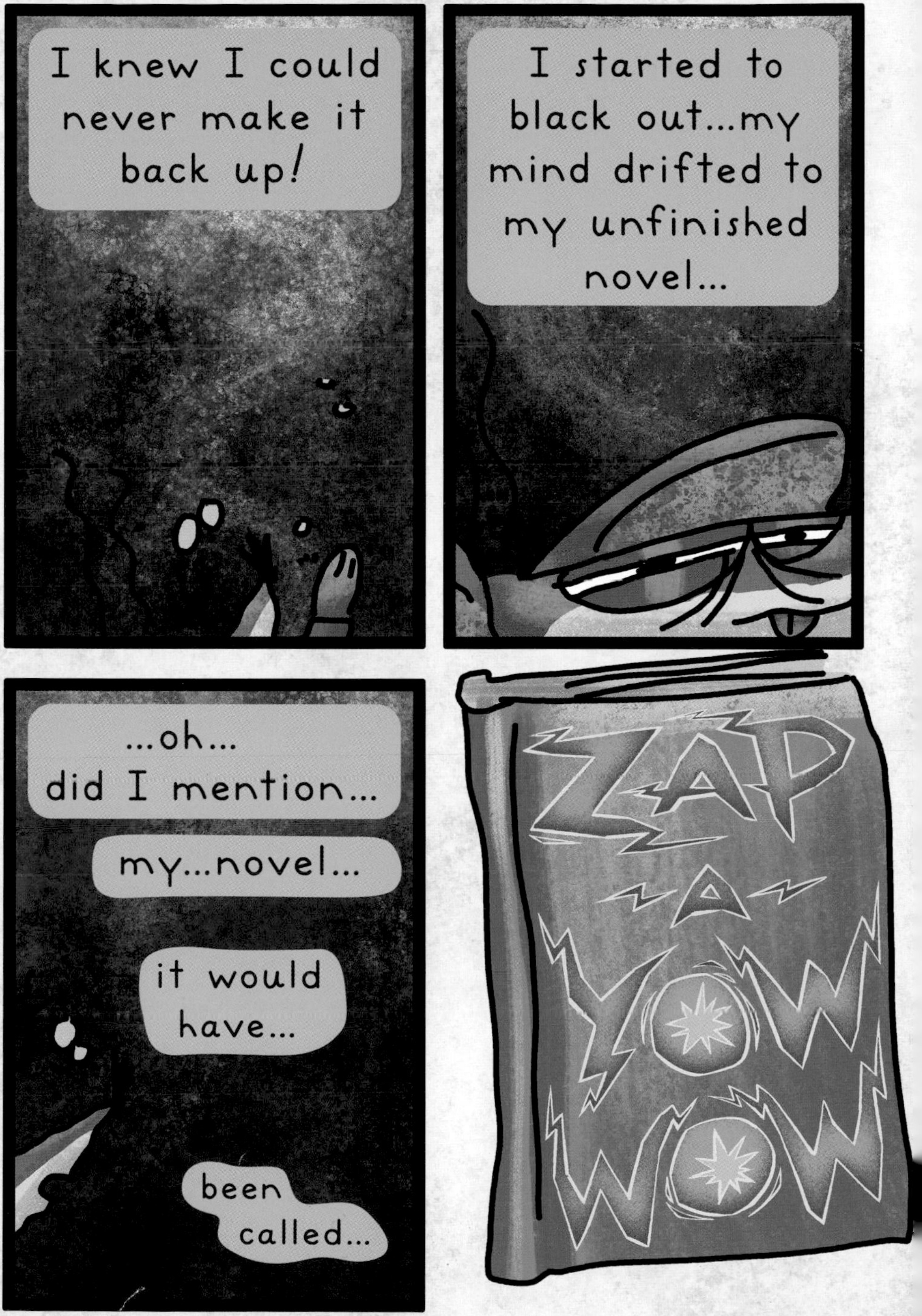
I knew I could never make it back up!
I started to black out...my mind drifted to my unfinished novel...
...oh... did I mention...
my...novel...
it would have...
been called...
ZAP
A
WOW
WOW

No, that's not the name of my novel*!!!*

That's the sound of me getting ***SHOCKED*** by an **ELECTRIC EEL!**

IT HURT!

Really bad*!!!*

But it woke me up enough to see something strange wiggling before my eyes. And it wasn't another eel*!*

CHAPTER TWENTY-FOUR

SAVED BY THE COMB

It was Hercule's giant comb!
With the last of my strength,
I **grabbed** it!
Hercule pulled us up!

Welcome back,
Gerry Berry!

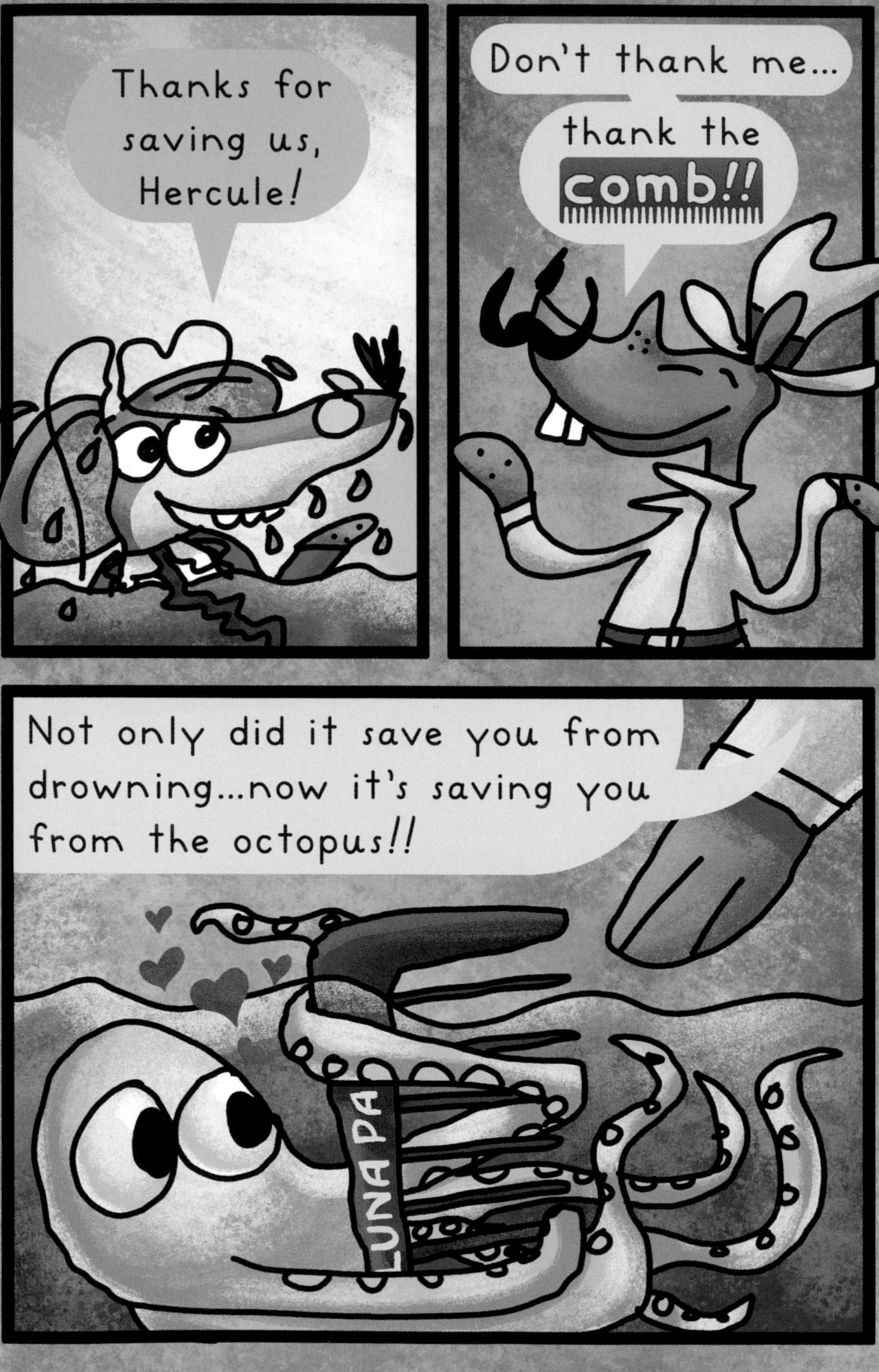
Thanks for saving us, Hercule!
Don't thank me...
thank the comb!!
Not only did it save you from drowning...now it's saving you from the octopus!!
LUNA PA

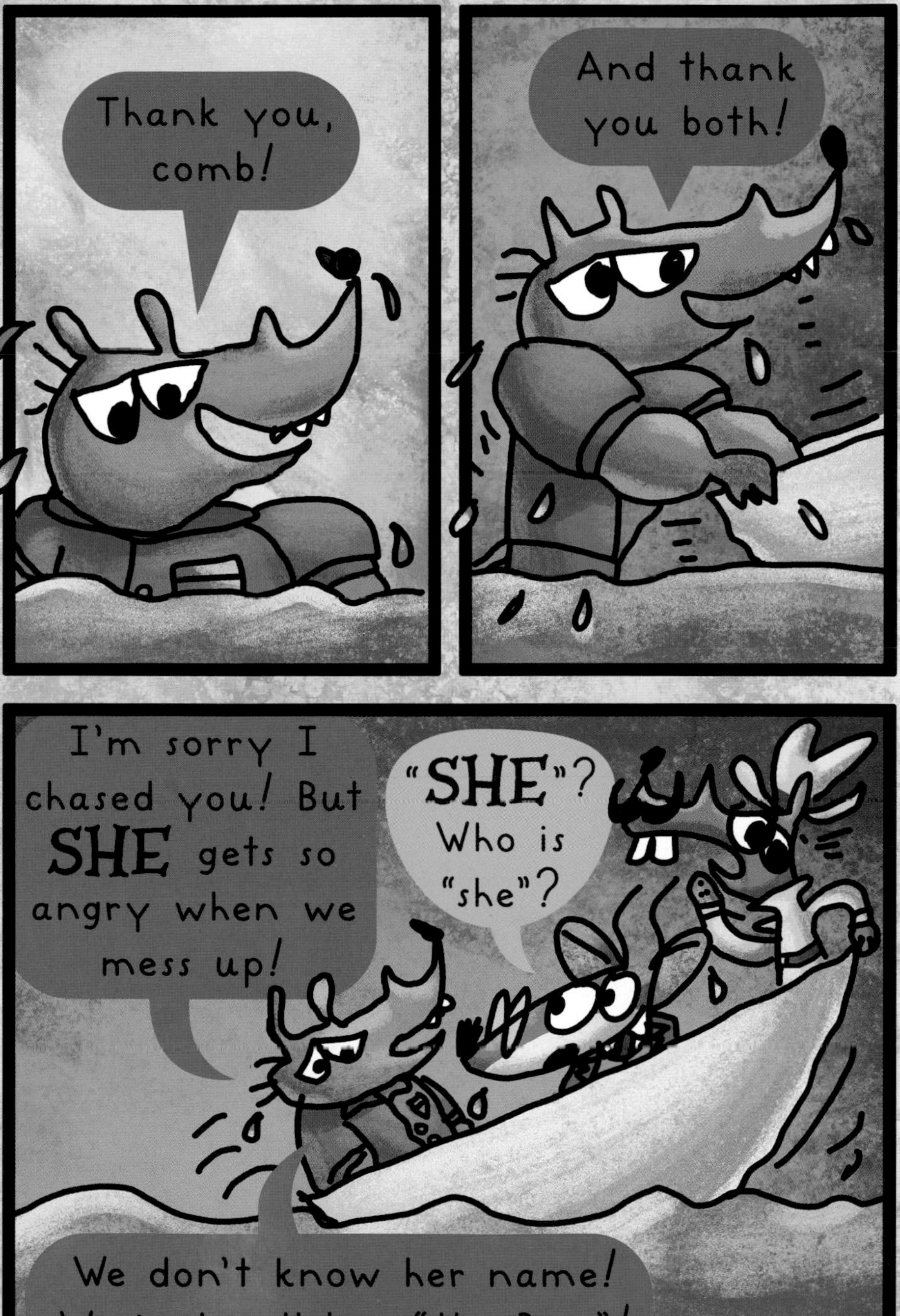
Thank you, comb!
And thank you both!
I'm sorry I chased you! But SHE gets so angry when we mess up!
"SHE"? Who is "she"?
We don't know her name! We just call her "the Boss"!

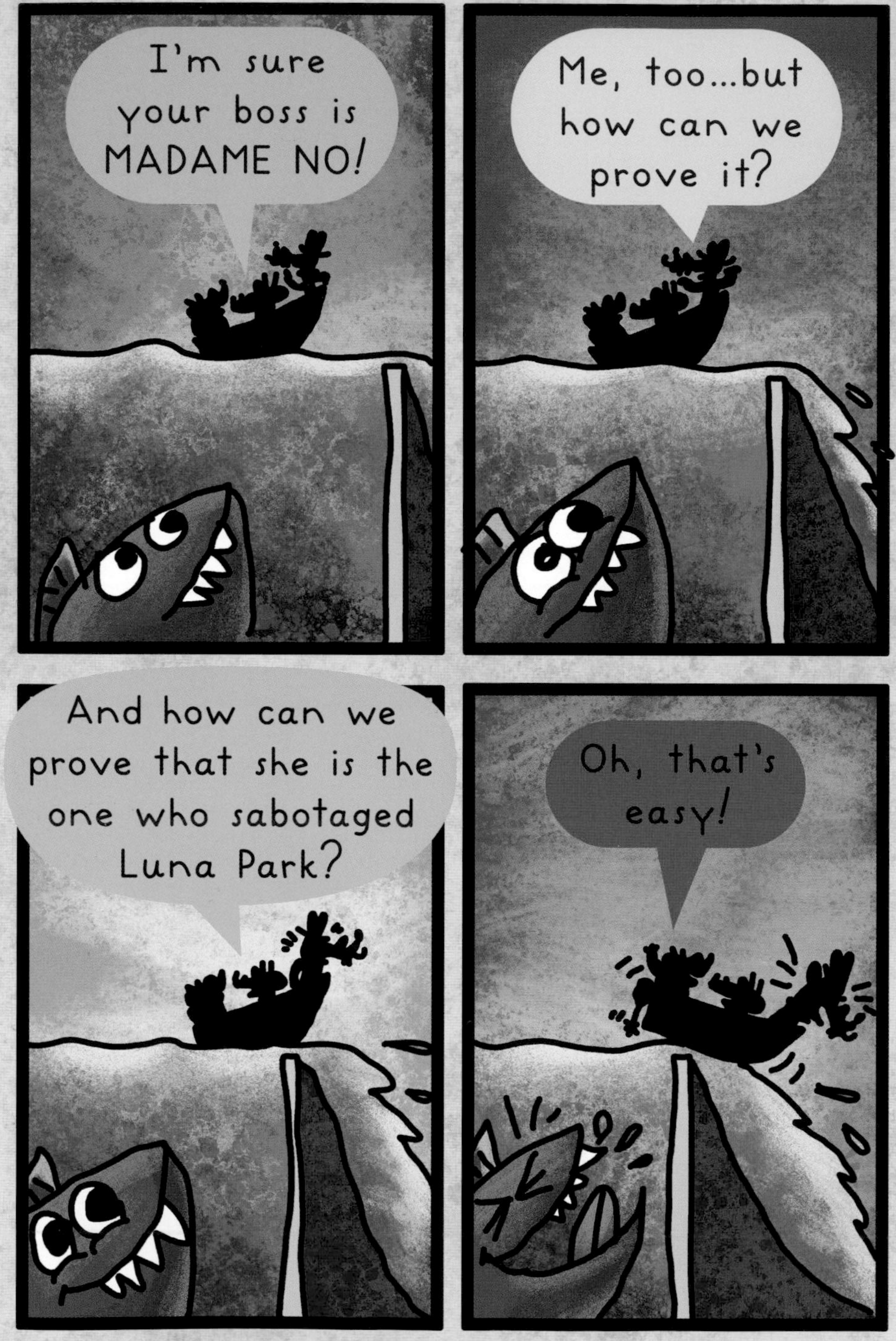
I'm sure your boss is MADAME NO!
Me, too...but how can we prove it?
And how can we prove that she is the one who sabotaged Luna Park?
Oh, that's easy!

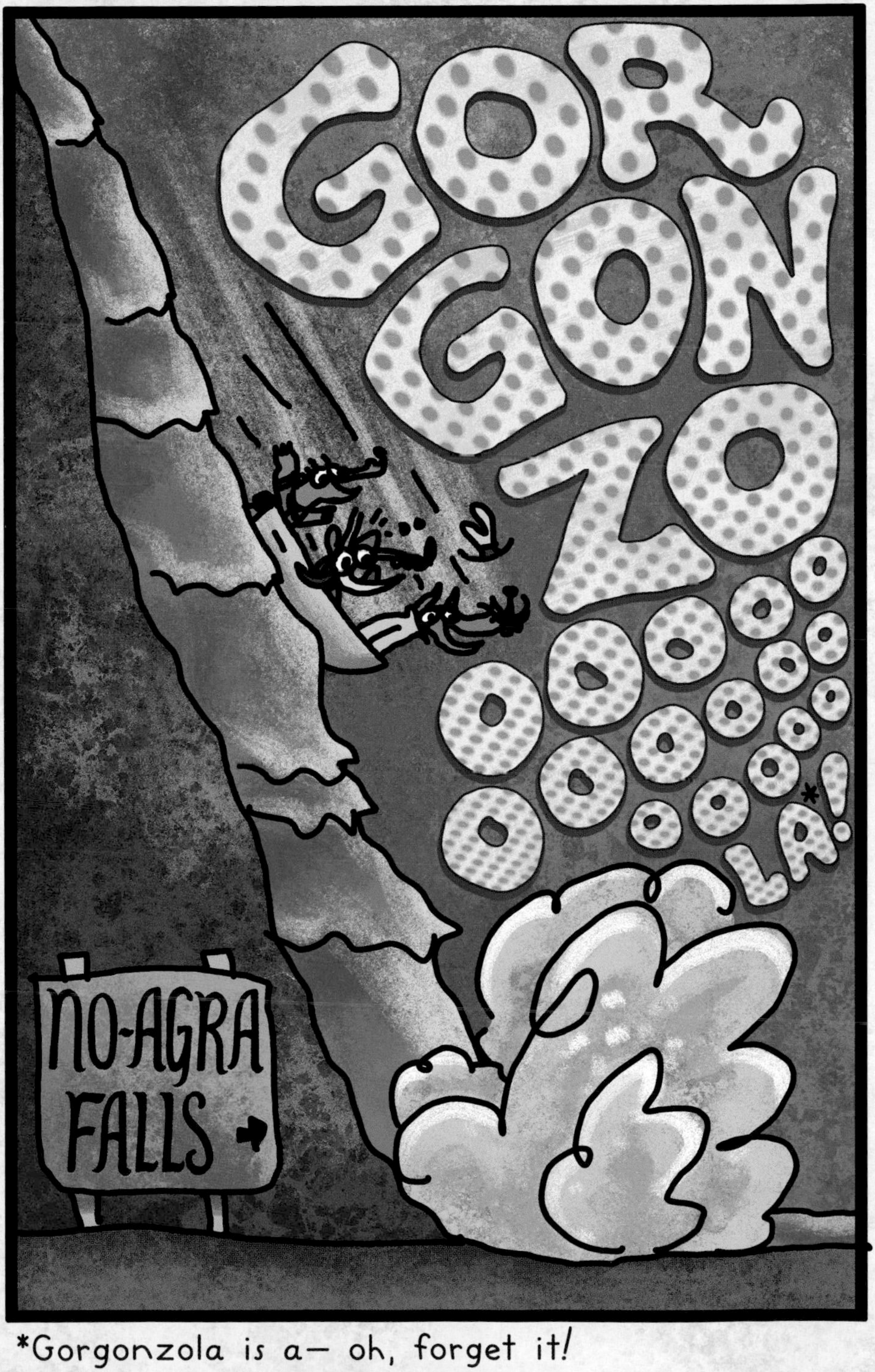
GOR-GON-ZO-OOOOOOOOOOOO-LA!*
NO-AGRA FALLS

*Gorgonzola is a— oh, forget it!

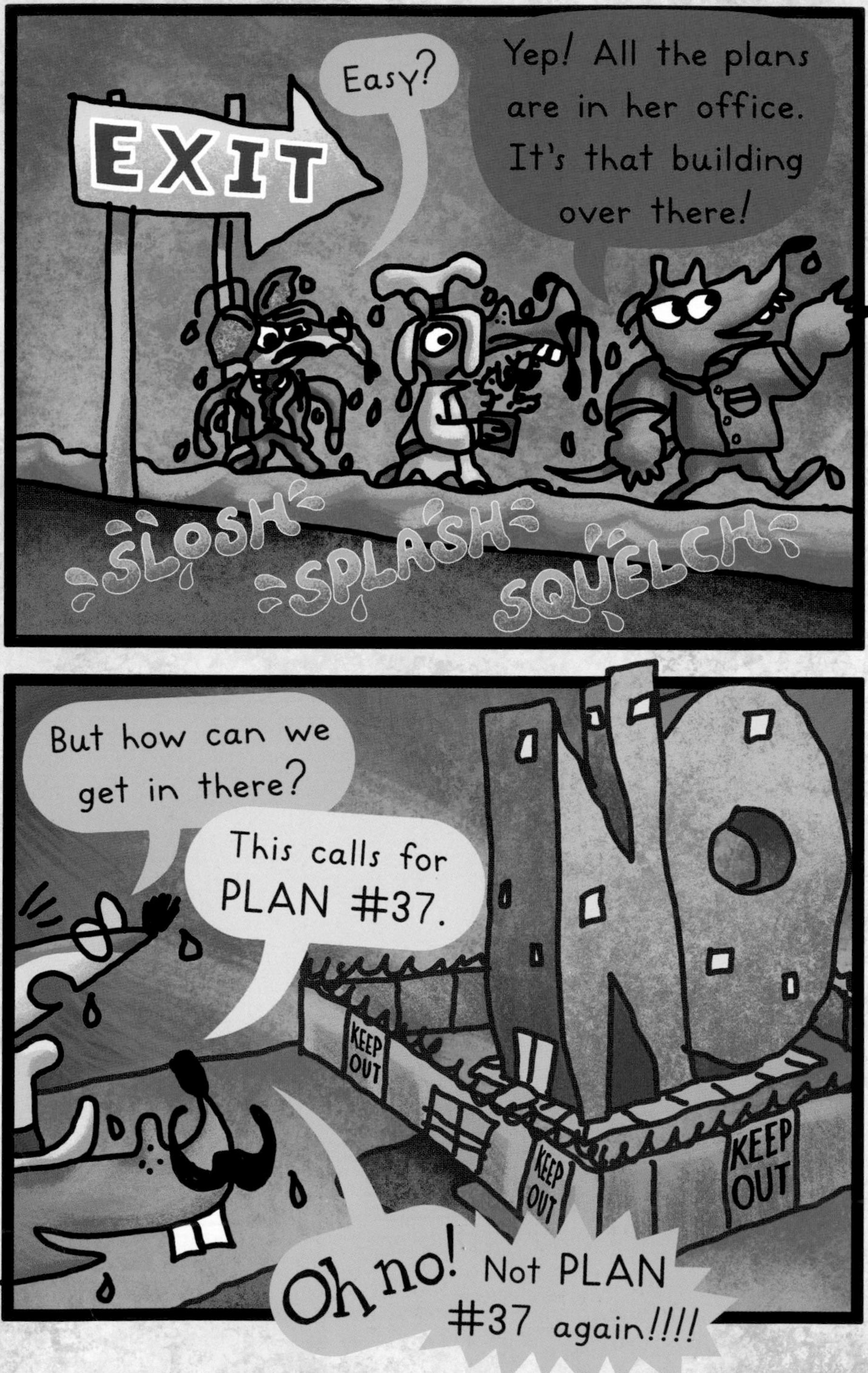
EXIT
Easy?
Yep! All the plans are in her office. It's that building over there!
SLOSH
SPLASH
SQUELCH
But how can we get in there?
This calls for PLAN #37.
KEEP OUT
KEEP OUT
KEEP OUT
Oh no! Not PLAN #37 again!!!!

CHAPTER TWENTY-FIVE

PLAN #37

Hercule's Plan #37 has gotten me into more scrapes than an automatic cheese grater! But there seemed to be no other way to save Luna Park. Plus, I was soaking **wet!**

So I agreed...

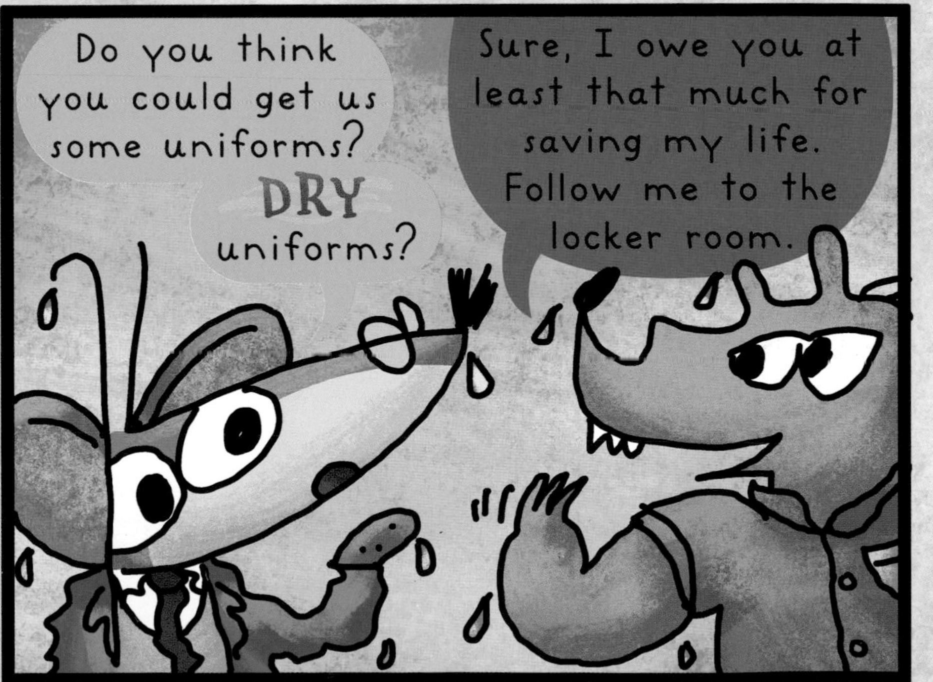
Do you think you could get us some uniforms?
DRY uniforms?
Sure, I owe you at least that much for saving my life. Follow me to the locker room.

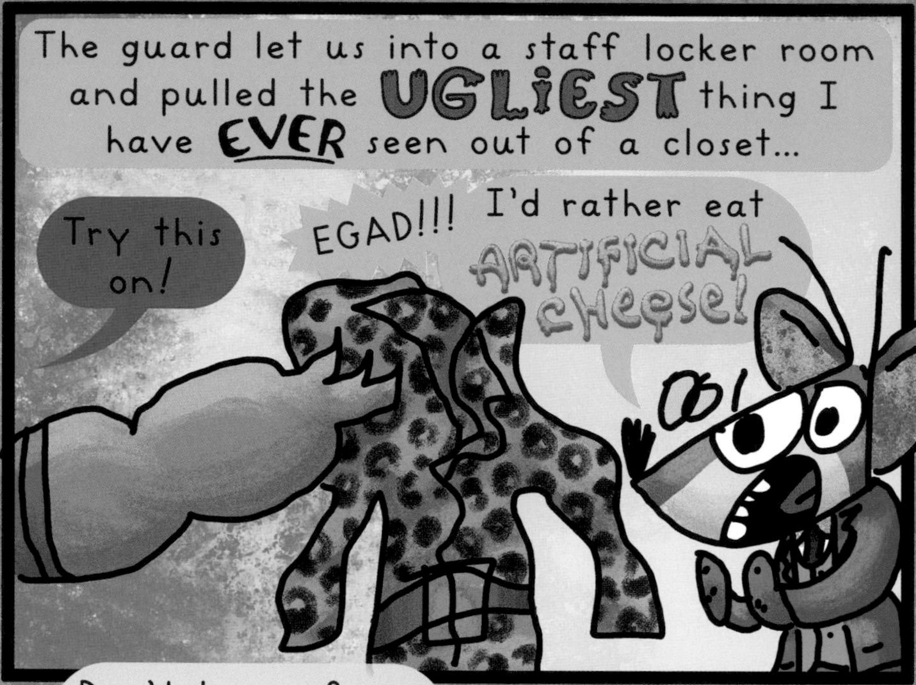
The guard let us into a staff locker room and pulled the UGLiEST thing I have EVER seen out of a closet...
Try this on!
EGAD!!! I'd rather eat ARTIFICIAL cheese!

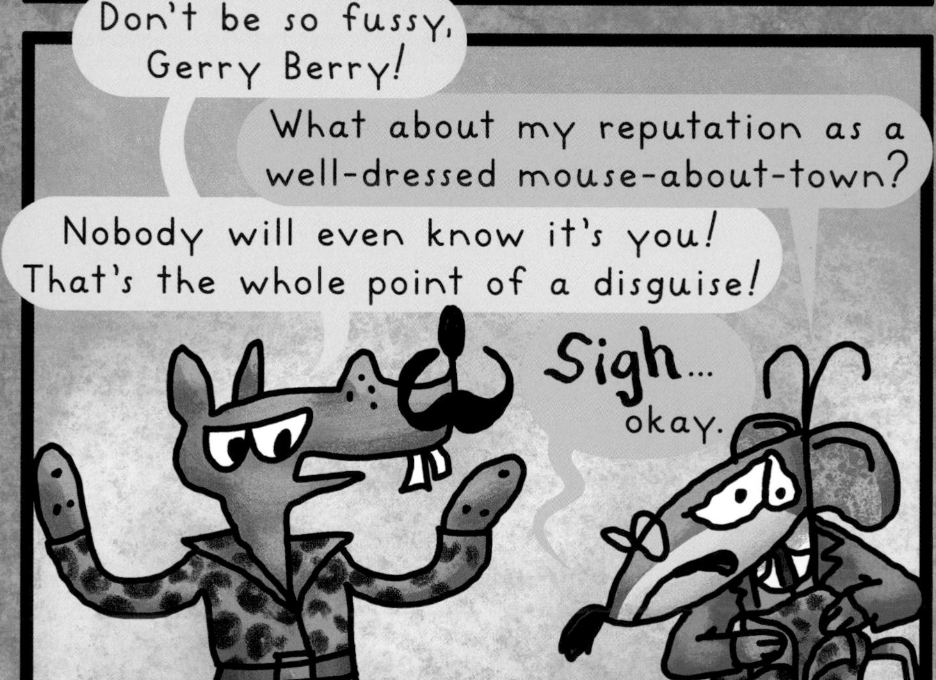
Don't be so fussy, Gerry Berry!
What about my reputation as a well-dressed mouse-about-town?
Nobody will even know it's you! That's the whole point of a disguise!
Sigh... okay.

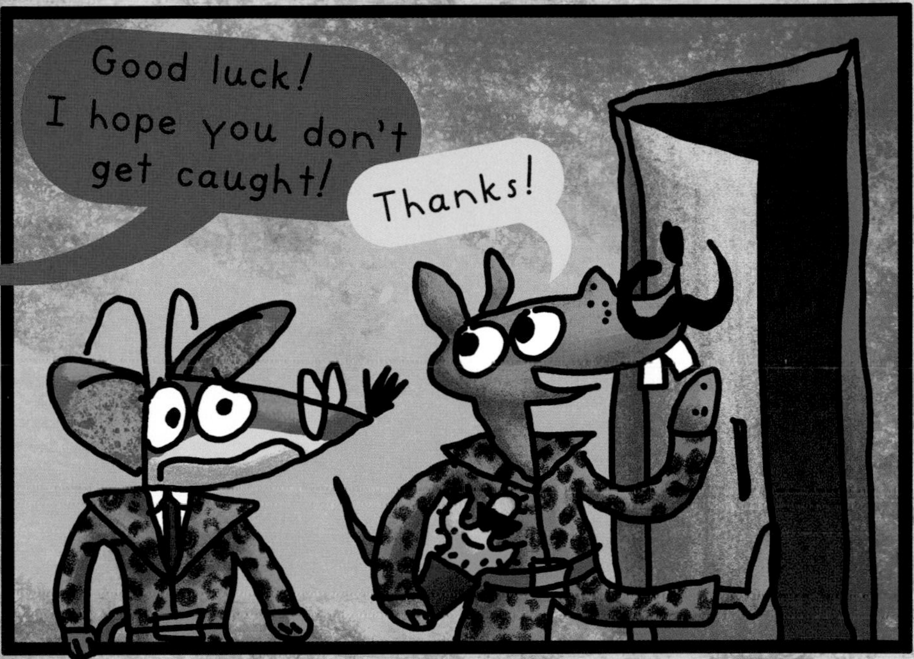
Good luck!
I hope you don't get caught!
Thanks!

We got caught.

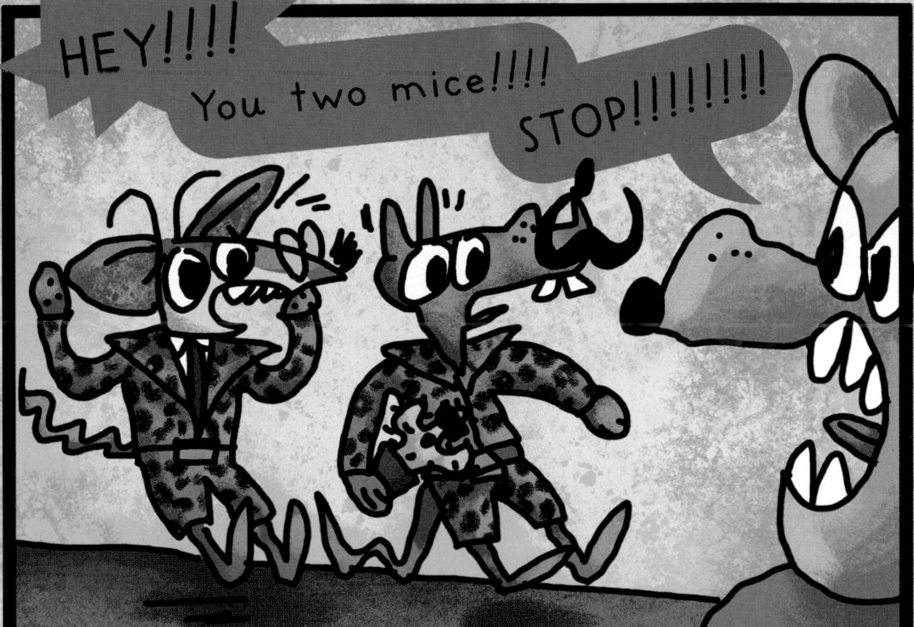
HEY!!!!
You two mice!!!!
STOP!!!!!!!!

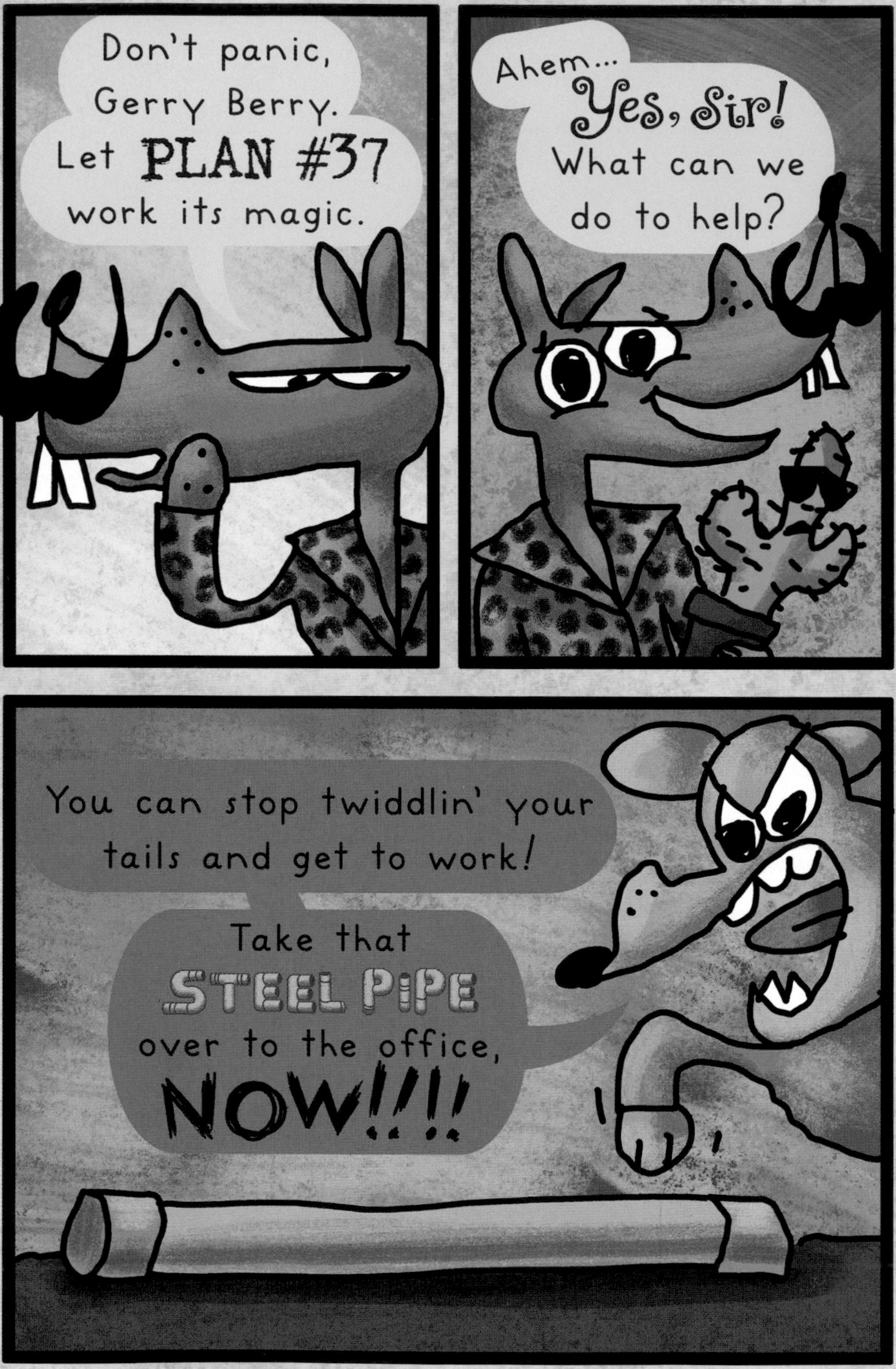
Don't panic, Gerry Berry. Let PLAN #37 work its magic.
Ahem... Yes, Sir! What can we do to help?
You can stop twiddlin' your tails and get to work!
Take that STEEL PIPE over to the office, NOW!!!!

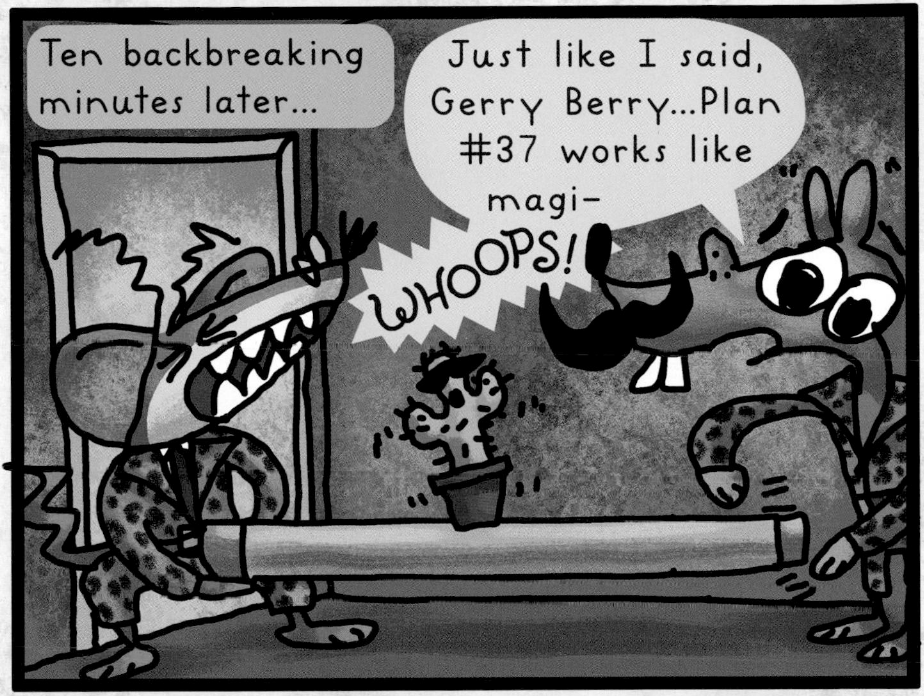
Ten backbreaking minutes later...
Just like I said, Gerry Berry...Plan #37 works like magi-
WHOOPS!

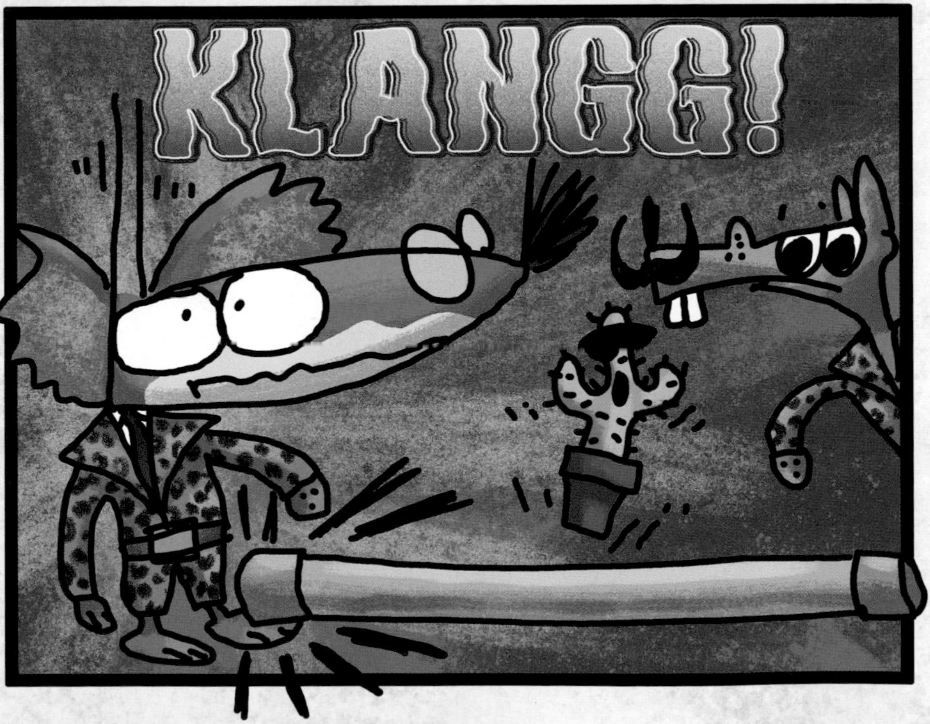
KLANGG!

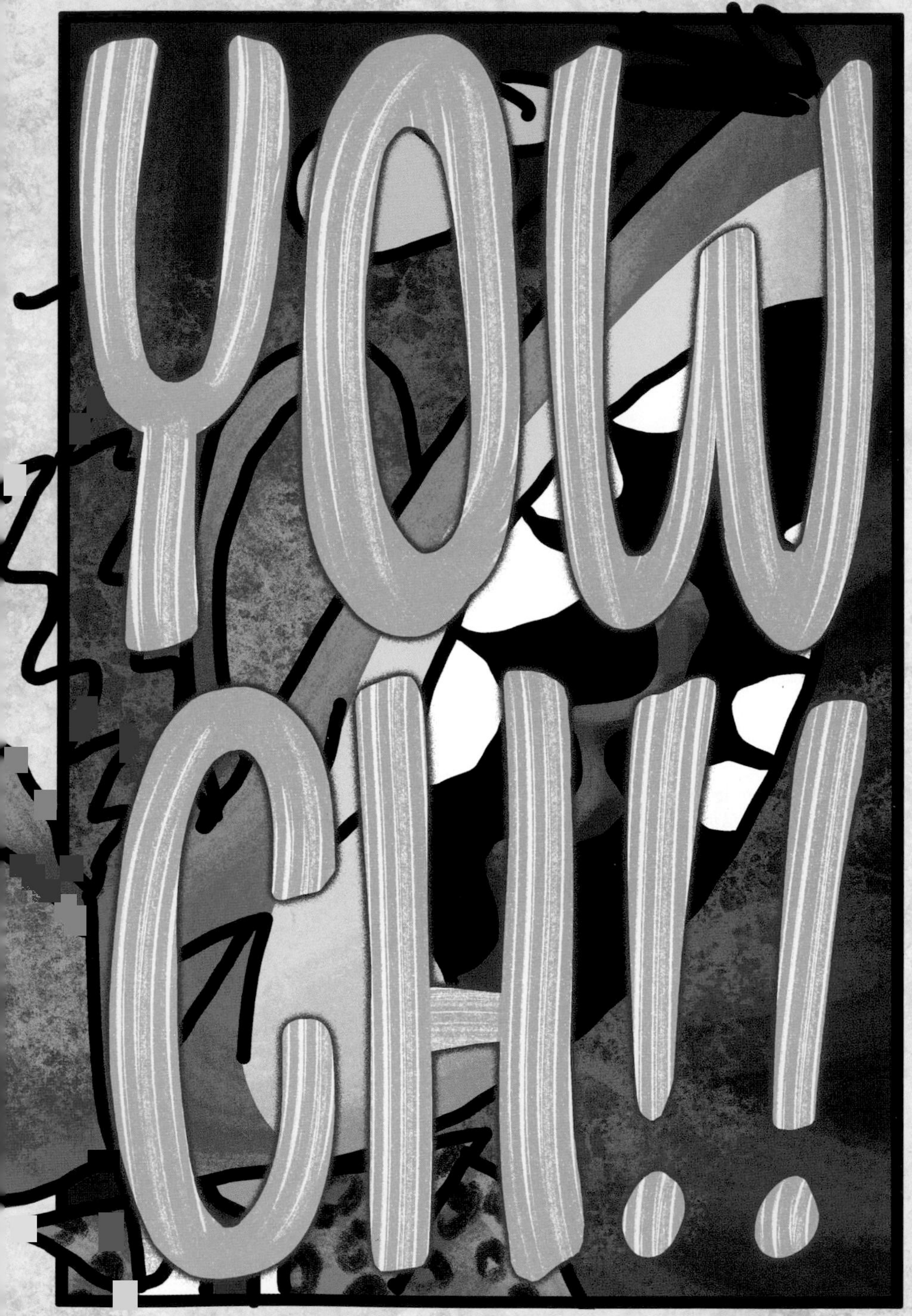
YOWCH!!

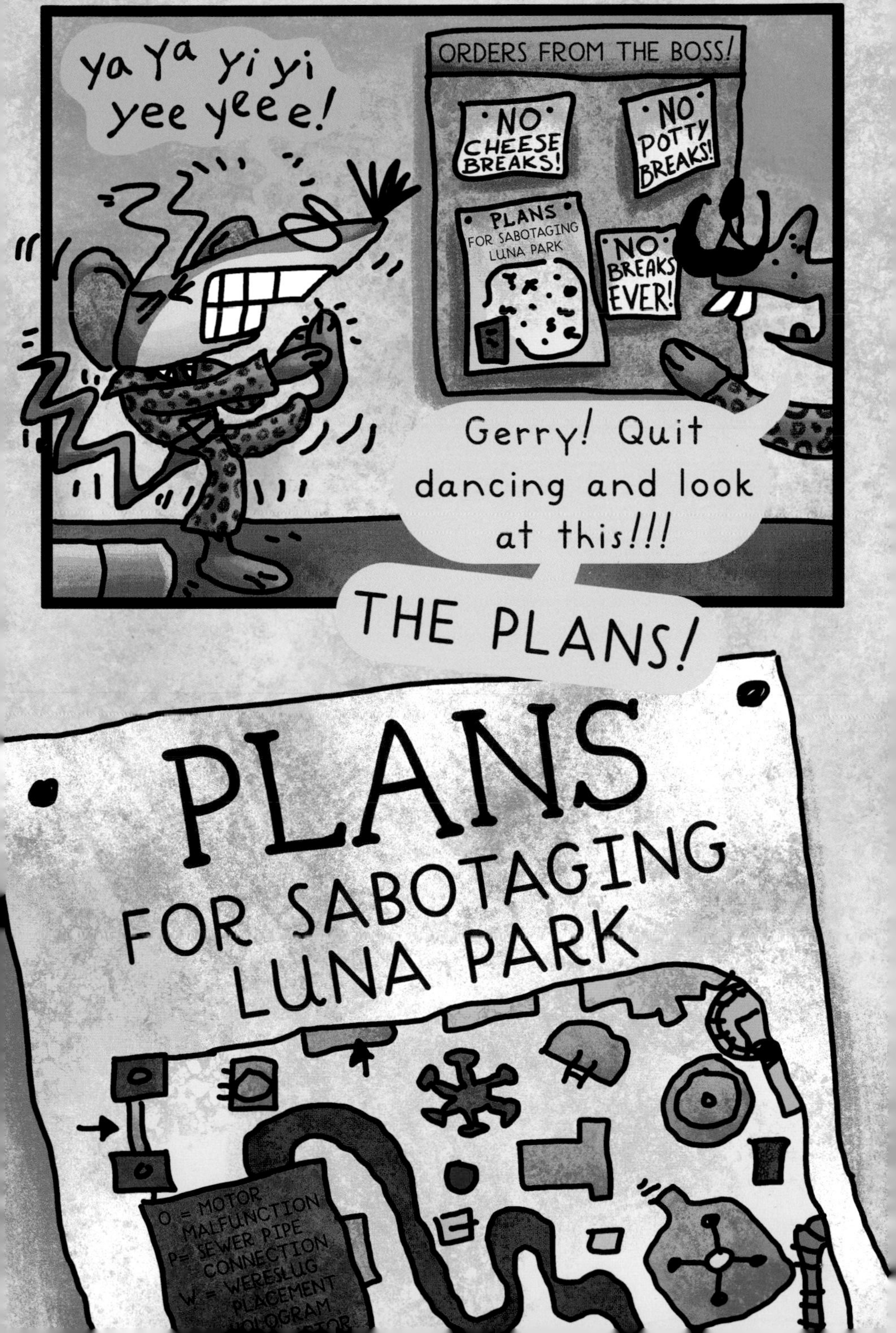
ya ya yi yi yee yeee!
ORDERS FROM THE BOSS!
NO CHEESE BREAKS!
NO POTTY BREAKS!
PLANS FOR SABOTAGING LUNA PARK
NO BREAKS EVER!
Gerry! Quit dancing and look at this!!!
THE PLANS!
PLANS FOR SABOTAGING LUNA PARK
O = MOTOR MALFUNCTION
P= SEWER PIPE CONNECTION
W = WERESLUG PLACEMENT

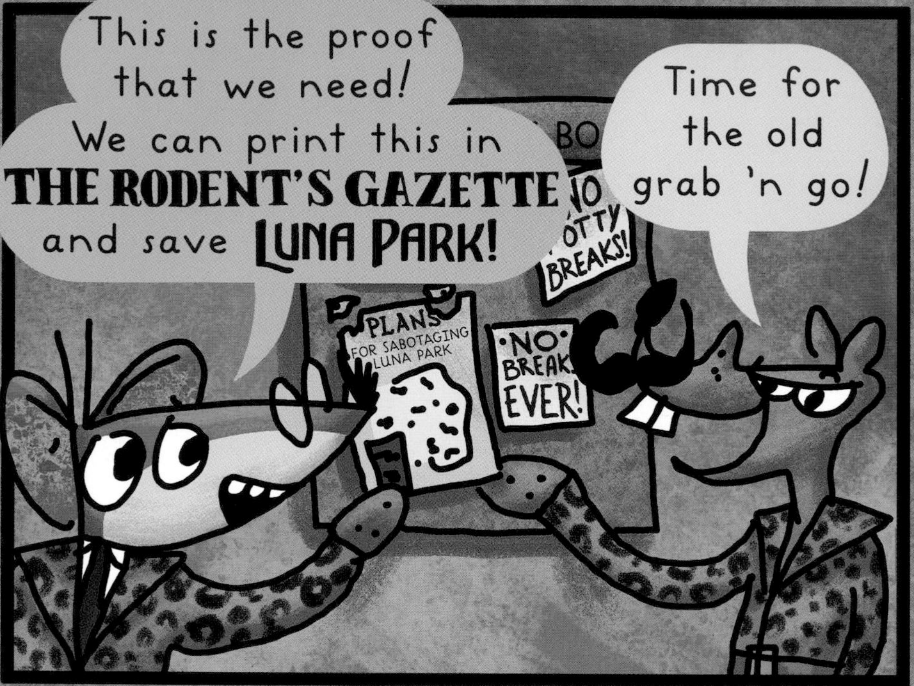
This is the proof that we need! We can print this in THE RODENT'S GAZETTE and save LUNA PARK!
Time for the old grab 'n go!
PLANS FOR SABOTAGING LUNA PARK
NO POTTY BREAKS!
NO BREAKS EVER!

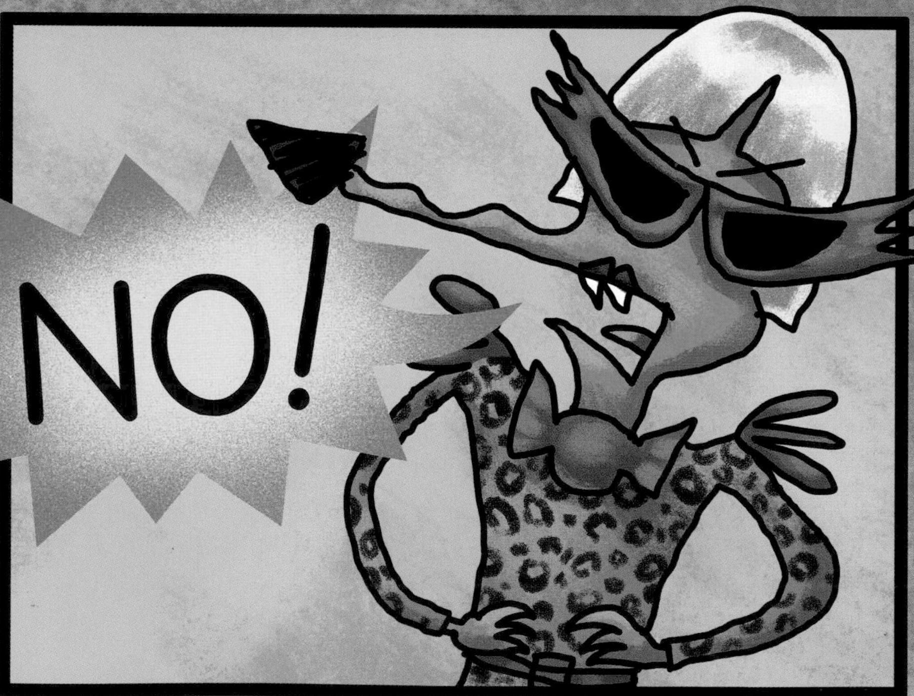
NO!

CHAPTER TWENTY-SIX

CAUGHT IN A MOUSETRAP!

It was Madame No

followed by two guards even **BIGGER** and **MEANER** looking than the other one!

Madame No!!! So you ARE the one who sabotaged Luna Park!
NO!!!!

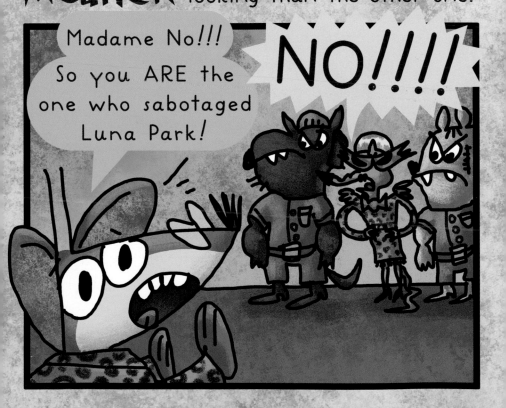

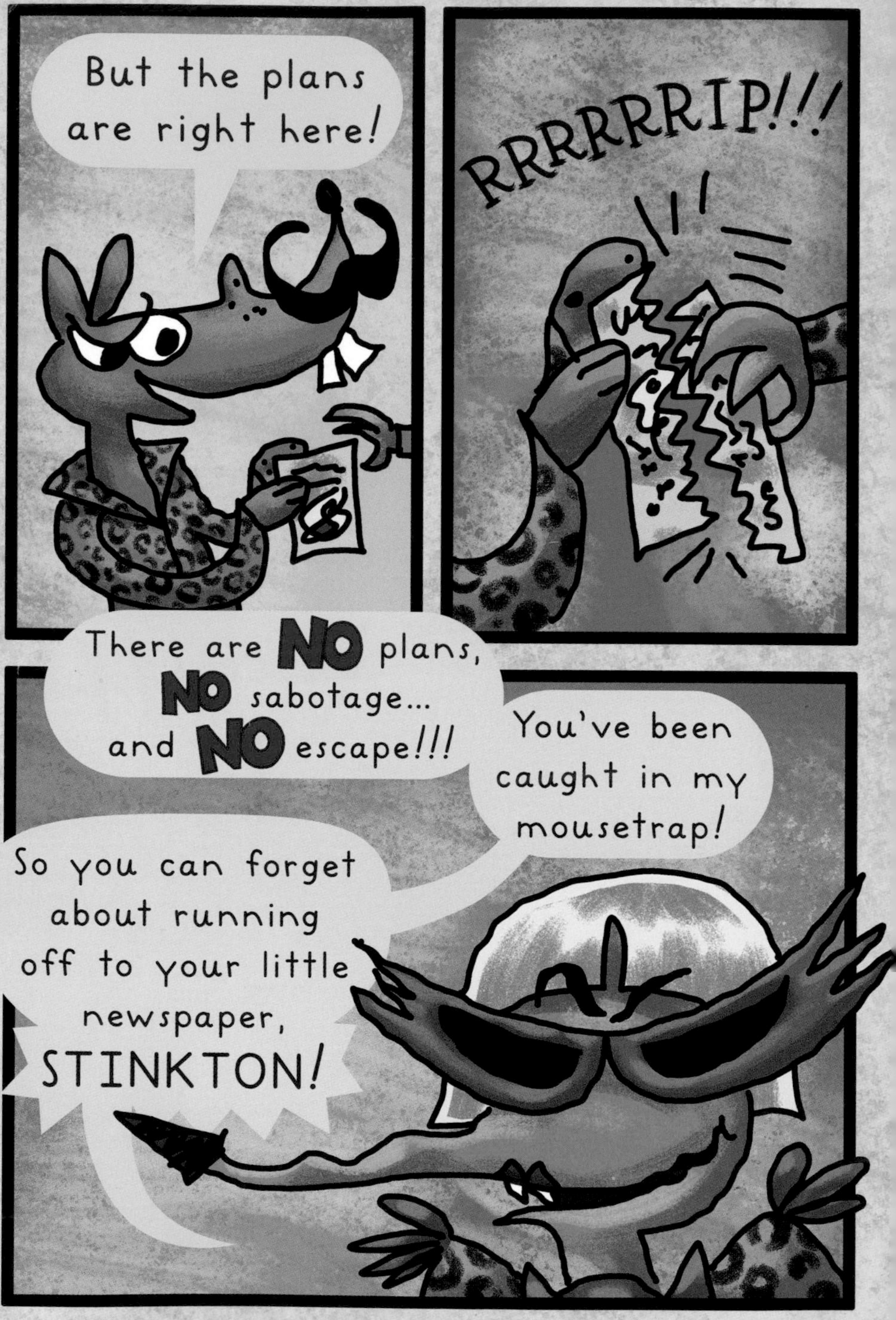
But the plans are right here!
RRRRRRIP!!!
There are NO plans, NO sabotage... and NO escape!!!
You've been caught in my mousetrap!
So you can forget about running off to your little newspaper, STINKTON!

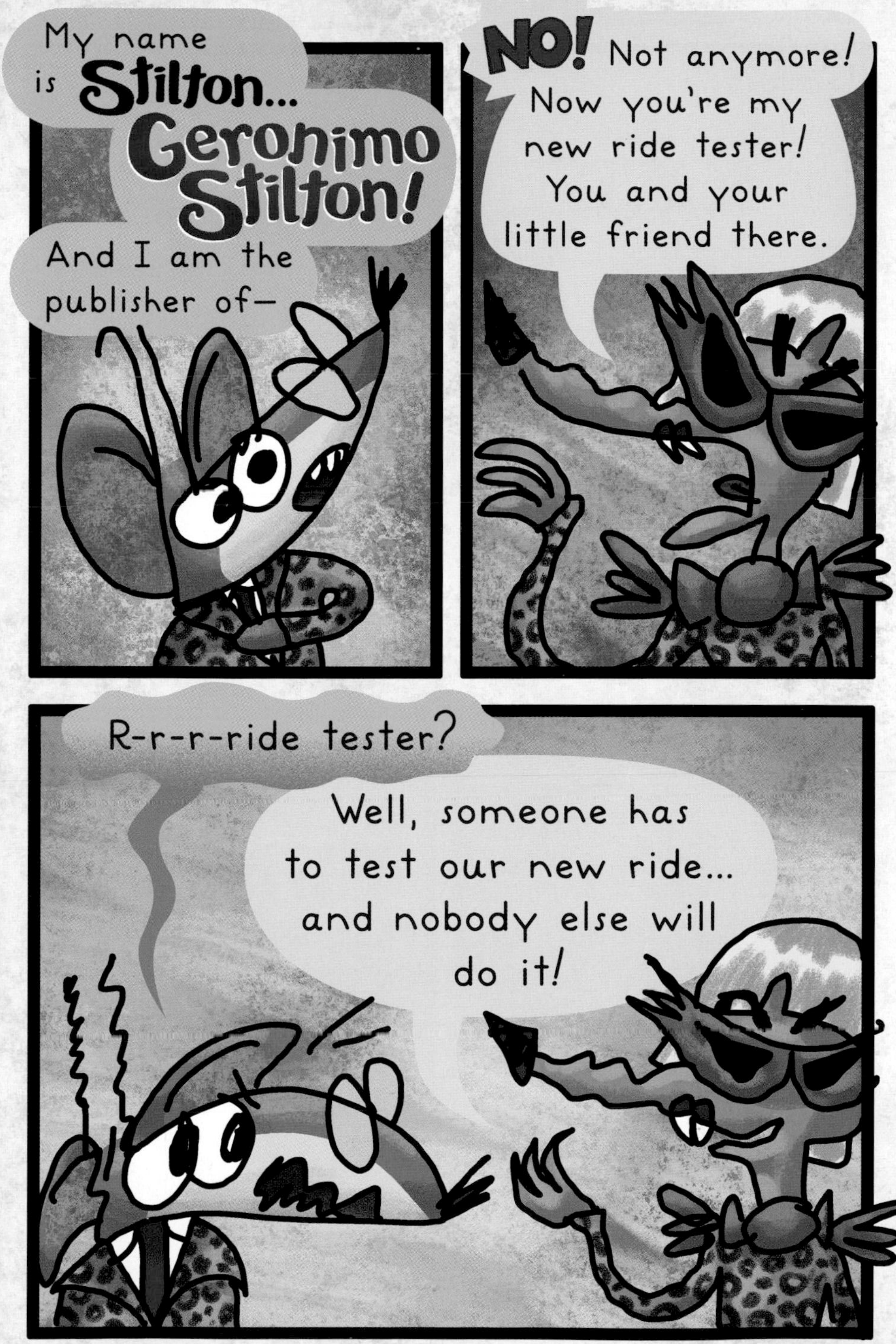
My name is Stilton... Geronimo Stilton!
And I am the publisher of—
NO! Not anymore! Now you're my new ride tester! You and your little friend there.
R-r-r-ride tester?
Well, someone has to test our new ride... and nobody else will do it!

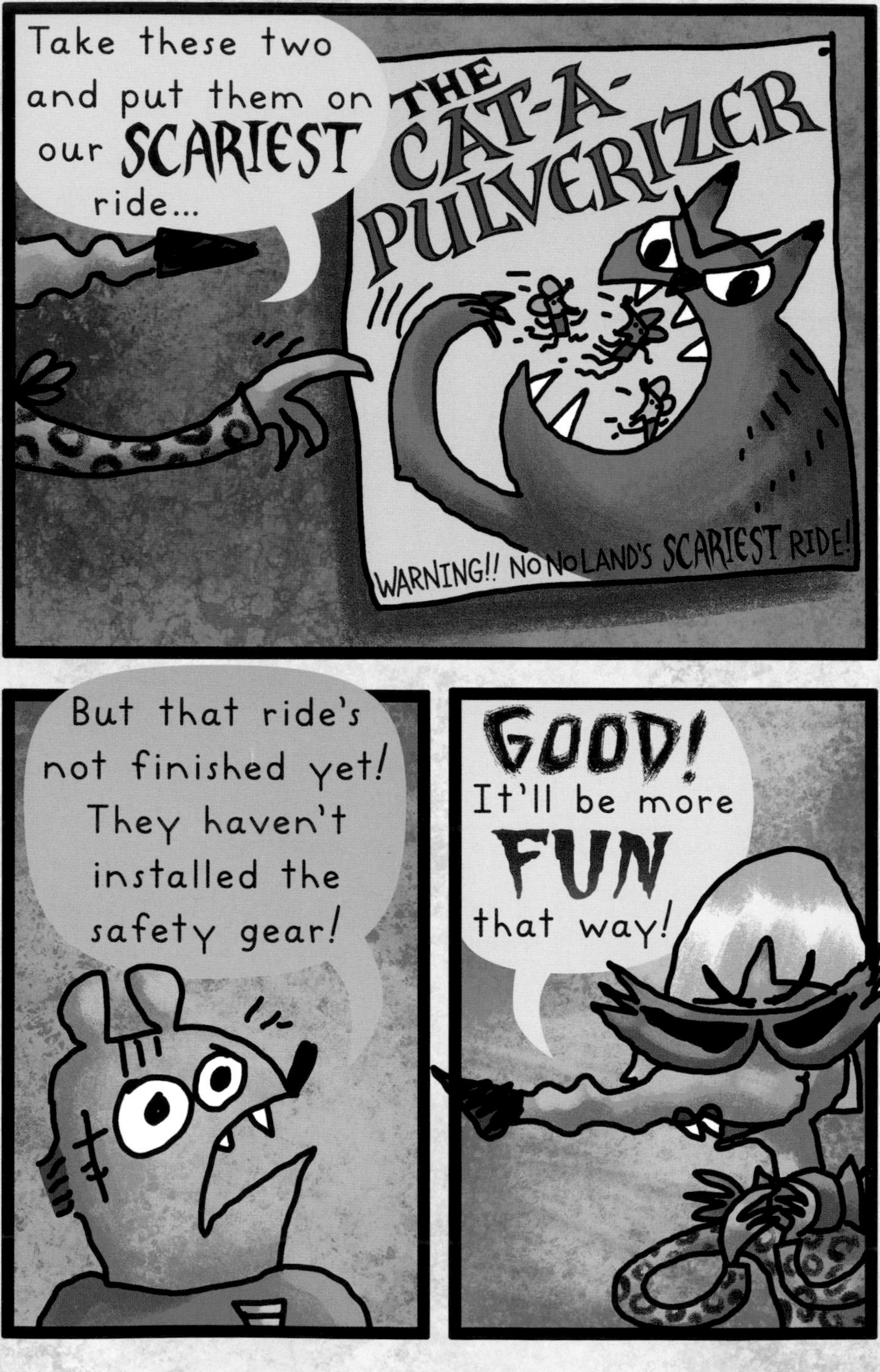
Take these two and put them on our SCARIEST ride...
THE CAT-A-PULVERIZER
WARNING!! NONOLAND'S SCARIEST RIDE!
But that ride's not finished yet! They haven't installed the safety gear!
GOOD! It'll be more FUN that way!

CHAPTER TWENTY-SEVEN

MONSTER ATTACK!!!!

The guards shoved us out of the office and across the park to a giant metal CAT CLAW. Then they clamped us in... ¡¡¡UPSIDE DOWN!!!

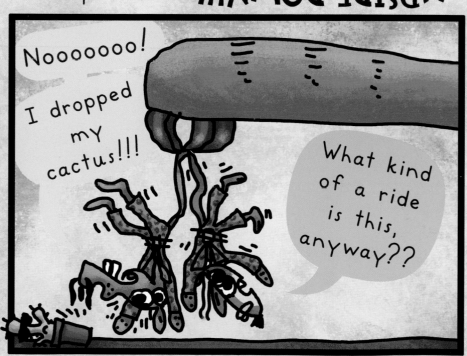

Nooooooo! I dropped my cactus!!!

What kind of a ride is this, anyway??

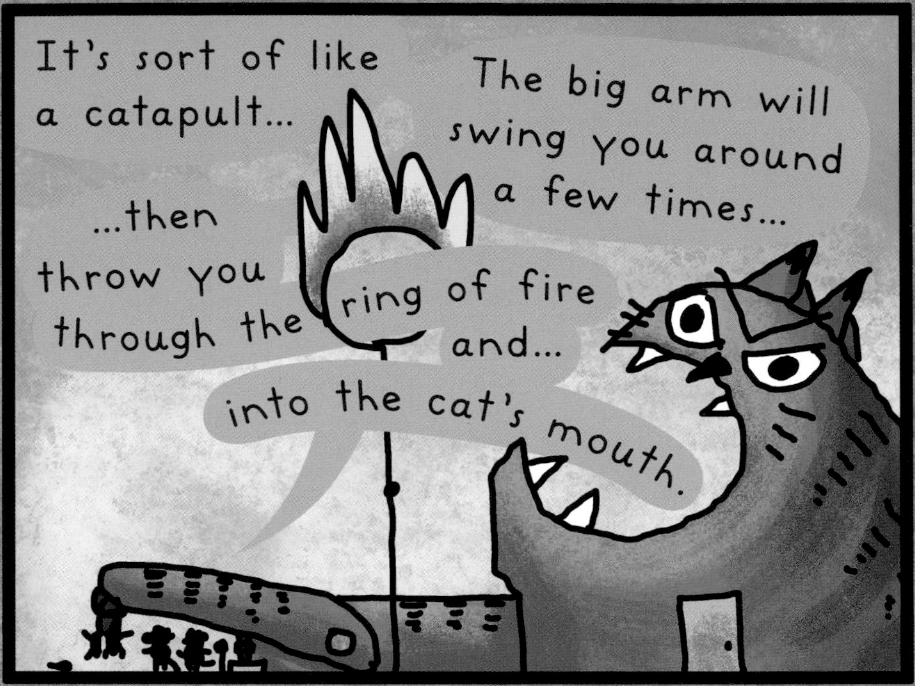
It's sort of like a catapult...
The big arm will swing you around a few times...
...then throw you through the ring of fire and...
into the cat's mouth.

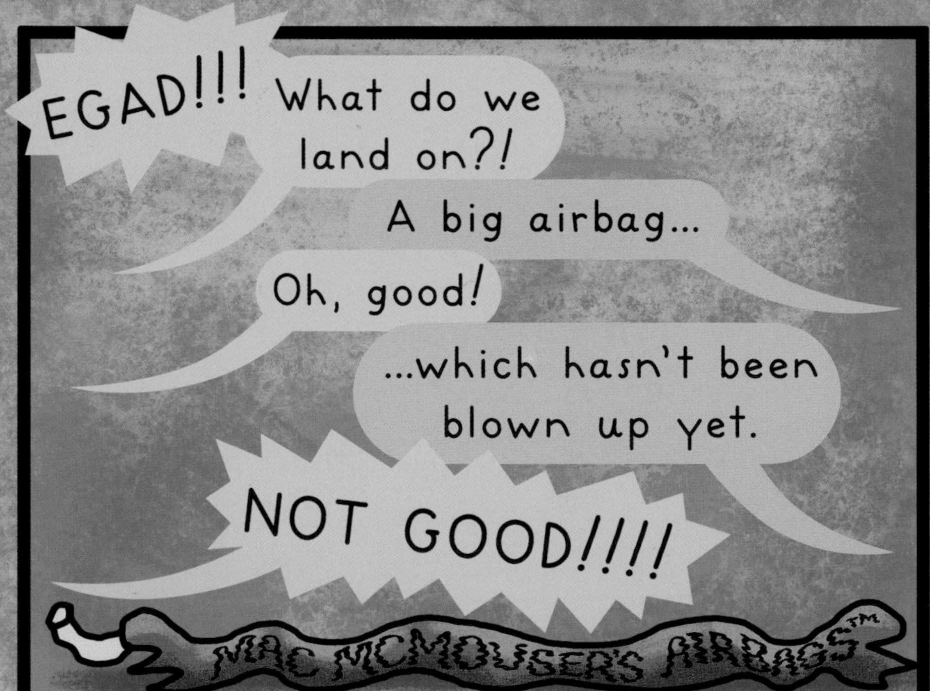
EGAD!!! What do we land on?!
A big airbag...
Oh, good!
...which hasn't been blown up yet.
NOT GOOD!!!!
MAC MCMOUSER'S AIRBAGS™

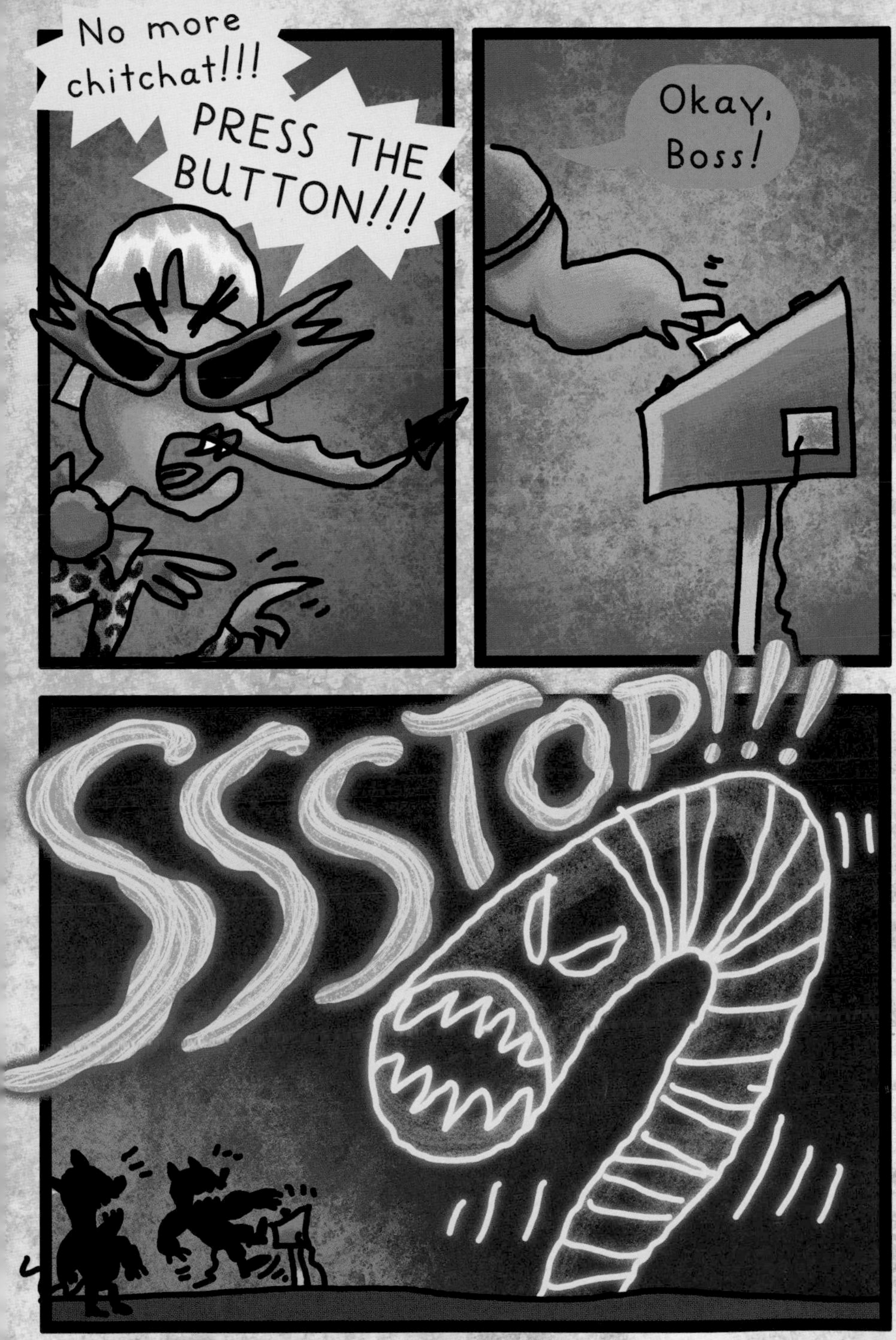
No more chitchat!!!
PRESS THE BUTTON!!!
Okay, Boss!
SSSTOP!!!

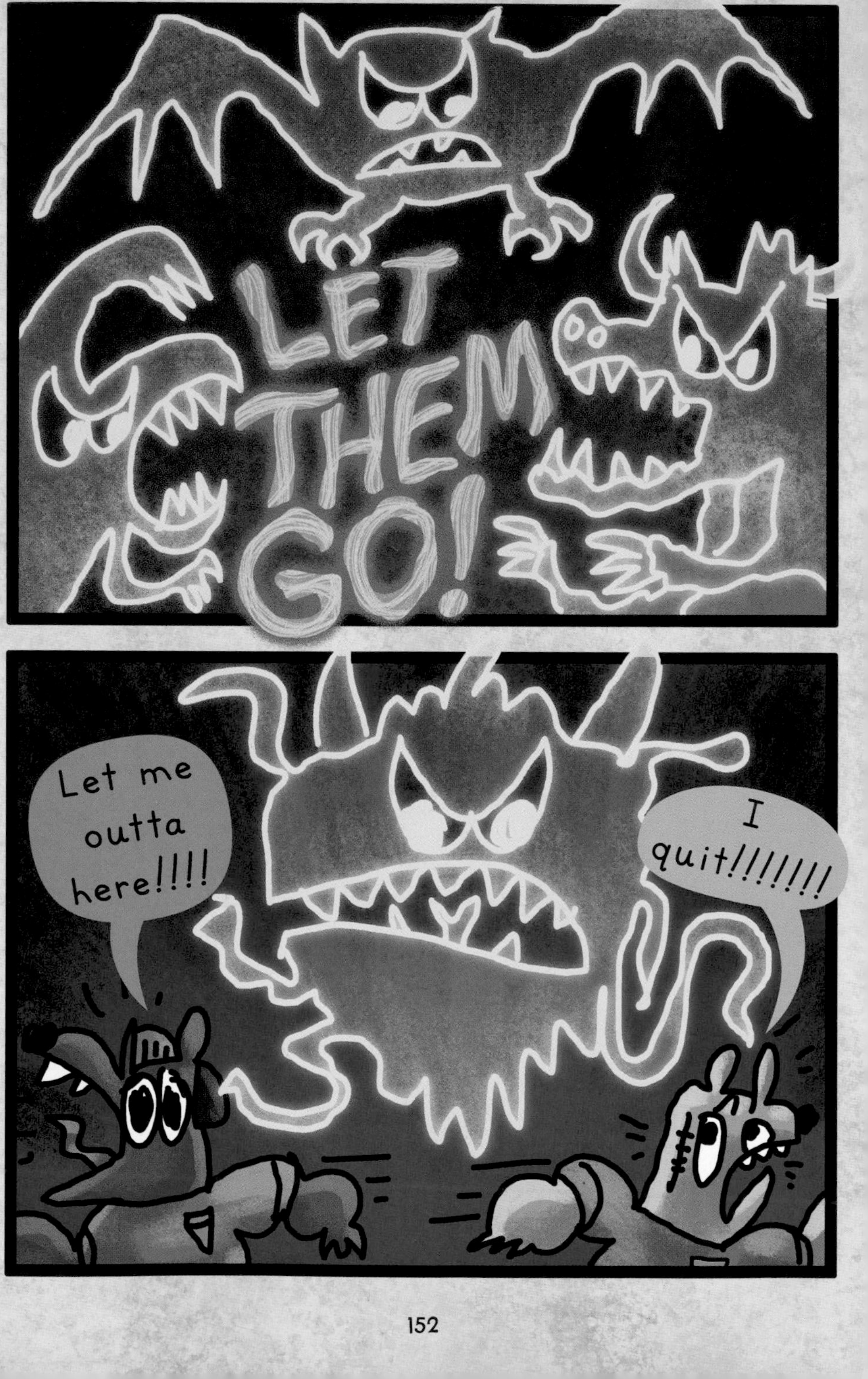
LET THEM GO!
Let me outta here!!!!
I quit!!!!!!!!

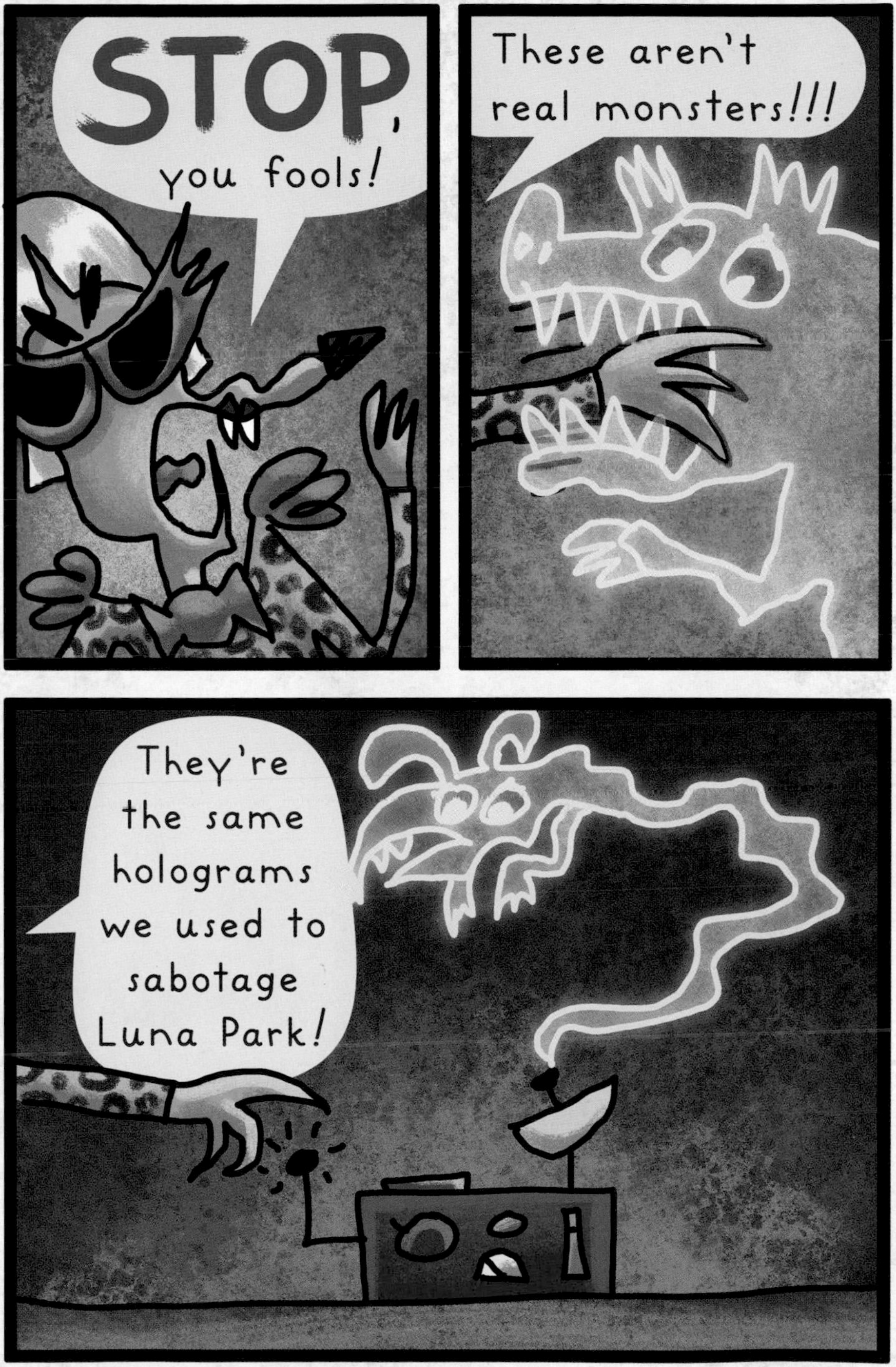
STOP, you fools!
These aren't real monsters!!!
They're the same holograms we used to sabotage Luna Park!

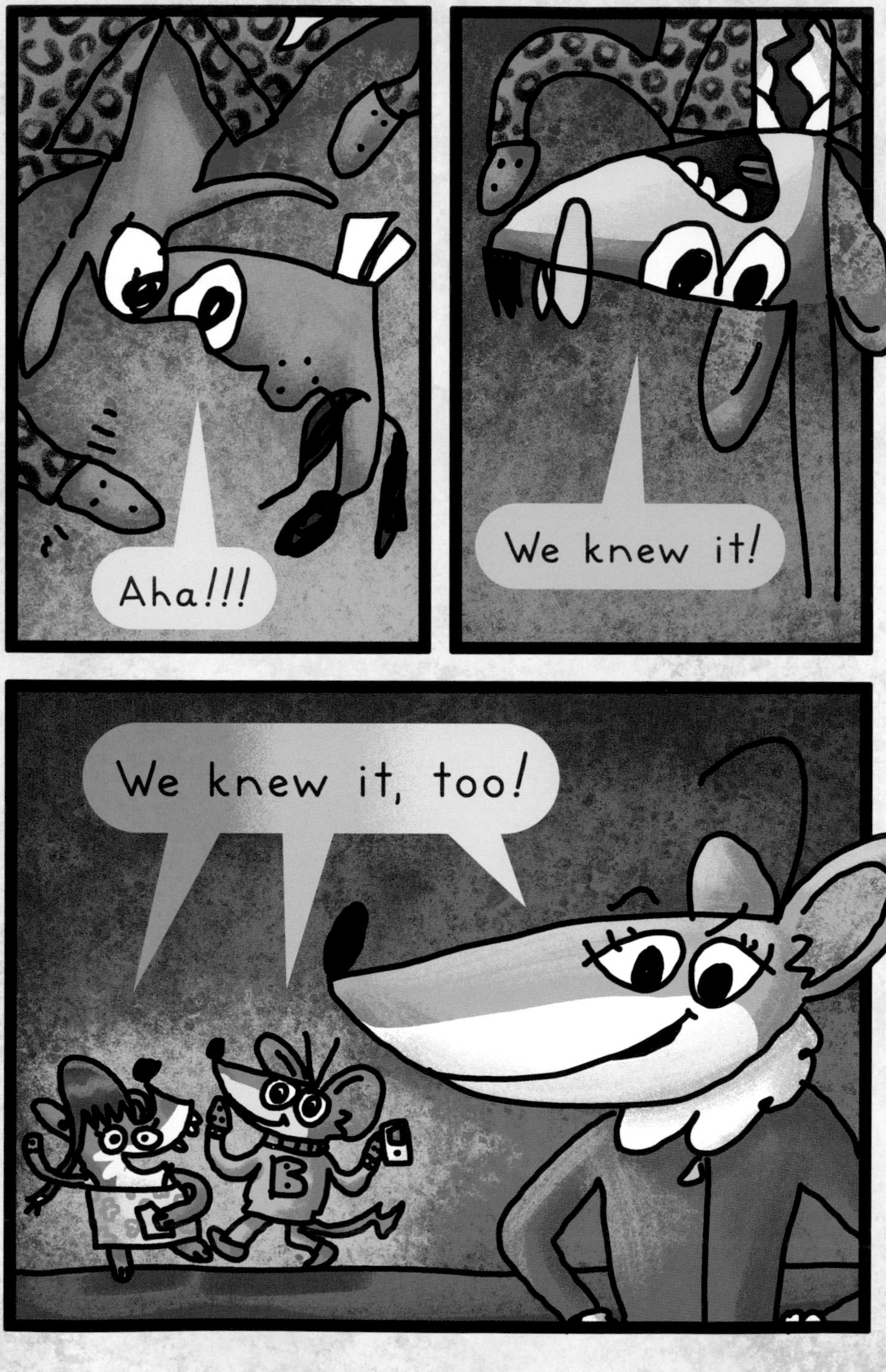
Aha!!!
We knew it!
We knew it, too!

CHAPTER TWENTY-EIGHT

H'YUK H'YUK

I was so **HAPPY** to see Thea! I was so **HAPPY** to see Benjamin and Trappy! I was so **HAPPY** to get unhooked from the cat claw and turned right-side-up again!!!

What in the **cheddar** are you doing here??

Saving your tails, Little Brother!!

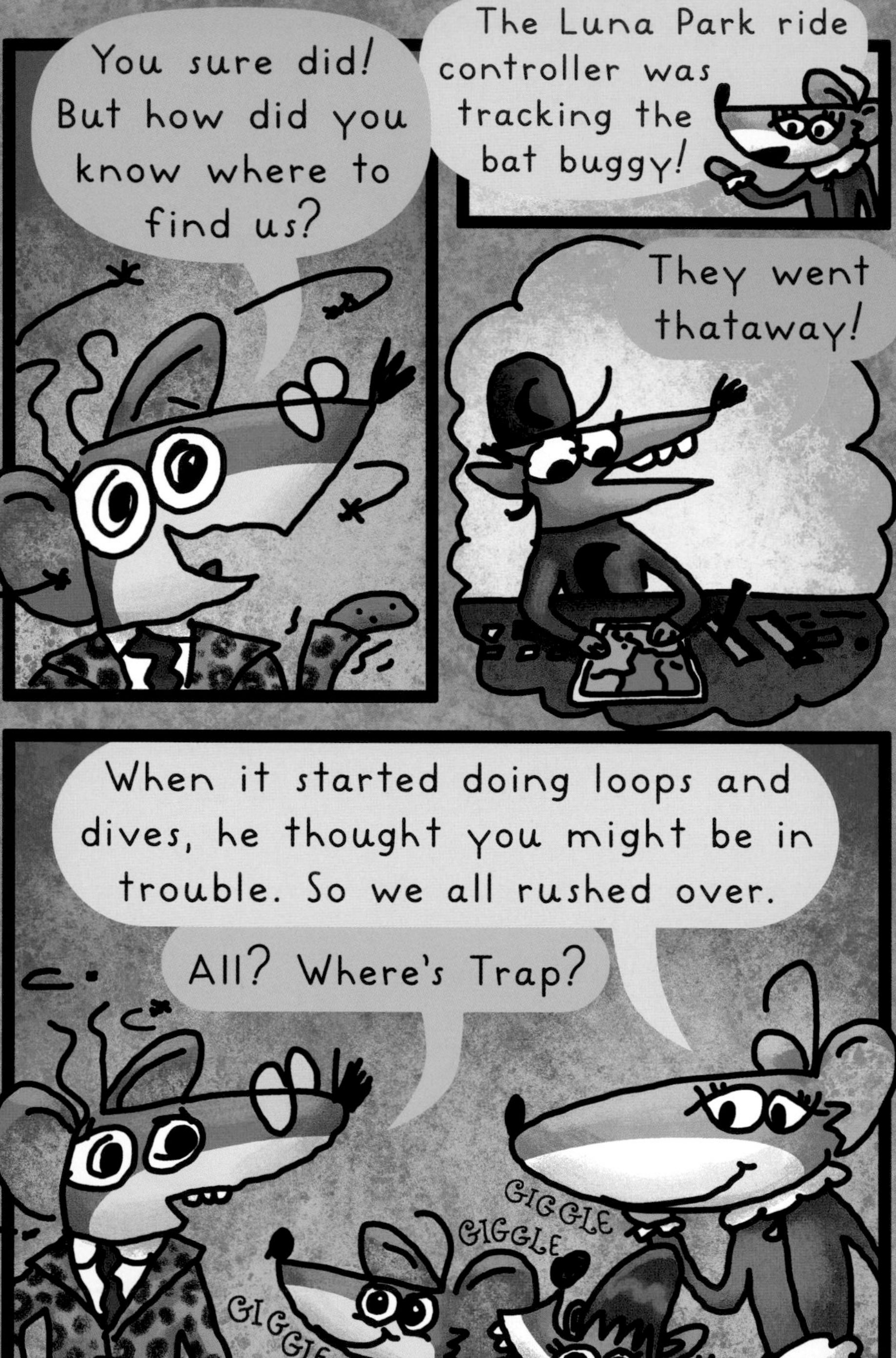
You sure did! But how did you know where to find us?
The Luna Park ride controller was tracking the bat buggy!
They went thataway!
When it started doing loops and dives, he thought you might be in trouble. So we all rushed over.
All? Where's Trap?
GIGGLE
GIGGLE
GIGGLE
GIGGLE

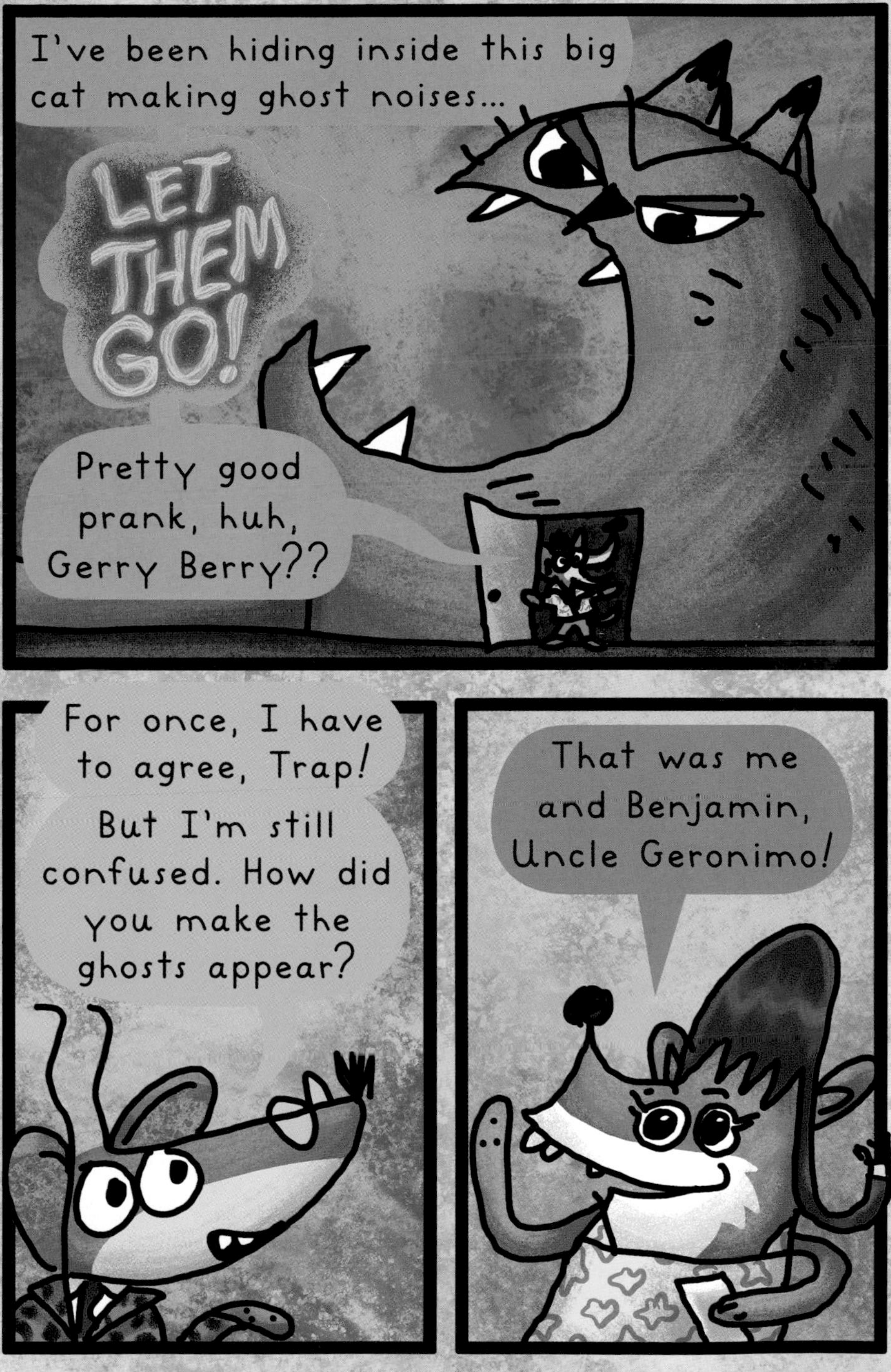
I've been hiding inside this big cat making ghost noises...
LET THEM GO!
Pretty good prank, huh, Gerry Berry??
For once, I have to agree, Trap!
But I'm still confused. How did you make the ghosts appear?
That was me and Benjamin, Uncle Geronimo!

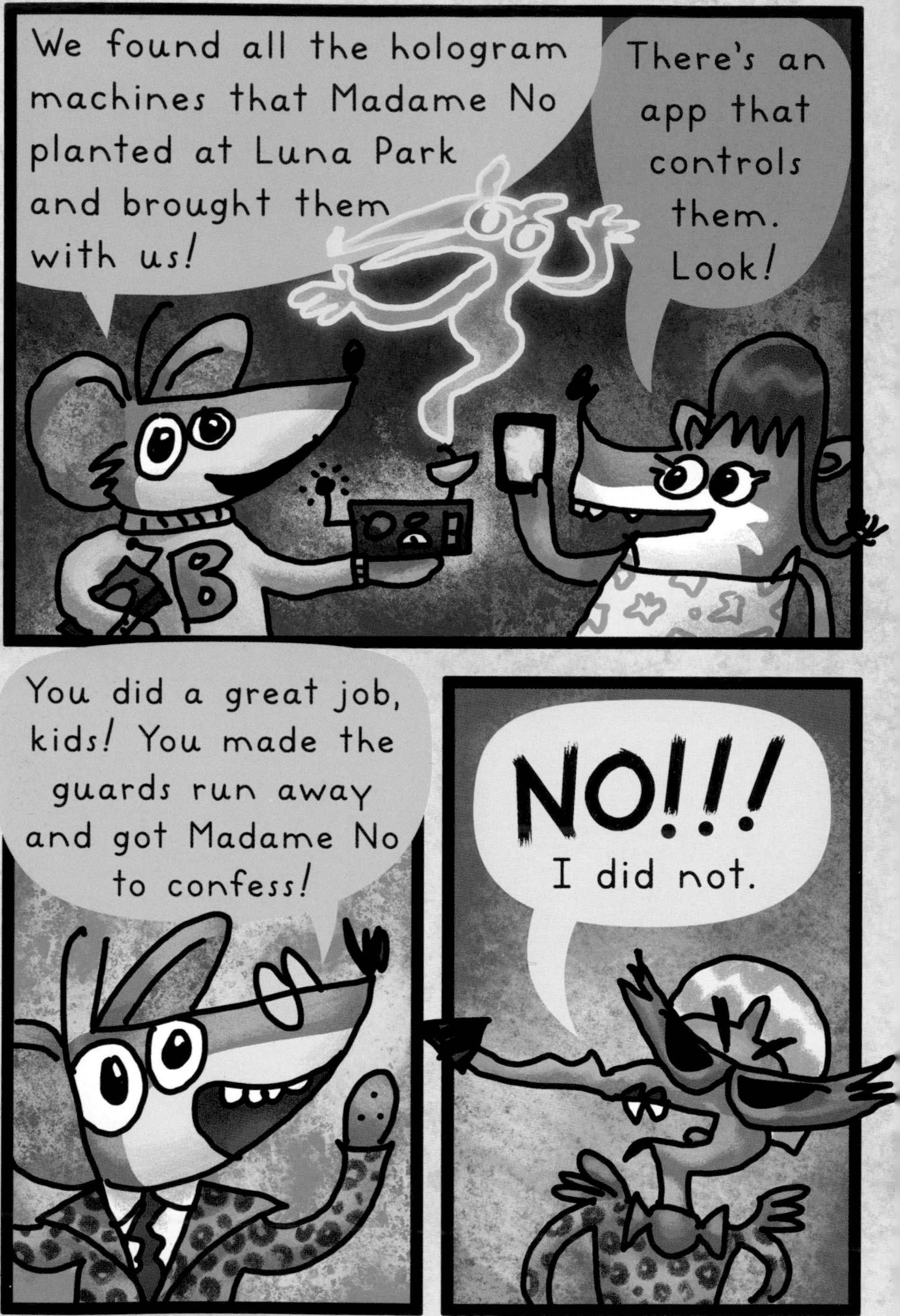
We found all the hologram machines that Madame No planted at Luna Park and brought them with us!
There's an app that controls them. Look!
You did a great job, kids! You made the guards run away and got Madame No to confess!
NO!!!
I did not.

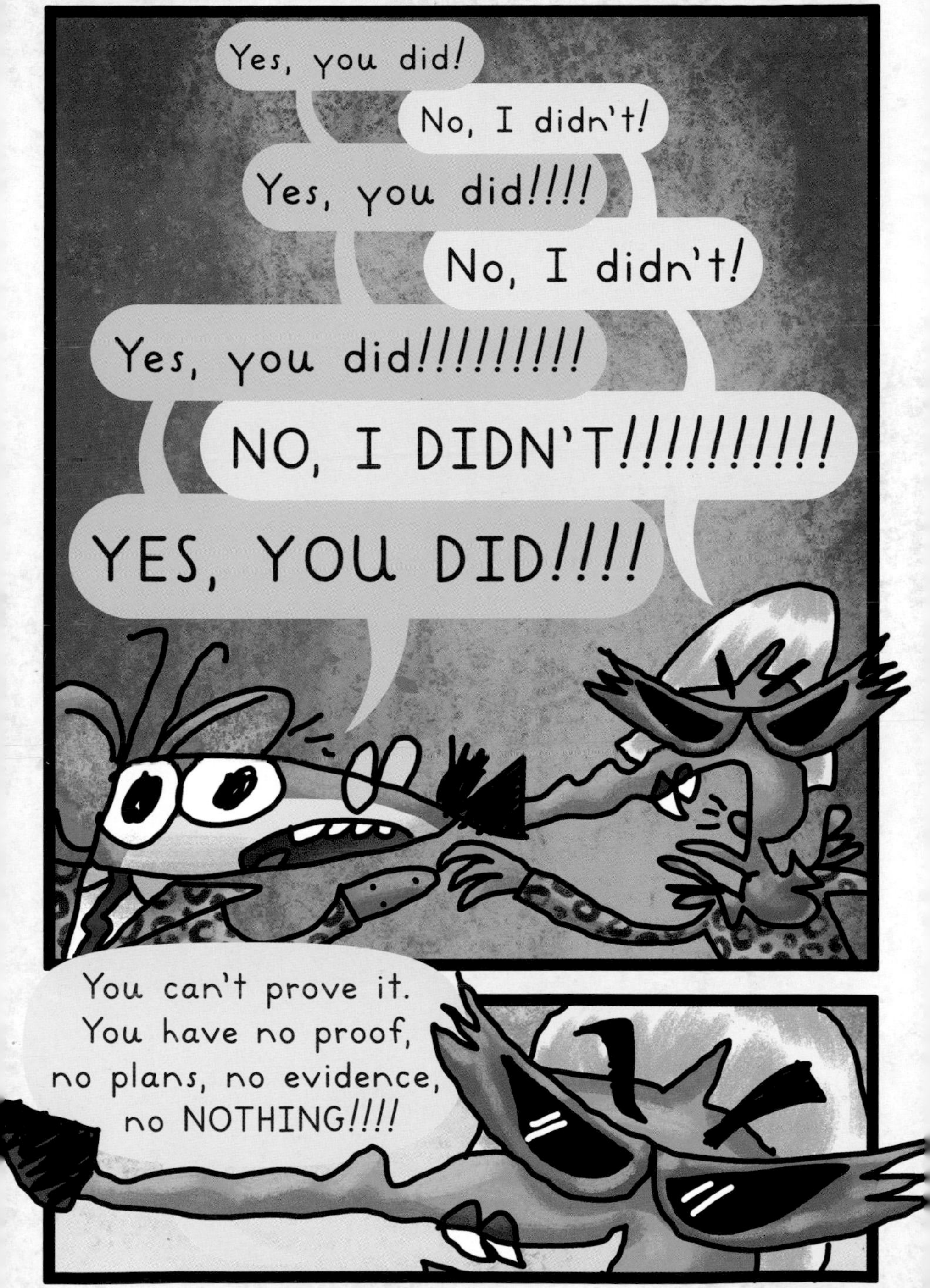
Yes, you did!
No, I didn't!
Yes, you did!!!!
No, I didn't!
Yes, you did!!!!!!!!!!
NO, I DIDN'T!!!!!!!!!!!
YES, YOU DID!!!!
You can't prove it. You have no proof, no plans, no evidence, no NOTHING!!!!

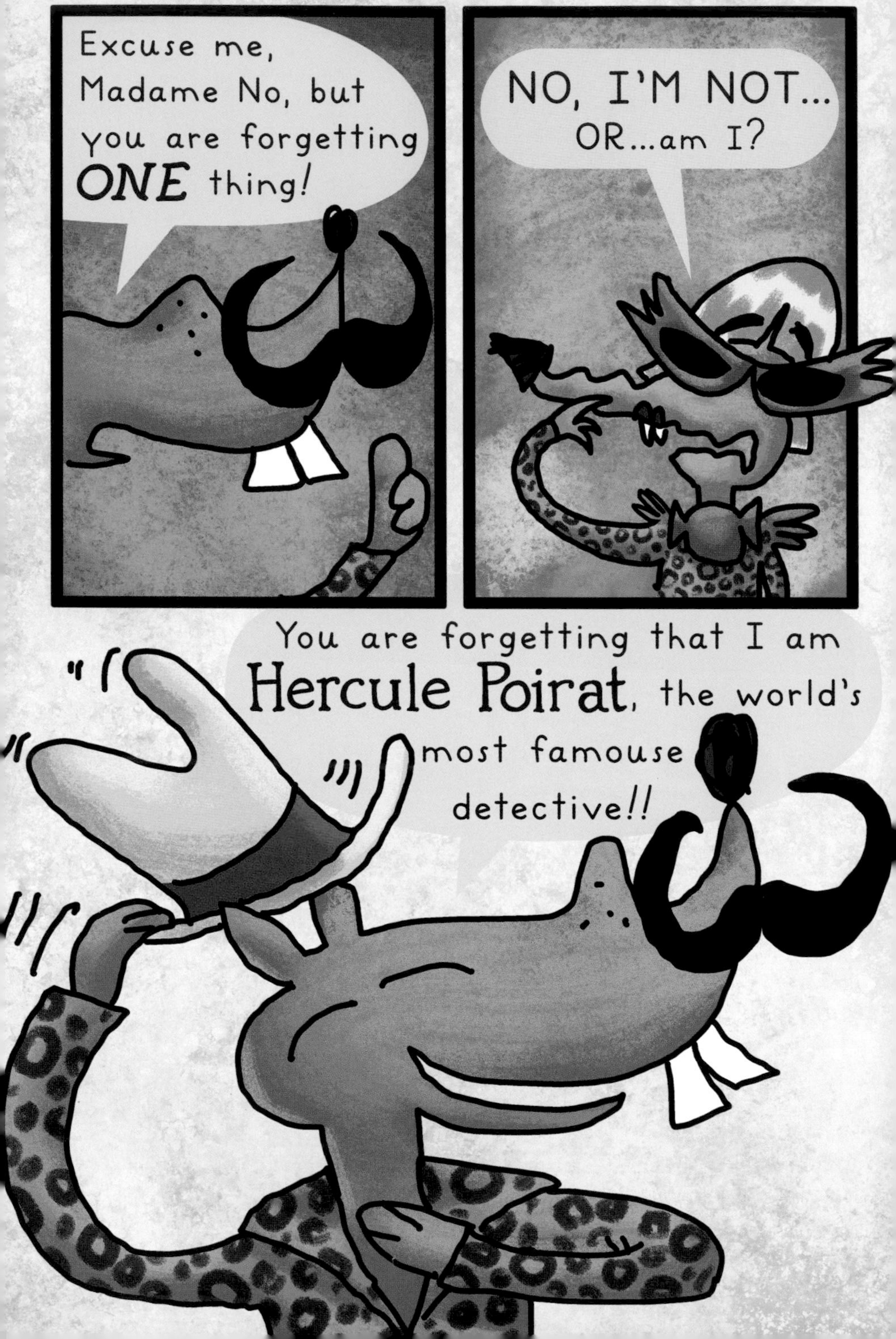
Excuse me, Madame No, but you are forgetting ONE thing!
NO, I'M NOT... OR...am I?
"You are forgetting that I am Hercule Poirat, the world's most famouse detective!!

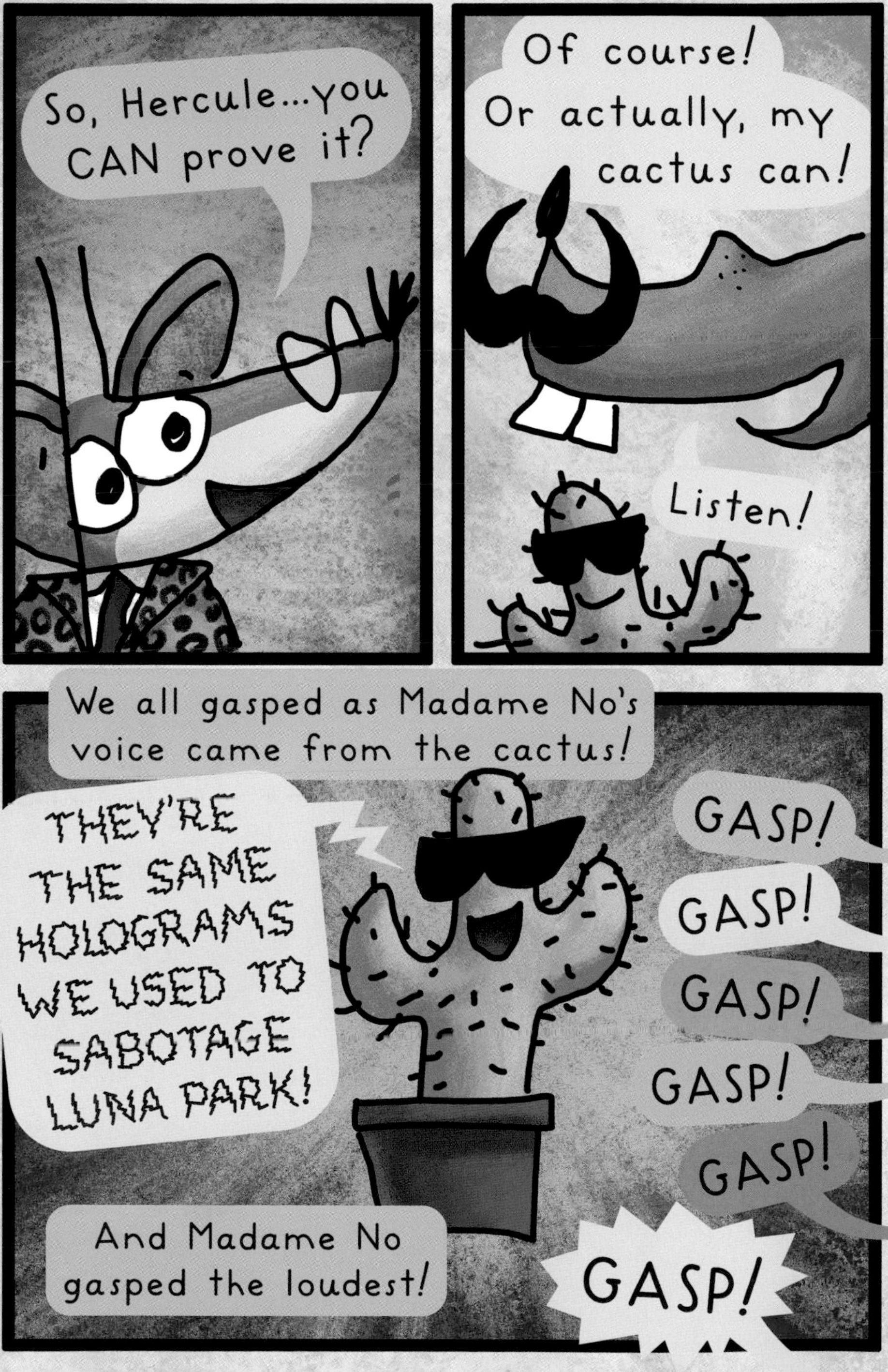
So, Hercule...you CAN prove it?
Of course! Or actually, my cactus can!
Listen!
We all gasped as Madame No's voice came from the cactus!
THEY'RE THE SAME HOLOGRAMS WE USED TO SABOTAGE LUNA PARK!
GASP!
GASP!
GASP!
GASP!
GASP!
And Madame No gasped the loudest!
GASP!

CHAPTER TWENTY-NINE

Have a NICE DAY!!!

Hercule had done it! The cactus had the proof we needed! Once we printed the proof in **THE RODENT'S GAZETTE**, everyone would know Luna Park was not really haunted!

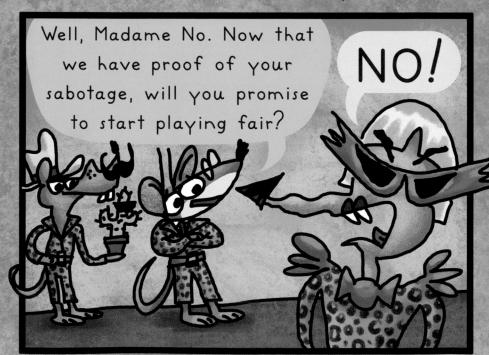

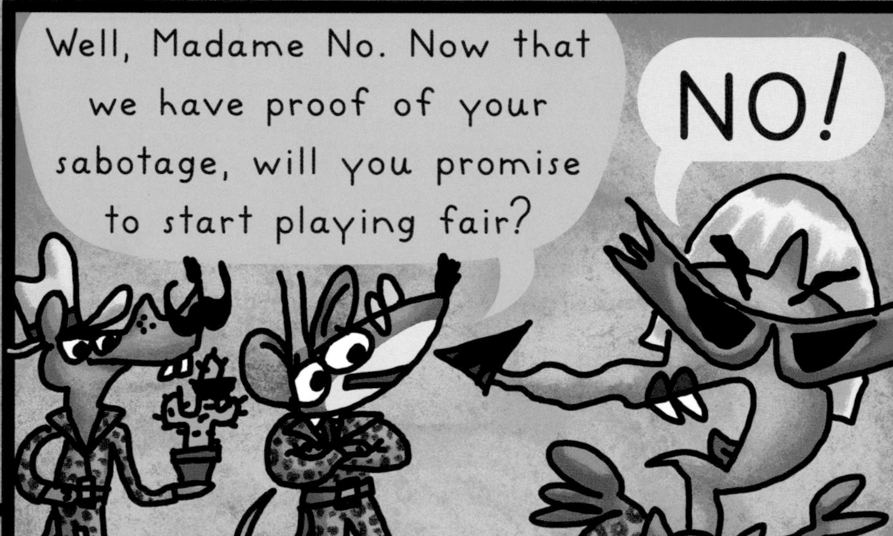
Well, Madame No. Now that we have proof of your sabotage, will you promise to start playing fair?
NO!

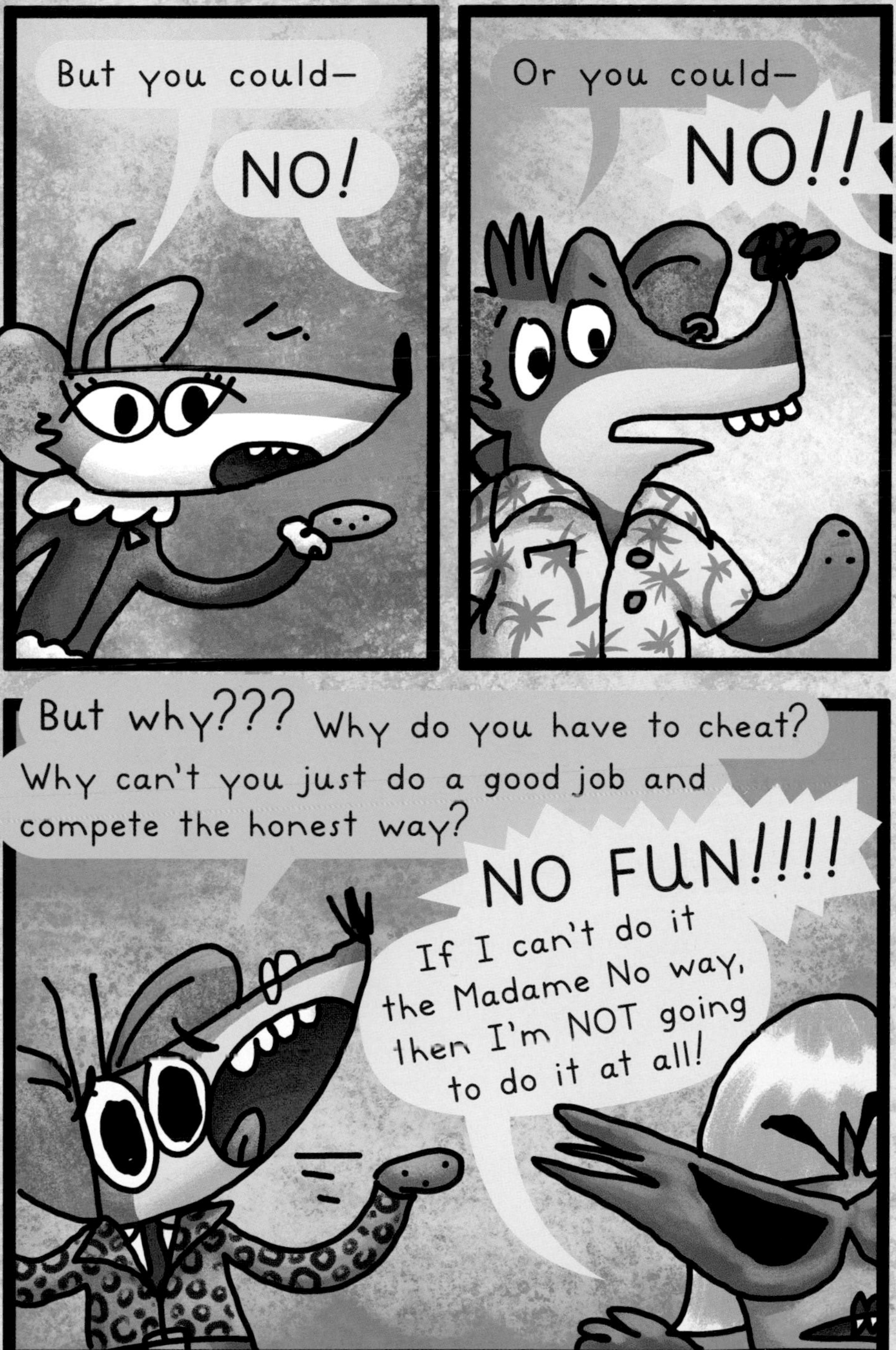

But you could–
NO!
Or you could–
NO!!
But why??? Why do you have to cheat?
Why can't you just do a good job and compete the honest way?
NO FUN!!!!
If I can't do it the Madame No way, then I'm NOT going to do it at all!

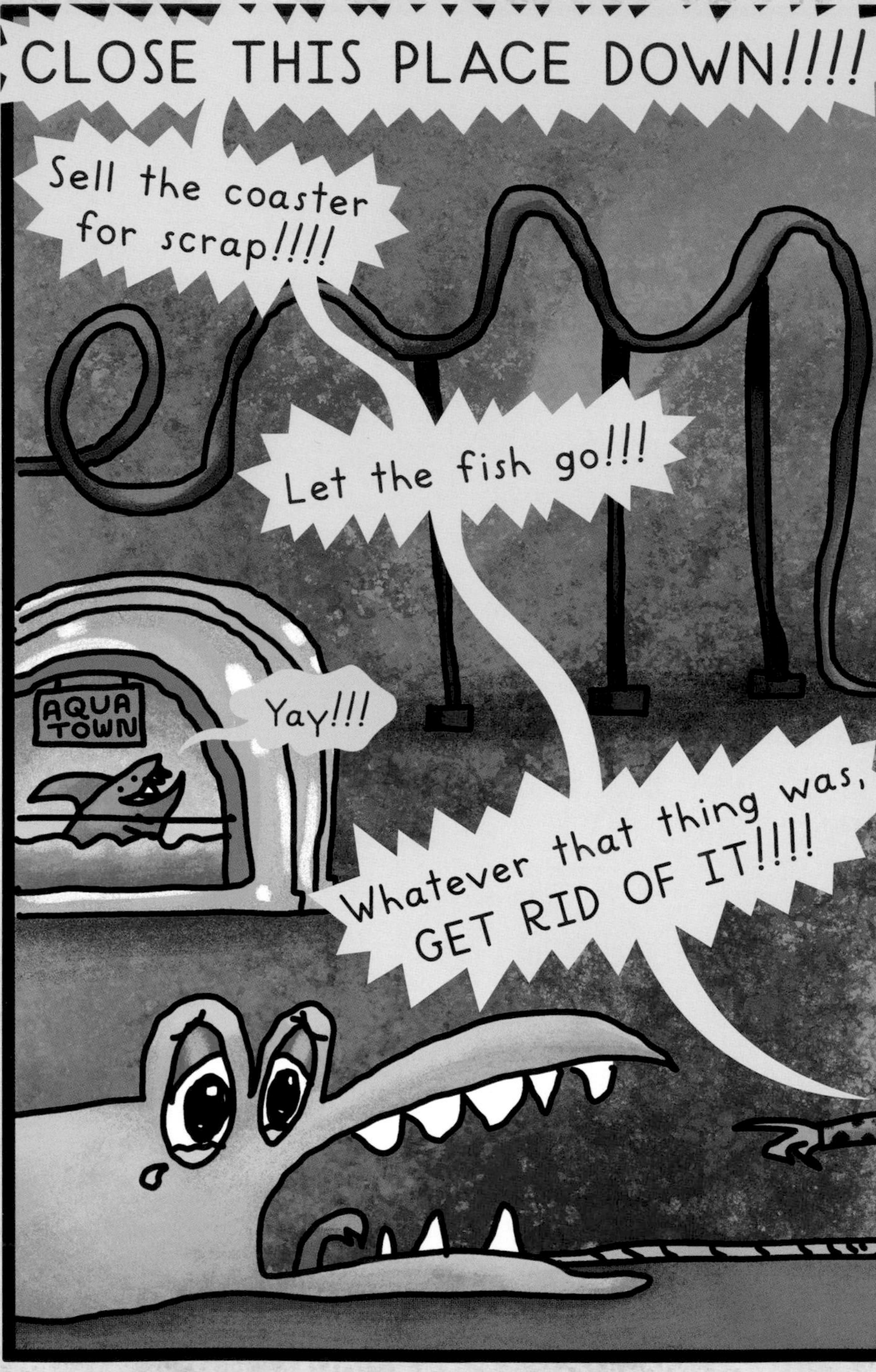
CLOSE THIS PLACE DOWN!!!!
Sell the coaster for scrap!!!!
Let the fish go!!!
AQUA TOWN
Yay!!!
Whatever that thing was, GET RID OF IT!!!!

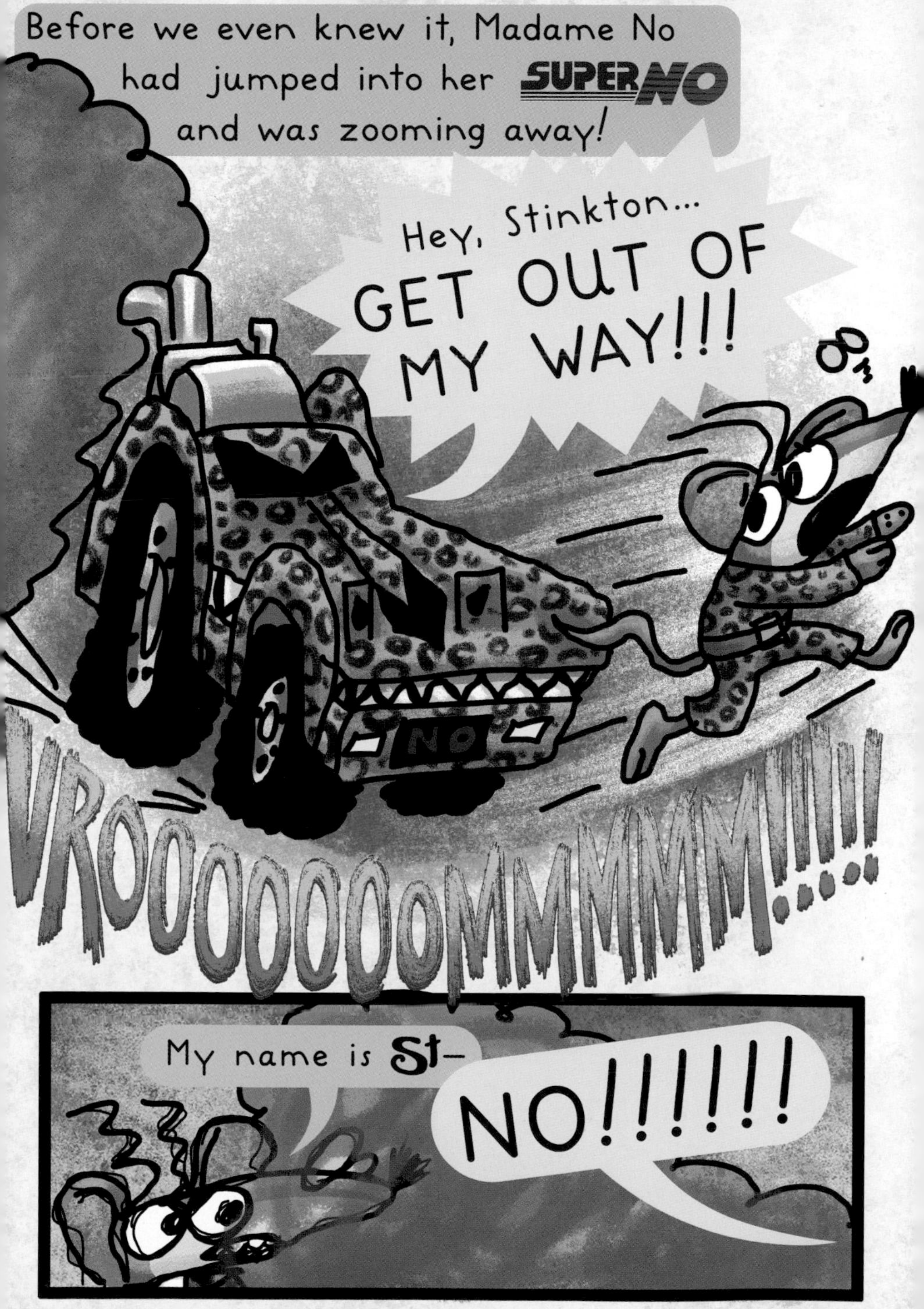
Before we even knew it, Madame No had jumped into her SUPER NO and was zooming away!
Hey, Stinkton... GET OUT OF MY WAY!!!
NO
VROOOOOOOOMMMMMM!!!!!....
My name is St—
NO!!!!!!

CHAPTER THIRTY

FOR THE STYLE SECTION

Just like that, Madame No was gone in a cloud of dust. None of the guards and workers seemed interested in chasing us. In fact, several thanked us!

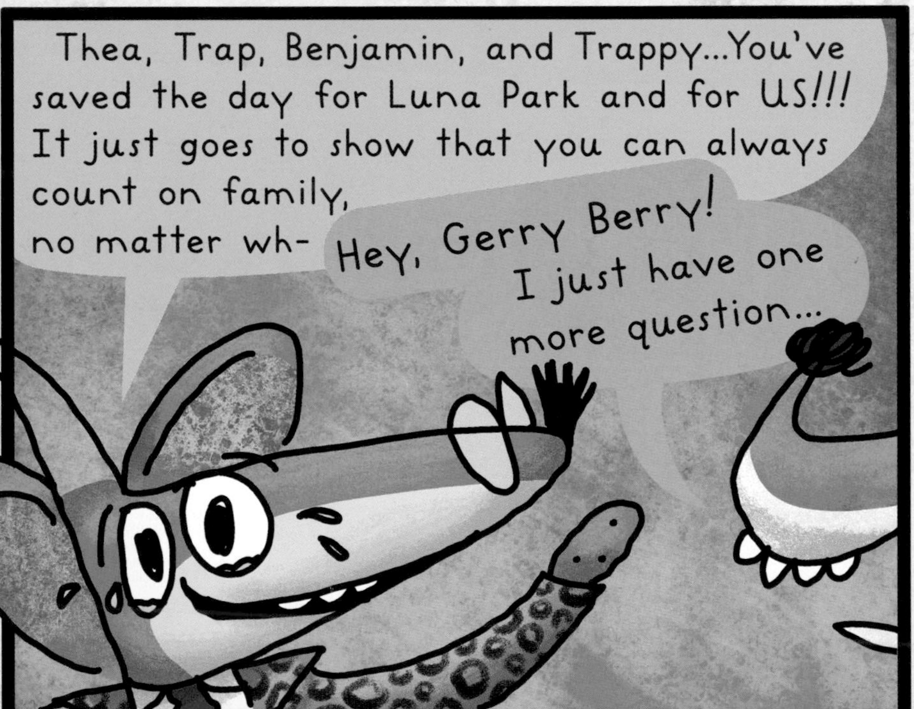
Thea, Trap, Benjamin, and Trappy...You've saved the day for Luna Park and for US!!! It just goes to show that you can always count on family, no matter wh-
Hey, Gerry Berry! I just have one more question...

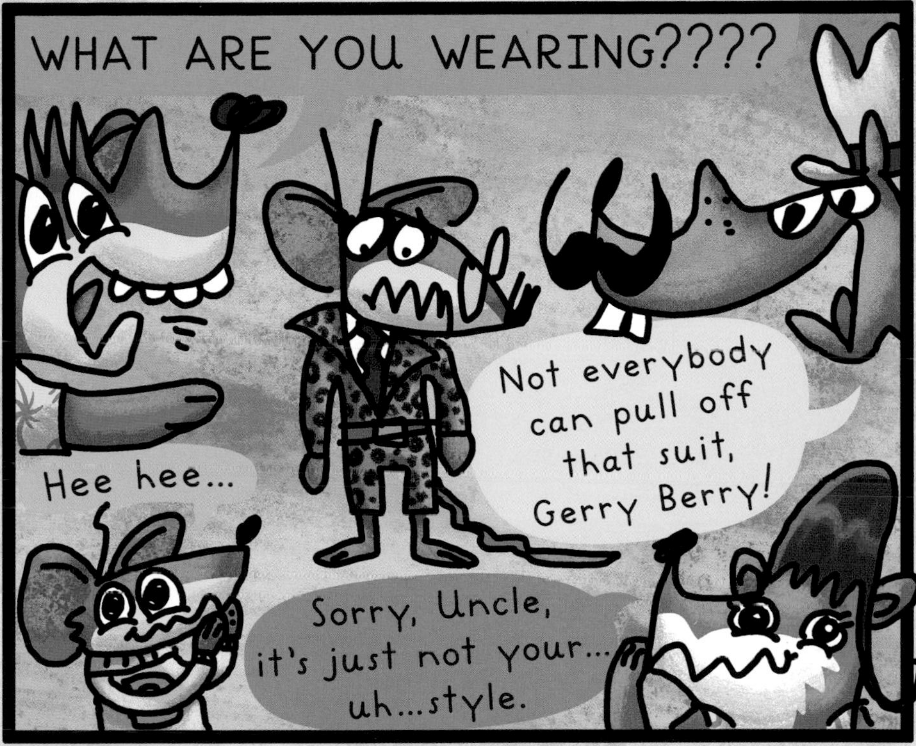
WHAT ARE YOU WEARING????
Not everybody can pull off that suit, Gerry Berry!
Hee hee...
Sorry, Uncle, it's just not your... uh...style.

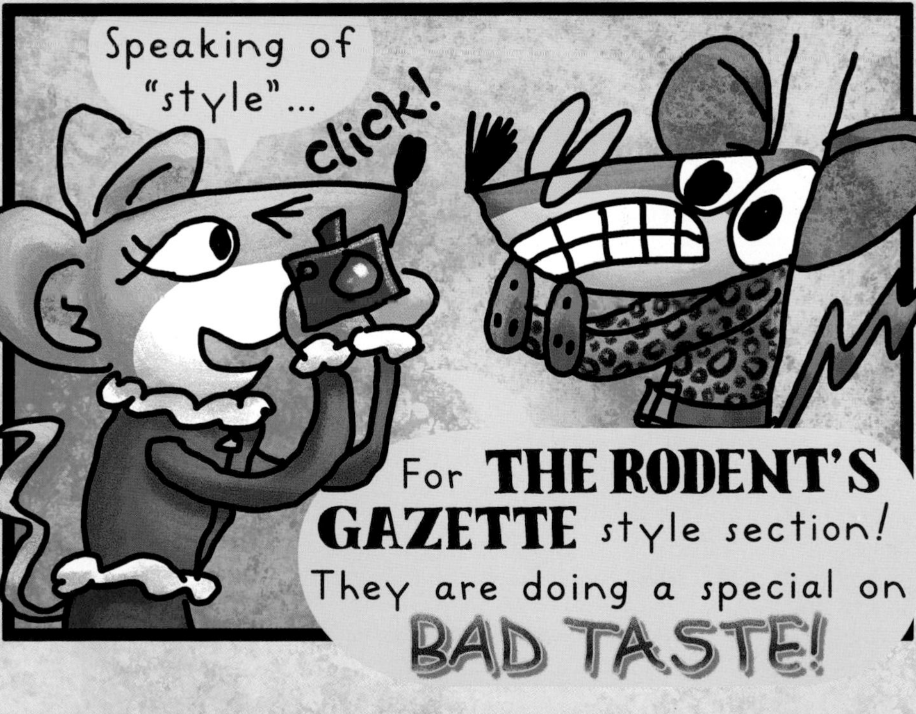
Speaking of "style"...
click!
For THE RODENT'S GAZETTE style section! They are doing a special on BAD TASTE!

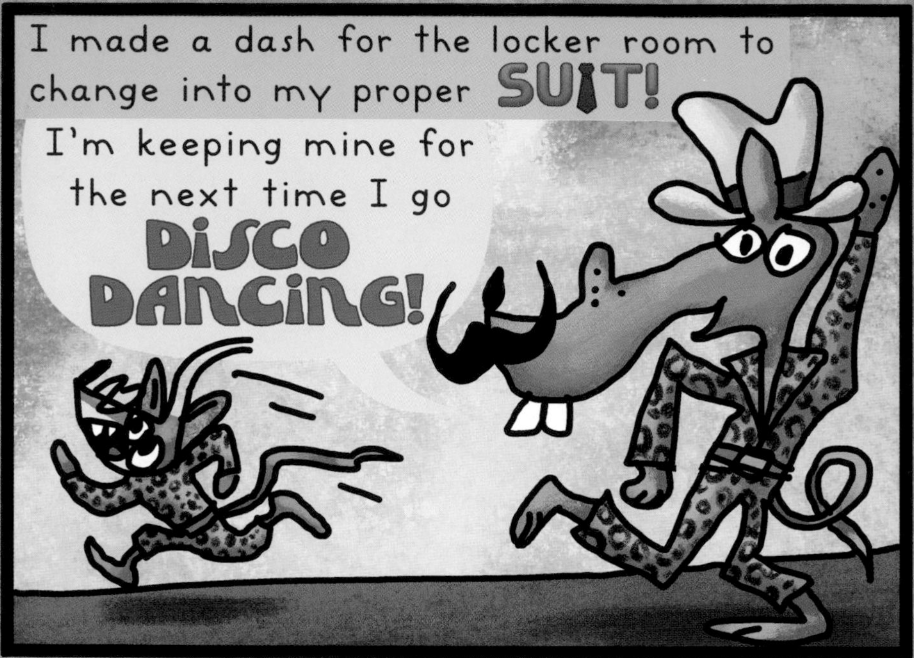
I made a dash for the locker room to change into my proper SUIT!
I'm keeping mine for the next time I go DISCO DANCING!

Five minutes later, Hercule was still DANCING, but I was looking a lot better...

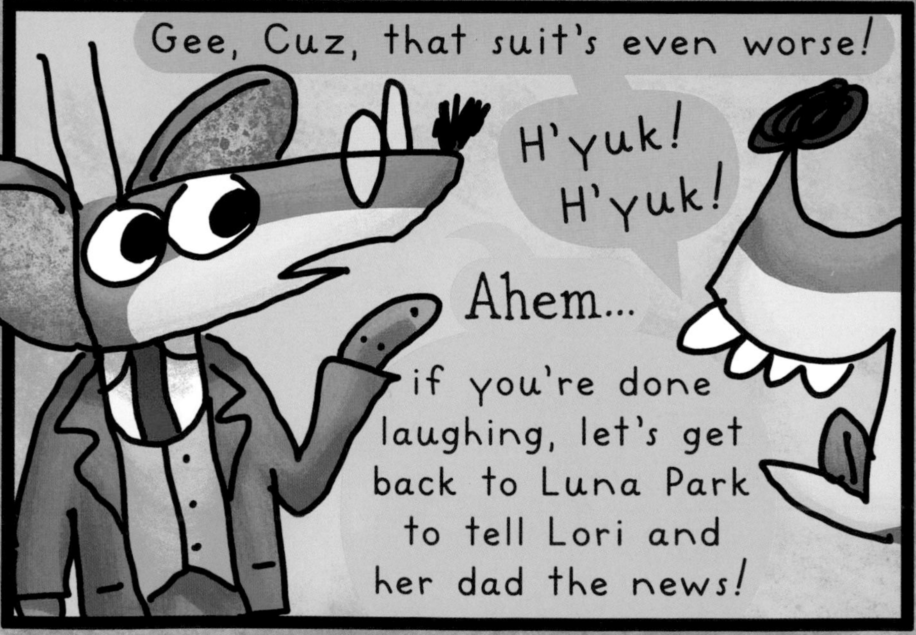
Gee, Cuz, that suit's even worse!
H'yuk! H'yuk!
Ahem...
if you're done laughing, let's get back to Luna Park to tell Lori and her dad the news!

CHAPTER THIRTY-ONE

BACK TO LUNA PARK!

We all headed back to **LUNA PARK**—
even Benjamin and Trappy, who were
up WAY past their bedtime.
But everyone wanted to be part of telling
Lori and her dad the good news!

Wallopin' whiskers!
You youngsters
have saved
Luna Park!

I had started to
give up hope!

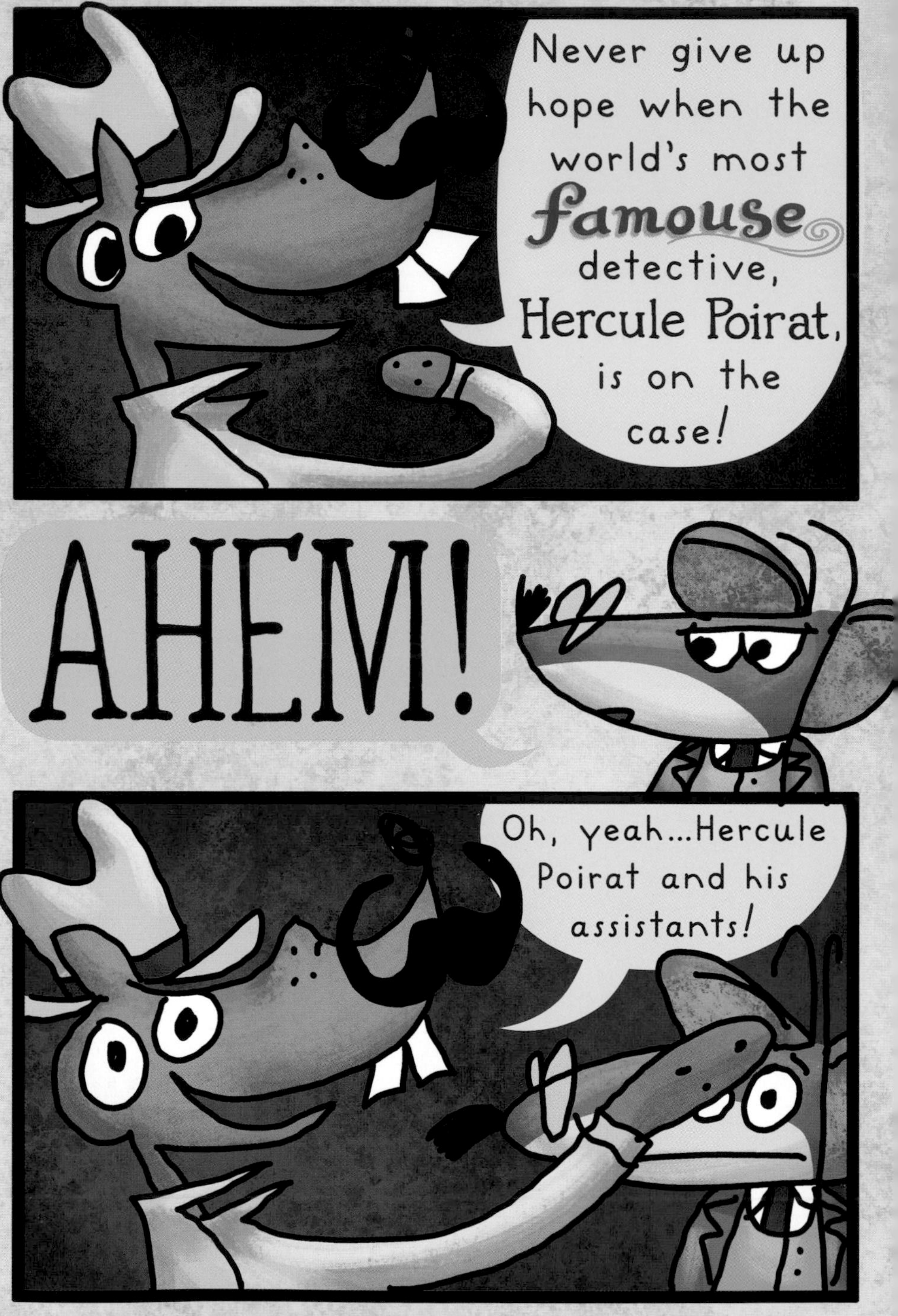
Never give up hope when the world's most famouse detective, Hercule Poirat, is on the case!
AHEM!
Oh, yeah...Hercule Poirat and his assistants!

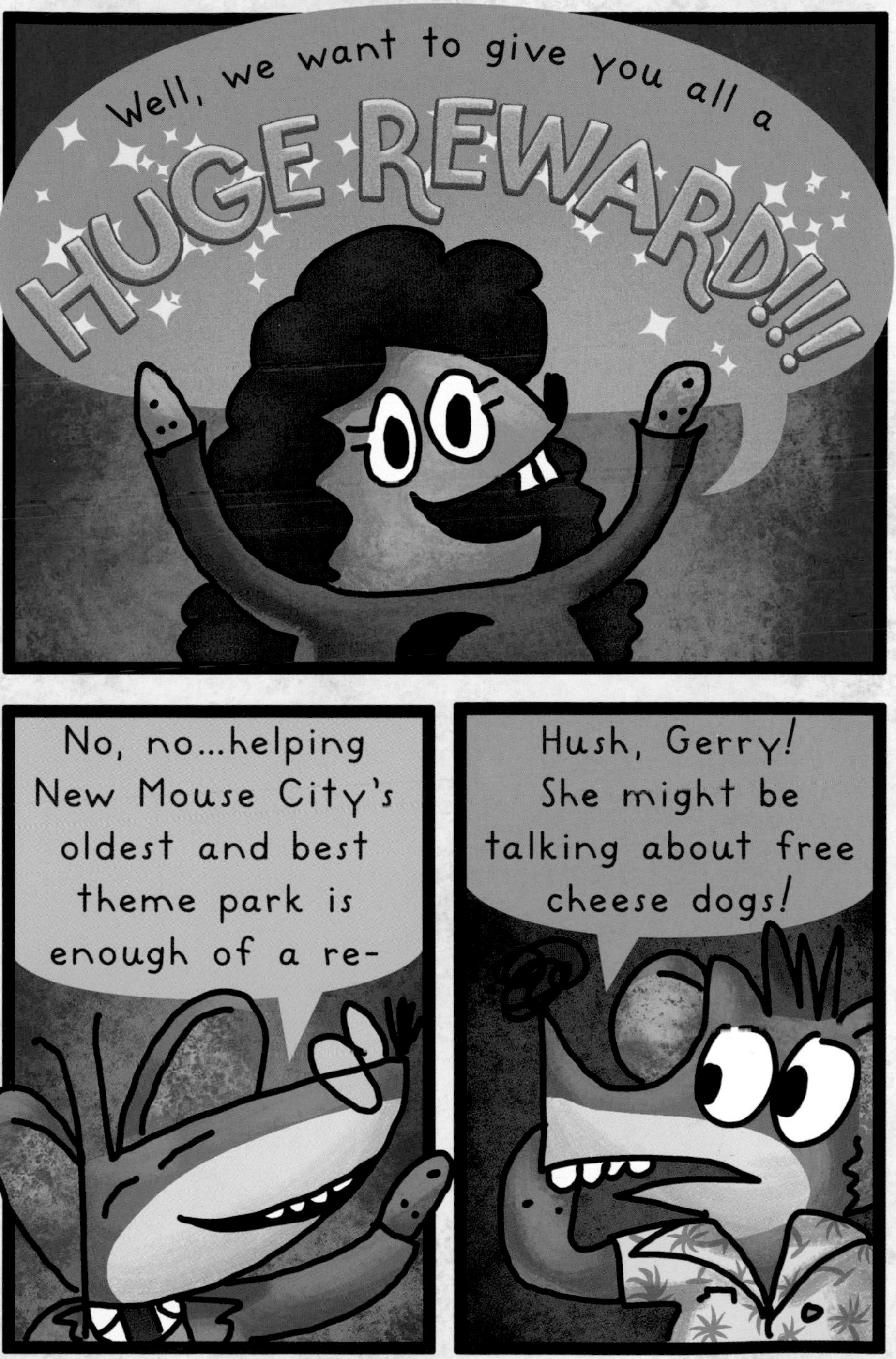
Well, we want to give you all a HUGE REWARD!!!!
No, no...helping New Mouse City's oldest and best theme park is enough of a re-
Hush, Gerry! She might be talking about free cheese dogs!

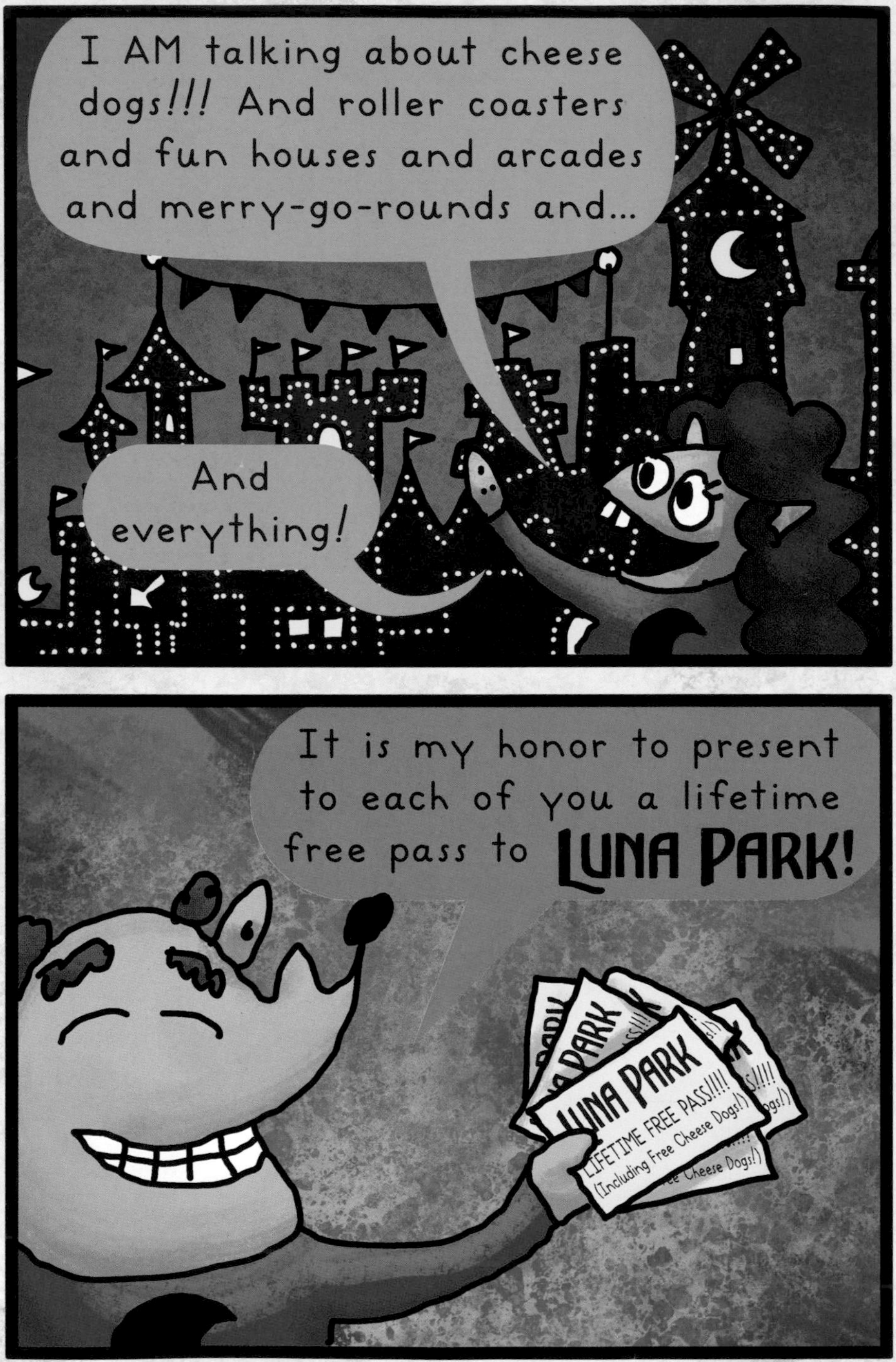
I AM talking about cheese dogs!!! And roller coasters and fun houses and arcades and merry-go-rounds and...
And everything!
It is my honor to present to each of you a lifetime free pass to LUNA PARK!
LUNA PARK
LIFETIME FREE PASS!!!!
(Including Free Cheese Dogs!)

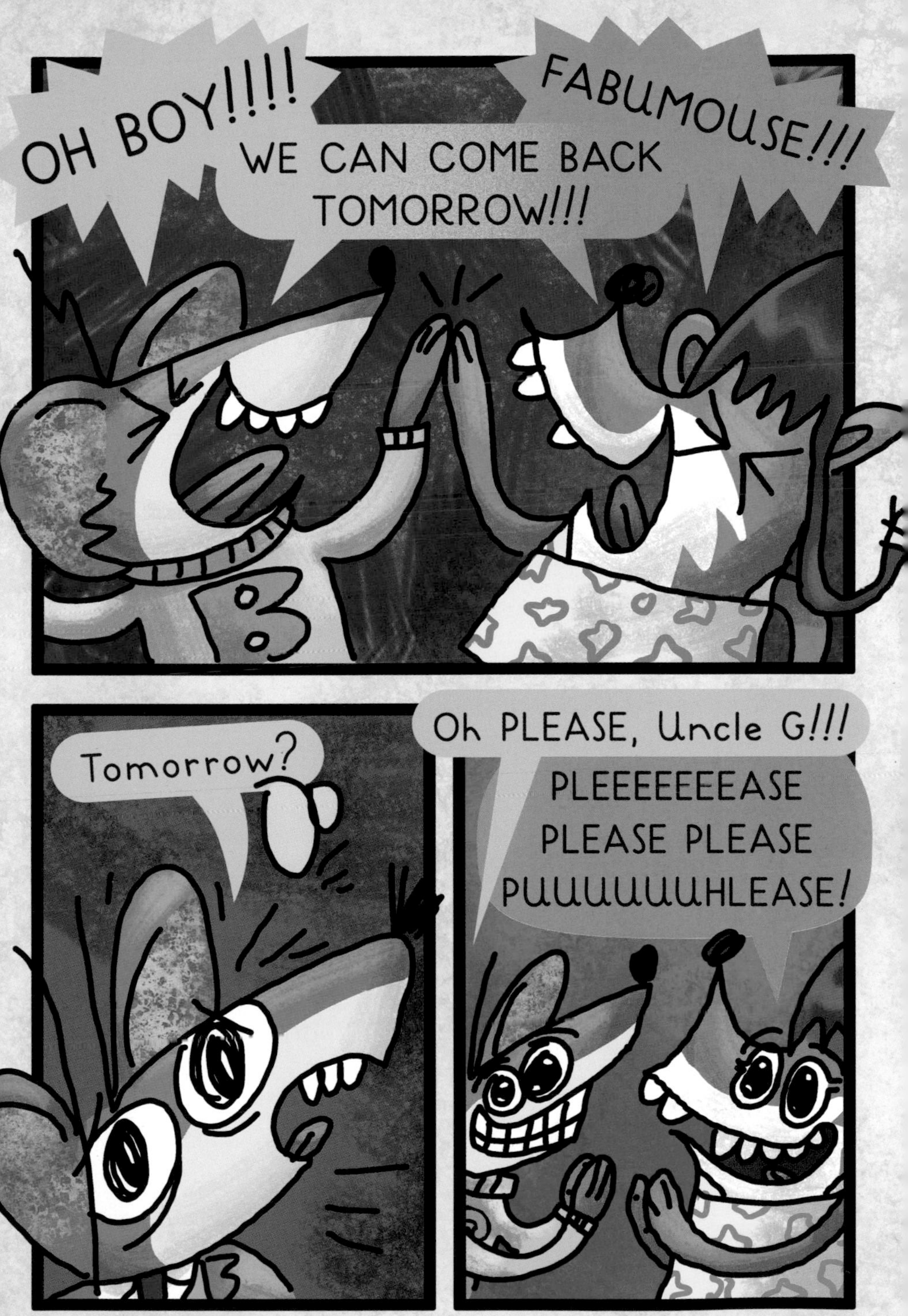
OH BOY!!!!
FABUMOUSE!!!
WE CAN COME BACK TOMORROW!!!
Tomorrow?
Oh PLEASE, Uncle G!!!
PLEEEEEEEASE PLEASE PLEASE PUUUUUUHLEASE!

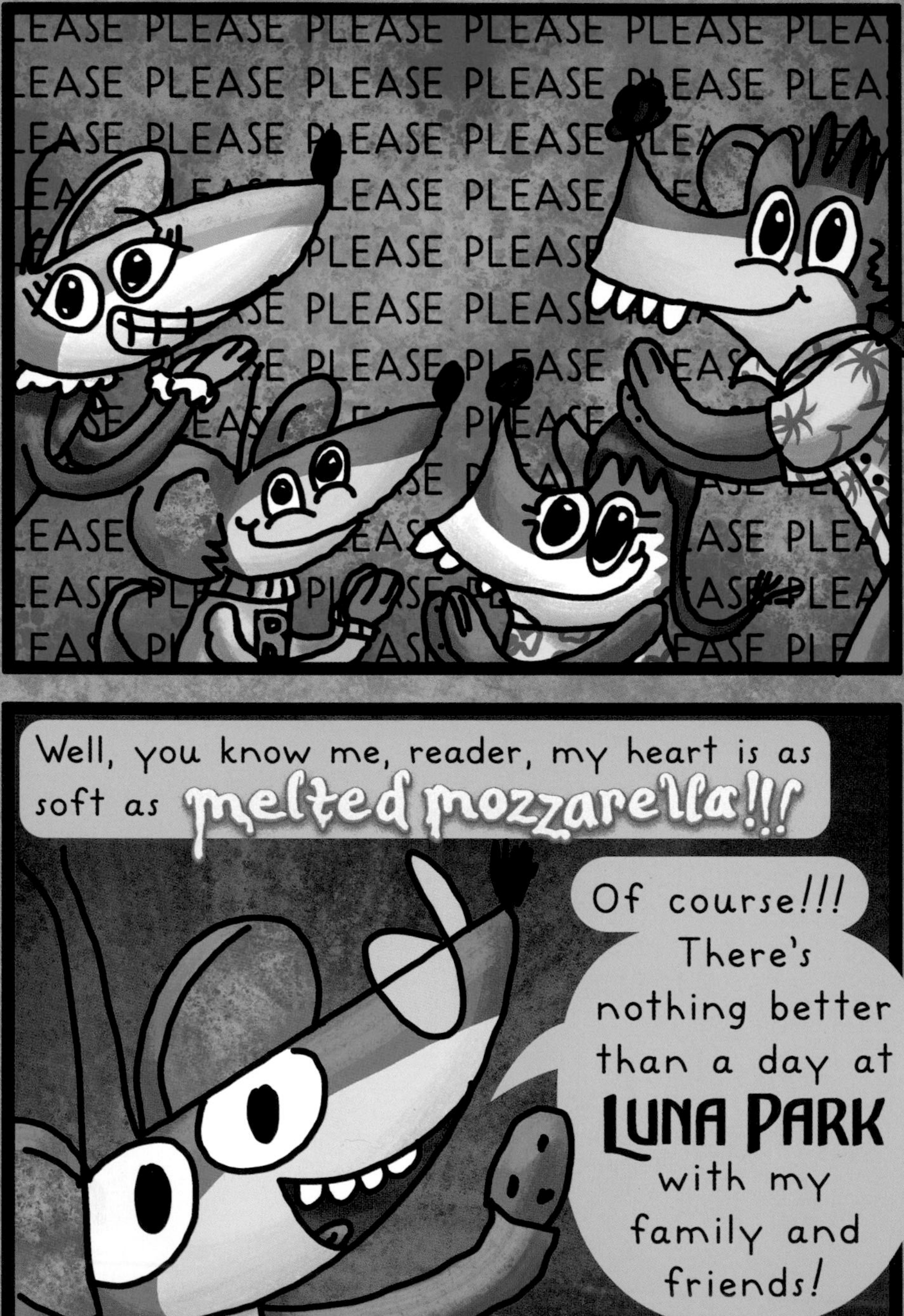
PLEASE PLEASE PLEASE PLEASE PLEASE
Well, you know me, reader, my heart is as soft as melted mozzarella!!!
Of course!!! There's nothing better than a day at LUNA PARK with my family and friends!

CHAPTER THIRTY-TWO

MONSTER SELFIES

When we got to **LUNA PARK** the next morning, it was even more crowded than it had been the day before. It seemed like every mouse in New Mouse City was there! Even my assistant, **Pinky Pick!**

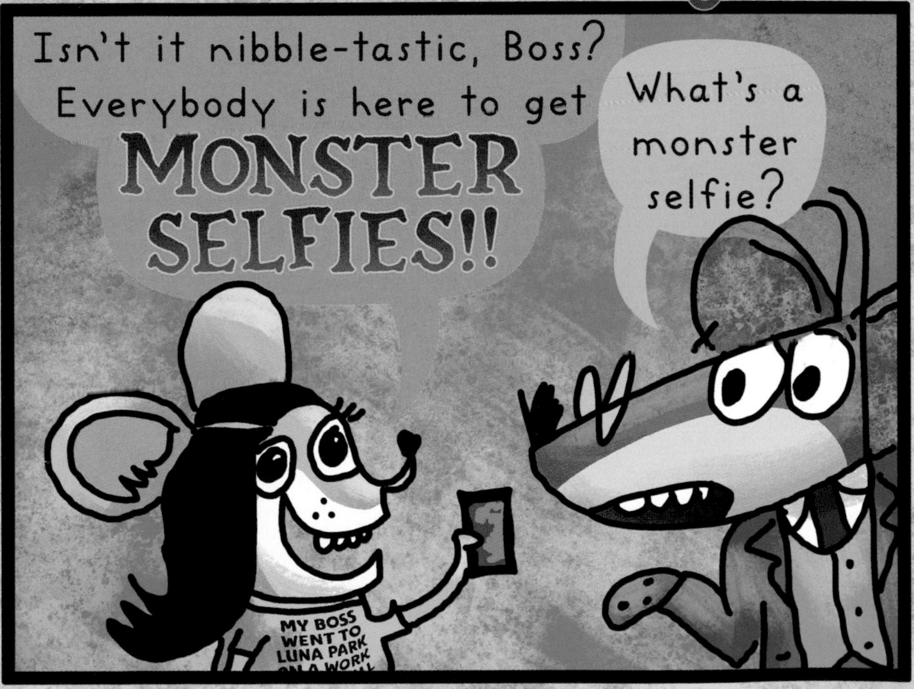

Isn't it nibble-tastic, Boss? Everybody is here to get MONSTER SELFIES!!
What's a monster selfie?
MY BOSS
WENT TO
LUNA PARK

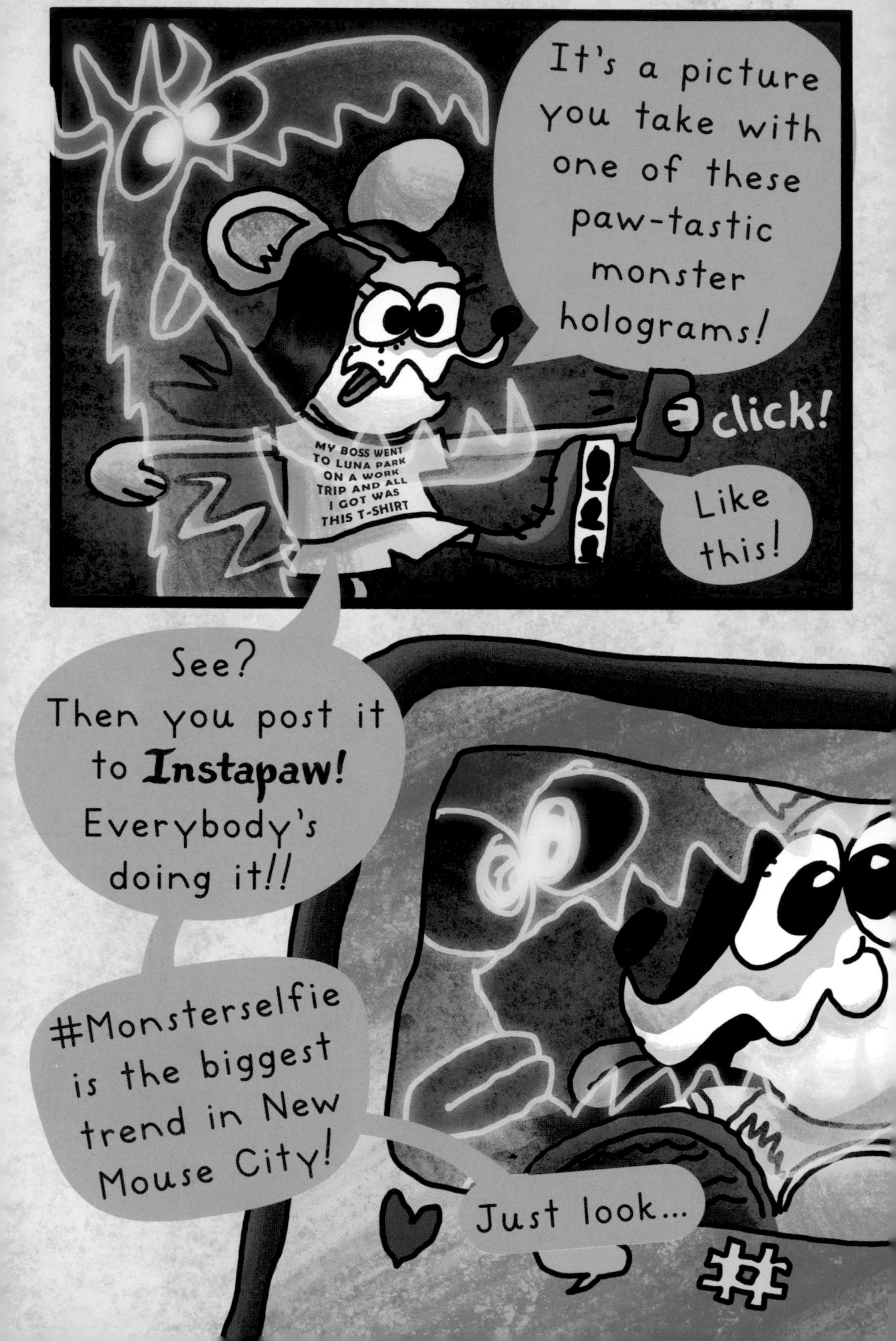
It's a picture you take with one of these paw-tastic monster holograms!
MY BOSS WENT TO LUNA PARK ON A WORK TRIP AND ALL I GOT WAS THIS T-SHIRT
click!
Like this!
See? Then you post it to **Instapaw!** Everybody's doing it!!
#Monsterselfie is the biggest trend in New Mouse City!
Just look...
#

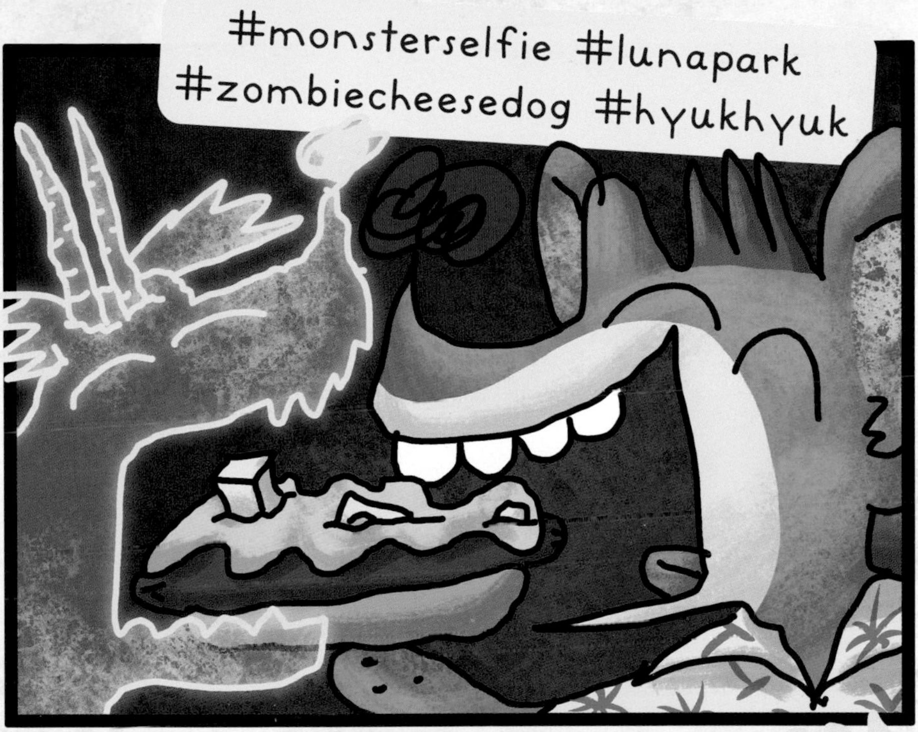
#monsterselfie #lunapark
#zombiecheesedog #hyukhyuk

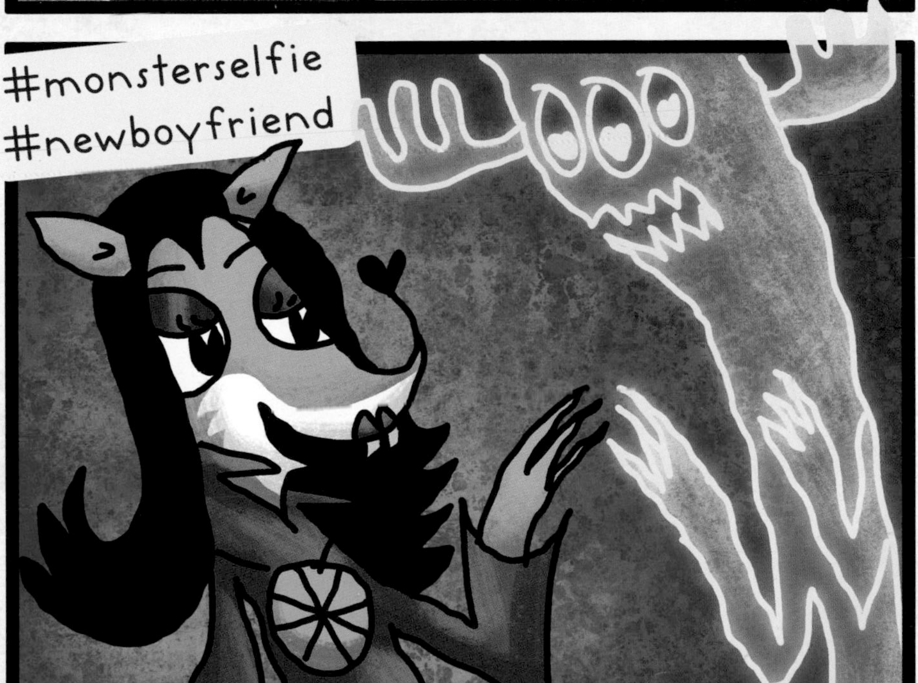
#monsterselfie
#newboyfriend

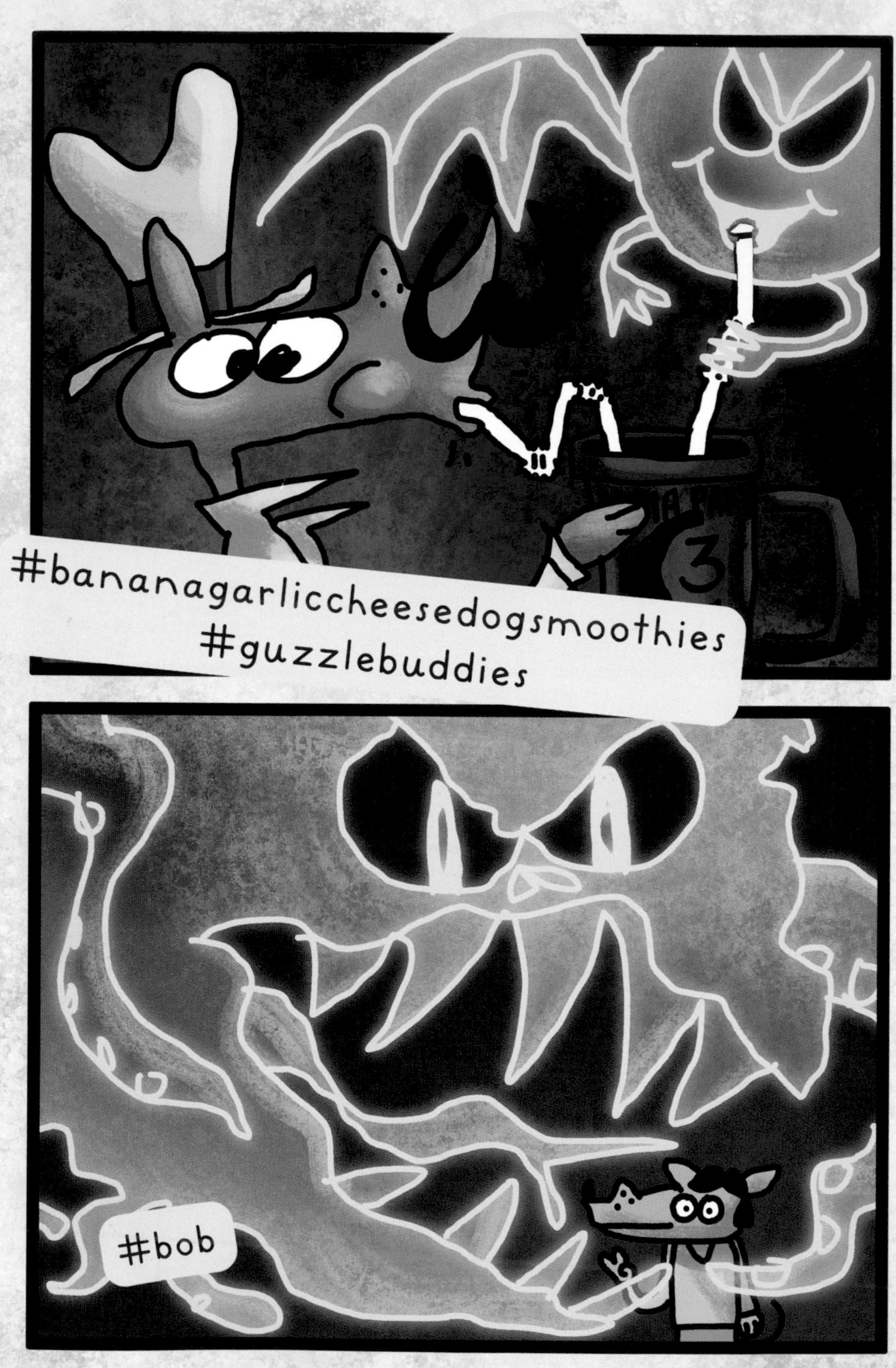
#bananagarliccheesedogsmoothies
#guzzlebuddies
#bob

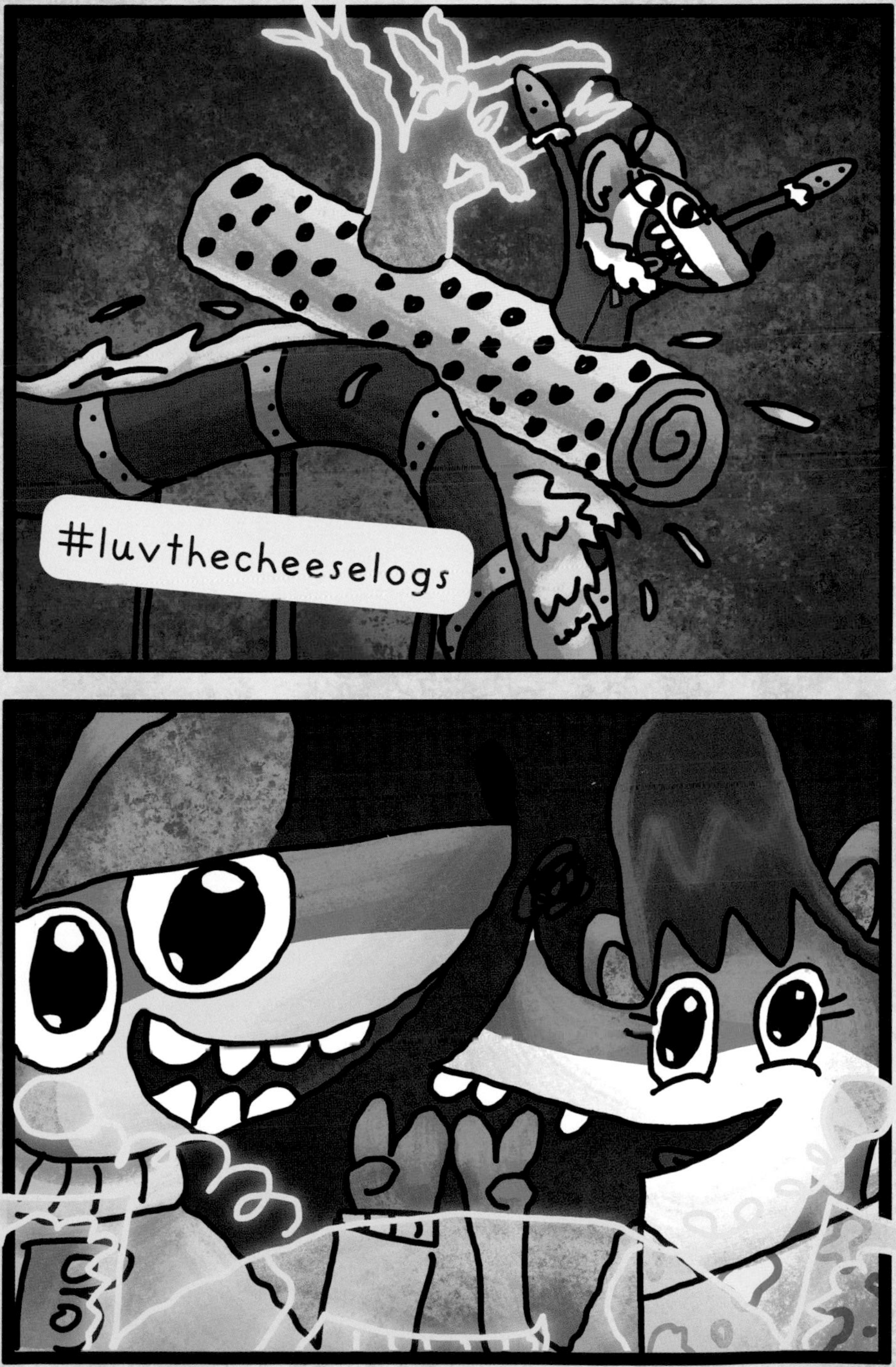
#luvthecheeselogs

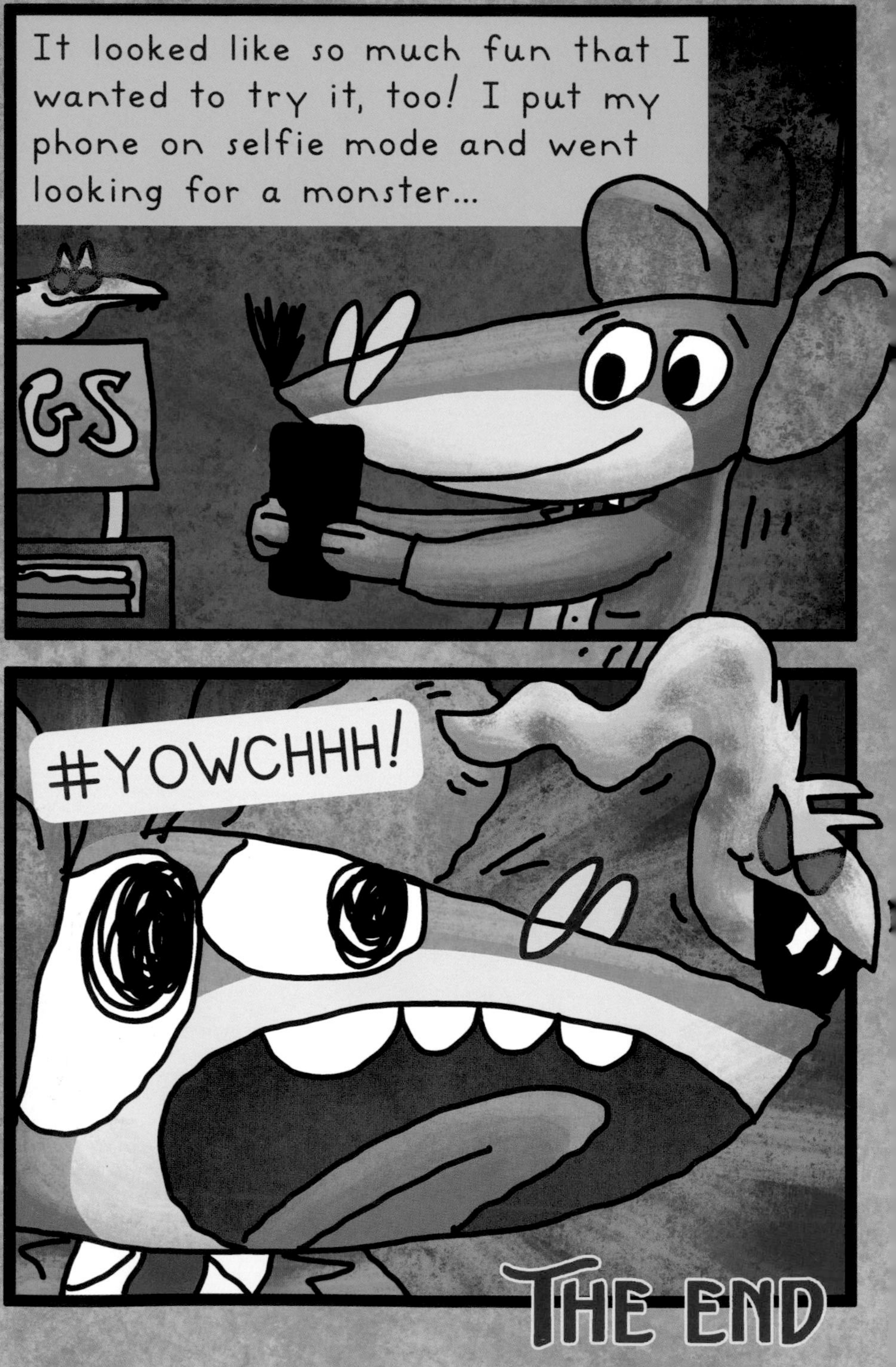
It looked like so much fun that I wanted to try it, too! I put my phone on selfie mode and went looking for a monster...
GS
#YOWCHHH!
THE END

Epilogue

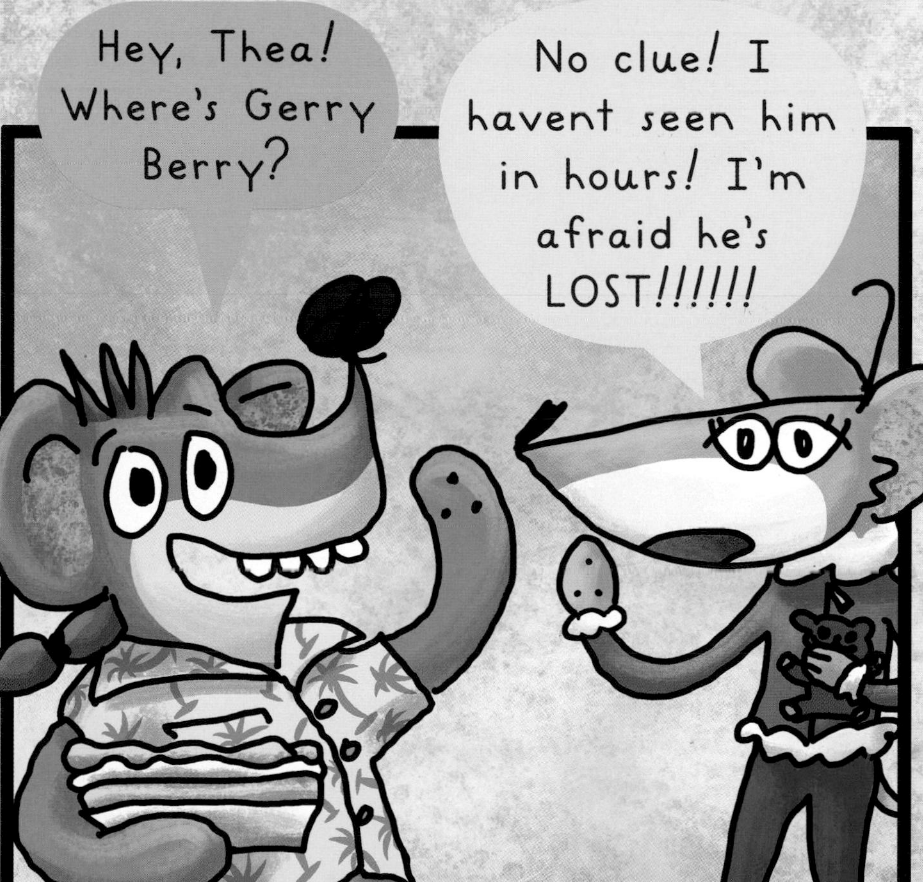
Hey, Thea! Where's Gerry Berry?
No clue! I havent seen him in hours! I'm afraid he's LOST!!!!!!

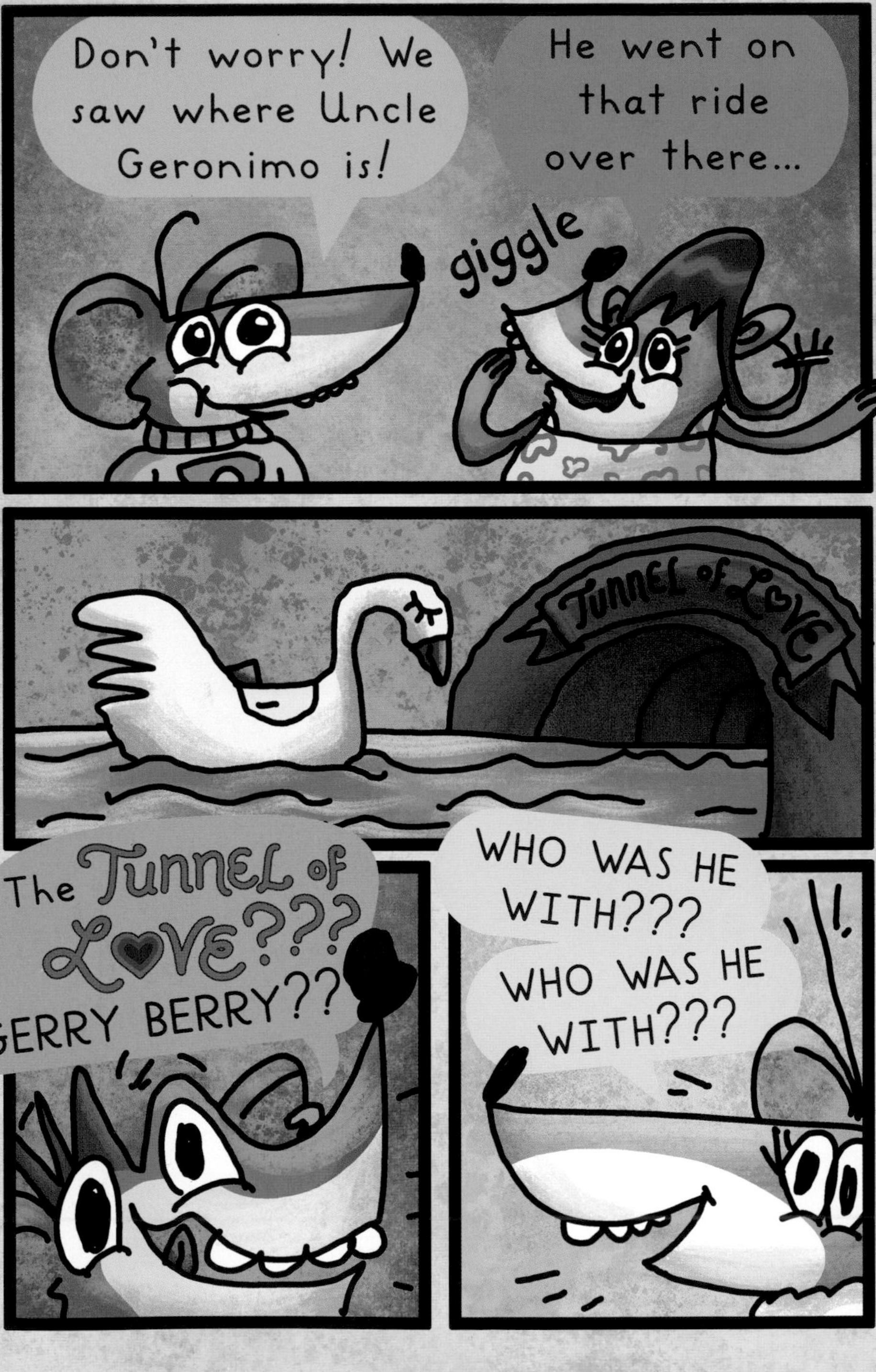
Don't worry! We saw where Uncle Geronimo is!
He went on that ride over there...
giggle
TUNNEL of LOVE
The TUNNEL of LOVE??? GERRY BERRY??
WHO WAS HE WITH???
WHO WAS HE WITH???

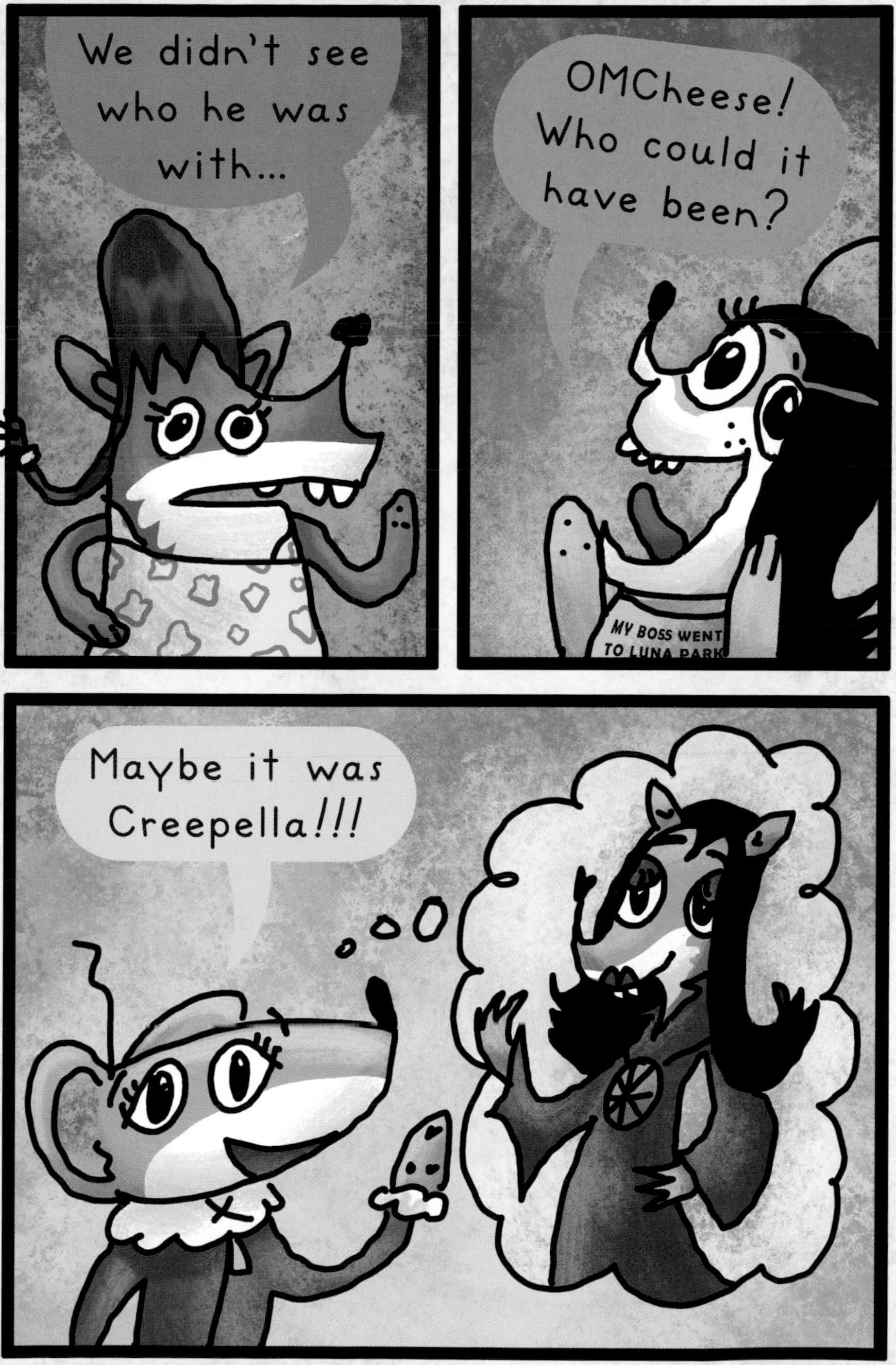
We didn't see who he was with...
OMCheese! Who could it have been?
MY BOSS WENT TO LUNA PARK
Maybe it was Creepella!!!

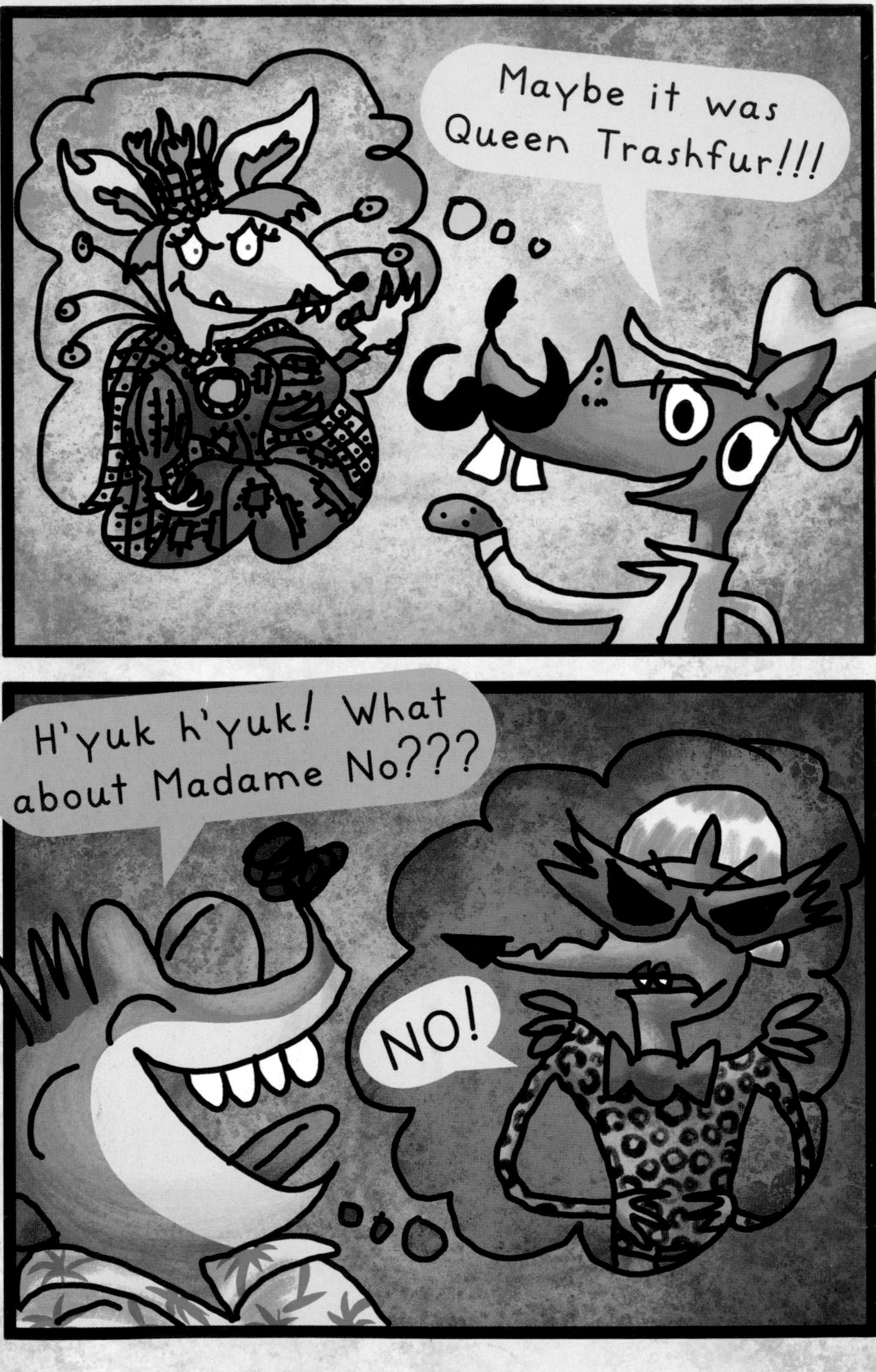
Maybe it was Queen Trashfur!!!
H'yuk h'yuk! What about Madame No???
NO!

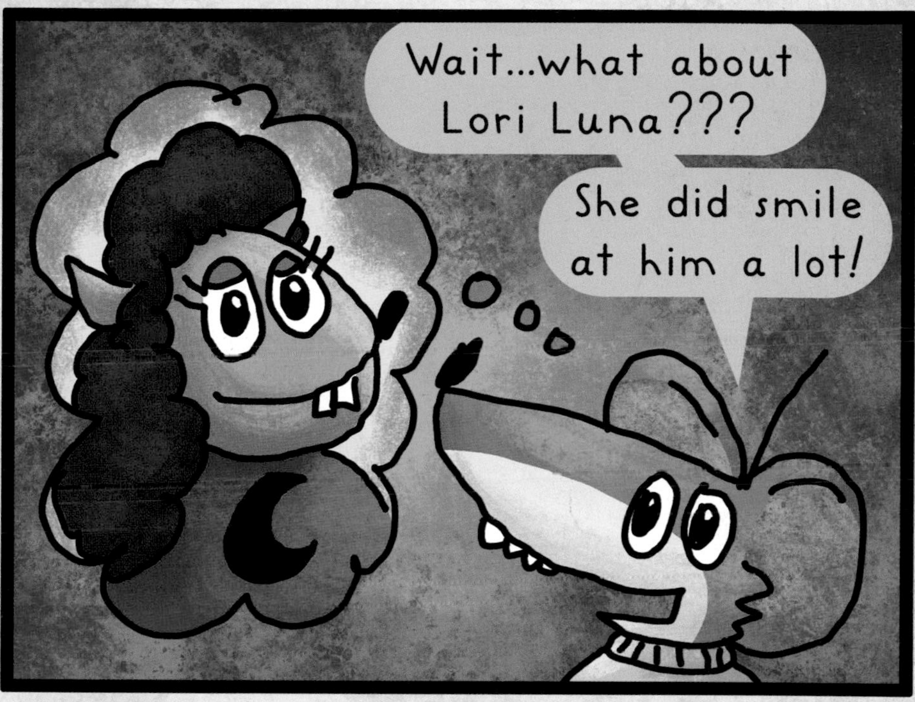
Wait...what about Lori Luna???
She did smile at him a lot!

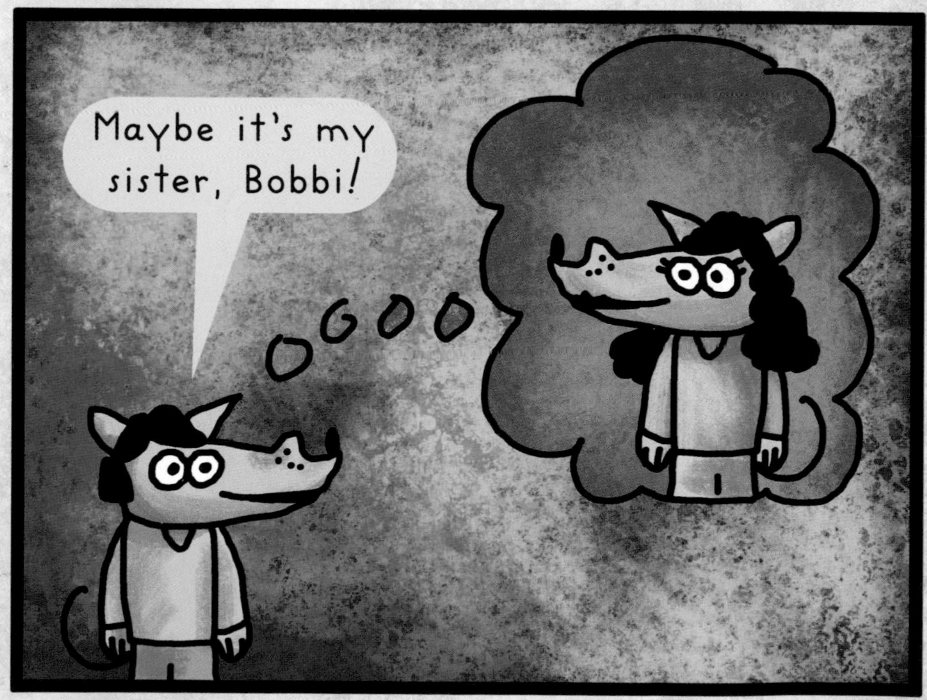
Maybe it's my sister, Bobbi!

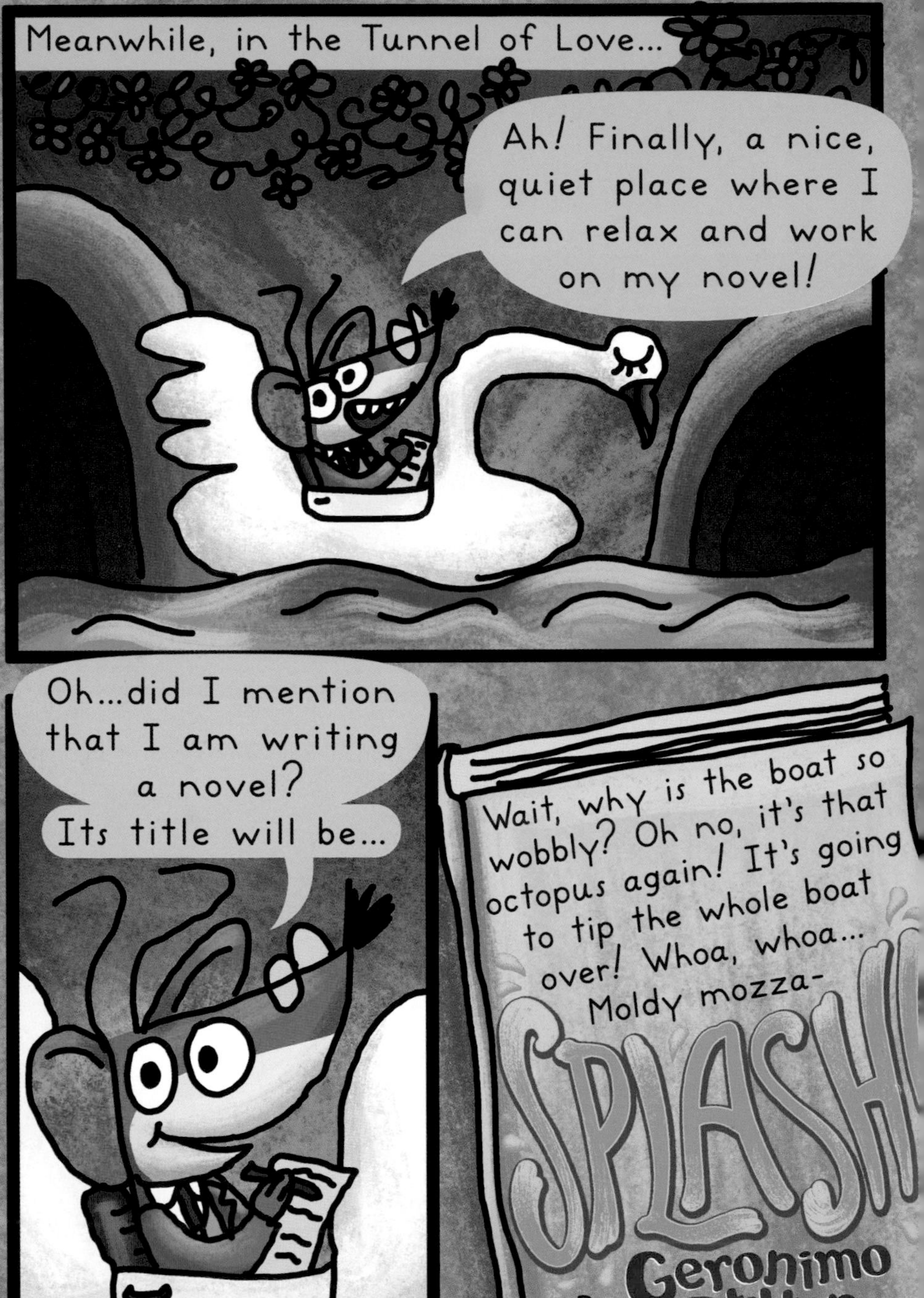

Meanwhile, in the Tunnel of Love...
Ah! Finally, a nice, quiet place where I can relax and work on my novel!
Oh...did I mention that I am writing a novel? Its title will be...
Wait, why is the boat so wobbly? Oh no, it's that octopus again! It's going to tip the whole boat over! Whoa, whoa... Moldy mozza-
SPLASH
By Geronimo Stilton

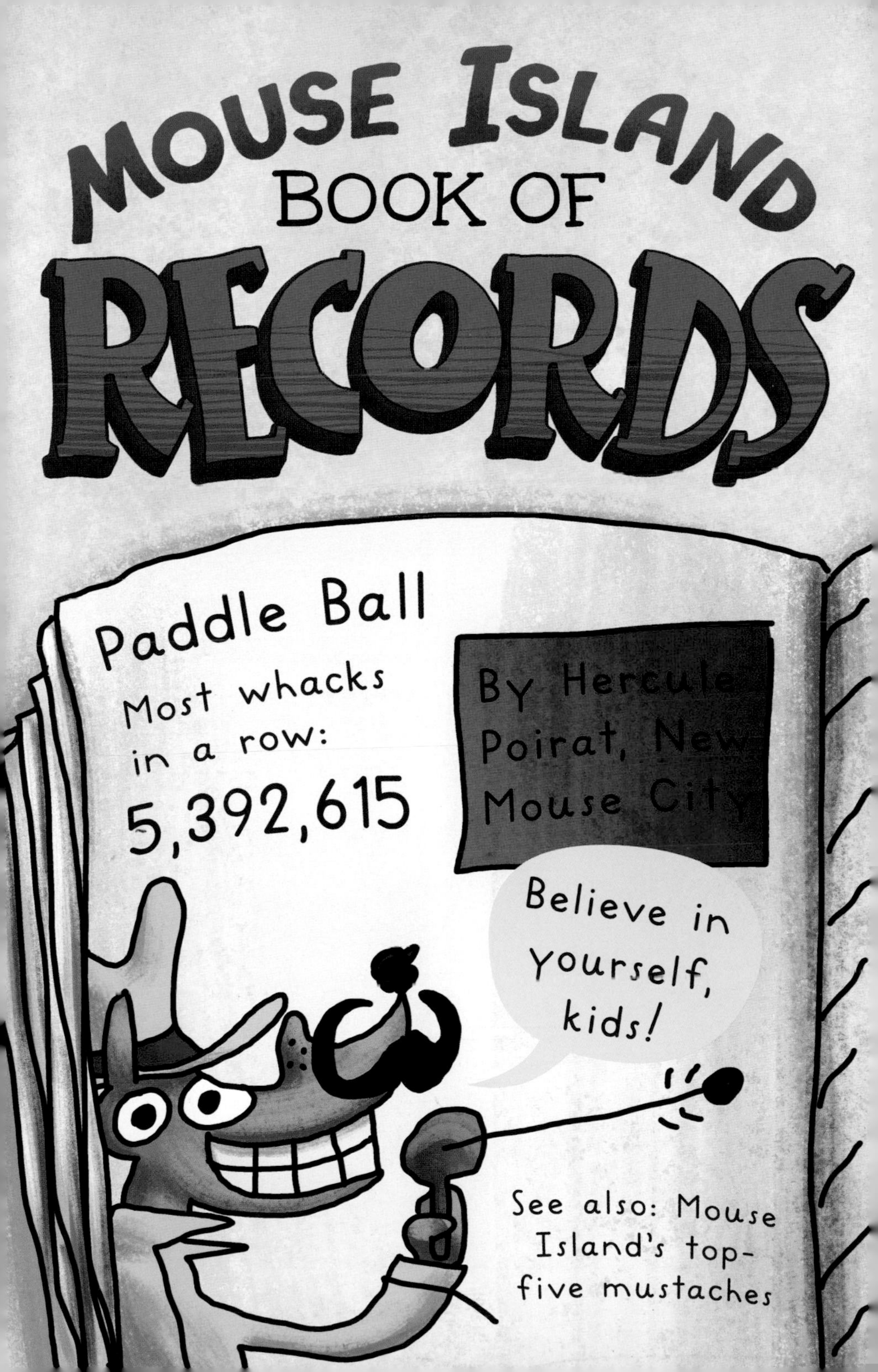
MOUSE ISLAND
BOOK OF
RECORDS
Paddle Ball
Most whacks in a row:
5,392,615
By Hercule
Poirat, New
Mouse City
Believe in Yourself, kids!
See also: Mouse Island's top-five mustaches

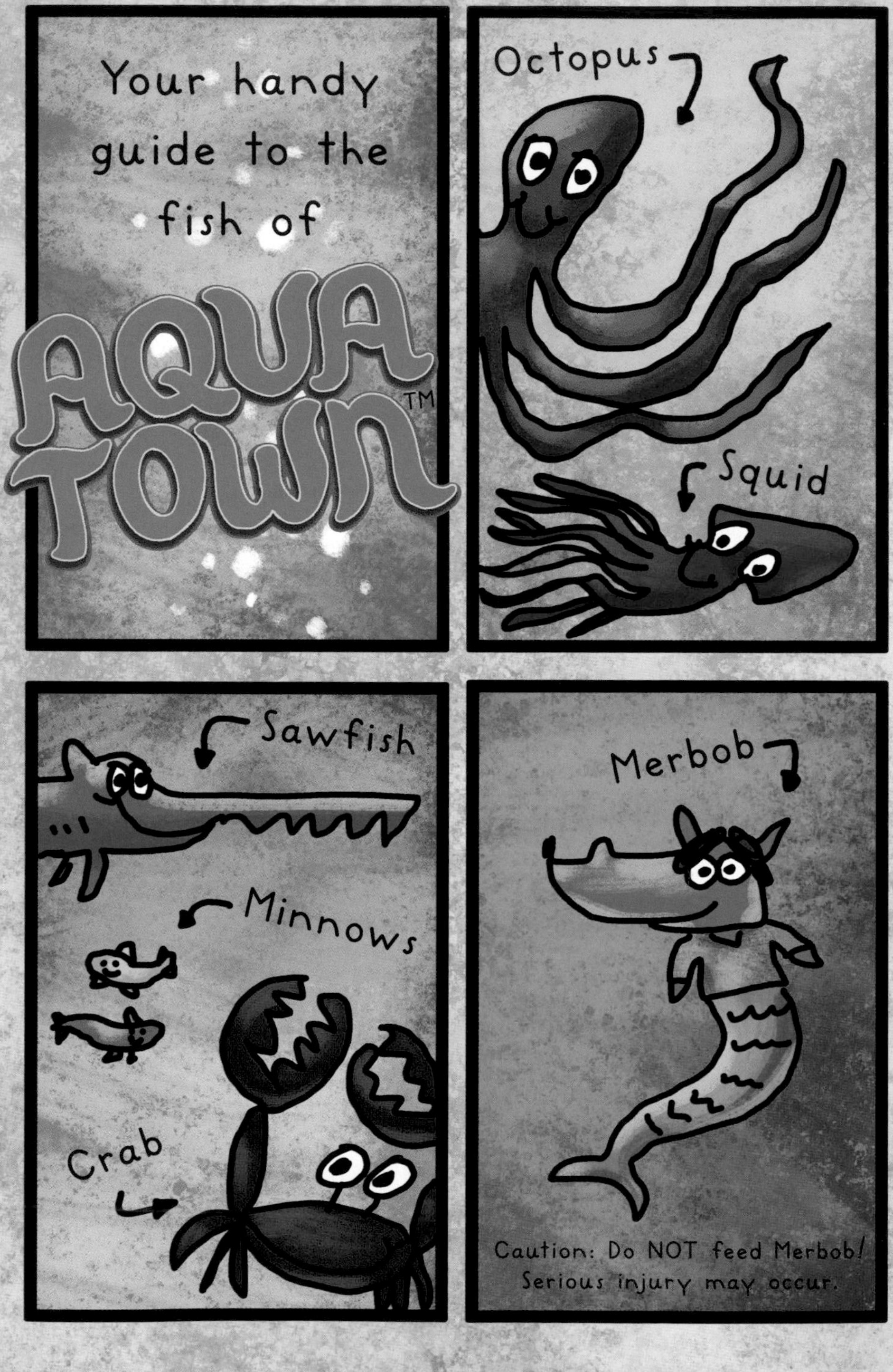

Your handy guide to the fish of
AQUA TOWN™
Octopus
Squid
Sawfish
Minnows
Crab
Merbob
Caution: Do NOT feed Merbob! Serious injury may occur.

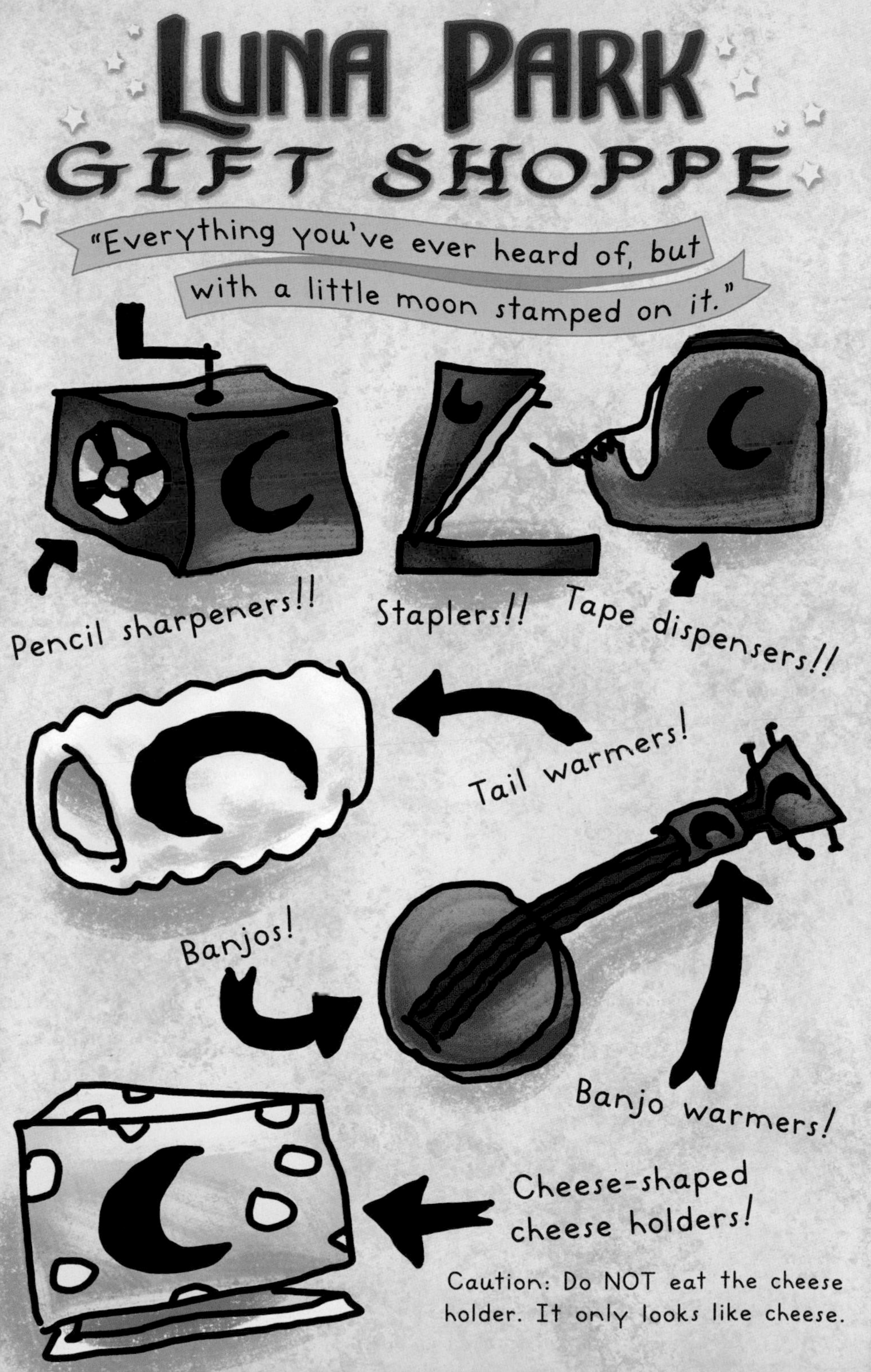

LUNA PARK
GIFT SHOPPE
"Everything you've ever heard of, but with a little moon stamped on it."
Pencil sharpeners!!
Staplers!!
Tape dispensers!!
Tail warmers!
Banjos!
Banjo warmers!
Cheese-shaped cheese holders!
Caution: Do NOT eat the cheese holder. It only looks like cheese.

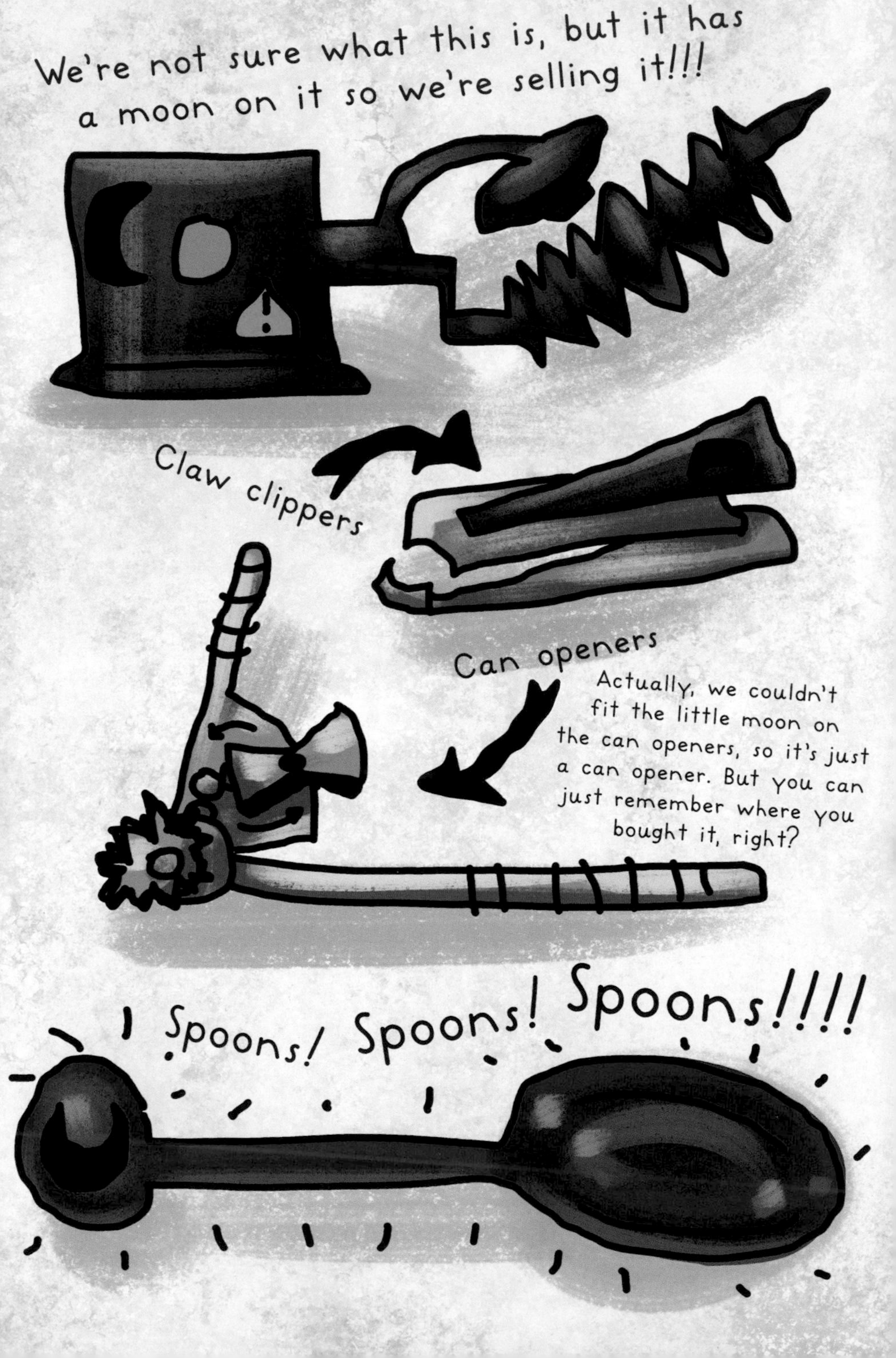
We're not sure what this is, but it has a moon on it so we're selling it!!!
Claw clippers
Can openers
Actually, we couldn't fit the little moon on the can openers, so it's just a can opener. But you can just remember where you bought it, right?
Spoons! Spoons! Spoons!!!!

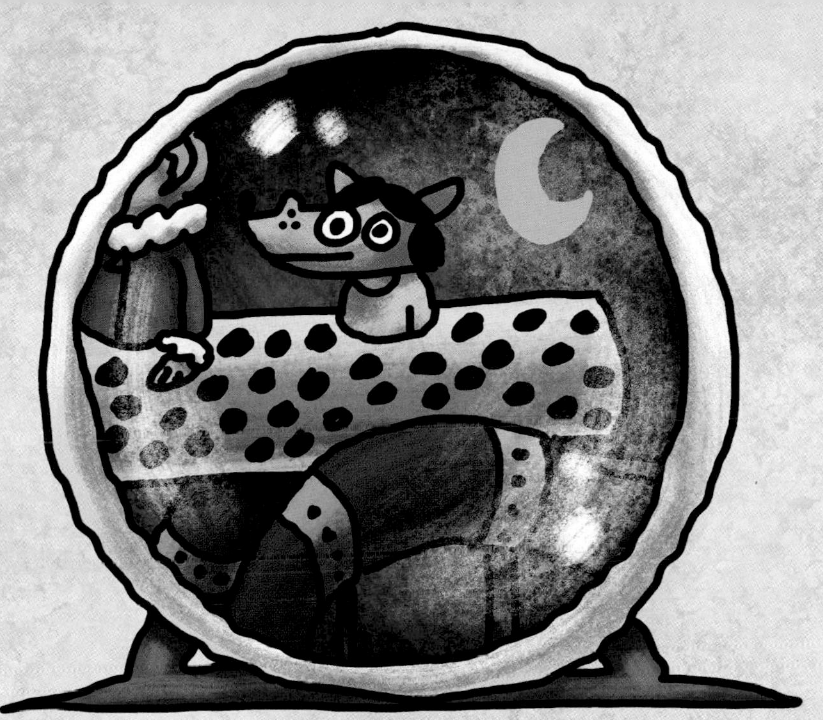

Remember that time Bob got stuck on the Cheeselogs? You'll never forget it with this lovely, brush-painted, solid-plastic collector's plate from the Mousepaw Mint! (Genuine collectible plate stand extra. A lot extra.)

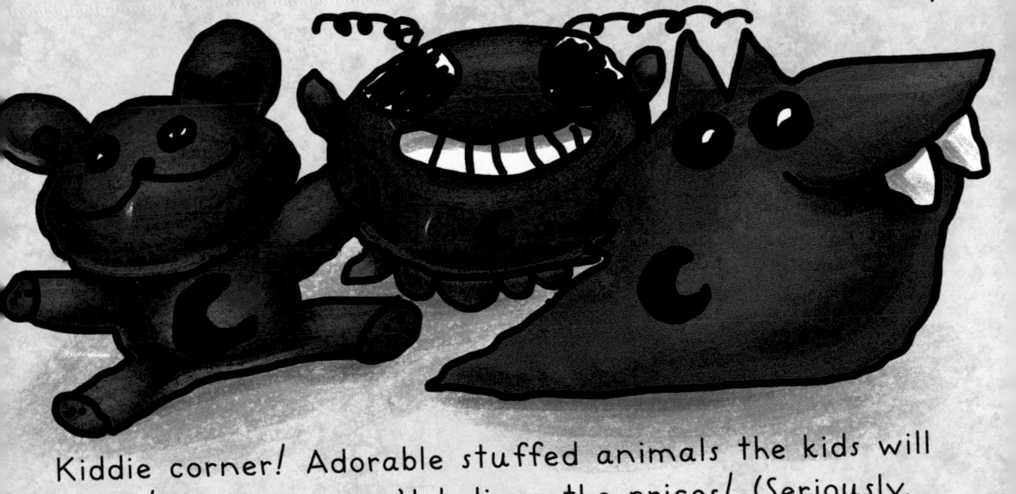

Kiddie corner! Adorable stuffed animals the kids will love! And you won't believe the prices! (Seriously, you won't believe them. Bring all your credit cards and a note from your bank. Car trade-ins accepted.)

OF GERONIMO'S ADVENTURES!

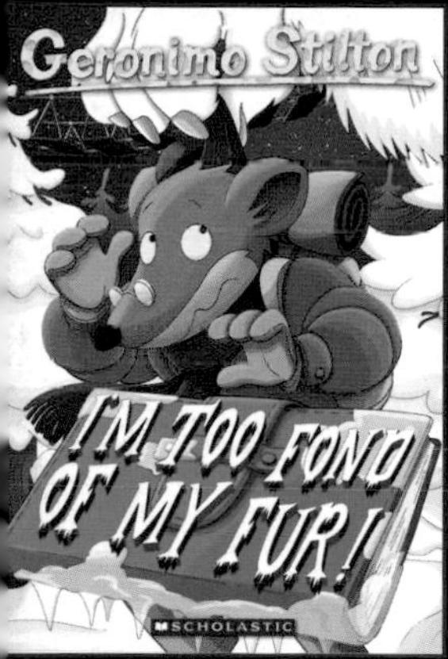
Geronimo Stilton
I'M TOO FOND OF MY FUR!
SCHOLASTIC

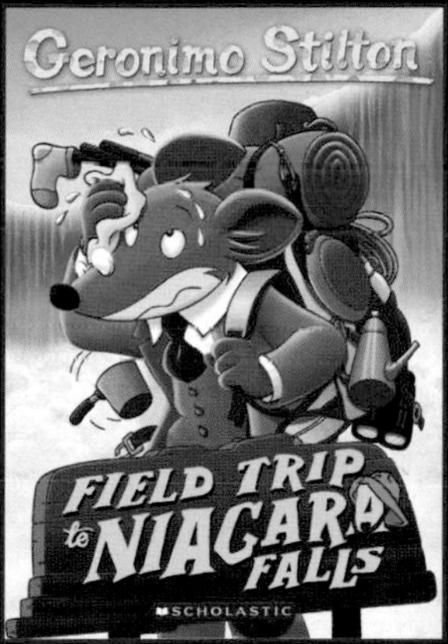
Geronimo Stilton
FIELD TRIP to NIAGARA FALLS
SCHOLASTIC

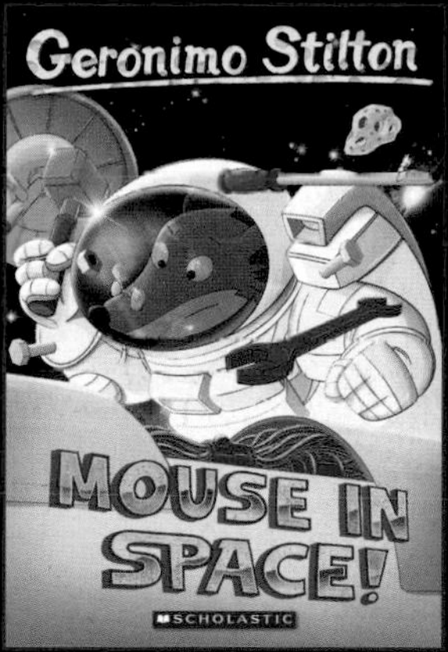
Geronimo Stilton
MOUSE IN SPACE!
SCHOLASTIC

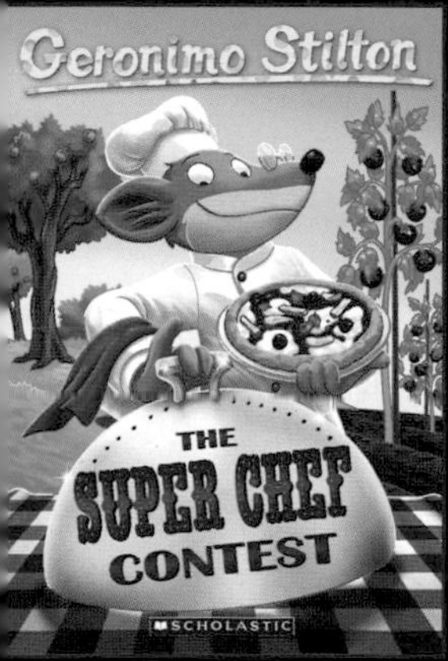
Geronimo Stilton
THE SUPER CHEF CONTEST
SCHOLASTIC

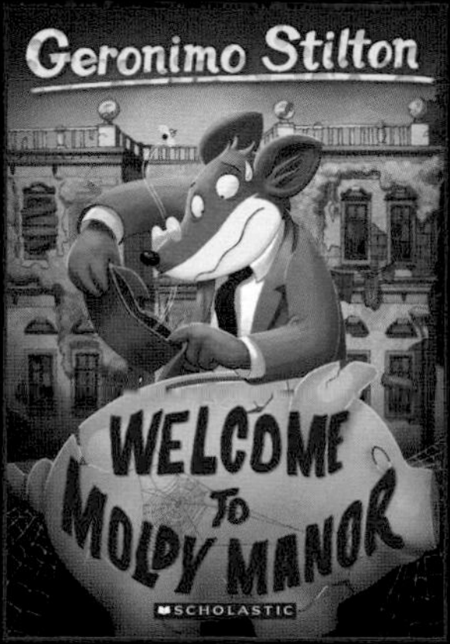
Geronimo Stilton
WELCOME TO MOLDY MANOR
SCHOLASTIC

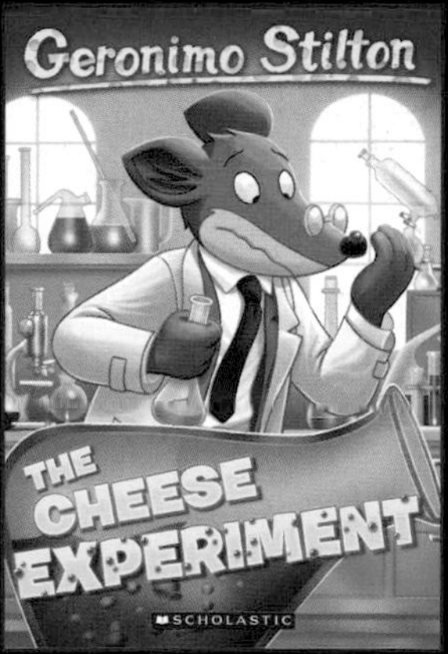
Geronimo Stilton
THE CHEESE EXPERIMENT
SCHOLASTIC

Geronimo Stilton

is an author and the editor-in-chief of *The Rodent's Gazette*, New Mouse City's most popular newspaper. He was awarded the Ratitzer Prize for his investigative journalism and the Anderson 2000 Prize for Personality of the Year. His books have been published all over the world. He loves to spend all his spare time with his family and friends.

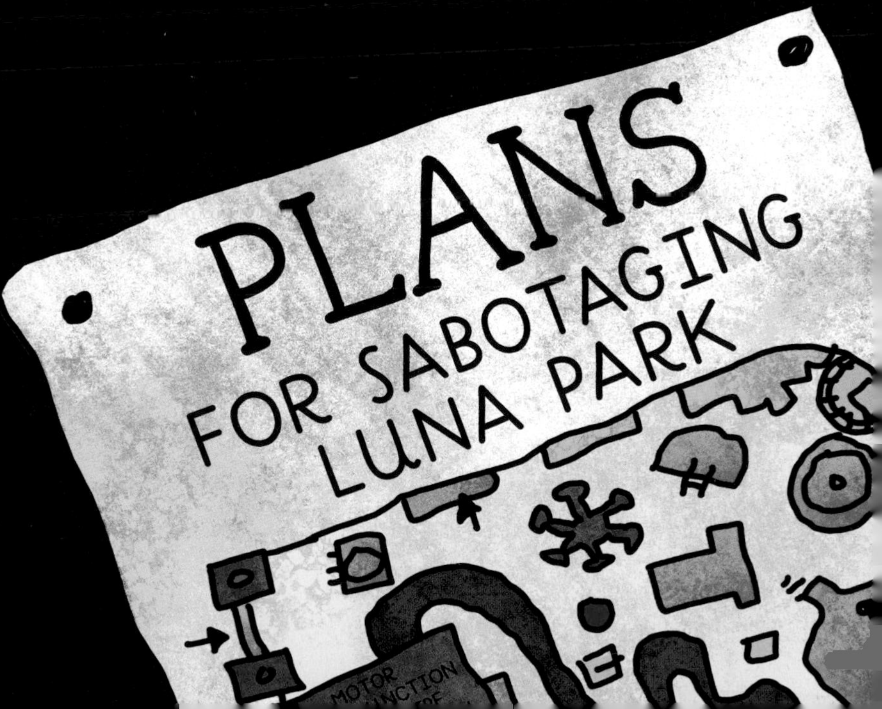
PLANS
FOR SABOTAGING
LUNA PARK
MOTOR

DON'T MISS ANY
ORIGINAL

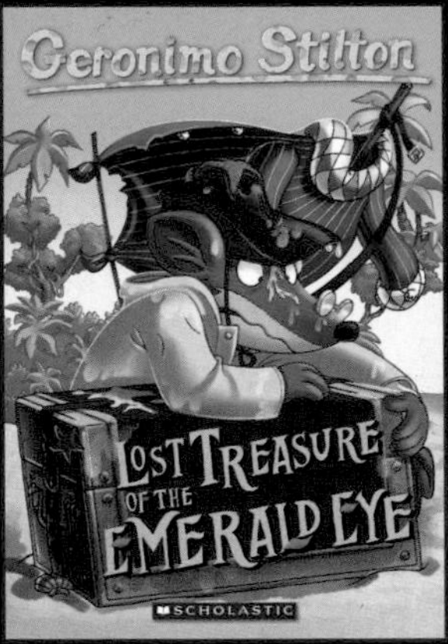

Geronimo Stilton
LOST TREASURE OF THE EMERALD EYE
SCHOLASTIC

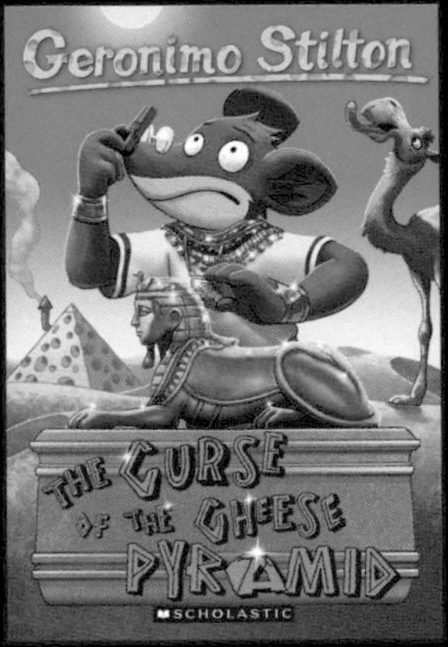

Geronimo Stilton
THE CURSE OF THE CHEESE PYRAMID
SCHOLASTIC

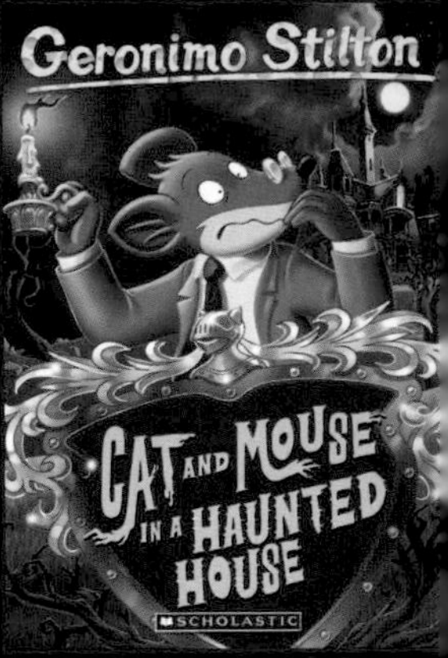

Geronimo Stilton
CAT AND MOUSE IN A HAUNTED HOUSE
SCHOLASTIC

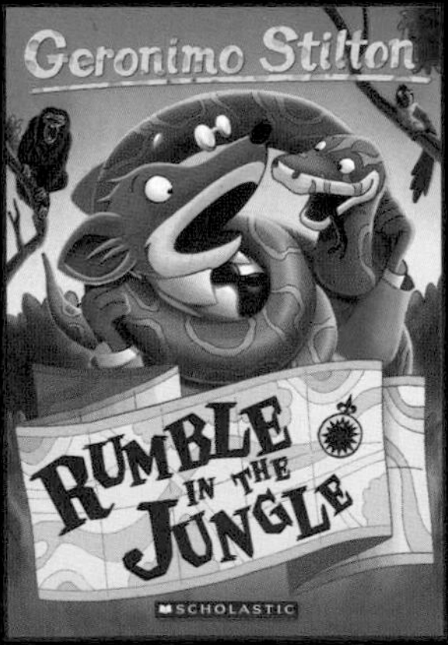

Geronimo Stilton
RUMBLE IN THE JUNGLE
SCHOLASTIC

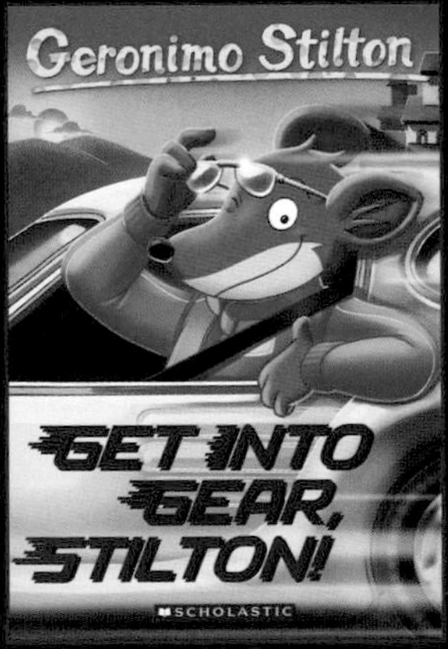

Geronimo Stilton
GET INTO GEAR, STILTON!
SCHOLASTIC

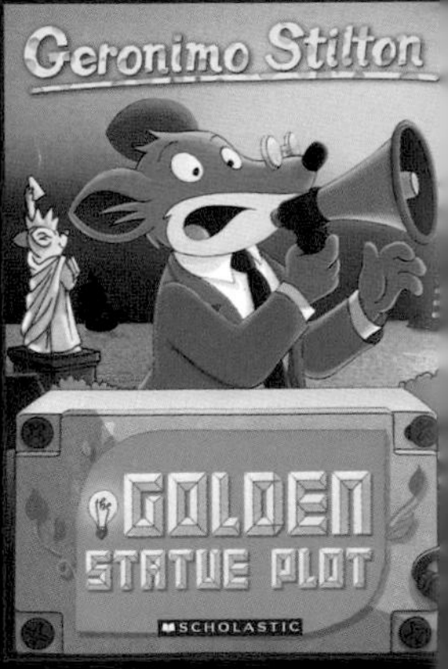

Geronimo Stilton
GOLDEN STATUE PLOT
SCHOLASTIC